8/27/04

FIC
Lak

Laker, Rosalind

To dream of snow

DUE DATE

To Dream of Snow

Recent Titles by Rosalind Laker from Severn House

THE FRAGILE HOUR
THE SEVENTEENTH STAIR
TO LOVE A STRANGER
NEW WORLD, NEW LOVE

B29
8/04

TO DREAM
OF SNOW

Rosalind Laker

This first world edition published in Great Britain 2004 by
SEVERN HOUSE PUBLISHERS LTD of
9–15 High Street, Sutton, Surrey SM1 1DF.
This first world edition published in the USA 2004 by
SEVERN HOUSE PUBLISHERS INC of
595 Madison Avenue, New York, N.Y. 10022.

British Library Cataloguing in Publication Data

Laker, Rosalind, 1925-
  To dream of snow
  1. French - Russia - Fiction
  2. Russia - History - 1741-1762 - Fiction
  3. Love stories
  I. Title
  823.9'14 [F]

  ISBN 0-7278-6042-9

Typeset by Palimpsest Book Production Ltd.,
Polmont, Stirlingshire, Scotland.
Printed and bound in Great Britain by
MPG Books Ltd., Bodmin, Cornwall.

To Jo and John in friendship

One

Her screeches of temper echoed back into the crowded ballroom like those of a trapped eagle. Neither hastily closed doors nor the playing of the orchestra within could drown the ear-splitting sounds until she had gone some distance away. Candlelight in wall sconces threw her shadow everywhere as she stormed through the enfilade of gilded portals that took her from one vast and glitteringly ornate room into another.

'Never again!' she shrieked, shaking her fists in the air.

Terrified servants prostrated themselves as she charged past while those younger and nimbler dived behind the open doors or pressed themselves against the walls of alcoves to keep out of her way. In her present mood she would be quick to strike out at any one of them and had once beaten a maidservant almost to death.

As Empress Elisabeth, Tsarina of all the Russias, approached her own private apartment the guards flung wide its double doors and she swept through. Snatching up a crystal decanter by its neck and a glass from a side table, she paced the magnificent room with its mural-covered walls. Pouring glass after glass of wine, she gulped it down, still engulfed by her rage. Now and again the wine slopped down the front of her bodice, but it was of no consequence since she never wore the same gown twice.

Richly framed mirrors reflected her image as she passed to and fro, catching the sparkle of diamonds in her dyed-black hair. Sometimes she wore it powdered in the new

1

fashion, but tonight she had chosen otherwise. She was a sturdily built, beautiful and full-breasted woman in her forties with a high forehead to her round face and magnificent dark-blue, almost violet eyes under arched brows. Those meeting her for the first time, when she was her most charming and gracious self, found it hard to believe that she could ever be as viciously spiteful and petty or even as enormously vain, avaricious and ruthlessly cruel as they had heard. But they were not long at court before they learned that all of it was true.

When Elisabeth replaced the emptied decanter and set the glass heavily beside it her hands were unsteady, but her thoughts were clear. Never again should the wife of that French diplomat draw eyes away from her! Tonight had been the final straw! The Frenchwoman's gown with its embroidered sprigs of lilac had seemed to shimmer as if the blossoms were moving in a light breeze. She, who always gowned herself magnificently, had never possessed a garment like it. If the Comtesse d'Oinville had been one of her own ladies she would have grabbed a courtier's dress sword and slashed the gown over and over again from waist to hem until it was in ribbons! – just as she had once slashed off the topknot of one of her ladies at court who had dared to wear a delicate arrangement of ribbons far prettier than anything that had ever been created for her.

Sitting down, Elisabeth drummed her fingers on the end of the sofa as she thought out a course of action. Now that it was spring and the snows had gone the Comtesse would be leaving for Paris very shortly. Naturally the woman would replenish her wardrobe while visiting family, but there was a simple way to prevent her from being the focus of all eyes in such a gown again!

Elisabeth smiled vindictively. Nothing should be rushed. She would bide her time until the moment was right. That Frenchwoman must have no advance knowledge of her plan. The Comte d'Oinville and the French Ambassador were both as anxious as each other not to upset her since she made no secret of distrusting French politics. The Ambassador, eager for a new trade agreement with his country, would be only too pleased to see that her wish was carried out. For the same reason, the Comte d'Oinville would endorse it no matter how much his wife might protest.

Her mood had changed. She rang a little silver bell and her maids-in-waiting came scurrying to undress her and prepare her for bed. Then she sent one of them to summon her current lover, a young officer new to one of her regiments, who had caught her lustful eye. Alone, she slipped off her silken robe and spread herself sensuously on the wide bed, her naked body creamy in the candle-glow. Through her seductively lowered lashes she watched the door for the young man's arrival.

In the upper room of a Paris atelier a young woman sat at her work. Her needle flashed with the speed of her stitching. In and out. Silk thread whispering and swirling. On the table at which she sat the glossy satin with its embroidered embellishment lay spread before her like a golden harvest.

Marguerite Laurent was alone at her task. As head embroiderer she was allowed plenty of space when working on a voluminous skirt or a cloak. Even when embroidering gentlemen's silk coats and waistcoats she had the luxury of this upper room to herself.

The late summer sunshine was pouring through the small-paned window, giving her a brilliant light, but like every other window in Madame Fromont's establishment it was kept bolted against dust and dirt floating in from the Paris streets to soil delicate work. It was for the same reason that her cap and apron had to be spotless and her mass of luxuriant copper-brown hair tucked completely out of sight.

These days she worked in silence, concentrating on her task. Yet before she had been plunged into an abyss of grief a few days before her marriage she had often sung happily to herself as she worked – an old remembered song from childhood or something she and Jacques had heard from a street performer. Her late sister, Anne-Marie, who had been twelve years older, had once told her that she had inherited their late mother's gift of a good voice and it made a link for her with the woman she could not remember.

A final stitch, a snip with the scissors and her task was done. As she stood to gather the mass of material together she heard the familiar sound of slow and heavy footsteps mounting the stairs. Then Madame Fromont, short and rotund with a permanently high purple colour in her cheeks, heaved herself into the room. She paused breathlessly on the threshold with a shake of her head, pressing a hand against her chest.

'I declare those stairs get steeper every day!' she sighed despairingly, more to herself than to the young woman, who had promptly pushed a chair forward for her. She lowered herself on to it. 'You've finished the skirt, Marguerite? Good. I have just had an urgent message from the Comtesse d'Oinville. She wants to see you now.'

Marguerite was surprised. 'But her latest order was delivered three weeks ago in good time for her journey back to Russia, and she was satisfied with everything.'

Madame Fromont shrugged her shoulders. 'I've no idea what she wants. Perhaps she needs yet another new gown to take with her. Let us decide which of your latest designs you should show her.' Then she nodded towards some small, elegantly gowned dolls lined up on a shelf. 'You can also take two of those fashion mannequin dolls dressed in the new styles you created the other day.'

A selection of designs, including some of embroidery, was made and put into a presentation folder, which was laid in a silk-lined, flat-bottomed basket. A swatch of Lyon silks was added and finally Marguerite placed the two fashion dolls carefully on top before drawing a cover over them.

As Madame Fromont went downstairs again Marguerite removed her cap and apron. Taking her flat-crowned straw hat from its peg, she put it on. It had been trimmed with scarlet ribbons until her bereavement, but she had replaced them with black ones and, more recently, with blue in her constant struggle to adjust to her loss. It was these that she tied back under her luxuriant hair, which she wore simply, drawn away from her face in one of the current modes into a clusters of short curls at the nape of her neck, a few tendrils wafting. Picking up the basket, she slipped it on to her arm and went swiftly downstairs and out into the sun.

There was a slight breeze that fanned her face as she set off along the street. The sights and sounds of the ancient city with its grand as well as its humble buildings and narrow alleyways, were intensely familiar to her, for they were all she had known in the nineteen years of her life. Various aromas, some pleasant, others nauseating, assailed her as she passed by wine shops and saddlers, flower sellers, butchers' stalls and coffee houses. At the corner of the cobbled street the smoky stench from the burnt-out shell of what had been a goldsmiths' workshop still seemed to assail her, even though she knew it was only the heart-wrenching memory of that terrible day that caused her mind to play tricks. Yet it was a daily torture to her that she could not escape, for there was no other route by which she could get to work.

Tall and slender, her step was brisk as she walked along, for the nobility did not like to be kept waiting. The brim of her hat shaded eyes that were more amber than brown in an oval face that was not conventionally beautiful but alert in expression with well-shaped cheekbones and a firm curve to the chin. There was also a vibrancy about her in spite of her grief that had lain so heavily on her heart for almost a year now. Previously her exuberance for life had shown itself in her love of dancing and laughter and good company, but losing her beloved Jacques had sobered her in a way that seriously concerned her friends.

After twenty minutes she reached a long avenue lined with fine mansions and her heels tapped across a paved courtyard to the servants' entrance of the Comte d'Oinville's city residence. He was a diplomat, presently in Moscow, where his wife was shortly to rejoin him. Marguerite had been to their house many times before, for fine embroidery on garments had never been more fashionable and the Comtesse liked always to have long discussions about the designs and colours before making a choice. At first Madame Fromont, although an amiable woman, had resented being bypassed, but the Comtesse was too important a patron to upset in any way.

As usual on these visits Marguerite was shown into a pink and gold boudoir. Normally she was greeted with a nod and an austere little smile, but today she found the Comtesse d'Oinville, an elegant, small-waisted woman with porcelain features, sitting grim-faced on a sofa, the fashionable side panniers of her gown extending her olive-green skirt over the width of it. Her beringed fingers were sparkling restlessly in her lap.

'You may sit down,' she said with unusual sharpness.

Uneasily Marguerite took a chair facing her. 'Is something wrong, Madame la Comtesse?' she inquired anxiously.

'Not with your work, but I have a matter of importance that I'm reluctant to put to you. You will remember the ivory-silk gown that you embroidered with the Persian motif in all those beautiful colours for my visit to Russia?' As Marguerite nodded, the woman continued. 'I wore it to my first ball there, but the Empress Elisabeth showed such hostility towards me that I was bewildered to know why! Earlier that day she had been most gracious and welcoming to both the Comte and myself on his appointment to the Russian Court. Then our ambassador explained to me afterwards that the Empress's colossal vanity makes it impossible for her to tolerate the presence of any woman

6

gowned more magnificently than herself!'

'Oh, Madame!' Marguerite breathed in dismay. It was a compliment that the powerful Tsarina of Russia should have admired her work, however unpleasant the consequences, but did it mean that the Comtesse had decided now at the last minute to abandon the equally embellished gowns made for her second visit to Russia? She knew that no payment had been received yet, for the nobility resented any request for money as if it were a privilege to work for them and a year usually elapsed before anything was forthcoming.

'The wretched woman was even worse towards me on another occasion when I wore the azure silk worked in silver thread! At the best of times we French are not exactly in favour at the Russian Court and after that second dreadful display of her vile temper our ambassador asked me to wear simpler gowns! He said that the Empress was so unpredictable that she could create an international incident out of an imagined slight.'

'How difficult it must have been for you, Madame!'

'It was indeed. I had to keep my best gowns for events when I knew she would not be there.' She sighed with exasperation. 'Just as I shall have to do this time.'

Marguerite breathed a silent sigh of relief. At least Madame Fromont was not going to find those garments back on her hands.

'I deeply resented the rule that had been imposed upon me,' the Comtesse continued. 'Then on the eve of my coming home at a Kremlin Palace ball in Moscow I decided to do as I wished and look my very best for my husband and everybody else. So I wore the lilac gown with the lappets that look like floating blossoms. I ignored the Empress's glowering expression, but when she stalked up to me in the middle of the dancing she was shaking with fury from head to toe. She even raised a fist as if she would strike me before she turned on her heel and stamped out of the ballroom!' Impatiently the Comtesse snatched up a letter from a side table. 'I would never have spoken of the matter if this letter had not come today by special messenger from our ambassador!'

Marguerite listened incredulously as it was read out to her. The Empress had demanded that the Comtesse d'Oinville's embroiderer should travel to Russia immediately. There she would be in charge of a spacious atelier and create exclusively for the Empress and, on a more moderate scale, for the Grand Duchess Catherine, wife of the heir to the throne. She was to bring with her four or five equally gifted embroiderers and they were to travel at the Tsarina's expense with the Comtesse's entourage. Comfortable living quarters would be provided, the head embroiderer's salary would be generous and her assistants well paid, and local seamstresses of her choosing would make up her work force.

'But there must be many skilled embroiderers all over Russia!' Marguerite exclaimed in bewilderment.

The Comtesse had lowered the letter to her lap. 'Of course there are, but the Empress thinks nothing of summoning foreigners to her court from all over Europe if they can be of some particular highly skilled service to her. She has an English head gardener, a Danish doctor and an Italian hair-dresser to name but a few. But with Frenchwomen such as Madame de Pompadour and myself leading the world in fashion,' she added smugly, linking herself with the most fashionable woman at Versailles, 'it is no wonder that the Empress has turned her greedy eyes towards Paris, no matter how much she dislikes us as a nation!' The woman's lips whitened beneath their paint as she compressed them, making a beauty spot by her upper lip quiver angrily. 'She is also making sure that I do not eclipse her again! I had to let you know the contents of this letter, but you need not concern yourself about it. I leave for Russia at the end of the week and it will give me great satisfaction upon arrival to let the Ambassador inform her that you declined her offer.'

Marguerite had turned pale. She was being given the opportunity to begin life again. In new surroundings the still raw anguish within her could give way to a healing. She would be able to remember all the happy times with Jacques without the horror of seeing him trapped at the upper window of that flame-engulfed building, which presently blocked out all else for her. Promotion with her own atelier and needlewomen of her choice, once her most cherished dream, was more than secondary now. All she could contemplate was this gateway to finding again in joyous memories the man she had loved so deeply.

'But I will accept the appointment, Madame la Comtesse!' she exclaimed swiftly.

The Comtesse was staring at her in disbelief. 'You would seriously consider obeying this demand for your presence?'

'Yes, Madame.'

'Are you aware just how far away Russia is?'

'Yes, indeed! I know that journeys there take many weeks.'

'But you still do not seem to realize what you would be accepting. The Empress is insatiable when it comes to clothes. Your hours would be long. On a whim of the Empress you might have to work twenty-four hours a day to finish something for her.'

Marguerite thought to herself that this aristocrat and others born to riches like her had no idea how often *grisettes* like herself slaved through many midnight hours until dawn to finish some garments ordered imperiously at short notice before continuing the normal day's tasks.

'I'm used to working hard,' she said quietly. 'When there are no immediate orders for embroidery at Madame Fromont's establishment I take my place with the other seamstresses and often have the dullest of dressmaking tasks instead of the creative work that I love.' She leaned forward eagerly, putting forward the only argument that the Comtesse would understand. 'In the Tsarina's employ I would have my own atelier and always have wonderful work to do. I'd take pride and pleasure in it. And I'm sure I should soon learn to speak Russian.'

'I'm sure you would. The Grand Duchess Catherine, who is only a few years older than you, mastered it early in her marriage and she is German by birth. Fortunately she is also fluent in French, which is the language of the Russian Court. But it is a barbaric court with a glittering veneer of great ceremonies and magnificent palaces and fine clothes that hides an abysmal lack of culture.' She shook her head disdainfully. 'It is as different from the Court of Versailles in that respect as chalk is from cheese. Several of the Russian aristocracy are common people to whom on a mere whim the Empress – just like Peter the Great before her – has given a title with property, land and probably as many as a thousand serfs. Naturally the old noble families dislike all the upstarts and yet few of the ladies, whether noble or otherwise, are literate! How the Grand Duchess, who comes from a cultured family, has adapted to such barren ground I do not know.'

Marguerite answered carefully. 'But I shall not be involved in the Court itself. My world will be on a different level with only the Empress and the Grand Duchess to please and I'm sure that I could do that.' She had had plenty of experience in dealing with difficult women to be confident on that score. Even the Comtesse had never been easy!

Although normally the Comtesse had no interest in working people beyond their capacity to wait on her, she felt it would be a great loss if this young woman's exceptional talent should be damaged in any way.

'Think carefully,' she urged, leaning forward. 'Let me emphasize again the Empress's terrible temper. As for the excesses of her immoral way of life, I cannot bring myself to mention them.' She passed a hand delicately across her lips in emphasis. 'She plays vicious and humiliating tricks on both her male and female courtiers. Her ministers all go in fear of displeasing her in case she should banish them to some distant place! She could send you back to France for the slightest error.'

'What kind of man is the Tsar? Why does he indulge her whims?'

'There is no tsar. The Empress has never married. She was a young woman when she lost the love of her life after he contracted smallpox and died. Then she seized the Throne of all the Russias through a conspiracy. The more rightful heir, a mere boy, Ivan VI, is shut away in a fortress somewhere.' The Comtesse paused dramatically. 'Surely you would not wish to be employed by such a cruel and wicked woman?'

'I will take my chance,' Marguerite answered firmly, 'and make sure she never has any cause to turn against my fellow workers or against me.'

The Comtesse sighed, seeing there was no changing the young woman's mind. 'Then you will need some instruction as how to address the Empress when you take designs to her and you must also be told about the customs that have to be observed by everybody. Before you leave here today talk to my personal maid. She will give you all the information and also tell you what will be needed in the matter of warm clothes and various necessities when travelling. It will be very cold in Russia by the time we arrive.'

The maid proved to be friendly and helpful, adding a few warnings of her own. Marguerite made a list of everything she needed to remember.

She kept up a quick pace as she retraced her steps back to work. The sooner she broke the news of her departure to Madame Fromont the better. Fortunately she had finished the major work on the gold-satin skirt and so she would not be leaving her employer with that task unfinished. Already new designs for the future were dancing in her head. She saw embroidering for the Empress as a challenge. It would be a French triumph to please her as well as a personal one. She welcomed the prospect wholeheartedly. Most important of all would be a new peace of mind in which she could find her beloved Jacques again.

Two

In her office Madame Fromont listened attentively as Marguerite recounted all that had taken place on her visit. Finally the woman gave a slow nod of her head and smiled at her reassuringly.

'I have no intention of putting any barriers in your way and I wish you well in this new venture, Marguerite. You need to get away from Paris for a while. You have never recovered from the shock of that day we all remember with great sadness. This opportunity could not have come at a better time for you or for me.'

'For you, madame?' Marguerite was puzzled.

'I'm not well and my doctor has advised retirement. I have been postponing the moment, but now you have helped me come to a decision. If any of my workers are prepared to go with you, they are all free to make a choice, except the young ones apprenticed to me. They must remain. I have had several offers for the business and the would-be purchaser I favour most has needlewomen of her own, but has guaranteed that she will take on those wanting to stay. So why not speak to your fellow embroiderers after work today and see what happens?'

Marguerite was astonished by the woman's magnanimity, even though – unlike the majority of others in her position – she had always been a considerate employer. 'You are helping me a great deal. Time is short as the Comtesse will be leaving in a matter of days. I had intended to try for volunteers among those I know in other sewing establishments.'

'There's no need.'

It was late evening when the day's work ended and everybody was impatient to get home when Madame Fromont gathered her embroiderers together in the largest workroom. She spoke first, explaining that she had decided to sell the business. Immediately there were cries of dismay, but quickly she changed their anxious and, in some cases, frightened expressions by reassuring them that they would be able to stay on under the new owner.

'But,' she concluded, 'Marguerite has a proposal to announce with my goodwill and some of you may wish to take advantage of it.' Then with a final glance at them all she left the room and returned to her office.

Marguerite knew that most of the women would have no idea where Russia was located or anything about it and she began by explaining how great the distance was from France. Then she put the facts forward as bluntly as the Comtesse had done to her, hearing gasps of astonishment and incredulity from those gaping at what they were hearing. She warned of inevitable homesickness and emphasized that she could not take anyone with family ties and responsibilities, for the obvious reason that travelling to and fro would be impossible and there was no way of knowing how long they would be expected to stay in Russia.

'Anyone interested must think it over carefully. I have to ask for a decision by the day after tomorrow at the latest,' she concluded, 'because the entourage will be leaving next week and travelling papers must be obtained.'

At first there was a stunned silence. Then came an outburst of refusal and derision, only a few remaining silent.

'No! You must be mad to think of it, Marguerite! That Tsarina sounds a monster! She could have our throats cut for a misplaced stitch! Leave home for that? Never!'

Ignoring the jibes of those already departing, some looking back over their shoulders at her as they laughed together,

Marguerite turned to see how many had remained in the room. There were only five. Like most of the embroiderers in the establishment they had been trained as dressmakers before specializing in the more delicate work. She would be glad to have any one of them in her team.

'Are you all considering the proposal?' she asked. Then, as they nodded, she added, 'But I did say that I couldn't take anyone with family responsibilities.' Her gaze had rested on one of the women, who stood with folded arms. She was solidly built, amiable and level-headed, and although she was only in her early forties her hair was prematurely white.

'I'll go on one condition,' she stated decisively.

'But you are married, Jeanne Dudicourt,' Marguerite pointed out.

'I'll be thankful to leave my drunken sot of a husband!' Jeanne replied forcefully. 'I should have done it years ago, but I had the two kids and nowhere to go. Now my son is a mercenary in the army and I haven't seen him since he marched off to a war seven years ago. I just hope to God that he's still alive somewhere!' Briefly she put her hands together in an attitude of prayer and shook her head anxiously. 'So I'll leave word with a neighbour as to my whereabouts in case he should ever turn up again. But I'll also make her swear never to let the drunkard know anything. Not that he'd ever be able to find me! But I'll only come if I can bring Rose, my daughter, with me. She's seventeen, a good little needlewoman. She works over at the Desgranges atelier.'

'If she's willing to come I'll accept her on your recommendation.'

'Maybe my sister Sophie would come too. She embroiders for a bitch of a woman at the Valverde place and I know she's been looking for a place elsewhere, but it's not so easy. If she's interested shall I bring her to see you?'

Marguerite nodded. 'Come to my place tomorrow

evening when everyone has had time to think things over. Bring Rose too. We'll have a glass of wine.'

Another voice, rich in throaty cadences, spoke up. 'I'm volunteering to go with you, Marguerite! It will break the monotony of this place and be an adventure if nothing else!' The speaker was Violette Narbonne, her attractive feline face full of amusement, her hair a mane of wild, corn-gold curls.

Jeanne gave her an amused glance. 'Have you run out of Parisian lovers at last?'

Violette laughed, her blue eyes twinkling. 'No, far from it, but a change should be interesting. I like the idea of a whole new field of handsome men.'

Although Marguerite could foresee some trouble in taking her there was no doubt that the young woman's buoyant good humour and ability to see the funny side of events could help enormously in times of gloom, which were bound to occur from time to time. Then, turning her attention to the remaining three women, who were whispering together, she said questioningly, 'Charlotte? Hortense? Berthe?'

'We're thinking about it,' they replied in unison, but there was a negative tone in their voices.

Marguerite bade them all goodnight as they left. It looked as though at the final count she would have four embroiderers to go with her. She went at once to report the result to Madame Fromont, who nodded approvingly.

'Well done, Marguerite. You'll need good company when you're far from home. I should not have liked to see you depart on your own.'

As Marguerite left the building she found one of the apprentices, Isabelle Pieron, waiting for her. 'Mam'selle Marguerite! Can you spare me a moment, please!'

'Yes, of course, Isabelle.' Marguerite knew her background. She was the only child of a weak, ineffectual mother and a brutal stepfather. Before coming to the Fromont establishment the girl had worked almost from babyhood with

16

her mother in a silk mill and bad conditions as well as a poor diet had taken its toll on her. Small and thin, she looked older than her sixteen years, her soft fair hair pushed back under her hat and her little face marred, not for the first time, by the fading yellow bruise from a black eye. 'What did you wish to speak to me about?'

'Let me go to Russia with you!' It was an impassioned plea.

Marguerite saw the desperation in the girl's light-blue eyes. 'How do you know I'm going to Russia? You were not in the room.'

'I heard the others talking and jeering about it as they left while I was sweeping up. Then afterwards Jeanne and Violette were discussing it as they put on their hats.'

Marguerite gave a little sigh. 'I know from what I have seen for myself over past months that you do excellent work, but I think I have four embroiderers now, which is the number I need. In any case, I feel sure your stepfather would forbid it and Madame Fromont would not release you from your apprenticeship. I'm sorry, Isabelle.' She would have moved on, but the girl caught her arm.

'Wait, please! My mother would want me to go! She knows how my stepfather has always abused me and there's nothing she or I can do to stop him! I've tried to get away from home more than once, but he has always found me and dragged me back again. In Russia he could never get me!' Tears suddenly burst out of the girl's eyes and she threw her arms over her head, crying out in anguish. 'I swear I'd work my fingers to the bone!'

'Hush!' Marguerite, moved by pity and shocked by the girl's torment, drew her into a doorway, for her noisy sobbing was attracting attention. Holding the girl to her, she saw under a pushed-up sleeve the black bruising on the girl's forearm. Remembering that the Tsarina's letter had said four or five embroiderers, she gave another little sigh. 'I can't make any promises, Isabelle. All I can say is that

17

I'll speak to your mother. Tell her to meet me here at this time tomorrow evening. If she gives her permission I'll also talk to Madame Fromont on your behalf.'

The meeting took place as arranged. After the matter had been fully discussed Marguerite agreed to take Isabelle, providing Madame Fromont could be persuaded to release her. To Marguerite's embarrassment the girl's mother snatched up her hand and kissed it in tearful gratitude.

Madame Fromont called Marguerite into her office again early next morning. On her desk were boxes of trimmings.

'I suggest you take a supply of these with you,' the woman said. 'You may have them at less than cost price. I'll give you some of the mannequin dolls too.'

'That's most generous!' Marguerite exclaimed. 'I had thought to take some emergency supplies.'

'It would be wise. After all, there's no telling how difficult it might be to obtain French trimmings and the Empress seems set on having a Parisian look to the gowns you are to make her. After all, what I have here may be surplus to the new owner's requirements and so you might as well have them.'

Together they spent a while making a selection of dainty ribbons, pearly sequins, delicate braids, colourful buttons and even a stock of embroidery silks in every hue. When it came to reckoning up the cost of these items Madame Fromont took only a token payment, refusing anything more. When Marguerite thanked her she merely shook her head.

'You've been a good worker ever since you first came here as a little girl in your late sister's time, starting with picking up fallen pins and matching silk threads. Nobody knew then what a fine design seamstress and embroiderer you would become. I had always hoped to gain business at Versailles, which would have given you the opening you deserve with your original designs, but with so many dressmakers in Paris that was not to be. The Comtesse d'Oinville has been like many other women of her class in never revealing the name of a dressmaker they wish to keep exclusively for themselves. But now you will have the chance you deserve at the Russian Court instead and you have a good team going with you!'

'There is an apprentice seamstress I should very much like to take with me if you would allow it.' Then Marguerite pleaded Isabelle's case. When Madame Fromont had heard all the details she agreed to a cancellation of the apprenticeship.

That evening the volunteers met at Marguerite's garret room, Isabelle included. Jeanne had brought her daughter Rose, who was an impish-looking brunette with a short, pert nose and a happy smile. She was full of excitement.

'This will be a real adventure, Mam'selle Marguerite!' she declared, green eyes dancing.

Jeanne's sister, Sophie Bouvier, had also decided to accompany her sister and niece. 'I've always wanted to travel,' she confessed, 'and this will be a great opportunity to see other countries.'

She was tall and willowy with glossy black hair, her only resemblance to Jeanne being that they both had velvety-brown eyes. Both she and Rose had brought examples of their embroidery for Marguerite to approve and she saw at a glance that she had two skilful needlewomen with her.

She served wine and cake before telling them all they would need to take with them for the journey and afterwards answering their questions to the best of her knowledge. Then she spread out a map borrowed from the Comtesse's maid and they gathered round as she traced the route for them.

'From Paris we shall travel by way of Rheims to Liège and after that we leave our homeland behind us to follow this route' – she traced it with her fingertip – 'until we reach Cologne. From there we travel on through many more German towns to get to Gotha. Then comes Leipzig followed by Dresden and Frankfurt-on-Oder. Afterwards there's a long stretch through Prussia, passing through the city of Königsberg and on again until we cross the Russian border to reach Riga. That's when we'll be on the last lap of the journey to St Petersburg!'

She straightened up triumphantly and then saw the uncertain expression on all their faces.

'Merciful heaven!' Jeanne exclaimed breathlessly. 'It really is a long way!'

'Any second thoughts?' Marguerite asked, suddenly anxious, but to her relief they all shook their heads. 'Good! Now we'll all have another glass of wine and drink to a safe and interesting journey!'

On the morning of departure Marguerite stood alone at her sister's graveside in a quiet churchyard, a bunch of flowers in her hand. Farewells had been said and now the last one was to be made. Normally she came here once a week, but now she did not know when she would be able to visit again.

It was Anne-Marie who had taught her to read and write, to sew and later to excel in embroidery, all while taking care of her after their mother had died and later when their father, faced with bankruptcy and imprisonment for fraud, had taken his own life. Until then they had had a good home. Anne-Marie would never speak of how she had managed to keep them both fed and sheltered after that terrible time, but Marguerite recalled dark hovels with a rag doll to keep her company whenever her sister went out at night. Then gradually their circumstances had improved. Anne-Marie had gained employment with Madame Fromont as an embroiderer and she herself, although only seven years old, had started the first stages of an apprenticeship under her sister's watchful eye.

'I've come to say adieu, Anne-Marie,' she said softly. 'It is through guessing what you must have endured on the streets that I've managed to get a young girl released from her apprenticeship to take her away to Russia with me. I'm so thankful that you knew better times and found some happiness again before you had to leave this world.'

She stooped down and laid the flowers carefully by the ornate headstone. Anne-Marie's married lover had paid for it as well as the funeral, for which she had been immensely grateful. Her own meagre savings would barely have kept her sister from a pauper's grave.

Jacques had been buried in his birthplace of Rouen where his parents lived. She had only visited his last resting place at the time of the funeral and had not seen his parents since that day. They had not approved of her, wanting more for their talented son than a seamstress for a wife. But Jacques had loved her as she had loved him. There would never have been anyone else for either of them.

She drew back a pace, and stood for a few more moments in reflective silence before slowly turning away to retrace her steps along the path. Outside the gates the noise of the city enveloped her once again.

Three

Marguerite had expected to be the first to arrive at the place of departure outside the gates of the Comtesse's home, but Isabelle was already there. The girl had not dared to enter the waiting coach assigned to the seamstresses. Instead she stood huddled by a gatepost, her face white and scared, a carpet bag clutched in her hand and a small valise by her feet. She was the only one not to have delivered a travelling box the night before, all of which were already securely strapped to the roof and on to the back of the coach. Marguerite gave her a reassuring smile.

'You may get in now, Isabelle. The others will be here soon.'

Isabelle promptly scuttled into the coach, which was a large, lumbering-looking vehicle. Although there was comfortable seating for six she huddled into a corner as if trying to make herself as small as possible. The coach with its six sturdy horses was one of a dozen equipages already in line, ready to accommodate the Comtesse's retinue of personal servants and her large amount of luggage.

Just then the rest of Marguerite's travellers began to arrive. Jeanne came hurrying along with Rose, both carrying some hand baggage and their sewing boxes. In addition Jeanne had a basket of food over her arm as all the seamstresses had to provide their own sustenance for the first day, although for the rest of journey their meals and accommodation would be paid for from the Comtesse's purse. Rose greeted Marguerite with a bob and a wide smile.

'Bonjour, mam'selle. I could hardly wait for this morning to come!'

'Yes, here we are,' Jeanne declared breathlessly. 'We left the old devil snoring after last night's binge.' Yet she was as eager as Isabelle to get into the coach out of sight and hustled Rose in with her as if she feared he might yet come in roaring pursuit of them.

Sophie arrived next. She had been hurrying to catch up with her sister and niece, whom she had sighted ahead of her. 'I'm not late, am I?' she inquired anxiously. 'Those two were keeping up such a pace!'

'No,' Marguerite assured her. 'There's still time to spare.'

Violette was last, sauntering along with swinging hips and gaily dressed in a scarlet cape and a straw hat with a curling feather, hand baggage in one hand and a basket in the other. 'Isn't this going to be fun!' she cried happily in greeting.

As soon as Violette had stowed away her belongings as the rest had done and seated herself Marguerite took the place by the window that had been left for her. With the exception of Isabelle all were chattering eagerly. Then there was a sudden flurry of movement in the courtyard and the last of the servants came hurrying to take their places in the coaches. It was clear that the Comtesse was about to leave. Her gleaming equipage had been brought to the steps of the entrance.

A few moments later there was the glimmer of a blue-velvet cloak as the Comtesse emerged from the house and stepped into the coach. Then the eight horses drawing it came clip-clopping out of the courtyard, the four postilions in the d'Oinville pale-grey livery, to sweep ahead of the waiting vehicles, four armed outriders in escort. With a lurch that nearly shot all the seamstresses off the seats their coach rolled forward.

'We're on our way!' Violette exclaimed joyfully, clapping her hands together as they all sat back again, laughing and talking. Isabelle gave a shuddering sigh of relief.

The merry chatter continued until the cavalcade of coaches had passed through the gates of Paris, for then everyone was quieter, gazing out at the passing countryside as if they feared it might be the last time they would see it. Before long another coach stood waiting by the road-side. The traveller spoke to the Comtesse, showing her proof of his identity, and gained her permission to follow her entourage, there being greater security travelling in convoy through many lonely places where there was always the danger of attack by highwaymen and other rogues of the road.

'How did that man know we were coming?' Rose asked.

'Word goes quickly by the grapevine,' her mother replied, 'but sometimes travellers have to wait days for an armed convoy going in the right direction, especially if they're going far afield. Most travellers have to go a certain distance with one convoy and then, if it's not going to their partic-ular destination, they switch to another to follow the route they want. The greater the number travelling together the better the security since every man carries a pistol.'

At noon the women shared their food. Isabelle had only two slices of stale black bread to offer. Rose grimaced.

'I'm not having a share of that!' she exclaimed in disgust. 'There's some mould on it.'

Her mother gave her a sharp dig with an elbow. 'We're having no nonsense from you, my girl! You'll eat your share like everybody else. From what the Comtesse's maid told Marguerite it isn't always possible to get food at times in some isolated places we'll be passing through. So eat up while you have the chance!'

Isabelle seemed to shrink more into herself, although the two slices were divided up and bravely eaten. Rose's eyes watered and she gagged but managed to swallow her portion.

Fortunately none of the seamstresses became nauseous with the sway of the coach over rutted surfaces, but three different times coaches ahead stopped for two maids and a young page to vomit in the bushes. As it was in the country others of both sexes took the chance to relieve themselves behind bushes and trees, men to one side and women to the other. The Comtesse never appeared, but her lady's maid discreetly emptied a small boat-shaped receptacle such as most ladies used on journeys. The seamstresses had discovered one in a cupboard under the seat, which had been supplied for them, but although it bore the d'Oinville crest it was thick white china and not like the Comtesse's own of flower-decorated Sèvres porcelain

That night the seamstresses slept at an inn where they were given supper. The Comtesse stayed at a nearby château with people whom she knew, and this was to become the pattern of the journey. Whenever possible, overnight stops were timed to enable her to stay in comfort at the home of an acquaintance. Yet the seamstresses were not forgotten, a senior servant paying as promised all bills for their food and lodging. Not that there was much comfort for them. If they were lucky there would be a wash-house where they could bathe themselves and dry their washing overnight, the very nature of their work making them all naturally fastidious about cleanliness, but this facility was not always available. Frequently they had to sleep three or four in a bed and were sometimes plagued by bedbugs, but the sense of adventure had not waned and they were up early each morning ready for the new day.

The journey rolled on with the days, but it was not until a week after the French border had been crossed and Aix-la-Chapelle left behind that Isabelle began to throw off her nervousness, no longer looking wide-eyed and scared at every halt. Rose persuaded her into a game of cards and after that the two girls gradually formed a friendship. Before long they had become close, talking non-stop and giggling together over private jokes. Marguerite was astonished and pleased by the change in the girl. It was as if Isabelle were blossoming like a flower in her newfound sense of freedom.

The other women passed their time by knitting, darning stockings, dozing and chatting as well as by playing cards and memory games. Occasionally they bickered when boredom set in, but never seriously enough for Marguerite to intervene. Sometimes she read to them from one of the books she had brought with her. There were also other diversions along the way. An exceptional one took place during a change of horses when two accompanying travellers drew their rapiers fiercely in a personal quarrel. The Comtesse promptly barred them from following her entourage any further.

Without exception all the travellers took exercise at any opportunity, even if it was only a short walk up and down during a temporary halt. Violette flirted with one of the armed guards, who frequently rode alongside the seamstresses's coach to exchange a few pleasantries with her.

It was always amusing when a flock of sheep or a herd of cows swarmed about the coaches, even if it did cause some delay. Once they were held up in a forest by a boar hunt as the prey doubled back and left the hunters crossing and recrossing the road in confusion. Rose, Jeanne and Violette jeered and shouted from the windows, clapping when the boar appeared to have got away. Then they collapsed laughing into their seats, kicking up a flurry of petticoats.

In any populated area there were always the pedlars, who ran alongside the coaches, offering their wares for sale. Most enjoyable of all were the street performers, who appeared from nowhere whenever the entourage came to a standstill in a town or city. So day after day went by for the Frenchwomen as wheels rolled over everything from rutted country roads to rubbish-strewn city streets while the voices of local inhabitants changed language as great distances were slowly covered. By now private mansions where the Comtesse could stay with acquaintances had become intermittent, and mostly she had to take her chance at hostelries with everyone else, although she always had the best room available.

It was always exciting for the seamstresses when the coaches passed through a town. They looked out at the shops, the fashions, and the different architecture. In Dresden they gazed up at the great cathedral as they were driven by. It was when the convoy halted for a change of horses at a post house in Frankfurt-on-Oder that one of the d'Oinville menservants came to the seamstresses' coach as they were about to alight and handed in six individual foot-warmers.

'You'll be glad of these when the weather gets cold,' he informed them cheerfully. 'We get them filled with hot coals from inns that we'll pass. There's a stock of fur knee-rugs for you too later on and you'll need them, believe me! I've done this journey before and I know.' He glanced at Violette with a mischievous wink. 'If you need any extra warmth you can always have my arms around you.'

'Impudent devil!' Violette retorted, but she was amused and flashed her eyes at him. 'How long before we move on again?'

'Only half an hour. So don't wander off too far.'

When the seamstresses returned from a short walk another coach was waiting to join the convoy when it departed again. Violette, inquisitive by nature, soon found out from the same manservant that the traveller was an English-woman, Mistress Sarah Warrington. Accompanied by her maid, she would be travelling all the way to the Russian city of Riga. Violette relayed this information to her companions as they settled themselves in their seats again. They were all interested as so far nobody else would be with the convoy all the way to Russia, other travellers coming and going along the route.

Marguerite was the first to see the new arrival from where she sat by the window. It was just a glimpse as the Englishwoman's coach rolled past to take its place in the convoy. She saw a pretty, delicately boned face, framed by soft brown hair before the moment was gone.

'What's the maid's name?' Rose asked as the wheels began to roll again. 'Is she English too?'

'No,' Violette replied. 'Blanche Chamier is a fellow countrywoman of ours, originally from Boulogne, but she's been with the Englishwoman for some time. She's a big, strong-looking woman and will be well able to lift her mistress in and out of the coach if need be.'

'Has the lady difficulty in walking?' Rose bit into half of the sweetmeat she had bought from one of the pedlars, the other half given to Isabelle.

'No, but she was taken ill after arriving here and had to be nursed for several weeks. She's come from France and is on her way to join her husband, but she had to stay on in this city until she'd recovered from whatever it was that ailed her. She hasn't fully regained her strength yet and in Blanche Charmier's opinion she shouldn't be starting out again for another couple of weeks at least. But the lady made a promise to her husband before he left for Russia that she would join him with the least possible delay and is anxious to continue her journey.' Violette threw up her hands merrily. 'What we women do for love!'

'We all know what you do!' Jeanne bantered good-humouredly, giving her a nudge with an elbow, and they both laughed.

'Why didn't she travel with him in the first place?' Sophie questioned, her arched brows meeting in a frown. She was intrigued by the thought of this lone woman making such a great journey with only a maid for company.

'He had to leave at short notice three months ago and she was left to see to the packing up of their home in France where they had lived for four years.'

'Where was that?'

'Near the Palace of Versailles. He is a special kind of gardener and was engaged in some project there and other of the royal parks,' Violette continued. 'Apparently he's quite famous for creating beautiful gardens and landscapes, which was why he was suddenly invited by the Empress to do some very important work in Russia. Just like she sent for you, Marguerite. Blanche says . . .'

She broke off as a rider galloped past the coach, shouting to those at the head of the line of vehicles to delay departure. Rose was the first to dart to the window and lean out to watch proceedings.

'There's some argument going on,' she reported delightedly. 'Now the horseman has approached the Comtesse's coach and is making his appeal to her through her window.' There was a pause. 'Oh, it's all right. She must have agreed to the delay, because he's smiling and nodding. What a fine-looking fellow he is! Who could resist a request from him?'

Violette was on her feet, pushing Rose aside. 'Let me see! Yes, you're right.' She gave an envious sigh. 'No wonder she's keeping him in conversation. Ah! He's leaving her now and coming this way again.'

She kept her position at the open window, but to her annoyance he rode past her without a glance and the rest of them saw briefly his well-cut profile before he was out of sight. Her commentary continued.

'We must find out all about him! He's handing his horse over to a groom now to be stabled.' Her head was still out of the window. 'Hey, I can see it's going to be a longish wait. The Comtesse is getting out and making for the tavern. Her maid is in tow, carrying the usual shawls and jewel box. Come along, girls! We can all go for another walk around the stalls and shops. I saw a necklace I'd like to take another look at.'

As Marguerite set off with the others on their walk she saw Mistress Warrington again. The Englishwoman's pace was slow as she crossed the cobbled square with her maid to a coffee house. She was as small and slight as her maid was big and broad. Blanche Chamier was in her thirties with a boisterously healthy look to her round kindly face. As Violette had said, care of the Englishwoman appeared to be in capable hands.

The delay requested proved to be a lengthy one. It was three hours before a carriage and two wagons, their loads roped down securely, finally appeared. The newcomer, who had been impatiently pacing up and down, darted into the tavern and solicitously escorted the Comtesse back to her coach. It had clearly been a longer wait than expected, but she seemed mollified by his attention, her frown of exasperation easing away until she was smiling at him. As soon as she was settled he left her to hurry across to his own newly arrived carriage. With the familiar discordant cacophony of cracking whips, shouts, creaking wheels and groaning springs the journey recommenced.

The seamstresses speculated amongst themselves as to what the wagons might be carrying. Surely there must be something vitally important under those covering tarpaulins for the Comtesse to agree to a delay? It could not be just the man's good looks that had persuaded her. Absurd suggestions were forthcoming and caused laughter. Was it a secret cache of arms? Jewels for the Empress? Then, as the suggestions became bawdier, there was even more laughter. Marguerite approved this new diversion. Anything that kept her companions' minds from boredom was greatly welcomed.

At the next halt for a change of horses at a country tavern Violette went immediately with her provocative, hip-swinging walk to laugh and flirt with one of the wagon drivers. When she rejoined the others, who were seated at a corner table in the tavern, she had found out all she wanted to know.

'That good-looking man is a Dutchman named Hendrick

van Deventer.' She tilted her head in his direction where he stood smoking a long-stemmed pipe by the hearth. 'He is on his way to Russia with those wagons to join his brother, Jan. They're art dealers with an important gallery in Amsterdam. More paintings were needed for sale in Russia and he is supervising the delivery of them.'

Marguerite was as interested in the Dutchman as the others. 'So he is going as far as Russia too?' she said. 'It must be a cargo of value if it can't be trusted just to wagon drivers.'

Her glance went again to the Dutchman. He was well groomed and well clad in a good cloth coat and knee breeches, his waistcoat a merry green, and his wheat-coloured hair unpowdered and caught back with a black ribbon. He looked every inch a prosperous merchant. She would have liked the opportunity to view those paintings in the wagons, but that could never be.

She turned her gaze to the Englishwoman, who was sitting with her maid on the opposite side of the room. By chance their eyes met and Sarah Warrington smiled and inclined her head in greeting. Marguerite responded, pleased at this friendly contact. Perhaps they would get to know each other as the journey continued.

The chance came to chat a week later when they met by chance on the landing of the stairs in the tavern where they had been staying for the night.

'You are certainly travelling in lively company.' Sarah Warrington had spoken in French and she indicated with amusement the crescendo of noisy chatter in the room that Marguerite had just left.

'I'm thankful to say we get on very well.' Then Marguerite added with a little laugh, 'Most of the time anyway.' They began to descend the narrow stairs, the Englishwoman going ahead.

'I've been informed that you are on your way to make gowns for Empress Elisabeth. Ah, the grapevine brings all the news to us travellers as you surely know.'

'That's true indeed.'

Sarah paused and looked up over her shoulder at Marguerite. 'I've been told that the Dutchman is taking a painting to his brother that is destined for the Empress. Have you heard that too?'

'No, but it would explain his presence with the wagons. I thought it must be a valuable load,' Marguerite replied, understanding now why the Comtesse had allowed the journey to be delayed for such a long time. She had been nervous of giving that powerful woman in Russia any further cause to turn against her through a painting's late delivery.

After that Marguerite and Sarah often talked together and, both having run out of reading matter, they exchanged books. When Sarah invited Marguerite to ride with her for a stage of the journey she changed places with Blanche, who sat with the other seamstresses, giving them all a change of company.

Marguerite's only encounter with the Dutchman came when they were standing side by side as the landlord informed them that there was only one room left. Hendrick van Deventer stepped back.

'For the ladies, of course. I'll stay somewhere else.'

The landlord shook his head. 'There isn't any other place around here, sir. I can offer you the stable-loft.'

'I'll take that.'

In the morning Marguerite asked the Dutchman if he had spent a very uncomfortable night.

'No,' he replied with a grin, grey eyes crinkled at the corners. 'The straw was clean and there was plenty of it.'

After that he always bowed and doffed his tricorne hat whenever they met, but they had no further conversation.

It was one morning not long afterwards that Jeanne sighed heavily as she joined her companions already in their seats. 'I have to admit that I've become very tired of this daily journeying. Wouldn't it be good if we could just have two or three days in the same place?'

There were murmurs of assent from all except Marguerite. For her it was the moment she had been dreading. Spirits had been flagging and now here was proof that the novelty of travel had finally worn off. From this moment on it was likely to be difficult to keep the women's spirits up.

Soon it was just as she had feared with the start of longer periods of boredom with quarrels breaking out with little cause. Violette, whom Marguerite had expected to be of help at such a time, was ill-tempered and depressed, her liveliness having deserted her through a falling-out with the armed guard.

Surprisingly it was Isabelle who found a way to cheer them all. She had become totally content as the journey had proceeded, never complaining about anything, and she began to sing for the first time one morning, never having joined in with the others when they had sung together sometimes. Her voice was very clear and sweet. When she came to the end of her song the others applauded spontaneously and urged her to continue. She blushed crimson at their praise, but obliged them. As the days passed she seemed to have an unending repertoire of songs, some comic that made them laugh delightedly, others of love lost or found as well as hymns and ditties from childhood that all the women remembered and sang with her.

'How did you learn all these songs?' she was asked.

'I just seem to hear a song and remember it. Not all the words, of course, but if I don't get the chance to hear the song again I make up my own words to the tune.'

From then on, whenever gloom set in, Isabelle would begin to sing softly as if to herself, but even if it did not always dispel the general depression it soothed pangs of homesickness, anxiety and even regrets over earlier happenings in the women's lives that were in their minds. It also banished for a little while an awareness of the physical weariness that coach travel induced.

* * *

As the journey advanced through Prussia it was no longer possible for overnight halts always to be made in towns, which were few and far between. Often accommodation was only to be found in farmhouses and cottages where conditions were frequently cramped and dirty.

It was in poverty-stricken areas that the changing of horses presented a serious problem. With never less than four and mostly six horses to a vehicle it meant that eighty were needed each time to relieve those that had covered the previous stage of the journey. There was always fierce competition among the coachmen and postilions as to which of them would get the best, and fisticuffs became commonplace. It was often a case of searching stables far and wide for replacements, which meant long delays. At these times Jeanne gained her wish to stay more than one night in a place, but inevitably these lengthier sojourns were in uncomfortable and sometimes rat-infested accommodation, any obtainable food being of poor quality too.

Until now, apart from the occasional shower, the weather had been good for travelling, although it had been getting colder all the time. Now it had begun to deteriorate seriously, the wind turning rougher with heavy rain that never ceased. Frequently coach wheels became stuck in deep muddy ruts and in the pelting rain men would push and shove until the vehicle was mobile again. By now the promised fur rugs had been handed in to the Frenchwomen, which with the foot-warmers, gave welcome warmth to feet and legs, although it was not everywhere that they could be refilled.

It was late afternoon along a rough road through a particularly dense forest when a band of brigands came bursting out of hiding, some on foot and the rest on horseback, waving swords and firing weapons. Immediately there was uproar, shouting and swearing, and responding gunfire. The door of the seamstresses' coach was wrenched open and two villainous-looking ruffians gave a shout of triumph at seeing the women within. Reaching forward like a flash they seized Jeanne by the ankles to send her crashing on her buttocks to the floor, one hauling her out like a sack of potatoes while the other grabbed at Rose by the petticoats.

Instantly all the women were shrieking and screaming as they threw themselves into the defence of their friends, only Isabelle left cowering in the corner. But as they almost fell out of the coach in their fury, Marguerite lashing out like the rest with fists and nails, they were sighted by other ruffians, some of whom came racing towards them.

By now the defence of the armed men with the coaches was taking its toll. Jeanne's attacker fell, screaming and clutching his arm, and the other was killed outright from a bullet in the head fired by Hendrick van Deventer, who yelled at the seamstresses to get back into the coach and keep down.

They obeyed him. The other villains, who had been aiming for them, had been intercepted, but bullets were flying and the women crouched together on the floor, arms about each other. Isabelle was shaking violently, uttering curious little whimpers, while Sophie and Rose sobbed from shock. Jeanne just swore quietly and repetitively in a monotonous drone of rage, knowing her bruises would make sitting painful for some time to come.

When the shooting ceased, all except Isabelle ventured rising to their feet. There was no longer any sign of danger and they alighted one by one into the cold air. The wounded man had disappeared, but they each had to step over the dead one. Somebody had already covered his face with a rag. The robbers had fled, taking their wounded but leaving their dead. Nobody in the convoy had been killed, but several men had minor injuries and a robber's bullet had smashed the bone of a manservant's leg.

Blanche came running up to the seamstresses with a flask of cognac. 'Are you all right? My mistress wants each of you to have a measure of this.'

'That's very kind,' Marguerite said, taking it from her.

'What of Mistress Warrington? Did any of those men come to her coach?'

'No, we hid down on the floor, but the Comtesse would have lost her jewels if her guards had not acted as quickly as they did.'

Sophie had gathered up their drinking cups and Marguerite poured the cognac. It was Jeanne who persuaded Isabelle to drink some, almost forcing it through the girl's chattering teeth.

Marguerite went personally to return the flask. Sarah immediately expressed her fervent relief that they were all safe.

'I have a small pistol in my muff,' she said. 'Tom insisted that I carry it with me at all times on this journey, but I forgot about it in my fright.'

'I'm sure Blanche would have fired it if it had been in her hands. Perhaps you should let her have it in future.'

'Yes, I'll do that.'

Marguerite left her to inquire after the Comtesse, but there was no chance. A lantern had been lit within her coach and the blinds drawn to discourage anyone from disturbing her. If she was in a state of shock it was not to be witnessed.

Turning back, Marguerite came face to face with Hendrick, who grinned at her with satisfaction. 'I think all acquitted themselves very well, especially you and your ladies, who fought those two villains like tigers!'

She gave a soft laugh. 'All is well now and that's what counts. No wonder travellers like to take the road together! A coach on its own wouldn't have had a chance. Are we likely to meet another ambush anywhere?'

'Who can tell? We've many miles to go yet.' He glanced up and down the line of vehicles. 'When we've finished binding up our wounded we'll be on our way.'

'Can I help?'

'Not this time. Everything is in hand.' He turned as somebody shouted to him and went hurrying away to see what was wanted.

As yet the seamstresses were still too subdued and upset to get back into the coach and stood talking everything over with other travellers, but Marguerite saw that Isabelle had not moved from her crouching position on the floor of the coach. Pitying the timid girl, Marguerite entered and drew Isabelle up beside her on to the seat, keeping a comforting arm about the thin waist.

'It's all over, Isabelle,' she said reassuringly.

'At first I thought law-keepers had come all the way from Paris for me,' Isabelle whispered as if her mind was far away.

'Why ever should you think that?'

Isabelle looked up, her pupils still dilated with fright and swimming with tears. 'Because the night before I left home I killed my stepfather!'

Marguerite stared at her in disbelief. 'Do you know what you're saying?'

'Yes! He was like a madman when he came home and discovered that my mother had left him.' Isabelle was stuttering as she unburdened herself of the terrible secret she had been keeping to herself. 'I had persuaded her to go, because there was no knowing what he would do to her after he found me gone. When he came at me in his rage I grabbed a kitchen knife and stuck it in his belly!' Her eyes were wild and she screeched out, her fists clenched, 'And I'm glad of it!'

'Hush!' Marguerite covered the girl's mouth with her hand, but nobody outside the coach had heard. 'Where did your mother go?' Marguerite hoped that the frail little woman would not be pursued by the authorities and blamed for the crime.

'To her brother in the country. Nobody will ever find her there. She thought I'd be leaving the house before that devil of a man came home and would be staying the night at your place, because that is what I told her. But he'd had no money left for drink and returned earlier than I'd expected. After I'd killed him I collected my things and spent the night in a church porch as I'd planned.'

'How long will it be before he is missed?'

Isabelle shook her head wildly. 'He lived by violence and robbery, so it may be days before the body is found. Then everyone will know I committed the murder and not my mother, because I left my bloodstained clothes with the knife.' Isabelle threw her arms over her head and rocked to and fro. 'Now you know why I can never go back to France! They'd hang me!'

Marguerite understood now why Isabelle had been like a frightened rabbit until France had been left far behind. At least the danger of any pursuit had long since gone. The arm of the law would never reach this far and in any case violence and murder were common enough events in the slums of Paris and given little attention.

'Listen to me carefully, Isabelle. This is our secret. Nobody else need ever know of it. The past with all its agonies is behind you. There is a new future ahead and I shall help you in any way I can.'

She broke off. Their companions were returning. She took the girl's hand into hers and held it in comfort. Isabelle's trembling only ceased when after a while she fell asleep. The seemingly endless journey continued.

They had crossed the border into Poland when intensely cold weather set in. Fortunately there were only light flurries of snow, which did not hinder wheels on frost-hard surfaces and, except for minor delays, progress was good. Small braziers were now lit daily and handed into all the coaches where they were suspended on chains from the ceiling. At least wherever the company stayed overnight, however humble the dwelling, there was always a wonderful warmth from the stoves that the inhabitants kept stacked with kindling from the great forests.

Sarah became noticeably more exhausted as the days went by. She felt the cold excessively in spite of being enveloped in furs. She no longer took walks, although everybody else exercised, their breath hanging in clouds as they became red-cheeked in the freezing air. Whenever she had to leave the coach for a night's accommodation she leaned more and more heavily on Blanche's arm until eventually two of the Comtesse's lackeys carried her in and out. Great areas of the land were poverty-stricken and when only stable and barn lofts were available for sleeping she was like the Comtesse in choosing to keep to her coach, Blanche staying with her.

'I'm worried as to how much longer my mistress can endure this travelling,' Blanche confided to the seamstresses. 'She seems to get weaker every day.' Her deep sigh conveyed her exasperation. 'I knew she should have had a longer convalescence before setting off on this journey, but oh, no! She would not listen to me.'

In spite of Sarah's listlessness she was always glad to see Marguerite and they talked of many things. Sarah had grown up in a comfortable middle-class home, but as she was one of ten daughters it had been important for her parents to find husbands for all of them. Tom Warrington was the son of neighbouring friends and as he and Sarah had known each other since childhood it had seemed natural that they should marry when his apprenticeship was over and he had established himself. After he had worked on the royal gardens at Windsor he had seized the chance to move to France, where he had assisted one of the royal garden designers for four years as well as gaining commissions of his own.

'I was happy living in the village of Versailles,' Sarah said one afternoon as she and Marguerite sat by the fire in the taproom of a hostelry. 'At least, as content as I could ever be away from my own country.'

They were passing the time during a wait for horses to be gathered in from the surrounding area. Blanche had gone to the privy, which was giving them a chance to talk again for a little while on their own.

'Did you miss England so much?'

'Oh, yes. Early mornings I often went into the park at the Palace when only the gardeners were about and where the blossoms and plants were the same as at home. The gates there stand open permanently, and as the guards knew me as Tom's wife they always let me through. Not that I ever distracted Tom if he was supervising something. I just wandered on my own along the secret paths into those lovely little groves and flower gardens. Once in one of the open-air ballrooms I met Tom by chance and we danced on our own there!' She lifted her chin and laughed delightedly. 'We have had many happy times and he is so good to me.'

Out of loyalty to him she did not add that she dreaded living in Russia, even though it would not be for ever, for she knew it would be alien to her in every way. In France she had made friends and people thought much along the lines of her own countrymen and women, but how would it be in a land so remote from all she had ever known? She envied the way the young Frenchwoman saw the future as a challenge, determined to be successful in whatever lay ahead.

A clattering of hooves coming into the courtyard announced the arrival of more replacements. 'That's a good sound,' Marguerite commented. 'Now we should soon be on our way again.'

A sudden uproar outside failed to capture the attention of those in the taproom, for it seemed like the usual outbreak of quarrelling over who should have the best horses. Then there was a sudden unnatural silence. The door burst open and one of the grooms came rushing into the taproom to glance around until he spotted Sarah. He darted across to her.

'Madame! There's been an accident! Your maid!'

Sarah turned ashen and sprang to her feet. 'Dear God!'

She was already stumbling on her way to the door. Marguerite was swift to catch up with her and supported her around the waist. Out in the courtyard a gathering of men parted quickly to let them through. Blanche lay on the cobblestones, her arms flung out where she had fallen, half her head gashed horribly. Hendrick was on one knee beside her and he looked up, his expression grim as he shook his head to show there was no hope. Sarah uttered a torn cry and flung herself down on her knees beside the dead woman, sobbing desolately.

'What happened?' Marguerite asked hoarsely.

Hendrick rose to his feet. 'There was the usual struggle to grab the fittest-looking horses, which alarmed one of them, causing it to rear and plunge like a mad thing, and a hoof knocked her flying. She was just waiting to go past to the taproom.'

The Comtesse, wrapped in a sable cape, was among those who had come outside to see what had happened and she spoke out clearly. 'This journey shall not continue until that poor woman has been given a Christian burial.'

Then she turned on her heel and went back indoors. There were those who muttered amongst themselves at this unexpected delay, but after the incident in the forest none wanted to continue without full security.

Marguerite and Hendrick helped Sarah to her feet and back indoors. Fortunately there were rooms available in the hostelry and Marguerite took Sarah upstairs to one of them.

'Blanche has been with me for four years,' Sarah sobbed as she lay down on the bed. 'She came to me soon after I arrived in France, because my English maid had become violently homesick and I had to send her home again.' She covered her face with her hands. 'Oh, my poor Blanche! She was such a good, kind woman. I must write to her sister. She had nobody else.'

'Shall I do that for you? You can tell me what to write and then sign it.'

Sarah clutched Marguerite's hand gratefully before sinking back into her grief. 'Thank you most kindly. Everything seems to have become such an effort for me recently and never more than now.'

Marguerite fetched paper and pen and wrote the letter while Sarah slept. It was the first of many tasks she was to carry out in her new role of unofficial attendant all the way to Riga.

'How is the Englishwoman today?' the seamstresses always asked when Marguerite came from Sarah's coach to ride a little distance with them. Her report was never good.

'We miss you,' Isabelle ventured, for Marguerite now shared Sarah's accommodation, unable to leave her on her own, and ate all meals with her. It had taken Isabelle quite a time to recover from the fright of the raid. It had not helped her when a lone highwayman had attempted to rob the coaches parked by the roadside for the night, only to take flight as disturbed sleepers started firing pistols in his direction.

'I have suggested that Sarah should see a doctor when we next stop in a town,' Marguerite said to the others in a hallway one morning as she was waiting for the Englishwoman to be carried downstairs, 'but she will not hear of it. I believe she is afraid he will tell her to discontinue her journey and rest until another armed convoy comes through. She has already had one delay and will not risk another.'

'Stubborn and foolish,' Jeanne commented.

Sophie laughed unpleasantly, having had sharp words earlier with her sister. 'You're only jealous because you don't love any man as the Englishwoman does!'

Violette intervened humorously. 'Hold on! In Russia we shall all find men to love as much as that!'

General laughter eased the tension.

It was that same night that they witnessed the curious phenomenon of streamers of light criss-crossing the sky. They had eaten their supper when Jeanne went out to fetch something she had forgotten from the coach, but stopped to gape upwards in nervous astonishment. After calling the others, she went back outside and they joined her.

'What's happening to the sky?' Isabelle asked fearfully.

Marguerite was able to enlighten them. 'Sarah guessed why Jeanne looked so bewildered and said it was sure to be the aurora borealis that she had seen. That's what those lights are called. They only appear at times of intense cold. Her husband told her about them. She said we'll see them often from now on.'

Sophie shivered. 'They look ghostly, don't they? I'm going back indoors.'

Marguerite took a last lingering look. To her they only added to the strange beauty of these snow-covered lands.

Four

There was a final overnight stay en route for Sarah before her destination was reached.

'You've been a wonderful friend to me in my hour of need,' she said gratefully as Marguerite helped her into bed. 'I don't know what I would have done without you.'

'I've been glad to do it,' Marguerite replied, smiling. 'Go to sleep now. Tomorrow we'll be in Riga and Tom will be waiting for you. We'll send word to him as soon as we get there that you've arrived.'

'I feel too excited to sleep,' Sarah declared, 'but I'll try.'

By the time Marguerite had undressed and slipped into the neighbouring bed, she could tell by Sarah's steady breathing that exhaustion from the day's journey had overcome all excitement. Before extinguishing the candle, Marguerite rested her head on the pillow and let her thoughts drift. She could empathize with her friend's glorious anticipation of being reunited with the man she loved. Had she not felt exactly the same whenever she and Jacques met again after a temporary absence from each other, no matter how short the time between?

A quiet sigh of surprise escaped her as she realized that for the first time her thoughts had gone past the day of tragedy to the many joyous moments when, full of laughter, she and Jacques, sighting each other from a distance, had rushed into each other's arms. How often he had swung her up off her feet to whirl her around with the speed of a child's spinning top.

She propped herself up on one elbow, scarcely able to believe that after so long in a black abyss of despair she was gradually emerging to find him again. With this comforting thought filling her mind, she took up the candle-snuffer from the table by her bed and put out the flame.

In the morning the Comtesse returned to the hostelry, having spent the night at the home of an acquaintance, and he and his wife appeared to have loaded her with gifts, for several boxes were being stowed away. They were there to see her off and she was very gracious and smiling. Everybody else had to wait impatiently until her final farewells were said. Never once throughout the whole journey had she even nodded in Marguerite's direction. Hendrick seemed to be the only fellow traveller to whom she had directed a smile since leaving Paris.

In heavily falling snow the frozen River Dwina was crossed and by evening the lights of the city of Riga twinkled through the flakes. As the whole convoy came to a halt in front of a large hostelry peasants came flocking forward in the hope of carrying baggage.

Once again Sarah was carried indoors where the welcome heat from a great stove met them in a comforting wave full of the aromas of food, pipe smoke and beer. As previously arranged by Tom, the landlord had only to be informed of her arrival and a message would be sent to him immediately. Marguerite had to wait ten minutes to gain the landlord's attention, for he was busy serving the swarm of new arrivals, and from how he addressed them in turn he appeared to have a smattering of several languages. When he finally turned to her he understood her request immediately.

'I'll send a boy now,' he said as he continued pouring beer for one of his many thirsty customers.

'Now we have only to wait,' Marguerite said as she rejoined Sarah, who had been seated in a high-backed chair in a quiet corner of the busy room.

'I know these minutes will be longer to me than the whole journey,' Sarah confessed smilingly. 'Do watch for Tom. I can't see the door from here.'

She lowered the hood of her cloak and fussed with her hair, which Marguerite had dressed specially for her that morning. Although she had tried to look her best, adding a little rouge to her cheeks, she could not disguise the gauntness of her face or the dark circles under her eyes.

Marguerite ordered tea while they were waiting and it was served from a samovar into little drinking bowls. They had just finished it when suddenly Marguerite saw that a tall man, wearing a Cossack-style fur hat and a thick greatcoat, had entered, snowflakes whirling about him as he shook them away. He had a fierce, dramatic-looking face with a strong nose and chin, his dark-browed, deep-lidded eyes scanning intensely the crowded scene before him. As he pulled off his fur-lined gauntlets his expression showed his impatience to find the person he sought.

'I think Tom has arrived!' Marguerite exclaimed, measuring the newcomer against Sarah's description given early on in their friendship.

Swiftly she left her chair and began threading her way through the tables towards him. She thought he looked a man of passionate, uncertain temperament, but she knew from all she had heard from Sarah that he was an exceptionally kind and devoted husband. No wonder he was anxious to find his wife immediately.

He had not noticed Marguerite approaching, for he had turned his searching gaze in the direction of an archway that led into another taproom. Just as he was about to move in its direction she caught his sleeve, happy to be the bearer of good news. 'Wait! No need to go in there!' She threw out her hands expressively. 'Your wife is here!'

He turned his head sharply and his penetrating greenish-grey gaze pierced into her for a matter of seconds before amusement reached his narrowed grey eyes and a smile tugged at his mouth. He answered her, low-voiced, in French, his intimate tone deeper and far warmer than it should have been.

'You're a very lovely woman, mam'selle.' He seemed to breathe his appreciation of her. 'Unfortunately I'm not looking for a wife at the moment. Another time perhaps?'

Embarrassed, she stepped back quickly. 'My apologies! I thought you were someone else.'

'So I guessed,' he replied, still amused. 'Now if you excuse me I can see my search is over. My brother has come to find me.'

He had caught sight of Hendrick, who was rushing towards him from the other room. They greeted each other exuberantly.

'Jan, you devil!' Hendrick exclaimed, not noticing Marguerite, who had drawn away. 'How are you?'

'Fine! What sort of journey have you had? No trouble with the paintings, I hope? Did you get the Rubens for me?'

Together they went into the other taproom. Marguerite paused to look after them for a few moments before she returned to give Sarah an account of what had happened. 'He turned out to be Hendrick's brother!'

Sarah hid her disappointment that her waiting was not over yet. 'What is he like?'

Marguerite thought for a moment, recalling those striking good looks and wickedly amused eyes. 'He fitted your description of Tom by being tall, good-looking and dark-haired. It's no wonder I made a mistake in identifying him. In my opinion, Jan van Deventer would be both entertaining and dangerous company.' Her sense of humour surfaced. 'But,' she joked in mock regret, 'as I told you, he turned me away!'

'That was surely the greatest mistake he has ever made!' Sarah declared, laughing with her. Then she saw Marguerite's expression change as if she had been suddenly hypnotized, stiffening in her chair, her gaze fixed across the room.

'Someone else has just come in.' Marguerite spoke in a curiously tight voice.

'Is it my husband now?' Sarah leaned forward and caught at her friend's arm. 'Tell me he is here at last!'

'Yes, I'm sure this is Tom,' Marguerite replied in the same constricted voice and she patted Sarah's gripping hand reassuringly while her eyes remained unwaveringly focused.

She had no doubt in her mind that this was truly Tom Warrington. He was just as tall and well built as Jan van Deventer, but in spite of his Russian furs there was an unmistakably English look about him. She had seen enough English travellers in Paris to recognize that totally confident, self-assured air natural to them as if they owned any place they entered or any street they trod, coming as they did from the richest and most stable nation in the world. Yet it was something else about Tom's appearance that had strangled her voice in her throat and made her feel that when she stood up her legs might give way.

'Then go to him!' Sarah was urging. 'Why are you waiting?'

Somehow Marguerite managed to rise to her feet and once more began making her way between the tables. Even from a distance she had seen an extraordinary resemblance to Jacques in the tilt of Tom's head and well-moulded features. He was looking eagerly about the room and it was almost possible to believe he was looking for her. As she drew nearer she realized the likeness that had hit at her heart was not entirely illusory as she had expected it to be at close quarters, for his eyes were the same clear brown, his nose as straight and his mouth as sensual. As often happens when a stranger's looks are similar to someone already known, the feeling remained with her that they were already long acquainted.

'Mr Warrington?' she said, almost catching her breath when he turned a smile on her that made attractive and all too familiar indentations in his lean cheeks.

'Yes, mam'selle. I'm Thomas Warrington.'

She heard herself answering him. 'My name is Marguerite Laurent and your wife is seated on the far side of the room. First of all, I must explain that I've been her travelling companion for the latter part of the journey. Although Sarah was not involved, there was an accident with one of the horses and her maid, Blanche, was killed.'

He was deeply shocked. 'The poor woman! What a terrible tragedy!' Anxiety rang in his voice. 'But you are sure my wife was unharmed?'

'Yes, have no fear about that, but she is not well. She was taken ill at Frankfurt-on-Oder and had to stay there for three weeks before she was well enough to continue the journey. Unfortunately travelling has taken its toll on her strength and she has difficulty in walking. I just wanted to prepare you and to advise getting medical help for her without delay.'

He frowned, deeply anxious. 'I shall do that, of course.'

'Come this way.'

She led him to Sarah, who was on her feet, joy radiating in her face at the sight of him, and her arms encircled his neck tightly as he kissed her. Immediately he asked her how she was feeling, showing his concern, and reassured her that there should be no more travelling until she had recovered.

'I have comfortable lodgings where you shall have every attention and only when you are well again shall we travel on to Moscow. You'll like the house we have there, but in the meantime we shall manage very well.'

'But your work?'

'I had plenty of serfs to help me finish the planting of the winter garden for the Empress before I left Moscow to meet you here. Until the snow gets too deep there'll be a grand show of tall and hardy foliage that will make a fine contrast of black and white for the Imperial lady to see from her window. But for now, until the spring thaw, it will be a matter of designing and estimating costs while I decide how many serfs I'll need to carry out each project. It's already kept me busy during my wait for you and I have much more to keep me occupied.' He scooped her up in his arms, ready to leave. She held out her hand to Marguerite, who caught hold of it.

'We must not lose touch, Marguerite! I'll write to you and we must meet again one day.'

'Take care, dear friend. I wish you well.'

'Adieu, Mam'selle Laurent,' Tom said with a smile that turned her heart over. 'I thank you most heartily for your care of my wife.'

She watched them go before sinking down on to the chair that Sarah had vacated and closing her eyes, desperate to recover from the devastating experience that she had just been through. What tricks Fate managed to play! All the time Tom had been talking to Sarah she had watched his face unwaveringly, catching those faint similarities that had stirred such joy and anguish within her.

Determinedly she drew in a deep breath. But it was over. Moscow and St Petersburg were very far apart and it was most likely that in spite of Sarah's wish their friendship would remain only in an exchange of letters with no chance of ever seeing each other again. Although it would spare her any more meetings with Tom it also saddened her, for she and Sarah had become good friends during the many trials and tribulations of the journey.

That night she dreamed of Jacques for the first time since losing him, and they were walking hand in hand by the Seine just as they had done so many times. A feeling of contentment stayed with her when she awoke, even after the dream had slipped away beyond recall. She was also aware of a sudden uplifting sense of freedom. It had been quite a responsibility looking after Sarah, not that she regretted a minute of it, but now she could look forward clearly to her own future.

It was a cold and bright morning. Downstairs at breakfast Marguerite and her companions were told that during the night all their baggage had been transferred to sledges for the rest of the journey to St Petersburg. There was no sign of the Comtesse, but a note from her was handed to Marguerite and a purse of money. She read the note through.

'The Comtesse has written that there was a message awaiting her from her husband yesterday evening. He is presently in Moscow with the Ambassador and so she is to meet him there. To speed our journey she arranged with the Master of the Port of Riga that a courier be sent ahead of us all the way to the capital to ensure that horses are ordered in time to prevent any hold-ups on the last lap of our journey.'

'Well, that's something, I suppose,' Jeanne commented. 'But the armed guards won't be with us.'

'The coachmen will be armed,' Marguerite replied reassuringly. 'Now if you've all finished eating let's get going without further delay.'

The seamstresses split up to ride in the two enclosed sledges allotted to them and tucked under heaped furs to keep warm as the fiercely bearded coachmen cracked whips and the runners sped swiftly along the snowy streets out of the city.

The countryside was dazzlingly beautiful in its winter cloak and hoar frost had robed the trees in diamonds. Frozen lakes gleamed blue and grey and silver while the sky was palest amber as if the fallen snow of the previous night must have come from some other source.

Now and again the sledges drove through poor-looking villages, the dwellings all built of log and wattle, a finger of wood-smoke arising from each. The inhabitants scurried out of their path while others paused in whatever they were doing to gaze at the brightly hued sledges shooting by. As with all peasants the men were bearded and most of them wore fur hats, and although some of the women did likewise the rest had bright scarves tied about their heads. Nearly all were clad in sheepskin coats tied with a leather belt or a length of rope around their waists, high boots on their feet. As for the little children, they looked like balls of clothes running about, their faces little round moons of laughter or shy curiosity. Yet many of the villagers had an emaciated look. Marguerite pitied them for their hard life, knowing that every one of them was some master's serf and owned body and soul like a chattel.

It intrigued the Frenchwomen when now and again they saw peasants sliding over the snow on what appeared to be long, narrow boards, a stout stick in hand to aid their speedy progress, but there was little else to relieve the monotony. In many ways this final stage of the journey was the hardest. In spite of the quick changing of the horses the journey still took almost four weeks. As well as the frequent heavy snowstorms that caused delays, there was the sheer boredom of travel day after day with nothing to occupy their minds other than gazing at the passing white-blanketed landscape. Christmas day would have passed unnoticed if they had not remembered previously to buy small gifts for each other.

By now they had lost interest in all their previous pastimes and a village or very occasionally a town looked the same as any other under its blanket of snow. It made them disagreeable and tired, quick to snap and to quarrel. They grumbled about everything. It added to their ill temper that most of their nights were spent in uncomfortable lodgings and often the food was barely edible. Once Violette and Jeanne came to clawing at each other and had to be separated for the rest of the way. It took all Marguerite's efforts to keep the peace as much as possible. Isabelle was the only one who never complained and Marguerite appreciated her loyalty.

The new year of 1753 was two days old on the moonlit evening when the sledges passed into the city of St

Petersburg, wall lanterns illuminating the wide streets and windows pouring out golden light from chandeliers. Here and there the braziers of the city's watchmen glowed red and gold and the whiff of hot charcoal hung in the air.

The seamstresses looked from side to side in wonder and strained their necks to look up at the great mansions, silvery in the moon's glow and all grandly ornamented, many with balconies and each with the look of a palace. It was obvious that by day these would be pastel-coloured, which would add to the charm of the architecture, and everywhere the spires and onion-domes of the churches soared into the stars. Linking everything were the wide sweeping curves of the great River Neva that presently lay frozen and austere with reflected light adding flickers of gilt to its opal surface. It was easy to see from branching canals that this was a city of waterways.

They all gave a spontaneous cheer as they reached the end of their long journey. They had arrived at the Imperial Winter Palace, which reared up before them like a beautiful cake of great size, every window aglow. The sledges came to a standstill by what they knew was the domestic entrance in spite of its magnificently carved portal and great door. Both coachmen sprang down from their seats, pulling away the thick scarves that had covered the lower half of their faces, but their beards, eyebrows and lashes were frosted white by their own breath. One man thrust open the door and disappeared into the glow of candle-lamps within while the other began to unload the baggage.

One by one the seamstresses alighted. They were all stiff and tired as well as being extremely hungry. Marguerite, equally fatigued, led the way indoors, and the others followed her wearily. There was an inner door to insulate against the cold outside and then they passed through a tiled vestibule before entering a wide hallway with doors on all sides, one of which stood open. There the coachman was talking rapidly in Russian to a thin-faced, severe-looking woman wearing a black gown and a lace apron and cap. She listened attentively to all he had to say, nodding her head, and then waved him back to his duties with an impatient gesture. Closing the door behind her as if denying admittance, she took a couple of steps forward and looked steadily at the Frenchwomen.

'I am Madame Rostova,' she announced imperiously. 'French is spoken throughout the domestic quarters as well as in Court circles. You need have no fear that you will not be understood. The coachman has already told me that you are seamstresses from Paris.'

Marguerite experienced a sense of foreboding, but did not show it as she introduced herself and her companions. The woman's expression did not relax.

'Your names mean nothing to me,' she replied crisply, 'and I have had no notification of your coming. We already have sewing quarters in the Palace with a full staff of needle-women.'

'But we're here at the request of the Empress herself.'

'Request? What insolence! Her Imperial Majesty does not request! She commands! You have papers endorsing such orders?'

'No. It was all arranged through the Comtesse d'Oinville, the wife of a French diplomat here in St Petersburg.'

'That name is unknown to me too. There are so many foreigners coming and going at court. This Comtesse must either present herself to the right official to speak on your behalf or else you must obtain an authorized statement from her without delay.'

'But she isn't here! There was a change of plan and she left us in Riga to join the Comte d'Oinville in Moscow!'

'Then nothing can be done at the present time. You must leave this palace at once.'

Behind Marguerite the seamstresses groaned loudly in despair and Isabelle's face crumpled as she began to weep silently. But Marguerite had no intention of being turned away. 'No! You have no right to go against your Empress's expressed wish that I should come here with some of the best needlewomen in all France to make her the loveliest gowns that have ever been seen in this city!'

A shade of uncertainty passed across the woman's eyes. The Empress was like her father, Peter the Great, in bringing the most unlikely foreigners from far distances to do some specialized work for her. It was highly likely that these Frenchwomen were the result of an imperial whim. What was most important was that she knew what her own fate would be if she sent them away in error. She dared not risk it.

'Tell me how it all came about,' she said stiffly.

'The Empress admired gowns worn by the Comtesse and wanted the talents of whose who had made them. Couldn't word of our arrival be taken to the Empress?'

Madame Rostova looked astounded at the suggestion. 'Certainly not! I need to make inquiries and discover if you are truly expected or if a great mistake has been made. However, out of charity I shall allow you all to stay here tonight.' She frowned as the drivers began bringing in the baggage from the sleighs and she indicated that everything should be set down in the hall. 'You may take out what you need from your travelling boxes tonight, but they must remain here until the matter of your presence under this roof is settled one way or the other.'

She turned sharply, her back very straight, and reopened the door to lead the way into a vast kitchen that was one of a series of kitchens, each opening through a wide archway into another as far as the eye could see. All the servants present looked at them, but carried on with their tasks. Two of the maids, who were folding cloths, were called forward.

'Take these Frenchwomen to one of the empty bedrooms in the servants' quarters and also show them where the privies are. See that the beds are made up and the stove lit. Then bring them back here.'

'Yes, Madame Rostova.'

The maids took lamps and led the new arrivals out of the kitchen. Immediately they showed a friendlier side as well as being full of curiosity. Although their French had a strong Russian accent they were fluent in the language.

'Have you come to work here? Don't be scared of that old scarecrow. She thinks she's as important as the Empress herself when she is on duty. Are you really here to sew for Her Imperial Majesty? How long has it taken you to get here?'

Marguerite and the others answered their questions up two flights of stairs and along many corridors until they were shown into a narrow, comfortless room with beds hung with simple draperies and with a rolled-up feather mattress at the end of each one. A crimson-tiled, floor-to-ceiling stove was in one corner and there were two washstands with ewers and basins, but in spite of the curtained windows the room was icy cold. Sophie moaned, shivering with cold as she rubbed her arms and sank down on the bare boards of the nearest bed.

'We're going to die of hunger or freeze to death before morning.'

'Don't fret,' the younger maid said cheerfully, going towards the stove with a tinderbox. 'You'll be given some supper and it will be hot in here in no time. If you stoke up the stove before you go to sleep it will still be warm in the morning. You'll all be as snug as bugs in a rug.'

Almost at once a fire was roaring behind the grating and soon afterwards a lackey arrived with a large basket full of logs, which he set down before leaving again.

Warmth was radiating pleasantly around the room by the time the maids finished making up the beds and led the way downstairs again. In one of the kitchens the French-women sat down to enjoy a thick and tasty bean soup with chunks of good bread and a light beer to drink. Well fed and tired in every limb they all slept as soon as they had climbed into bed.

Marguerite was the first to wake in the morning at a pounding on the door and a voice shouting that it was time to get up. Some of the women stirred, but tucked down again. She slipped out of bed and stoked up the stove, which crackled as the embers leapt into flames around the logs. There was no telling what time it was, but the window, in spite of a web of frost, enabled her to see out. The skyline of the city was almost ethereal in the dawn light.

'I'm here,' she whispered triumphantly, 'and here I'm going to stay!'

Five

It was not good news that awaited Marguerite after breakfast. Madame Rostova informed her that in spite of extensive inquiries nobody knew anything about seamstresses coming from Paris.

'Until you have made contact with the Comtesse d'Oinville nothing can be done. You must all leave now. Come back when you have a declaration from her.'

Marguerite made a last appeal. 'At least allow me to visit the French Embassy before we leave! I could ask when the Comte and Comtesse are expected to return and perhaps gain some help in this matter.'

The Russian woman hesitated. In her own mind, knowing the Empress's passion for clothes, she was certain now that these Frenchwomen were here at an imperial whim, but she had to have proof. She glanced around at the seamstresses. Apart from Marguerite, who was standing her ground, they were a dejected-looking bunch, one girl red-eyed and dissolving again into soundless tears.

'Very well,' she conceded reluctantly, 'and since you don't know your way about the city I'll let you have one of the lackeys as a guide.'

He was a cheerful lad named Igor with a swagger to his walk. Fifteen years old, he had worked at the Palace since he was eight.

'Anything you want to know just ask me,' he said with supreme confidence as Marguerite went with him from the Palace.

58

In spite of her present troubles Marguerite was keenly interested to see the city by day, but they had not gone far when she paused to look back at the Winter Palace. It was not as large as the Palace of Versailles, but with its many windows and pale walls it looked almost luminous in the snow-bright morning light.

'It's a very fine building,' she commented admiringly.

'Yes, but we've heard that all those buildings are to be demolished to clear a site for a new, far larger Winter Palace. You can be sure that it will be even grander than the present one when it is finished.'

She looked in the direction that he was pointing in. A palace as large as Versailles could be built on the vast site, where it would be facing the Neva. 'It will be an enormous building project.'

'It's said that some part of it will be the Empress's new hermitage, where she can entertain friends privately and without fuss.'

'Her new hermitage?' Marguerite asked with interest as they continued on their way. 'Have there been others?'

'Yes, but her father, Peter the Great, built the first one at Peterhof out in the country at Tsarskoe Selo. They say he got the idea from your country when he toured Europe.'

Marguerite thought that was probably true. The late Louis XIV had had a retreat, as did the present King Louis XV, but those were away from the hub of Versailles and also not in the heart of a city, as this new palace would be.

She looked about eagerly as they walked along, enjoying the sight in daylight of the pastel-coloured mansions, pinks, blues, greens, yellows, amber and apricot. Igor made sure that he kept her well out of harm's way, for although the streets were wide the passing traffic paid little heed to pedestrians. Often coachmen and other drivers drove so arrogantly that people were forced to press themselves against walls to keep out of danger. On the frozen surface of the Neva branches of trees had been laid to make routes for traffic to use and there the sledges and carriages and troikas passed one another with great frequency. Farther up the frozen river there was a fair, music drifting from it. Here and there on the ice high mounds of snow had been built up and children and adults paid a man-in-charge to slide on tray-like objects down the twisting route to land laughing at the bottom.

Marguerite smiled at their pleasure, but there was something else she wanted to ask the lad. 'Why wouldn't Madame Rostova have word sent direct to the Empress about our arrival?'

Igor gave a snort of laughter and explained. 'Nobody would do that without some evidence to show our grand lady, because if she'd been drunk at the time of sending for you she wouldn't remember anything about it.'

'Does she drink heavily?'

'Not all the time, but too often for her own good. She would be furious if reminded of something she'd done that she couldn't recall. I've only seen her in a temper once and luckily I was at a safe distance. Once in a rage she had the tongues cut out of two ladies of her own court, because she thought they had plotted together against her! So you'd better not put a stitch wrong if ever you do get to sew anything for her.'

'At least I can thank you for the warning,' Marguerite remarked wryly. 'If all goes well we'll be sewing for the Grand Duchess Catherine too. Is she as temperamental?'

'No! You've nothing to worry about there. She's as different from the Empress as she could be. She's never shouted at anyone and is a kind lady, but she has dangerous enemies at Court. Her life isn't easy.'

'Why should that be?'

'All sorts of reasons. Worst of all for her must be having Grand Duke Peter for a husband. He's strange in all his ways, dancing jigs and shouting and laughing when nobody else has even a smile.' He shook his head in sympathy with the unfortunate Catherine. 'All he wants to do is to play at being a soldier.'

'Do you mean he is childlike?'

'In some ways, but not in others. Far from it! He makes no secret of hating the Empress and wanting to be Tsar. Yet I'm sure he's frightened of her too.' He grimaced soberly. 'Well, everybody's scared of her.'

'I was told that before I left Paris,' Marguerite replied, recalling the Comtesse's warning. 'I can see that life must be hard for the Grand Duchess.'

'Yes, but she never shows it. She and the Grand Duke have their own court for those more their age and there are always parties and balls and entertainments. For a while now one of the chamberlains, Sergei Saltykov, has been paying her a deal of attention, but so have lots of men before him without success.'

Marguerite glanced at him with raised eyebrows. 'Is there anything you don't know?'

He grinned widely. 'We get to find out everything sooner or later in the domestic quarters. Those upstairs in the salons and private apartments have no idea how much we who wait on them see and hear.'

The French Embassy was located on Vasilievsky Island that split the Neva into two forks. They crossed the ice along a marked path and there was easy access up to the island's wharf. From there they followed the street that would take them to the gates of the Embassy, passing on the way many more great mansions, and all were pastel-coloured like those in the city itself.

'You should feel at home here on this island,' Igor remarked with a grin. 'This is where German and particularly French people settle when they come to St Petersburg.' He indicated their immediate surroundings. 'You'd find your fellow countrymen and women living in all these streets in this section. As for the English, they live in an area on the mainland that spreads out from the embankment and that's a close-knit community too. The Italians have their own area as do the Dutch, but in the tailoring section of the city, there's every nationality under the sun that's able to cut cloth and wield a needle.'

'I hadn't realized St Petersburg was so cosmopolitan.'

'Foreigners have been coming here ever since Peter the Great started building this city and needed every kind of skilled craftsmen. So it has gone on ever since. Take yourself, for example.'

They had reached the gates of the Embassy. French guards were on duty, but after Marguerite had produced her identification papers they allowed her to enter. At her request they let Igor accompany her.

There was a long wait before Marguerite was shown into the office of a minor official. He did not know when the Ambassador and the Comte d'Oinville would be returning to St Petersburg, nor could he help her solve her problem at the Palace.

Outside the gates again Marguerite clenched her fists angrily. 'I'll not tolerate this treatment! I'm responsible for five of my fellow countrywomen and somehow I have to keep them housed and fed.' She still had money in the purse that had been given to her in Riga, but it would not last long. 'Is there some way I could appeal to the Grand Duchess? You say she has a kind heart. Surely she would listen to me. How could I get to see her, Igor?'

He looked uncertain. 'I've never been in the grand ducal apartments and in any case they are in a part of the Palace where I don't go very often.'

'But could you get me there without discovery? I give you my word that I'll never let anyone know that you had anything to do with it.'

He showed his dismay and drew back a pace from her. 'I can't do that! If it came out I'd get a terrible flogging and it would be the end of my working days at the Palace!'

'You're my only chance!'

'No!' He stumped ahead of her, his head down and his shoulders set as if plunging physically against her request.

She followed in silence, knowing he was angry with her for asking so much of him, but she dreaded the moment when she would have to face her friends and tell them the bad news. She wondered wildly if Madame Rostova could be persuaded to let them all work as maids until the Comtesse returned. Then, when they were almost back at the Palace again, Igor halted abruptly and swung round to face her.

'You swear you will never tell?' he demanded fiercely.

'Never!' she replied on a flash of hope.

'Do you have any samples of your work?'

'My embroidery? Yes, I have many that I brought to show the Empress and judge what she liked. But they're all in one of my travelling bags that were left in the hallway.'

'Describe it. Is it labelled? Good! You wait here.'

He went off at a run. She waited anxiously, but before long he returned with her bag. She opened it quickly and took out some samples, but he saw she had more in the velvet-covered folder in which she had kept them.

'Bring the lot,' he instructed. 'Now we'll go back to the Palace.'

He snatched up her travelling bag and when they were back in the domestic hallway again he set it down with the rest of the luggage. Opening a door opposite the one into the kitchens, he beckoned to her, a finger to his lips. A narrow stairway led upwards and she followed him, realizing that it gave servants secluded access to each floor. Eventually he opened a door into a narrow corridor and she saw by its length that it was one that ran parallel to a number of rooms where servants could traverse without intruding on the people within.

'We're outside the grand ducal apartments now,' he whispered. 'I don't even know if the Grand Duchess is in her suite there. She rides in the mornings and you may have to wait hours. I'll cook up some tale for Madame Rostova. I'll tell her I left you waiting at the Embassy and you'd said you could find your own way back.'

'Describe the Grand Duchess Catherine to me, so that I'll recognize her.'

He frowned thoughtfully. 'Not very tall. Brown hair unless she has it powdered. Her nose is a bit long, her fore-head high and her chin is sort of pointed. Her eyes are blueish.' There was a pause as he searched his mind for further description. 'Not exactly pretty, but a nice, sparkling kind of face.'

A shrug of his shoulders indicated he had done his best and he led the way on again. In the gloom ahead something scurried away.

'What was that?' she asked quickly, fearing that she knew already.

'Only a rat,' he replied casually. 'They're everywhere, but mostly near the kitchens.' He did not see her dismayed expression as he pressed on. At the end of the corridor he turned into another one, counting the doorways as he went past. Halfway along he stopped.

'A tapestry on the other side hides this door. It opens into a kind of hallway, which the Grand Duchess has to pass through whether she's coming or going. Wait there and, if she comes, give a curtsey and show her your handiwork. She loves beautiful things – paintings and porcelain and that sort of stuff. If you're in luck she might like your embroidery too.'

He gave her no time to thank him, but thrust her through the door and closed it after her.

She looked about her. This was wider and longer than any hallway she had ever seen, with a large window at one end, the walls enhanced by tapestries that were larger than the narrow one that she had held aside when coming through the door. Along its length were two tall, patterned-tiled stoves that gave a good warmth, but failed to counteract a cold draught that came from somewhere. There was a damp patch on the ceiling just above her head and she could see that one of the windowpanes was cracked. She had noticed the previous evening that nothing was as pristine as would be expected in a palace and it seemed that an air of neglect prevailed even in the imperial quarters.

Slipping off her cloak, she made a cushion of it on the floor beside a large cupboard, where she sat down, hoping she would be unnoticed by anybody other than the Grand Duchess when she happened to come this way. She also listened for the slightest scuffle of a rat, ready to spring to her feet.

Opening the folder, she sorted through her embroidery samples, which varied in size, and wondered which to display if the chance came. Then, on impulse, she sprang up to spread them all out like a brilliant carpet over a wide section of the floor, the incorporated pearls and beads and sequins gleaming and twinkling, the stitched flowers and ferns and feathers giving their own variety of colour. Hoping for the best, she sat down again and rested her head against the cupboard as she waited. Somewhere a clock chimed the hour.

Studying the tapestries for diversion, she shuddered at their sinister and frightening themes and decided they must be very old. The clothes of the warriors wielding their scimitars and the torturers with their hot irons were what she knew to be the old Russian styles worn before Peter the Great had wrenched his great country into line with the rest of the world.

Closing her eyes to shut out the sight of them, she dozed until suddenly she jerked alert as there came the sound of a sharp tap of heels. She took a cautious look, not wanting to make the same mistake as she had done with Jan van Deventer and Tom, but there could be no mistake about the identity of the young woman approaching. Igor's description could not be faulted. Catherine was quite short, slim and narrow-waisted, clad in blue riding attire and carrying her gloves and whip. Her face was flushed healthily by her exercise and she was walking swiftly, looking ahead and seemingly lost in thought.

For a few tense moments Marguerite feared that those hurrying feet would scatter the samples without one being seen, but suddenly Catherine stopped abruptly, staring down at the colourful carpet spread before her. Then she knelt down, picking them up in turn to examine each one closely and sitting back on her heels when she placed each one on to her lap. Then, having studied the last one, she collected them altogether in her grasp and rose to her feet again to continue on her way, still looking at them. Marguerite stepped out of her hiding place.

Startled, Catherine turned and looked back at the young woman. 'Who are you?' she demanded. 'What are you doing in my private apartment?'

'I'm the embroiderer, Madame. I've taken an unorthodox way to show you my work since the Empress seems to have forgotten that she sent to Paris for me and five of my fellow embroiderers.'

A smile twitched across Catherine's mouth and she regarded Marguerite steadily for a few moments. 'Is that so? What's your name?' Then she gave a nod as she was told. 'Come with me. Your talents shall not be kept waiting any longer.'

Six

C atherine led the way through several of the many rooms in her apartment, passing through her own library, which held books from floor to ceiling. Everywhere reflected her high intellect and her love of beautiful things. Marguerite, who loved to read, noticed in passing that a book lying open was on philosophy and beside it was a tome on the history of the world. There were many paintings on the walls and here and there a beautiful icon, depicting the Virgin and Child or one of the saints, radiating gold and scarlet and lapis lazuli blue. On shelves and display tables there were artistic arrangements of pretty shells, figurines of porcelain, small jade animals, exquisitely enamelled boxes in rainbow colours as well as engraved gems and ivory carvings.

'I can see that you like my little treasures,' Catherine said smilingly when they reached her favourite salon. She had seen how the Frenchwoman had been glancing at them, enraptured.

'Yes, indeed I do!'

'I find it hard to resist collecting small and beautiful objets d'art. They seem to call out to me when I see them.' Catherine thought to herself that it was a great pity that the Empress, although she had her own collection of fabulous treasures, only viewed hers as yet another wild extravagance. All had started out so well when she had first come to Russia at the age of fifteen to marry Peter, but after a while the Empress's approval of her had turned to vindictiveness. She knew that it was not just for her so-called extravagance or her debts, which had been incurred when she had failed to realize that the income allowed her had been stopped by the irate Empress. The blunt truth was that her unforgivable crime in that woman's eyes was her failure so far to give Russia an heir. But this was not the time to think of that side of her unfortunate marriage.

'Your embroidery is some of the loveliest I've ever seen, Mam'selle Laurent,' she praised sincerely, going across to a round rosewood table where she sat down to spread the samples out before her. 'Are these your own original designs?'

'Yes, Madame.'

'Any one of your samples could be framed to make a beautiful picture. Come and stand opposite me.' Then she sat back in her chair and regarded Marguerite with interest. 'First of all I want to hear the circumstances of how you were sent for and what has been happening.'

Under Catherine's direct and steady gaze Marguerite gave a full account of how she had been summoned to Russia through the Comtesse d'Oinville and concluded with an account of how her visit to the French Embassy had been in vain. All the time she was thinking how right Igor had been in his description of Catherine. There was something dazzling about this young duchess, for she radiated charm, not only in her smile but also in her whole personality.

'I remember the evening when the Comtesse d'Oinville wore that lovely lilac gown,' Catherine said reminiscently when she had heard everything. 'But what is most important to me now is that I see you as a very straightforward person.' She considered herself to be a good judge of character and liked the way the Frenchwoman held her gaze openly, but respectfully. 'I think your seeking me out will prove to be providential. Am I right in believing that you know how to be discreet?'

'Yes, of course, Madame!' Marguerite answered on a note

close to affront that her integrity should ever be in doubt. 'I've never in all my life betrayed a confidence!'

'I believe you.' Catherine continued to look hard at her. 'The whole Court is soon off to Moscow for the religious celebration of Christmas and the festivities of the New Year. The resident seamstresses have made me the gowns I wanted, but I believe that with all the banqueting that will take place during the festive season I shall start to put on a little weight about the waist. It is something that nobody else must notice.' She paused deliberately. 'So far I have been fortunate and kept myself well corseted. But time will eventually run out. You understand me?'

Marguerite nodded. So Catherine was pregnant by her lover! 'Perfectly, Madame,' she replied evenly. 'I have done such special work before and there are many variations. I could even make changes to the gowns already made. But I would need my own atelier where my fellow seamstresses and I could work privately and unhindered, with everything on hand.'

'You shall have it!'

'But what about the Empress?'

'She has scores of new gowns to take to Moscow. When the moment is right I shall inform her of your being here. My gowns must be made before anything else. I'll arrange everything this very minute.' She waved a hand towards the wall. 'Give that bell-pull a tug. Then we must discuss your ideas.'

It was a senior manservant who came almost at once. He was white-wigged and in crimson livery like all the manservants that Marguerite had seen, but extra silver braid on his coat denoted an elevated position. Catherine told him to write down everything that Marguerite would list for him. He promptly produced a notepad from his pocket and stood with a pencil poised.

While Catherine sifted through the embroidery samples again Marguerite transported herself mentally back to

Madame Fromont's establishment and, going through its rooms, began to list everything necessary that she saw in her mind's eye from flat irons, wide wooden tables, plenty of candle-lamps with reflectors for dark days, and dummies, which in this case must be shaped in the figures of the Empress and the Grand Duchess. Although all her needle-women had their own sewing boxes with their favourite thimbles and all else they would normally need, there always had to be extra supplies and she added many small items such as pins, pincushions, needles and scissors.

Marguerite would have listed beads, spangles, fringes, braids and silk threads in every colour, but was told that these were all to be had from one of the sewing storerooms. There were already many bolts of beautiful materials in stock, for both Catherine and the Empress chose from swatches brought to them on a regular basis. As for the atelier itself, that was to be in a remote part of the Palace alongside a set of rooms for the seamstresses' own living quarters, which Catherine insisted must be made comfortable.

'I want everything made ready by this evening,' she declared emphatically. Then, as the manservant bowed his way out of the room, she sat down at the table again and turned her attention back to Marguerite. 'Now tell me your ideas.'

When these had been fully discussed Marguerite was allowed to leave and, once outside the doors of the apartment, went rushing off on flying feet to tell the others that all was well.

Catherine sat on at the table, deep in her own thoughts. Would Marguerite's skills be enough to conceal her condition to the end? The Frenchwoman's suggestion of starting a new fashion with long scarves of lawn, silk and later velvet to swathe about her was a good one. Somehow she would have to give birth secretly and hope that her personal maid, Chargorodskaya, whom she could trust, would be able to whisk the infant away to a good foster-home afterwards.

Abruptly she sprang to her feet and paced the floor, letting her clasped hands rise and fall agitatedly as she pondered her dilemma. If only Peter had been a true husband to her from the start! Then this baby in her womb would have been his and they could have rejoiced together.

She had been on a family visit with her parents to Kiel when she and Peter had first met as children. Then Peter, a weedy-looking boy, had been growing up under the strict supervision of army officers in a military environment and for a short while they had enjoyed each other's company as they played with his toy fort and wooden soldiers. Much later she had been pleased to hear that the Empress of Russia, whose nephew he was, had chosen him to be her heir. She had not known then that he would hate Russia and loathe the Empress for taking him away from his beloved Prussia, which meant everything to him.

She had been even happier when told she was to marry him, for she visualized the glorious day when they would be the Tsar and Tsarina of Russia and together would rule wisely and well. Yet there was a shock awaiting her when they met again at the Imperial Court. She could have overlooked his growing up to be an ugly youth, badly scarred from the smallpox that had almost taken his life, but he was so changed in his nature. With wisdom beyond her years she had realized instantly that if she let love grow out of her childhood fondness for him her life would be totally wretched till the end of her days.

He had become eccentric in all his acts and mannerisms, often giving loud bursts of maniacal laughter at anything slightly untoward. Ruthless German discipline and harsh punishments in his upbringing seemed to have given him a taste for cruelty and he ill-treated his servants and his pet dogs almost daily for the perverted pleasure of it. Once he had hanged a rat in her room and she shuddered at the

71

memory of his excitement and high-pitched taunting at the creature's struggles.

It was because he came often to her bed that it was thought by all but the most discerning that relations were normal between them. The truth was very different. He always came with his dressing-robe pockets full of toy soldiers to play war games with her, the hobby of his child-hood now an obsession, and the humps of their knees under the covers made the hills and valleys of the battle areas. She often thought to herself that there was not a fighting stratagem or battle manoeuvre that she did not know.

Peter had liked to lie boastingly to her and to others of his conquests of women, covering up his own inadequacy, and loyally she never derided him in private or in public. But it was reports of his supposed sexual rapacity that had convinced the Empress that she had a barren daughter-in-law. It was only recently, after it had been disclosed to the Empress that her heir was impotent, that a simple cut of a surgeon's knife had finally enabled Peter to perform his husbandly duties. Fortunately he preferred other women, for which she was thankful.

Easing her agitated pacing, Catherine went across to the window. It gave her a fine vista of the city, but she hoped that when the new Winter Palace was built she would have a view of the Neva, where there was so much to see at all times of the year.

Catherine sighed softly. She hoped so much that the Frenchwoman's fashion devices would keep her secret. Her greatest fear was that the Empress might discover that her pregnancy was more advanced than it should be, making it impossible for the offspring within her to be Peter's child. Her punishment would be banishment from this vast and wildly beautiful country with its great forests and steppe land. She loved Russia and had done everything to make herself one with it, learning the language and adopting the Russian Orthodox religion, neither of which Peter had ever

72

done. He had never attempted to make himself likable to her or anyone else except his mistresses. In fact, jealous of her popularity, he had come to hate her as much as he loathed the Empress.

From the early days after she had arrived at court, despite her young age, she had had the wisdom to see that she would need to gain the loyalty of all the people, whatever their station in life, if she was to help her erratic husband rule successfully when the time came. She also learned how to hide from the world all the hurt and disappointments she suffered. It was a valuable lesson and, even now, none could tell how much in love she was with a court chamberlain named Sergei Saltykov.

At the age of twenty-three, after she had endured eight years of unconsummated marriage and resisted many advances from other men, Sergei's persistent and amorous pursuit had finally won her. He had awakened her intensely sensual nature to ecstatic realms and she was forever finding new ways of her own to pleasure him in his turn. In many ways she had never been happier or more despairing.

The atelier was all that Marguerite had hoped for, consisting as it did of two large rectangular rooms painted a creamy colour with plenty of windows and a great stock of candle-lamps. Long tables gave ample room for cutting and pressing while the chairs were padded and comfortable. Dressmakers' dummies of the Empress's and the Grand Duchess's figures had been brought from among those in the established sewing rooms elsewhere in the Palace and were up to date, one with an ample bust line and the other youthfully slim. There were minor additions to be made to the atelier before Marguerite was entirely satisfied, but these were only a matter of extra shelves, better ironing facilities and more chests of drawers and cupboards, for she liked work space to be kept as clear as possible.

The Grand Duchess had emphasized comfort for the seamstresses' own rooms and this had been faithfully carried out. Redundant furniture that had seen better days enriched the three bedrooms and the living room. There was still the gleam of gilt in the ornate frames of slightly patchy mirrors and a touch of splendour in the faded silk curtains at the windows, the bed draperies caught back by great golden tassels. The dining table, its surface ringed from wine and scored by careless treatment, nevertheless still had a polish and six accompanying chairs arranged around it. There were three sofas offering more comfortable seating and wide rugs, slightly moth-eaten in places, had been rediscovered somewhere to cover the floors. An ormolu clock and two figurines had been placed on a side table.

Catherine, ever concerned with the well-being of those who worked for her, had not overlooked the necessity of the newcomers' wages and Marguerite was called to the office of a palace official to receive the seamstresses' first wages in advance. Her own salary was particularly generous and the others were overjoyed to find they were to earn more than ever before. To Marguerite's relief they were equally pleased with everything else. As there were three beds in one room Jeanne chose it to share with her daughter and Isabelle, the two girls wanting to be together, while Violette and Sophie took another, leaving Marguerite to have a room on her own. It was small, but that was unimportant. After constant company over so many weeks it was a relief to have space to herself and some solitude.

In spite of Catherine's wish to have new gowns there proved to be no time to make them. The Empress, deeply pious in spite of her licentious ways, suddenly decided she would leave for Moscow sooner than planned, as she wanted to go first to the great church of Kiev for penance and prayers. Her decision resulted in Marguerite and her fellow seamstresses working long hours and finally overnight to alter the gowns for Catherine that had already been made.

Bodices had bones removed and a more pliable stiffening added where necessary while fringes, frills of lace, ruffles, flowers and bunches of ribbons were either changed or added, the sparkling beads and spangles having their own trickery for deceiving the eye. There were even button loops that could be loosened to expand.

Just before the day of leaving St Petersburg the Empress sent for Marguerite. As she guessed, Catherine had chosen her moment to tell Elisabeth of her arrival with her team of seamstresses and that they were now installed. Entering the imperial presence, Marguerite curtsied deeply before she straightened up again and looked for the first time at the woman who alone ruled over all the vast lands of Russia.

Elisabeth, dressed in midnight-blue velvet trimmed with fur, turned from her reflection in a mirror, the wide, side panniers of her gown making her skirt extend far beyond her hips. A tall woman of immense presence, she was startlingly beautiful. The depth of her handsome blue eyes was echoed in the sapphires that encircled her throat and glowed in her powdered hair.

'So it was you who made that lilac gown for the Comtesse d'Oinville,' Elisabeth said almost accusingly in a deep rich voice. 'Tell me, what have you made for her since?'

Marguerite was startled. It was always expected of a seamstress that she would be priest-like in her silence over what had been made for a client. No woman wanted anyone else to know what she would be wearing for special occasions. She answered evasively. 'Many gowns in a variety of colours and fabrics, Your Imperial Majesty.'

'Whatever their style I want you to make even more beautiful creations for me!'

Her meaning was entirely clear to Marguerite. Whatever the Comtesse wore the Empress wanted to be sure of outshining her and Marguerite had all the fore-knowledge to ensure it.

There followed a tense half-hour for Marguerite as she

made suggestions that were either received with a nod or rejected with an impatient gesture. She had made some sketches to illustrate her ideas and had dressed several mannequin dolls to display styles in miniature. Fortunately Elisabeth's love of clothes enabled her to picture every idea presented to her. Eventually she dismissed Marguerite with instructions that all the gowns were to be ready for her by the time the Court returned from Moscow.

Outside the apartment Marguerite paused to regain her breath after the strain of the Empress's demanding attitude. Since the date of that imperial return from Moscow was not yet known Marguerite decided that work must start the next day on these new clothes. It was far better to have everything ready as quickly as possible than to be caught out with half of it unfinished.

On the day of the Court's departure the seamstresses gathered at upper windows to watch the scene below. The Empress's sledge, painted in scarlet and gold with the Romanov arms of the double-headed eagle emblazoned on its sides, had a sleeping compartment, as did those occupied by the Grand Duke and Duchess. A thousand horses from the great stables were hitched to the grand sledges as well as to those that would be transporting servants and goods, Igor having told them that household effects always went too. Porcelain dinner services, bed linen, tapestries and even favourite furniture went from palace to palace to supplement what was already there.

It gave Marguerite a better understanding of the neglect she had seen in the Palace. Organization and getting things done on time, no matter how many servants were available to do it, was something that became lost in the general mêlée of court life. Perhaps those who should have been responsible left it to others or, even more easily, always postponed everything till the morrow.

The great procession started forward. In the streets people bowed low, many falling to their knees and some prostrating themselves in the snow in the old tradition as the imperial sledge approached. Elisabeth was seen as the mother of their country and they loved her loyally and unquestioningly, even the poor serfs in their ignorance never daring to question her abundant wealth and their own hand-to-mouth existence.

The seamstresses were not alone in watching the magnificent departure. Sergei Saltykov stood at another window on a lower floor. Tall and good-looking, his dark brows were clamped together in a worried frown. He found it surprising that he was still violently attracted to Catherine, for the collapse of his own marriage of less than two years ago had been yet another example of how he lost interest after conquest. Yet her spell remained and now her pregnancy threatened terrible consequences for him. If it came out that he was responsible he could find himself either behind bars for years or sent to some godforsaken place for the rest of his days.

He swore under his breath. If only that wretched Peter had agreed six months ago to that simple operation none would have doubted that he was the father, but the snivelling coward had had be made dead drunk after an evening carousing with friends before it could be performed by a waiting surgeon. Now, all because of that delay, he himself had to be prudent and stay away from the Court for a while to avoid being seen with Catherine and arousing suspicion. It meant missing the nights of gaming for high stakes that he so enjoyed apart from all the festivities and riotous merrymaking.

Groaning, Sergei slammed a fist against the wall before swinging away from the window and leaving the room.

Seven

Two weeks had gone by since Marguerite and her seamstresses had been given their own quarters. It had been a busy time, but they were getting accustomed to working in their new environment. On the first day she had been given a key to access the store of fabrics destined to become imperial garments, and she had chosen a rich gold silk for the Empress's first gown in the French style. It had already been cut out from one of her own designs and the basic work had been done in the making of the sleeves, bodice and skirt, which would remain separate until the embroidery on them was finished. She had yet to visit the other atelier, and had asked Madame Rostova to arrange a meeting for her with the supervisor there.

Before that took place Marguerite planned to give her seamstresses a full day to enjoy themselves. They had not yet been out of the Palace and her only outing had been the day Igor had guided her to the French Embassy. They all needed a chance to look around the city and get their bearings.

They greeted the news of it with excitement and some trepidation. All well wrapped up, they set out with Marguerite into the ice-cold air. There was much to see and admire, but it was the busy markets that drew them. Street performers supplied music and a ragged old dancing bear was doing its best. Never before had the Frenchwomen seen such a strange sight as the food stalls. There was plenty of dried and salted meat and fish for sale, but otherwise the

78

fresh joints of meat were frozen hard, as were chickens, geese and game, all stiff as boards and aglitter with frost. Isabelle and Violette tried to prod them, astounded as they all were that food could be sold in such a way, but they realized that in such a cold climate anything would freeze and it was to be expected.

There were also stalls full of brightly coloured, very Russian wares as well as those more familiar, including displays of second-hand clothes, furs and boots. Violette bought two skirts for work and a long fur cape that was worn bare in places but warmer than her own woollen cloak. The others followed her example or bought furs that they could use as linings to their cloaks. The stallholder, like those they had observed on other stalls, used beads on a frame to add up the price of their purchases, each bead representing a certain value. Jeanne was interested in the lace stall, but could see nothing to compare with the fine lace that she made.

On the outskirts of the market was a pathetic cluster of women, nearly all with little children, offering simple home-made things for sale. Out of compassion Marguerite bought a small wooden bowl, brightly painted, and Jeanne a straw-plaited basket. Isabelle chose a rag doll.

At midday they went down some steps into a small cafe where they each had a bowl of steaming borsch, served with wedges of dark rye bread, which warmed them through. Here again the price was settled with a rattling of beads. Before returning to the palace they went into Kazan Cathedral and stood together in a little group, taking in everything from its glorious gilded height to the jewel-coloured frescoes and the great golden altar that shone like the sun before them. There was nowhere to sit, but they had heard that all congregations had to stand. Each of them chose a place to kneel privately on the vast marble floor for a few minutes on her own.

When they were back in their atelier again, taking up

their needles, there was plenty of chatter about what they had seen and Marguerite left them to work without her for a while. There was a meeting arranged with Madame Markarova, supervisor of the long-established sewing rooms, that she could delay no longer.

From directions she had been given she found her way to it in another part of the Palace, not knowing how she would be received. Neither Madame Markarova nor her seamstresses were resident, coming and going by an entrance far from that which Marguerite and her companions had been allotted.

The kitchens where they might otherwise have met at mealtimes were forbidden territory to all of them. It was to ensure that they and their clothes and subsequently their delicate work were kept free of cooking odours and the greasy atmosphere that permeated the kitchens. It was also why cold food was taken to both ateliers during the day, hot dishes only served in the evenings when work was over and the sewing rooms closed.

Madame Rostova had arranged with Madame Markarova that she and her women should continue to make the imperial garments, except for all elaborately embroidered gowns and accompanying accessories, which would be under Marguerite's supervision.

'Madame Markarova speaks French,' Madame Rostova had informed her, 'and so do some of her workers, but the majority know only Russian.'

Marguerite paused for a moment and took a deep breath before entering Madame Markarova's atelier. There were at least forty women of varying ages seated at four long sewing tables and every face in the room looked up with an expression of intense curiosity. Although none of them had seen her before they all knew that she was the Frenchwoman from faraway Paris. Just for a matter of seconds needles were idle and a variety of rainbow threads hung suspended in mid-air.

Agrippina Markarova, who sat at a small worktable on her own, was the only one who did not look up immediately, even though she was expecting this visitor. She finished a stitch before putting down her work and rising from her chair. She was tall, very upright and sternly good-looking in her late forties, her fair hair streaked through with grey and topped by a frilled white cap. Then to Marguerite's relief she smiled, her whole face softening, as if thankful to see that there was no arrogance in the newcomer's attitude, no haughty disdain as if nobody could match the skills of a Parisian seamstress and embroiderer.

'I'm pleased to see you here, Mam'selle Marguerite. I heard that you did not get a very warm welcome from Madame Rostova when you first arrived.'

'There was a misunderstanding for a little while,' Marguerite admitted carefully.

'You and your fellow countrywomen must have thought you'd come to the most inhospitable country in the world! I know that you were even threatened with being turned out into the street before you'd barely crossed the threshold! I want to assure you that we in Russia are friendly people. As soon as I heard what had happened I was determined to make amends.' She crossed to a cupboard and brought out a little painted bowl that held bread and salt. 'It is an old tradition in Russia to welcome strangers with bread and salt, and may your days in this country be long and peaceful.'

All the women in the room stopped work to applaud with smiles and a little chatter among themselves as Marguerite gladly accepted the offering. She had feared animosity and even aggression, but instead she had found quite the opposite. 'Thank you so much, madame. You have made it easier for me to make a request.'

'Yes? What is it?'

'There will be occasions when I shall need extra hands. In fact I should like to start off with at least three more

81

seamstresses and at least two apprentices for the mundane tasks. Would you be able to help me in this matter?'

Agrippina nodded. 'Yes, that can be arranged. But first of all I expect you'd like to see the work we're doing here.'

All the women had resumed their tasks and Agrippina guided Marguerite around the room, giving her the chance to see everything. The stitching was exquisite, some sewing delicate petticoats, nightgowns and chemises, others at work on bodices, skirts and drapery destined to become new gowns for the Empress and the Grand Duchess. In an adjoining room the younger and less experienced seamstresses were engaged in the embroidery of bed linen and other such tasks. Agrippina spoke quietly to Marguerite.

'The work of all the girls here is full of promise. I can have a choice of new workers any time I wish and I soon sort the wheat from the chaff. At the moment I can spare you two seamstresses, but they speak only Russian.'

'I'm sure it will not be difficult to demonstrate what I shall require.'

'I'll let you have the apprentices later.' She waved aside Marguerite's thanks. 'In the meantime I'll send the two young women I select along to you this afternoon.'

'How many gowns do you make a year?' Marguerite asked with interest as they returned to the main sewing room.

'It's difficult to say. We make many for the Grand Duchess, but for the Empress there have to be several new gowns ready for every single day of the year. No gown is ever worn twice, but they are only thrown away afterwards if they are irretrievably soiled in any way. It is my personal responsibility to check each one, and if they are not fit to be saved I salvage the good material out of them. As I do all the designing, it can often be incorporated advantageously later on. I doubt that the Empress realizes how I save her money in this way since economy is of no importance to her, but I cannot bear to see exquisite fabric wasted.'

Her glance was inquiring. 'Would you like to see some of the gowns that have been kept?'

'Yes, indeed!'

Together they left the atelier and went up a flight of stairs to double doors at the end of a corridor. Agrippina put a key in the lock.

'I have access here as it is my task to supervise the care of the gowns. Most of them are encased in panels of Venetian glass, which keeps them free of dust.'

Marguerite followed her into the dark room. Agrippina began opening the inner window shutters and light flowed in to reveal an amazing sight. Marguerite stood still in amazement, looking incredulously at the sight that had opened up before her. It was like being in a great ballroom full of headless women. Hundreds of dummies in glorious gowns stood four or five deep with many more encased in glass on both sides of the enormously long room.

'However many gowns are here?' Marguerite exclaimed in astonishment.

Agrippina looked over her shoulder as she opened yet another shutter. 'In this room? Fifteen hundred, but this is only one of several rooms where the gowns are stored. Four thousand were destroyed last winter in a fire at the palace in Moscow, but altogether there are many thousands more. None of them will ever be worn again. The Empress loves finery and everything to do with it. In her own private apartments there is an adjacent room where she has the choice of five thousand pairs of shoes in every conceivable colour and at least as many pairs of gloves.'

Marguerite continued to be amazed. She was already wandering along past the cases, gazing at the gowns. There were watered silks with a lovely sheen, autumn-shaded taffetas, velvets of imperial scarlet, forest green and sapphire blue that were dramatized with trimmings of sable, as well as a variety of rich gold and silver brocades. It showed Marguerite that the Empress had no preference for one colour or fabric over another. She was most interested in the beautiful embroidery that encrusted the bodices of a number of the gowns and spread down and over the skirts, but lacked the imaginative use of it that had made the Empress lust after the Comtesse's gowns.

Agrippina came to stroll alongside. 'If ever you should make a gown for anyone except the imperial ladies, always remember that only they have the right to wear silver silks and brocades. It is a long-established tradition in the Romanov family.'

'Thank you for telling me, but I doubt if that situation will ever arise.'

'In another of the rooms on this floor there is the Empress's male attire. She never wears those garments a second time either.'

Marguerite showed her surprise. 'When does she first wear them?'

'Occasionally there are balls when she commands the men to dress as women and vice versa. As everybody in the Palace knows, the Empress likes showing off her figure and displaying her legs in tight breeches and knee stockings. The older ladies with less than perfect figures detest these occasions. So do most of the men, many of them proud, high-ranking and courageous officers. They often get their skirts wedged in doorways or knock into others while dancing and feel thoroughly humiliated.'

'That would never happen at our Royal Court in France!'

'I'm sure there are many differences nowadays,' Agrippina agreed, 'but perhaps not so many in Peter the Great's time. When he returned from Europe he wanted everything modelled on what he had seen at the Palace of Versailles, which is why French became the Court language and French fashion swept away Russian styles; also it was no longer permitted for any man of rank to be bearded. Some men still wear richly embroidered caftans on occasions, but mostly for less formal wear.'

Marguerite, remembering the carting away of furniture when the Court had departed and the general neglect of the Palace that prevailed, thought that in spite of Peter the Great's great influence lingering on, it was clear that the transition had still not been successfully completed. She also recalled what the Comtesse had first told her of the whole country's lack of culture, which contrasted so sharply with France's richness in the arts and literature.

When the room was locked up again Marguerite thanked Agrippina for showing her the gowns. 'I'm very grateful. I was so afraid before we met that you would view me as an intruder.'

Agrippina smiled, shaking her head. 'Far from it! The old saying about many hands making light work is true, and you and your seamstresses are relieving my women of the embroidery that takes so much time.'

'Tell me a little about them. I'd like to know how they are selected.'

'There is always a tremendous choice. Some of my needlewomen are the mothers, wives and children of serfs. Although they themselves are of no intrinsic value – only the male serfs count in an estimate of wealth – the Empress still owns them and I can bid any one of them to join my work force.'

'I knew about ownership, but I never realized the lot of serfs was quite so hard.'

Agrippina shook her head in surprise. 'Hard? No. Why should you think that? Admittedly there are still instruments of correction in the cellars here as there are in many great houses, but they're only used for cases of thievery or brutal assault. Usually a flogging is enough for slackness or a task poorly done, and plenty of that punishment goes on.'

'Surely not here!' Marguerite glanced in dismay at the busy seamstresses.

'Oh, I never have any trouble with my workers, who are glad to be in my charge. On the whole, most serfs do well enough if obedient to an owner's will. Many have small-holdings to keep them and their families fed while working their masters' land. They also carve or make little things out of clay and so forth for sale in the markets. Whenever a serf dies in the streets, it's usually the result of punishment for sloth or spending whatever they have on vodka.'

Marguerite felt that a great void had opened up between her and this woman, who looked at life so differently, seeing nothing untoward in centuries steeped in slavery. She was thoughtful as she found her way downstairs again. Beneath the veneer this was still a barbaric land! The lot of the French peasants was hard and many existed on the edge of starvation, but at least they could raise a voice against injustice as had happened in rumbling little outbreaks from time to time.

She was almost back to her own sewing rooms when she decided, almost on a rise of rebellion on behalf of the serfs, to see something of this great warren of a place that was only one of the Empress's many palaces from which so many millions of people were ruled.

It took her several attempts before she found her way into the state apartments, coming suddenly upon a vast entrance hall that dazzled with gilt and marble. There was nobody about. She went slowly up the great staircase, her reflection in mirrors showing her as a tiny figure in a glittering gold embrace. Who would ever have suspected, coming into this glorious setting, that cruelty, indifference and tyranny lay behind its sparkling façade?

At the head of the staircase she went to a central pair of gilded doors and opened them cautiously. There was nobody about. She entered the great salon with its silk-panelled walls the colour of a summer sky, huge crystal chandeliers suspended from the ornate ceiling and the shining parquet floor wonderfully patterned in different woods. Enthralled, she wandered across to the next double doors and passed from one grand salon into another. Each one showed signs of having been robbed of its furniture for the journey to Moscow, but it had all been done in a haphazard way. A few chairs had been taken from a row placed against walls or one of a pair of side tables removed. Gaps showed where pictures had gone and some rooms were still in disarray where carpets had been taken up.

She had come into yet another salon when she saw that the next set of doors stood open and there was the sound of movement within. Thinking that it was probably a servant or two beginning to tidy up, she went to push the doors wider and saw a shoulder-caped coat and a fur hat thrown down on a sofa. Her gaze went swiftly to the tall man, his dark hair drawn back and tied with a black ribbon, who stood on some library steps, hanging a painting. She recognized him instantly.

Jan van Deventer spoke without looking in her direction. 'What do you think of the subject matter, Mam'selle Laurent? This is the portrait of a Dutchman like myself enjoying life.'

She realized he must have caught sight of her reflection in a pier glass. He jumped down from the steps, still assessing the painting with narrowed eyes. Curiosity spurred her forward. Standing level with him, she studied the portrait carefully and it made her smile. It showed a merry-looking man with sparkling eyes and red cheeks, wearing a wide hat fashionable a century ago and holding up a goblet of wine as if in a toast to the viewer.

'He'd be good company,' she declared, 'but noisy too. I can almost hear his bellowing laughter and it's quite infectious.'

Jan laughed. 'My opinion exactly! Do you suppose the Empress will approve of him? I understand she enjoys a hedonistic life herself.'

'I couldn't answer for the Empress, but I like him.' She met his eyes, which were piercing into her as at their first meeting, and was very aware of his height and fine physique. 'I'm surprised that you remembered me.' Then at the same moment she regretted her words, which had sounded coquettish to her own ears and not what she had intended.

Fortunately he did not seem to think the same, laughter in his voice. 'How could I have forgotten? It was the first time I had been offered a wife so unexpectedly and in Riga of all places.'

She laughed too, relieved. 'I suppose your brother Hendrick told you my name.'

He was nodding. 'Yes, on that same evening in Riga. Did you ever find the person you were looking for?'

'Yes, he came shortly afterwards to join his wife. I left next morning with my companions for St Petersburg.'

'Hendrick told me why you had come to Russia. He and I stayed in that hostelry for a couple of days. Then he set off for home again, and I brought the paintings he'd delivered on to St Petersburg.' He shrugged in frustration. 'Only to find the imperial ladies have gone to Moscow.'

'They went to Kiev first. Shall you follow them?'

He shook his head. 'No, I've other business in the city from orders taken on my previous visit. The English merchants and their wives, as well as other foreigners and also my fellow countrymen, who are engaged in the diamond and shipping business here, are always eager to buy.' His gaze travelled disparagingly over the other paintings on the walls and he waved a hand at them. 'None of these Russian works is outstanding. I look forward to the day when this country can produce her own great artists, perhaps as my own birthplace of the Netherlands did in the last century.' He smiled. 'That extraordinary age of art! If I had a glass of wine in my hand now like the fellow in the portrait I'd raise it in a toast to the glory of those golden years.'

She knew something about those times, for her sister's lover, who had had an extensive library, had lent her some books on art after she admired his paintings, but she would have liked to know more. Although she could see nothing wrong with the pictures he had dismissed, she also saw that his Dutch painting shone out from the rest, seeming to vibrate with laughter and life. She moved slightly to stand squarely in front of it.

'Is it a self-portrait by the artist?'

'No. Personally I think this fellow was one of Rubens's many drinking companions.'

She nodded sagely. 'Then this is the painting that you asked about when you met your brother at the Riga hostelry.' And, she thought, it was one of the ones that had caused the long wait that the Comtesse had permitted at Frankfurt-on-Oder. All because the Empress was not to be kept waiting excessively long for her latest acquisition.

'You heard me question him, did you?' he asked. 'Yes, I had a letter from Hendrick last time I was here, letting me know it was for sale and he hoped to secure it.' He narrowed his eyes at the painting. 'Although Rubens died over a hundred years ago I see his influence still in the work of today's artists everywhere.' He glanced at her. 'Even in France.'

She turned to him almost eagerly. 'You know my country?'

'Very well. It's full of beautiful women.'

Yes, she thought wryly, that's how he would judge any place he visited. Her interest waned. 'I must go. I shouldn't be here, but I was curious. How did you know where to hang the painting?'

'I was shown the place when I was last here. The Grand Duchess, who is interested in art, had just bought a still life from me when I told her about this painting. Immediately she was eager to have it for the grand ducal apartments.' Then his tone became ironic. 'Unfortunately the Empress overheard our conversation and stepped in, accusing the unfortunate young woman of further extravagance and saying that she would have it for herself.'

She wondered what clash he had witnessed between the two imperial ladies. Greed seemed to one of the Empress's great faults. 'You'll have to find something else to please the Grand Duchess. Now I really must go.'

'Wait! Not yet! You should see the great Dutch master-piece in the next room before you leave!' He caught her hand in his and she went willingly with him into the next room, he throwing the double doors wide with his free hand. Then he came to a halt, releasing her.

'There!' he exclaimed triumphantly. 'Rembrandt's *David's Farewell to Jonathan*! Peter the Great bought it himself at an auction years ago when he was in the Netherlands.'

It was the first time Marguerite had ever seen a truly great painting. Nothing her sister's lover had possessed came anywhere near the magnificence of what she was viewing now. Jan was talking of brushstrokes and dramatic colour and the deep humanity of the painting, but she was simply gazing her fill of the great picture.

'Peter the Great bought many Dutch paintings on both his visits,' he continued, smiling at her rapt gaze. It pleased him to see such enormous appreciation in her, but then everything about her pleased him. She was no ordinary woman, seeming to hold the promise of endless discoveries if only it were possible to break through to her. She intrigued and fascinated him. 'There's a Jan Fyt still life on the wall over there,' he continued. 'That's one of Peter the Great's purchases, although none can be compared with the Rembrandt.'

But she had only time to give the still life a fleeting glance, having heard someone approaching from the far room. 'I must go!'

'That will only be the official who received me,' he said reassuringly.

'But I don't think I should be here! Goodbye!'

She flew out of the room, back through the many salons

until she came to the great staircase. It took her a long time after that to find her way back to her own atelier.

Far away in a sledge travelling in the entourage between Kiev and Moscow, Catherine experienced the first arrow-sharp pains of a miscarriage. She wept with relief.

Eight

That afternoon the two Russian seamstresses arrived, their cheeks bright crimson with nervousness at being sent to work with foreigners. They were both in their twenties and about the same height with broad, pretty faces, Nina with straight, moon-fair hair and Lise with brown curls. As they stood side by side in dresses of similar colour, their aprons crisp and white, they looked like a pair of the dolls that slotted into each other, which the seamstresses had seen in the market place.

'Bonjour,' the two young women said together, having obviously rehearsed their greeting. Although neither spoke French they had heard enough of the language to know a few words and also grasp the meaning of what Marguerite said to them. Soon they had settled to sewing the underskirt of the Empress's gown while the others returned their attention again to their embroidery, using rich-green, sapphire-blue and gilt threads in the intricate pattern of peacock feathers that they were creating.

By the end of the week Nina and Lise had lost their shyness sufficiently to exchange Russian words for French ones as a general learning of one another's language evolved around the sewing tables. Agrippina came to see if they were proving satisfactory and brought twelve-year-old twins with her to be the new apprentices. They were named Julie and Marya, both bright-eyed as little mice with yellow hair, their tasks to include threading needles, heating irons and keeping the floor swept and clean, tasks that Marguerite had carried out herself when first starting her apprenticeship with Madame Fromont. The new arrivals were not in the least shy, and Marguerite soon had to reprimand them for being noisy and chattering too much, although she allowed them to join in the exchange of French and Russian words, for that was to everyone's benefit.

Igor, who sometimes came to see Marguerite, arrived just before supper one evening after work was over for the day to tell her that she had a visitor.

'His name is Mynheer Jan van Deventer.' Then, mistaking the reason for her quick frown, he added with the intention of being helpful, 'He's a Dutchman. From the Netherlands.'

She smiled. 'Yes, Igor, I know. Did he give his reason for calling?'

'He just asked to see you.'

'I think you had better tell him it is not convenient at the present time.'

Igor looked doubtful. 'He'll only send me back to you again. I can tell he's not a man to be easily turned away.'

She thought that Igor had summed up Jan van Deventer quite accurately, and she gave a sigh. 'Very well. I'll see him.'

A feeling of uncertainty took hold of her as she went along corridors and down flights of stairs, nor did it leave her when she came face to face with Jan again. He came forward, his gaze seeming to absorb her.

'Mam'selle Laurent! How good to see you again! You rushed away so quickly when we last met that there was no chance to settle a time and place to meet again.'

She raised her eyebrows at his assumption that she would have agreed to a meeting. 'It would have made no difference. I'm far too busy to make any social arrangements.'

He dismissed her statement with a shake of his head. 'But that was nearly two weeks ago. I think you will have organized your working routine by now. Nobody can sew twenty-four hours a day. Not even for an empress!'

'Perhaps not at the moment, but those times will come, I'm sure. It happened often enough when I was in Paris.'

'But you are free to have supper with me now while you're able to do whatever you wish! The lackey said you were about to sit down to a meal and so I know you haven't eaten.'

'That's true, but—'

'But you're tired of Russian food,' he interrupted, finishing her sentence in a way she had not intended, 'and I know a hostelry where French dishes are served.'

She showed her surprise. 'Here in St Petersburg? It must be on Vasilievsky Island.'

'That's right.'

'I was in the French quarter there the morning after my arrival in the city, but I was too worried then to take much notice of my surroundings.'

'Obviously you haven't had a chance to fully explore this city yet. So let me take you back briefly to France tonight in the very heart of St Petersburg. At the same time I can probably answer anything you want to know about the city.'

His invitation was enticing. It was a chance for a little self-indulgence in allowing herself to enjoy all things French again for a very short time.

'I'll come and I thank you,' she said decisively. 'I do want to know everything possible about this extraordinary city.' It had been a revelation to see it as she had done first in moonlight and then by day in all its multi-pastel colours and its gilded spires and domes – first impressions she would never forget. 'All I really know is that it was built through Peter the Great's whim to create a new capital on wide and desolate marshes.'

He grinned. 'So fetch your cloak. I've a troika waiting.'

When she was back upstairs dinner was already being served and her companions were all at the table, except Violette, who had gone to meet one of the footmen.

'We shall want to hear all about your evening when you get back,' Jeanne called out merrily as Marguerite bade them goodnight.

Wrapped in her cloak with the hood over her head, she went with Jan out into the starry night to where a coachman and his three-horse troika were waiting. Jan tucked a fur rug around them both and they were swept on their way. There were enough street lanterns for her to glimpse the various places of interest he pointed out that ranged from the Admiralty to various churches.

'Over there,' he said, pointing in the direction of what she knew to be the Peter and Paul fortress, 'is the little house where Tsar Peter lived like a peasant while this city of his was taking shape.'

'I was told about that, but I wasn't sure where it stood.'

'Perhaps I could take you to see it one day. Did you know he stopped building work everywhere else in the land to gather hundreds of thousands of workers here to fulfil his dream?'

'What a dedicated and powerful man he was! Tell me more.'

She enjoyed listening to him as they crossed the frozen river to reach the island and shortly afterwards the troika drew up outside what appeared to be a private mansion, except for the painted sign hanging above the entrance. It showed an unmistakably French vineyard.

Inside there was the golden glow of candlelight, the warm air rich with the aroma of good food, and the place was crowded. Several Russian officers were carousing noisily at one of the tables. The landlord, who seemed to know Jan well, showed them to a table in a quiet alcove, where her cloak and his greatcoat were taken away by a serving maid.

'We are very busy this evening, Mynheer van Deventer,' the landlord said, 'but I shall see that you are well looked after.' He then listed several dishes and they made their choice. A waiter came with the wine Jan had selected and then there was the chance to continue their conversation.

'It was like a revelation to me when I saw the city by moonlight upon arrival and then next morning saw it again in all its pastel colours with its gilded spires and domes. First impressions that I'll never forget. To me there is something jewel-like about St Petersburg as if Peter the Great saw it glittering in the mud of the marshes and scooped it out with his bare hands.'

'I like what you've said,' he acknowledged seriously. 'I'm reminded of a famous quote from a traveller seeing St Petersburg for the first time. He said that the beauty of it – and with Heaven to come – was too much joy for anyone.'

'I can identify with that thought,' she replied with a smile, just for an instant aware of total rapport with him. 'But there's one thing that puzzles me.'

'What's that?'

'Although he completed all his fine buildings it seems to me that since his time nothing is ever properly dealt with or finished.'

He laughed quietly. 'You've noticed that already, have you? Well, Russians get full of enthusiasm about a project, whatever it may be, but as that interest wanes they'll move on to something else. What wasn't done yesterday can be kept for another day. The poor serfs are like flotsam caught up in the tide, forever being swept here and there according to their masters' whims.'

'What you have said explains a lot to me,' she commented thoughtfully.

'I expect you've seen that the embankments along the Neva are still unfinished, although they must have been started years ago, maybe even in Peter the Great's time. The streets are another example, because when the packed snow melts away you'll see that some are fully paved, others half-finished and some not at all.'

'So this vast nation with all its resources has its weak-nesses too.'

'Never doubt it! It could be said that the Empress personifies her own country. On the one hand she has abol-ished capital punishment, but allows cruel chastisements to continue. She is a highly intelligent woman, but although she has a great library herself she tolerates appalling ignorance among those in her court. There are exceptions, of course, particularly among the old aristo-cratic families, as well as the younger up-and-coming intelligentsia, who cleave more to Catherine because she is in every way their match.'

'How do you know so much about the Empress?'

'I have a Russian acquaintance at court.'

Almost certainly a woman, she thought, but his next words corrected that assumption.

'He knows Amsterdam well, having spent some time in the Netherlands on diplomatic affairs, and he bought several paintings from my gallery when he was there. I had not thought of Russia as a possible market until he suggested it, saying there was a dearth of great art here. That is how I gained an entrée to sell that Rubens to the Grand Duchess, who – unfortunately – was not destined to have it after all.'

So, she thought, even though she had been mistaken in thinking at first that his court acquaintance was a woman, it had not changed her first impression of him in any way.

'Where did you live in Paris?' he asked with intense inter-est. 'And whereabouts did you work?'

She told him and, when he wanted to know how her working conditions here compared with Paris, she answered that there was very little difference. 'Except, of course,' she added, 'that it is more spacious and I am now in charge. Yet it all still seems strange to me.'

'That is only because it is taking you a little time to settle down,' he said. 'When you've been here long enough to really get to know the Russian people I'm sure you will like them. They have a great sense of humour, a huge national pride, and are stoic in every kind of adversity.'

'I have met kindness from almost everyone already.'

'Do you think you will be able to adapt to Russian ways?' he questioned closely, his fierce eyes never leaving her face. 'Does the climate alarm you? It will get even colder than it is now.'

'I can adjust to everything, including the weather, but not to the state of millions of men owned body and soul by masters who are free to flog and work them however they wish.'

He gave a nod, his expression serious. 'I agree with you, but there is oppression everywhere in the world in one form or another. That doesn't mean things can't change for the better in the fullness of time. I like to think that just one serf, dreaming of freedom, could set a ball rolling towards it that would never be stopped, no matter how long or how difficult its path.' He paused, smiling seriously. 'But I'm an optimist. Everything is possible if one sets a course and never turns from it.'

She sensed a sexual undercurrent in his tone and turned it aside by asking him how successful he had been in selling his pictures. He was interrupted in answering her by the arrival of the waiters with covered dishes, each one announced in the old traditional French way as they were uncovered with a flourish. There was foie gras enhanced by fried apples and a salad dressed with walnut oil, which was followed by lamb with grilled crêpes. Finally an apple tart decorated with candied violets.

'It was all delicious,' Marguerite said appreciatively. She had no complaint against the Russian food served at the Palace, which was plentiful and usually quite tasty, but often it was heavy and extremely filling as befitted the needs of those living and working in a harsh climate. Yet in every way it was far from the standard of this evening's dishes. The memory of much bad food eaten on the journey from home had also made this occasion seem like a celebration of French cuisine and it had lifted her spirits. There had been times in the past when she had dined in similar style, but that had been when Anne-Marie was still alive and her lover had occasionally extended an invitation to dine in their company.

The good wine had eased away the tension she had felt earlier and as they lingered over a final glass, Marguerite found herself telling Jan about her sister.

'Anne-Marie would have liked me to live with her in her fine apartment. She was often lonely when her lover was with his wife and family, but he would not allow it. He wanted her to himself whenever he had time to spend with her. It was only on special occasions that I was allowed to be there. Sadly she contracted sickness of the lungs and was not yet thirty when she died.'

'That was terrible for you,' he said compassionately, seeing the shadow that passed across her eyes. 'I have two brothers: Hendrick, whom you know, and Maarten, the youngest, who is following in the footsteps of our late grandfather, a well-known artist in his time.'

'Is Maarten's work as good?'

'It's maturing. I've sold several of his early works, but the best is yet to come.'

'Does he look after the gallery when you and Hendrick are away?'

He laughed, shaking his head. 'He'd get so lost in his painting that everything else would go out of his head! No, it was exceptional for Hendrick to travel as far away from home as he did in coming to Riga that time. Normally he manages my gallery in my absences, and if he should be away somewhere to buy for me his wife Cornelia takes charge. She's a good businesswoman as well as being the daughter of an established artist. So she knows a great deal about good art and is capable in every way.'

'Do you follow in your grandfather's footsteps too?'

He smiled. 'Yes. One day when I've set up a studio and gallery here, which I may well do eventually, I'll paint a picture for you. A landscape, perhaps.'

Her delight showed in her face. 'Just a little picture that I could hang in my room?'

'What would please you most? A landscape?'

'Could it be a view of St Petersburg?'

'That's exactly what I had in mind.'

At a nearby table a couple were rising to leave and Marguerite was reminded sharply of the passing of time.

'I should be getting back now,' she said anxiously, pushing back her chair. 'I was warned that doors to the domestic quarters get bolted and barred.'

He glanced at his gold fob watch, although he rose to his feet with her. 'You've no need to worry. There's another half an hour yet and we'll get there before time is up.'

Back at the Palace the guards, their fur hats down to their eyes with flaps over their ears and their high collars covering the rest of their faces, let her pass, but stopped Jan, it being too late to admit visitors at the domestic entrance.

'It's been a wonderful evening,' she said sincerely to him as they parted, their breath hanging in the frosty air between them.

Jan stood watching her as she hurried away along the cleared path in the ice-crisp snow to reach the domestic entrance. Just before she went into the Palace she paused on the lantern-lit steps to cast him a smile over her shoulder. He waved in return, resolved to have her sooner or later.

As Marguerite had expected, her companions had waited up as promised to hear about the evening. There were laughter and exaggerated moans and groans of envy as she described the food and wine. Only Violette was silent. She had enjoyed her evening too and had done a little delicious moaning of her own, but had no intention of telling anyone what had taken place.

Nine

S arah had kept her promise to write, although the first letter did not come until she was feeling better and able to take up a pen again. Marguerite replied promptly and their letters began to cross as the weeks went by in an exchange of all their news.

During this time the seamstresses had begun to form social relationships. Violette had finished seeing the footman, who had become too serious, talking sentimentally about marriage, which was the last thing she wanted. She had transferred her interest to a sergeant of the guards, whom she thought very handsome in his red and green uniform. He took her dancing and sometimes out to supper, which she enjoyed. Once in a crowded cafe, after drinking a little too much, he had performed a Russian dance on his own for her with bent knees and kicking feet, which had made her shriek with delight.

Yet Isabelle and Rose were the first to make friends outside the Palace. They were having rides down one of the built-up snow mountains when they met two English girls, Joan Pomfret and her sister Lily. They were the twin daughters of a hydraulic engineer from London, who was working on extending the city's canals. What started as shared laughter on the slides soon became a steady friendship with invitations to their home in the English settlement. Their mother, a very maternal woman, pitied the two young French girls' being far from home, even though Rose had her mother and aunt at the Palace. She made them welcome whenever they were free from work to visit.

Sophie had found a beau for herself quite by chance. She had taken a shoe to a cobbler's shop, needing to get a heel mended, but found it impossible to understand what the cobbler said to her. A middle-aged Russian, who was collecting a pair of boots, acted as an interpreter for her.

'He is saying that if you will take a seat he'll mend your heel while you wait, mam'selle.'

She turned shining eyes full of gratitude on him, her smile wide, and saw a kindly, rugged face with fair brows under his wide fur hat, his clean-shaven chin showing that he was above peasant status.

'Thank you for your help, monsieur,' she replied. 'I have yet to learn your language. So far I only know the Russian words for scissors and sewing silk and so forth.'

She looked about for a seat and he indicated a bench by the wall. To her surprise and pleasure he sat down beside her. 'You are a seamstress?' he asked. 'How long is it since you came to St Petersburg?'

She had much to tell when she took up her sewing again in the atelier. He had walked her back to the Palace and they were to meet again. He was a fifty-six-year-old widower, an apothecary by profession, with a grown-up son and daughter, both married, who lived in other parts of the city. His name was Valentin Vaganov.

'I told him that I'd come to Russia through your persuasion, Jeanne,' Sophie said, smiling at her sister, 'and that my niece is here too. He was very interested.'

'He sounds a nice type of man,' Jeanne said approvingly, hiding the sudden twinge of envy. It was not that she wanted any romantic nonsense in her life, but she would have liked some male conversation for a change and to inhale again the aroma of a real man with a strong arm to put around her waist and a laughing mouth to kiss her. But all that belonged to a long time ago before her disastrous marriage.

She sighed reminiscently as she lowered her gaze again to the flower she was embroidering.

A few weeks later it was Sophie who proved instrumental in opening up a more social life for Jeanne. 'Valentin is having a family party for me to meet everybody,' she said, her sparkling eyes full of secrets, 'and he wants you and Rose to be there too.'

'Is there to be a betrothal announcement?' Jeanne demanded sharply.

'No! But I'm hoping a path is being set.'

'Just don't rush into anything as I did.'

'Don't worry. Just say you'll come.'

Jeanne was pleased to find that Valentin had a comfortable home with servants and she noticed everything with interest. She could understand why he was attracted to Sophie with her graceful movements and thick-lashed, heavy-eyed good looks. Twenty-five members of his family were present, all ages represented, including his three-month-old grandchild. There was much talk and laughter with plenty of vodka and wine to drink at a long table full of good food. Not many spoke French, but Valentin's sister-in-law Olga, who was seated beside Jeanne, was fluent and spoke two or three other languages as well.

'It is necessary for me,' she said to Jeanne, 'because my husband only speaks Russian and we have a shop selling fabrics and lace where so many foreigners come to buy.' She had a round, pleasing face with smiling eyes and her friendliness shone through. 'So in our mutual knowledge of fabrics you and I have much in common, madame. You must come and see the shop at your first opportunity. I always have a samovar ready and we shall drink a cup of tea together.'

It was to be the first of many cups of tea shared there and led to Jeanne being invited into Olga's social circle, the Russian woman showing every sign of becoming a staunch friend.

All these developments were a great pleasure and relief

103

to Marguerite, for they gave all her seamstresses new interests and fresh topics of conversation, banishing the boredom that could have made them all desperately homesick. Naturally there were moments when longing for their homeland would hit them, Marguerite included, but for the time being there was not one who wished herself back in France.

Marguerite continued to enjoy Jan's company, although she tried not to see him too frequently. Yet his male conversation was so different from the never-ending female chatter she heard day after day, and he had shown her the city, including the log hut that had been Peter the Great's first home. He took her for supper in cellar cafes with arched ceilings where singers entertained and there was the music of violins or balalaikas. He taught her to skate and by the light of flaring torches they joined other skaters on the frozen river and canals. One Sunday afternoon they rode in a troika that he drove himself out into the country where they ate blinis with both red and black caviar in a good hostelry. One evening when they had had a particularly happy time together she gave him a very fine cravat that she had made him and he put it on at once, extremely pleased.

She liked to hear him talk of his homeland and its customs and how it had been to grow up there with daily lessons from a strict tutor, as well as being taught to draw and paint by a far more lenient grandfather. He and his brothers had competed in skating races along the canals in winter and had gone fishing and boating in summer. It sounded an idyllic boyhood that he had shared with Hendrick and Maarten, except that they had lost their father early on and their mother soon afterwards, leaving their grandfather as the centre of their lives.

She also encouraged him to talk of his favourite Dutch artists of the previous century. On an evening when they were having supper together he explained the symbolism that was to be found in so much of their work, making sketches of some examples for her.

'In a picture such as this,' he said, sketching it out, 'a broom would denote that the woman in the painting is a good housewife while a musical instrument or even a few sheets of music may mean that love is in the air.' He continued giving her examples while she watched how skilfully he drew. 'Many paintings hold a moral warning, the use of shadows sometimes conveying the nearness of evil or its temptations. In a still life there may appear to be no hidden meaning until you notice a fallen petal from a flower or maybe a piece of half-peeled fruit about to topple down from a table, reminders of the briefness of life.' Then he saw how absorbed she was in all he was saying, which pleased him.

'I'm learning so much about art from you that I never knew before.' She looked down at the sketches he had done for her. 'May I keep these?' she asked, studying them anew.

'Yes, if you wish.'

'You spoke well about your brother's work, but I believe he would speak more highly of yours.'

He shrugged. 'I paint whenever I have time, but I'm leaving it to Maarten to make our surname known in the art world!'

He was having no difficulty in selling the other paintings he had brought with him. Then one day he spoke of returning to Amsterdam to collect more works of art to sell in what he said was becoming a very lucrative market. She knew she would miss him and was thankful that he had seemed to accept that she wanted nothing more than friendship. When eventually he told her one evening that he had sold his last painting she knew his departure must be imminent.

'When will you leave?' she asked.

'The day after tomorrow. The next time I come to Russia I'm hoping to get a passage with a Dutch ship sailing direct to St Petersburg. All too often trading vessels call in at other ports in Prussia or Sweden or elsewhere, delivering one cargo and taking on another.'

'So it could take as long as going by road?'

'Sometimes longer.'

'But perhaps instead of all the changes of horses and those areas of poor accommodation and food you would have more comfort if you came by sea?'

He shook his head. 'Quite the reverse. Most of these trading vessels really haven't any room for passengers. One lives with the crew and much depends on the ship's cook whether the food is good or bad. It's different with ships making long voyages. They have cabins.'

'So you're setting off by road. At least the thaw should soon come.'

Again he shook his head. 'You mustn't expect to see an early spring here. This is not Europe. The saying is that there are only two seasons in this part of the world: winter and summer. You'll be lucky if all the snow has gone by mid-April, but unless the weather is exceptionally mild it's likely that some will still be lingering in shady hollows and slabs of ice floating on the water everywhere.'

She laughed. 'You're not exactly cheering me up! You're departing and the snow stays.'

He loved to see her laugh. She had a way of tilting her head, exposing the white length of her throat, which made him long to let his lips roam over it.

They were back at the Palace and alone in the hallway. Now that the guards had become used to seeing him they allowed him through. He took her gently by the shoulders as he looked down into her upturned face. 'Don't forget me while I'm away, Marguerite.'

'I've enjoyed the time we have spent together, so why should I do that?' she asked, smiling.

His expression remained serious. 'Because something or somebody stands between us. I've seen it in your eyes.'

She had never mentioned Jacques to him and was caught off guard for a moment. Although she knew Jacques would have wanted her to move on with her life, Tom's resemblance had somehow given her a brief extension of being with him. She was yearning to see him again just for that reason. The previous day she had received another letter from Sarah, saying that she and Tom would soon be on their way to St Petersburg.

'I came to Russia to move on with my life,' she said.

Somehow her simple reply seemed to confirm his supposition, but he could no longer resist taking her into his arms. Drawing her to him in a strong embrace, he bent his head and kissed her deeply, tenderly at first and then with an explosion of long-controlled passion.

Jacques flew into her mind, for nobody had kissed her since his last kiss, but then Jan seemed to blot out even that memory as she gave herself up to the sensual pleasure of his ardent mouth on hers. It had been so long since she had been held and loved as this man seemed to love her. Her intense response increased his ardour and he pressed her still closer to him until, unbidden, the wish came to her that it could have been Tom holding her in his arms to let her recapture the past. Instantly the flame died down in her. She sensed Jan's disappointment. His kiss eased immediately and slowly he released her. Exasperation and anger were blended in his face.

'I love you, Margeurite! That's why I'll be coming back for you!' Then he turned on his heel and strode away. At the gates he paused to look over his shoulder at her. He saw she was still standing in the doorway, silhouetted by the candle-lamps behind her.

There was still no sign of spring when the Warringtons arrived in St Petersburg. Marguerite received a note almost immediately from Sarah, asking her to visit as soon as possible. They had rented a house in the English quarter and directions as how to find it were included. But there was to be a delay to their reunion.

Marguerite sent Igor with a reply that gave the

explanation. A courier had arrived at top speed one afternoon with the news that the Empress and the Court had left Moscow on their way back to St Petersburg. Since Marguerite wanted every garment in hand to be completed, no matter that many finished gowns were waiting for the two imperial ladies, she and her seamstresses would be working late every evening and when they were normally free.

It was not only in the Frenchwomen's atelier that work had taken on an extra spurt of activity. In Agrippina's sewing rooms it was the same. As for the Palace itself, it had leapt into life as lacklustre daily cleaning gave way to a thorough spring clean with dusters and brooms, washcloths and beeswax polish used fiercely in every room where more rat traps were set. News of the Court in Moscow had trickled through from time to time, but there had never been any mention of a baby and Marguerite supposed that Catherine had given birth without discovery.

Not all the gowns that Marguerite had designed were elaborate, although she had kept in mind the Empress's need always to dominate any scene with her presence and her attire. So some of the gowns were simply beautiful through the glorious fabric used, but each had an original touch, such as the hundreds of emeralds used in the peacock gown, one fastened into the eye of each embroidered feather. It was because of the value of the jewels that Marguerite had had to apply for them from a treasure chest kept by a senior official in the Palace. The same rule had applied to the pearls and other precious gems that she had incorporated into the embroidery on some of the gowns.

Marguerite was thankful for a respite before visiting Sarah. It gave her time as she sat with her needle to adjust to the prospect of seeing Tom again. By the time she had considered and dissected her feelings in every way, she was totally calm and confident that nothing untoward would ever happen again.

Ten

On the day the imperial family arrived back at the Palace Marguerite saw Grand Duke Peter for the first time. He had come charging up the great staircase and took a short cut, normally used only by servants, to reach his own apartment. He did not notice her halting at once with a bolt of red silk in her arms, but she had a full view of a gawky, white-wigged young man with a sly-eyed, oval face deeply pockmarked beneath the paint and powder, and a loose, thin-lipped mouth. His stale body odour reached her even as he disappeared from her view.

By now she had heard enough about him to know that he was not only always reluctant to bath but also by nature as unpleasant as his looks. Maids had told her that although he often caroused drunkenly with his own band of menservants it amused him to throw wine over them when he was at table or – far worse – his urine whenever he had the chance, never losing the opportunity to play vicious tricks. None of them envied his menservants, who had to dress up in uniform and parade whenever he played his war games. Shaking her head, she continued on to the atelier.

As she had half-expected, the Grand Duchess sent for her shortly after arrival, and she took with her one of the gowns finished from designs they had discussed before the departure to Moscow. Entering the apartment at her bidding, Marguerite found her pacing thoughtfully up and down. Coming to a halt, Catherine waited until the door was closed before speaking.

109

'Put aside that gown you're holding, Mam'selle Laurent, and listen carefully to all I have to say. First of all, were you surprised when no news of the birth came from Moscow?'

'I drew my own conclusions, Madame.'

'Ah, yes.' Catherine sank down on to a chair and smiled wryly.

'My lips have been sealed, Madame.'

'Yes, I know. Had you even whispered once about my advanced pregnancy to anyone, word of it would have reached the Empress. She has spies everywhere. I want to show my gratitude.'

Marguerite flushed with embarrassment. 'Oh, no Madame!'

Catherine nodded understandingly, holding up a placating hand. 'I would not insult your integrity by offering you money or anything else. That was not my intention. I just want you to know that from now on I feel that in time of trouble I could always turn to you in total confidence.'

Marguerite was astounded. 'I'm honoured, Madame.'

'Whenever I send for you and whatever the hour, always come without delay. It may only be for the discussion of a garment, but it could also be for something much more serious. Do you understand?'

'Yes, I believe I do,' Marguerite replied, remembering when Igor had said that the Grand Duchess had enemies at court. She could not help pitying this unfortunate princess even while realizing that she herself had been drawn into a dangerous game that was being played. 'I'll not desert you, Madame.'

'That's what I had hoped to hear!' Catherine spoke gratefully, for she had known that Marguerite as an independent foreigner could easily have decided against any involvement. Her relief echoed in her voice. 'But now we can discuss more mundane matters, although there is nothing ordinary about that gown that is lying across that chair. Show it to me.'

Marguerite, still stunned that Catherine had confided to her, switched her mind to the gown. 'I have allowed good seams to the bodice, because I was not sure if you would have regained your figure quickly after your pregnancy. Now that the situation has changed again I can make the necessary alterations when needed.'

She displayed the beauty of the gown with its ample skirt and embroidered yellow roses enhanced by delicate beading as they cascaded down to encircle the hem. 'The gowns I have made for Her Imperial Majesty are a little more eye-catching, but I've taken a more subtle approach with yours, Madame.'

Catherine's eyes twinkled suddenly with amusement and her mood lifted. She was highly pleased with Marguerite's grasp of the situation. No other dressmaker had had the wit to realize on her behalf that it was possible to keep the Empress's jealousy at bay by always making her gowns a touch more flamboyant.

'More than once at a ball the Empress has sent me to change my gown on the pretext that it does not suit me.' She chuckled mischievously. 'As we know, the moon must never outshine the sun.'

'It should never happen again.'

'I don't believe it will. Bring me the rest of the gowns you have made me.'

It took several trips, even when assisted by Violette and Sophie. The Grand Duchess approved all the gowns. Marguerite was the last to leave again, having stayed to discuss some minor details. Carrying one of the garments carefully across her arms, she set off along the main corridor of the grand ducal apartments. She took no notice when a door opened somewhere behind her. Then suddenly there came a shout and footsteps running after her.

'Wait! You with the bronze hair!'

Turning, she saw in dismay that it was Grand Duke Peter. 'Sire?'

111

'Yes, you'll do, girl!' he shouted exultantly, grabbing her by the arm and snatching the gown away to throw it heedlessly to the floor. In spite of his weedy appearance, his grip on her was vice-like and he began dragging her back along the corridor.

'I have duties to perform for the Grand Duchess! Your Imperial Highness, please listen to me! Let me go!'

He stopped abruptly and hit her fiercely across the face. 'Shut up! I can't endure whining women!' Then he lurched her on again, heedless that his rings had cut her cheek and she was gasping from the stinging pain, her eyes watering. He hauled her through the doorway that had remained open and at first she thought the vast salon was full of soldiers. Then, in a matter of seconds, she recognized a face or two and realized they were his menservants dressed up. They stood in formation around a table of a gigantic length, but she had no more than a glimpse of it before Peter had grabbed a spare uniform from a chair and threw it at her.

'Put this on and be quick about it! You'll be a gunner on the cannons!'

One of the uniformed menservants opened another door and gave her a sympathetic glance as Peter shoved her into a large library where the shelves were stacked with books behind glass from floor to ceiling. Although she began to unfasten the hooks at the back of her bodice, curiosity drew her to study some of the titles. They revealed Peter's reading taste, for those in French were all about various wars, military tactics or the crimes of highwaymen and cutthroats. She guessed that the volumes in his native German dealt with the same subjects.

A deep male voice broke the silence at the far end of the library. 'I advise you not to dawdle. His Imperial Highness doesn't like to be kept waiting.'

Startled, she swung about to see who had spoken, her heart still thumping from the rough treatment she had received. At the far end of the long room an army officer had emerged from one of the reading alcoves, a book open in his hand. He was tall and well built, wearing the red and dark-green uniform of the imperial guards with gilt epaulettes, his gold buttons gleaming. His hair was formally dressed and powdered in the current fashionable style of a roll over each ear and tied behind his neck by a wide black bow. His face was well cut with a bold nose and a finely arrogant chin, his fair brows straight and thick, and his handsome, worldly mouth widened by an amused smile.

'I didn't know anyone else was here!' she exclaimed, but she was glad to have someone to question and, in spite of his aristocratic air, he seemed approachable. 'Please tell me! What's expected of me in that other room? The Grand Duke says I'm to be a gunner.'

'Don't worry. You won't come to any harm. Obviously he's short of a gunner for one of his military battles. You'll have to fire one of the miniature cannons, that's all.'

'No harm!' she echoed fiercely, her anger directed against the Grand Duke as she darted into the seclusion of a reading alcove to change into the uniform. 'I can't embroider for the Empress with burnt fingers!'

She heard him laugh. 'Say that to Peter!' he called to her. 'He loathes her, but he'll know better than to come between her and her gowns by ruining the fingers of her embroiderer.'

She put on the uniform as quickly as possible and, seething inwardly, clamped the black tricorne with its regimental rosette on her head and tucked her hair under it. As she emerged from the alcove, the officer spoke to her again from where he was leaning a shoulder against a bookcase, and there was laughter in his voice as he looked her up and down.

'Very smart! Now forward march, Corporal – what is your name?'

She told him, for in spite of her fury at the Grand Duke's brutal treatment of her, she felt no hostility towards this stranger, who was being helpful. 'And you are . . .?' she added, wanting to know his identity.

'Captain Konstantin Dashiski of the Empress's own body-guard, at your service.' He bowed with a click of his heels. 'Shall you remember that?'

'I'm getting used to Russian names.'

'I'll certainly remember yours, Marguerite.'

She had already turned away to press down the door handle and re-enter the other room. Instantly Peter jerked her in and slammed the door behind her. She had not real-ized she still had blood on her cheek from the cut that Peter had inflicted on her and he was viewing it in triumph.

'Look! Our tenth gunner has been wounded already! What a brave fellow!' Then he gave her a shove. 'Get over there! Your place is at that spare cannon.' He pointed to a container of spills on a side table. 'Take one of those spills, light it in the candle flame and use it to ignite the wick of the cannon when I give the command.'

She took her allotted place behind a model cannon on the table. Her anger against the Grand Duke strengthened her courage and she followed Konstantin's advice. 'Her Imperial Majesty wouldn't wish me to burn my embroidery fingers!'

Her mention of the Empress had an immediate effect on Peter, who was momentarily taken aback. To her exasper-ation he did not dismiss her, but hesitated only briefly before snatching up a spare pair of white gloves from a side table.

'Put these on! You should have had them on in the first place.'

They fitted, and she guessed they were of the size worn by the row of young drummer boys, who stood lined up on a dais beyond the table.

She examined the cannon and saw the protruding wick, which she would have to replace from a bowl of wicks if this objectionable Grand Duke should demand a second volley. Her neighbour showed her what to do.

'The ends of these wicks have a substance on the end. Be sure not to put two wicks in by mistake,' he warned, 'or you'll blow your hand off.'

She knew this could not be true, having caught the flicker of amused glances that passed along the faces of the menservants. As they stepped forward at Peter's suddenly barked command she viewed the table quickly. It was laid out realistically in hills and valleys with miniature villages, silvery rivers and winding roads. Battalions of model soldiers and cavalry were in position, stiff little banners representing individual regimental colours showing brightly here and there.

'Fire!' Peter roared.

Instantly it was as if chaos had been let loose. The cannons fired with puffs of smoke, the drummers drummed, and all the time realistic screams, groans and yells came from those hidden from view under the table for the realistic sounds of the injured and dying on the battlefield. Strips of brass attached to the table were being shaken, accurately representing the sound of shells exploding. She had fumbled a little in lighting her cannon the first time, hindered by her gloves, but afterwards she was quick enough.

'Charge!' Peter almost screamed the command this time, dancing with wild excitement, and the menservants controlled the advance or retreat of the foot soldiers with a wide-ended propelling stick and sent the cavalry in two different directions. Peter himself had a long thin rod with a silver tip in his hand and kept leaning forward to knock down those that he had decided were wounded or killed. Once, when one of the servants made a clumsy move, inadvertently misplacing some cavalry, Peter screamed with rage, slashing down on the man's hand with his rod and causing blood to burst forth through his white glove, the sight of which seemed to excite Peter still further. 'On your knees! Traitor! Spy! Coward!'

The man obeyed and Peter beat him forcefully across the shoulders before ordering him out of the room. The mad war game continued unabated, and another hour went by before Peter declared on a raucously triumphant shout that victory belonged to the Holstein battalions.

'It's always the Prussians that win,' Marguerite's neighbour muttered angrily to her.

The room had filled with smoke and on the table lay the fallen military, but the game was not over yet. Peter drilled the menservants for another half an hour, making them march up and down the long room before he finally halted them. Then the drummer boys received an order to march away. Marguerite, remaining with the other gunners by their cannons, was astonished to see that on the order to 'Fall out!' the menservants began to relax, talking amongst themselves as if Peter were no longer in the room; but then the explanation came in his exuberant shout.

'After such a great victory we must celebrate, my brave warriors! Get out the vodka! Some carousing is in order!'

The footmen, including those playing the part of gunners, were loosening their high-necked collars, some tossing their uniform jackets aside to relax in their shirtsleeves. All started ambling through a far pair of doors into a neighbouring salon with Peter skipping ahead to lead the way. As she watched she saw the men throwing themselves down into the sofas, one hooking his leg over a chair arm where he sprawled, a booted leg swinging. It seemed as if one of the drunken bouts that the Grand Duke enjoyed with his servants was about to take place, although she had heard that he punished them quickly enough if they took liberties he did not condone.

She hesitated no longer and seized the opportunity to slip back into the library. Konstantin Dashiski was no longer there and for a few moments she rested her back against the door as she thought over all she had witnessed. What sort of tsar would Russia have in Peter when the time came?

Apart from his eccentric behaviour and his lack of feeling for others, he seemed to care only for war. She feared for the Russian people under his rule and was filled with pity for Catherine being married to such a man.

Abruptly she began throwing off her uniform and when dressed again she left the library to hurry away down the corridor. The gown was still lying where it had been flung and appeared to be unharmed. She gathered it up quickly and continued on her way. Back in her own room she cleaned the dried blood and the grime of the cannon fire from her face. Knowing the smell of smoke must be hanging on to her, she put her garments to be laundered, bathed herself and washed her hair vigorously. She hoped never to be involved in any of the Grand Duke's war games again.

In contrast, many pleasant sessions followed with Catherine as they discussed future garments. There were other meetings, quite daunting in some ways, with the Empress herself. As at their previous meeting, Elisabeth did not enter into any discussion, but stated what she required, leaving Marguerite to make each garment beautiful and more eye-catching than anything she had worn before.

The peacock gown had been a total and delightful surprise to Elisabeth. She saw immediately what a sensation it would cause. Privately she thought it the most glorious garment made for her since her coronation splendour of silver brocade and gold lace. Immediately she had planned to wear it at a forthcoming great occasion when she would be hosting a grand assembly of foreign dignitaries, including two crowned heads.

When that evening came Agrippina, who had generously praised the finished garment and all the work that had gone into it, showed Marguerite where she could see the Empress enter the gilded ballroom where the glittering assembly was gathering. It was a spy-hole that could be used for watching or listening, which made Marguerite realize how easily the Empress's spies could discover palace secrets apart from more subtle methods.

She had a splendid view just a little above head height. The gilded room was a magnificent setting with its marble pillars and the shining parquet floor set in an elaborate pattern of many different woods, which was a characteristic feature of all the palace rooms and hallways. The great chandeliers, dripping with crystal, made the jewels and decorations of the company sparkle gloriously and shone on the gold and silver lace that lavishly trimmed the elegant clothes of both sexes. Marguerite could see that this was a highly fashionable event that could equal any royal occasion at Versailles.

Suddenly there came a fanfare from the trumpeters. The doors opened and Elisabeth appeared, looking as proud and beautiful as a peacock herself. Always graceful, she paused to bow her head forward and to the right and to the left in the Russian way before advancing slowly towards the canopied throne on the dais. The double-headed Russian eagle was emblazoned in gold on the crimson drapery behind it.

Her wide-panniered skirt flowed with the embroidered feathers, the glow of the jewelled eyes echoed in the emerald and diamond fan-shaped Russian headdress she wore at the back of her powdered head. She knew she was a truly magnificent sight and that none present would ever forget seeing her in the glorious gown. There was added satisfaction in glimpsing the Comtesse d'Oinville's tight-lipped expression.

At the spy-hole Marguerite sighed with satisfaction. She thought of the many hours that she and her companions had spent on the gown – the thousands of long and short stitches, the variety of stem, satin, fly and fishbone ones and the hundreds of French knots. There was also the delicate work with couched gold thread, all of which had created it. Thankfully it had been worthwhile. She knew without doubt that she had established herself as a designer on whom the Empress could rely for an outstanding garment at any time.

As the Grand Duke and Duchess followed the Empress in the procession Marguerite was shocked to see that instead of appearing in Russian uniform Peter was wearing the pale-blue uniform of a general in the Holstein Dragoons. He was the administrator of the German Duchy of Holstein and she had heard how he loved to wear this particular foreign uniform. But tonight it was an insult to the Empress as if he were aligning his loyalty with her enemy Frederick II of Prussia and his German empire in the very heart of Imperial Russia.

Marguerite wondered how Catherine felt about his act of contempt, knowing from how she had talked sometimes that she truly loved her adopted country. Her husband's disloyal obsession with Prussia was surely a constant irritant to her, although she never showed it.

In Elisabeth's wake, Catherine smiled in acknowledgement of the rustling curtsies and deep bows given to her and Peter in their turn, but inwardly she was full of sick dread as to what would happen when the Empress saw what her heir was wearing. He had been late joining the procession and as yet his choice of uniform had gone unnoticed by her. He was in one of his good moods, looking forward to the violin recital he would give later to the assemblage, being quite an accomplished violinist, and he only made the occasional grimace at the Empress behind her back. That day he had received a whole new collection of model soldiers from Prussia, the uniforms accurately portrayed, and had promptly donned his present uniform to be in command of them. It was playing with this whole new battalion that had made him late for the procession and he had had no inclination to change his attire for the Empress or anyone else.

119

Marguerite watched until the Empress had mounted the dais and sat down gracefully with a glorious spread of her skirt on the gilded throne. Then she returned to tell her fellow seamstresses all that she had seen. She missed the moment when Elisabeth's gaze fell on her nephew for the first time that evening.

Elisabeth, her colour soaring, intense fury blazing in her eyes, threw out her arm to point her finger at him and screeched one word: 'Go!'

He went happily, totally unembarrassed, and hurried back to his new toys. It was only those among the foreign aristocracy, present for the first time, who felt shocked and uncomfortable. Some wondered momentarily if their eyes and ears had deceived them, for the Empress was treating them to her delightful smile again. It was almost possible to believe that the extraordinary incident had never happened.

Only Catherine guessed that the peacock gown had induced such exultant pride in Elisabeth that it was overcoming all other emotions, even lasting rage.

Marguerite was able to visit Sarah at last. Early one evening when work was over for the day she set off and was passing the Admiralty when she saw that people were crossing the Neva by the bridge. Then she noticed that after four frozen months multiple cracks had at last appeared in the ice and so all foot and wheeled traffic across it had been stopped. Now and again there was a sharp sound like a pistol shot, which startled her until she realized that it was just another splitting of the ice.

She soon found the Warringtons' house, which was painted a pale yellow. Although it was the Russian custom to dine at two o'clock and the English at five, Sarah had written that dinner would be delayed until she arrived. The door opened promptly at her tug on the bell-pull.

Sarah came running into the hall at her entry, her arms

held out. 'My dear, dear friend!' she cried in welcome. 'We meet again at last!'

'It's wonderful to see you after all this time!' Marguerite declared warmly as they embraced, kissed each other's cheeks and then caught hands, laughing in pleasure at their reunion.

'I've so enjoyed your letters,' Sarah enthused, 'but it's not like being together and chatting together. Come into the drawing room and sit down. Tom sends you his apologies, but he is very busy at the moment and is at a meeting that will keep him until late. Tell me, how have you adjusted to life here? Have you found this winter very long? I know I have! Don't you think I look well now?'

'Indeed you do!' Marguerite declared happily, thinking that Sarah had put on a little weight and did look well, although there was – and probably always would be – a fragility about her and a delicacy of colouring that gave her a vulnerable look as if she were made of porcelain. 'And this evening I've seen that the Neva is beginning to crack, which means that the winter you have found so wearying will soon be at an end.'

'That's splendid news! There's so much I want to ask you and to talk about.' Then Sarah shook her head slightly and her eyes suddenly brimmed with sentimental tears. 'After all you did for me I see you as a sister, Marguerite. Say that is how it will always be between us.'

'I couldn't wish for anything better.'

'That makes me so happy!' Spontaneously she sprang up and gave Marguerite another hug. Then she sat down again, wiped her eyes and, with a smile, chatted on. 'You must forgive my tears. As you will remember, I do get very emotional at times. Tom is so tolerant. I don't know how he puts up with my highs and lows. But I don't want to talk about myself. I heard from a fellow countrywoman next door to us about the peacock gown that the Empress wore at that grand ball. Although my neighbour wasn't there to see it herself, her daughter was present in the company of a Russian beau and had described how beautiful it was. I told her that I was sure that I knew who had designed it. I'm right, am I not?'

Marguerite nodded, smiling. 'Yes, you are.'

'I'm so glad Tom and I will be living in St Petersburg now. I shall be able to hear about all your achievements. He will soon be busy with a new layout for a section of the park at the Palace of Oranienbaum, which is quite a way from here on the shores of the Gulf of Finland. The Empress seems to have palaces all over the place.'

'I know she has quite a number.'

'That's not all,' Sarah continued excitedly. 'In Moscow he showed the Empress some designs for a special garden on a section of the roof of the new Winter Palace that is soon to be built. Under glass and with heated stoves in winter a variety of flowers would bloom all the year round!'

'What a splendid project!'

Before they went in to dinner Sarah showed Marguerite around the house. It was noticeable that, although she had many small objets d'art, which she had bought when living in France, she was happiest in having around her again all the items that were originally from her first home with Tom after their marriage. It had not been far from Windsor Castle, where he had been working and becoming quite well known for his creativeness.

'You have managed to give this very Russian house quite an English look to it,' Marguerite commented with interest, 'even though you've only been here a very short time.'

Sarah nodded happily. 'That was my aim. I wanted this house to look like home. Did you realize that the footman who took your cloak is from England? His former employer recently died. In addition, I've an English lady's maid, who came to me in Moscow, and best of all' – she clapped her hands together like a child – 'I've an English cook! Now

Tom can have his favourite roast beef which he so enjoys just as if we were really home!'

Over the tasty dinner served with an excellent wine Sarah confessed to suffering agonies of homesickness when they were in Moscow. Even now she was missing her parents more than ever and also her married brother David, who was an officer serving with the Royal Navy. Just speaking of her family made her dab at her eyes.

'David has such a pretty wife named Alice. She has a baby every time he has shore leave, and I miss seeing the little ones. But now I have you here,' she added with a brave attempt at a smile again, 'I'll not be as lonely as before.'

'But you always have Tom with you.'

'He is out so much! In Moscow he was ever at the Empress's beck and call.' She sighed. 'Now he's going to Oranienbaum and will only get home occasionally.'

When they returned to the drawing room they sat opposite each other as Sarah made tea for them both in an English teapot, adding the tea leaves from a canister before pouring the hot water from a dainty silver kettle on its own stand.

'I suppose you must have learnt some Russian by now?' she said inquiringly as she handed a cup to Marguerite.

'Yes, I have recently increased the number of Russian seamstresses assisting me to eight and I encourage the exchange of languages.'

Sarah sat back triumphantly with her tea. 'Then I shall teach you English as well! Then when Tom and I are home again some time in the future you shall visit us and I will have found a delightful man for you to marry!'

Marguerite flung back her head and laughed. 'Then start my lessons at once!' she joked. 'What was the name of that English dish we had this evening?'

'Shepherd's pie!'

Marguerite repeated the words very accurately before

adding with amusement, 'English shepherds must live very well if that was an example of their diet.'

Sarah laughed, shaking her head. 'The meat was lamb. That's the reason why the dish has that name. But let's try some other words.'

The impromptu lesson continued, Marguerite genuinely interested in learning, for she had discovered from the amount of Russian she was mastering that she had an ear for languages. Then Sarah paused in her teaching, hearing Tom's voice in the hall.

'Tom has come home sooner than expected!' she declared joyfully. 'I begged him to try to get away from the meeting in time to see you.'

Marguerite was totally calm as they awaited his coming into the room, feeling quiet anticipation. But when he opened the door, even without turning her head, she felt a curious current pass through her. It was as if she had become totally aware of him with every nerve and fibre of her being, no matter that her mind battled with equal strength to reject it. When he greeted her, bowing over her hand, she saw again all that had caught at her heart the first time she had sighted him. Yet most dangerous of all was the guarded look in his eyes and the reason for it exploded in her mind. He had felt the same insane attraction for her in that Riga hostelry as she had felt for him and that had not changed for either of them.

'Good evening, Marguerite,' he said evenly. 'How are you?'

'I'm well indeed.' She kept her outward composure. 'What a comfortable home you have here! Sarah has shown it all to me.'

He smiled at his wife, sitting down beside her on the sofa. 'Yes, now that we've hung the pictures from home, placed some items of our well-travelled furniture and set out our books – as well as everything else we've taken around with us from place to place – it does begin to feel like our own home.'

124

Marguerite hoped her voice would not reveal the tension within her. 'But Sarah has told me that you're going to be some distance away from St Petersburg for a while.'

'Yes, I have work to carry out in the park of the Palace of Oranienbaum. The Empress is anxious that the park should not be neglected, which is why it has been included with everything else I'm doing for her. Her coffers will settle the account, but this particular palace is the one that she gave to the Grand Duke and Duchess as a marriage gift. I have been to view its setting extensively already. I'm pleased to say the park retains a natural rustic beauty in some of the more distant areas, which I shall maintain. There are also some splendid groves of trees that will be left untouched. I never compete with nature when I consider it impossible to improve on her work, although naturally there is always some tidying up to be done.'

'It sounds just the sort of lovely, quiet place that I should like for myself.' Sarah looked up at him lovingly as she held out her hand and he took it between both his own. 'You must take both Marguerite and me there to see it when everything is done.'

'At the first opportunity,' he promised. Then he glanced across at Marguerite. 'I hope you will keep Sarah under your watchful eye again all the time I'm away.'

'I'll do that with pleasure.'

He asked her how she found life at the Palace and somehow conversation flowed until the evening passed and it was time for her leave. Tom had his own carriage brought to the door for her. It was as he handed her into it that his fingers held hers slightly longer than was necessary and he gave them a moment of deliberate pressure. She took her seat swiftly and through the glass saw his intensely serious expression and the deep look in his eyes. Alarmed, she turned her face away and at the same instant the carriage moved forward.

All the way back to the Palace her mind grappled with

the desperate situation that had arisen. There was no doubt Tom loved his wife, which was obvious in his whole caring attitude towards her. Yet now she recalled how his gaze had lingered on her significantly in those few last moments at Riga before he had carried Sarah away. He had allowed himself those few seconds to absorb her into his memory, never expecting to see her again. It was far from the first time that men had been instantly attracted to her and it had been tiresome at times, but never dangerous as it was now, when her own feelings were involved.

If Sarah had not become such a good friend it would have been easy to dissolve the relationship between them just by giving her time to make other friendships among the wives in the English community. Then it would have been possible to make a gradual withdrawal from her life and Tom's too. But now that was impossible. Sarah's last words to her that evening had been an eager request for them to meet again soon.

Marguerite had a sickening feeling of being trapped. She had even promised Tom that she would be responsible for Sarah in his absence! If only this situation had not arisen! Everything had been going so well. She was enjoying her work as she had always done, her companions seemed content, and she was beginning to feel the same as Catherine towards Russia and its people. It was a relief to know Tom would be away now for some time and she could only hope that when he returned to the city he would have come to his senses. Neither of them wanted what had happened and there would be no lack of effort on her part to regain sanity.

Her thoughts turned to Jan van Deventer. When he returned she must try to make Tom believe that the Dutchman was important in her life. Although at first she had judged Jan to be a 'here-today-and-gone-tomorrow' man as far as women were concerned, she was not now quite so sure as far as she herself was concerned. But

Jacques was too much with her to think seriously about anyone else, which was all due to Tom stepping into her life. He must come to accept that their mutual attraction was pointless. Then her own struggle, however long it took, would be a completely private matter.

Eleven

As soon as Tom had left for the Palace of Oranienbaum Marguerite and Sarah met often. Sometimes it was at their favourite coffee house or at one of the chocolate-drinking establishments, when not dining together at Sarah's home. There were occasions when Marguerite was kept away through working late on some special task. One evening Sarah spoke sadly of her failure to have children.

'It is such a disappointment to both Tom and me. He has resigned himself to the fact that I'm barren, but for me there is a great gap in my life. My yearning for a child is a constant ache in my heart. I no longer speak of it to him, but it never goes away.'

'My poor Sarah,' Marguerite said sympathetically. 'I hadn't realized that you felt it so keenly.'

Sarah looked at her gratefully. 'You are always such a compassionate listener. I knew you would understand.'

Now that the snow had gone, taking with it the last of the bitter cold and the strange aurora borealis from the night sky, the sun sometimes gave a gentle warmth. Yet although it was mid-April the trees still had naked branches and the grass remained winter-brown. The flower beds had been dug, but nothing had been planted yet. The only replanting to be seen was that of certain trees, which had been removed before winter into storage to save them from dying in the bitter cold. Some of the side canals had not yet thawed and along the Neva jagged clumps of ice, glittering and dancing, still swept along from the lake of their source out to the Gulf of Finland where they would finally melt away.

Marguerite, strolling with Sarah on a fine evening, thought what a contrast it all was to Paris where the trees would all be fluttering with fresh green foliage and spring flowers blossoming everywhere. Jacques had always given her a posy of the first violets.

Yet there was plenty of activity to watch on the river. Every kind of vessel was now coming and going while the ferryboats plied their trade again. Tall-masted ships were arriving from the outside world, discharging cargoes at the wharves and filling up their holds again with furs, coal, fish, grain, timber and iron. Sometimes the sight of an English ship filled Sarah with such homesickness that she felt almost ill from the force of it. Marguerite viewed the arriving vessels in a different light, wondering how soon it would be before a Dutch ship brought Jan back to St Petersburg.

By now Sarah had met many other English people, for not only did they all live in the same district, but they also gathered to play cards, hold soirées, musical evenings and parties. Since all the husbands were merchants or otherwise linked with trade their wives welcomed the Empress's embroiderer, who had made the now fabled peacock gown, with Sarah, into their social circle. They also enjoyed trying to pair her off with some of the single men, but Marguerite, who was still having tuition in English from Sarah, was privately amused by their efforts. Although the young men were pleasant enough, she only wished to extend her knowledge of the English language in conversation with them. Sarah was as disappointed as the rest of the wives.

'What about that nice man you partnered at cards yesterday evening?' she said once.

'Sarah!' Marguerite exclaimed genially, but warningly. 'Leave matchmaking to others! Jan van Deventer should be returning to St Petersburg before long. I don't think he would be pleased to find I was seeing anyone else.'

'Oh!' Sarah beamed with pleasure. Although Marguerite had spoken of him she had not suspected romance.

Marguerite gave a silent sigh of relief. The seed had been sown. She was certain Tom would be told in Sarah's next letter to him.

As April gave way to May the weather grew warmer, trees and grass became green, blossom burst forth in pink and white clusters on branches and flowers bloomed. There were also signs that the Court would soon be on the move again. When Marguerite was summoned by the Grand Duchess she was not expecting to receive some unwelcome news.

'I have just heard that the Grand Duke and I will be leaving for Oranienbaum very soon.' Catherine had just returned from her daily ride and was still in her riding clothes. Although her face was flushed from the exercise, which she enjoyed so much, she seemed slightly distrait. 'You shall come too. I have an informal gown there that I've always liked. It is so light to wear in summer. I want you to see it and make me some more in a similar style.'

Leaving the room, Marguerite sighed in exasperation at the instructions she had received. Firstly, Tom was still at Oranienbaum and he was the one person she least wanted to see again for a while. He had been home twice and on both occasions she had used work as an excuse to avoid seeing him. Secondly, such a simple task of copying a gown made by others should have been given to one of Agrippina's seamstresses and not to her.

In fact, there was no need for anyone to make the new garments at Oranienbaum since the original could have been sent for by now. In reality, Catherine most surely wanted her there for some other reason altogether. Was it possible that she suspected that she was with child again? An imperial heir this time whether or not it was Peter's or Sergei Saltykov's child. Marguerite shook her head. Catherine's love life certainly had its complications.

The following week the great exodus from the Palace began again, but only Catherine and Peter were going with their entourage to Oranienbaum. The Empress and her Court went off to the Summer Palace. It would be for the period of what was called the 'White Nights' when summer daylight never left the sky and the sun kept the long hours of the north.

Marguerite, travelling with three maidservants in the grand ducal entourage, carried a letter and small package for Tom, which Sarah had given her, saying how much she wished she were going too. Marguerite also wished it, but for another reason entirely. Before departing she had left a good number of designs with Jeanne, who would deputize in her absence and could be trusted to see that everything was done to the peak of perfection.

As the journey neared its end it soon became apparent to Marguerite that the Palace of Oranienbaum would have splendid views of the Gulf of Finland, for they had been following a road alongside its shores for quite a way. When finally the Palace came into view with its many pillars and delicately moulded ornamentation it was as pretty as a porcelain piece, but on a vast scale with a pavilion topped by a golden pinnacle at each end. The sun was highlighting the intense blue of its walls and making the roof gleam silver from an earlier shower of rain.

Only the imperial and court coaches entered by the main gates, but as the rest took Marguerite and the others to an entrance to the rear of the Palace she could see that the great park was as pristine as if Tom had terrified every weed out of the ground. The beautiful trees, which he had mentioned, were all aquiver in rich green leaf and through the silvery gleam of birch groves there was the shimmer of a lake.

Watching the passing vistas, Marguerite inhaled the fresh, clean scents of grass and fern and damp bark that drifted in through the open window of the carriage. It made her realize how accustomed she had become to the city odours of St Petersburg and it was wonderful to be free of them.

Catherine was happy to be at Oranienbaum again, where she kept formal occasions at bay. All in the grand ducal court were young and lively, matching her and Peter's age, and apart from the usual pastimes of dancing and gambling there would be picnics, boating on the lake, riding through the sun-shadowed forests as well as taking part in innumerable open-air games that would make the summer slip by all too quickly. There was also the hilarious enjoyment of the Switchback Pavilion where rides could be taken on tray-like seats with wheels all the way down its outdoor switchback in a twisting and turning ride while spectators could watch and cheer from railed platforms. Catherine joined in every activity with energetic enthusiasm.

All too often the Empress in spiteful mood had restricted the grand ducal couple's social activities, wanting to isolate them from other young people whom they liked, often dominating them with her presence in their own palace. Yet this time they had been able to come freely to Oranienbaum. To add to Catherine's pleasure she knew she would have little contact with Peter, who – away from the Empress and the duties she imposed on him – would be able to devote as much time as he liked to his model soldiers as well as drinking himself insensible with his friends or his servants whenever the mood took him.

Every day from early morning she went riding, galloping off on her own into the forests and across the countryside. Nobody was concerned, knowing how she had always ridden alone whenever the opportunity had come her way. It had been the same ever since she had first come to Russia, having loved horses and riding wildly since childhood.

Speed exhilarated her. Feeling the wind whipping into her face as she urged on a fast horse, hooves thundering, and the leaping rise over obstacles in her path always replenished her joy in life, no matter how cast down in spirits she had been by Elisabeth's spite or Peter's petty harassment. There was an additional ecstasy in these present rides out of Oranienbaum. None suspected that each day they culminated at a certain meeting place in a forest of silver birch. There she flung herself out of the saddle into the waiting arms of Sergei Saltykov.

Before leaving St Petersburg a strange little interview had taken place at the Winter Palace. One of the Empress's ladies-in-waiting, although she had talked in a roundabout way, had made herself perfectly clear to Catherine. Elisabeth had accepted that Peter, in spite of the operation, was sterile. Therefore she was willing to accept a future heir to the Russian throne to be fathered by either Sergei Saltykov or another courtier whom she had also named.

Catherine had rejoiced in telling Sergei this news, but he had seemed less enthusiastic than she had expected. Uneasy doubts stirred in her mind as to whether he still loved her as much, but since her passion for him was far from assuaged she shut those uncertainties away.

Since only the aristocracy could wander in the park Marguerite, having nothing to do since she had not yet been shown the garment that Catherine wanted her to see, often went beyond the environs of the palace grounds. She would walk along the shore and stop to watch the ships passing along the Gulf and the local fisher folk busy with their nets. Sometimes she would follow paths in the forest, once glimpsing Sergei Saltykov riding on his own through the trees.

So far she had had no meeting with Tom, for she did not feel ready yet to see him again. On the first morning she had given Sarah's letter and package to a lackey for delivery to him. That would have told him she was here, even if Sarah in her innocence had not informed him in a letter, wanting them to spend time together.

Marguerite was never away long on her walks in case Catherine should return earlier than usual and remember to send for her, but it refreshed her to be on her own. This palace was like any other in being full of people, all members of the Court each having scores of servants. Fortunately she had a room to herself with a small sewing room adjacent to it, which so far had remained unused.

She was on her way back from one of her wanderings when a party of riders overtook her, also returning to the Palace. Then one wheeled his horse about and rode back to rein in as soon as he reached her. It was Konstantin Dashiski.

'I thought it was you, Corporal Laurent!' he declared, smiling down at her. 'Have you been taking part in any more battles for His Imperial Highness since I last saw you?'

She laughed, holding back a strand of her hair that was flicking in the breeze. 'No, I'm thankful to say.'

He dismounted and, leading his horse, fell into step beside her, the other riders disappearing in the distance. This time he was in riding clothes and his wheat-coloured hair was unpowdered. 'What are you doing here? I thought you were always shut away somewhere with a needle and thread.'

She explained and added, 'I haven't been as idle as I am now for a long, long time.'

'Then something must be done about that,' he said firmly.

'You'll remind the Grand Duchess that I'm here?' she asked hopefully. 'I haven't been able to get near her as she has been so occupied and everybody else has brushed my inquiries aside.'

He grinned. 'No, that's not my intention. I mean it's our chance to spend time together. Do you ride? No? I'll teach you. You dance, I'm sure, and as there's dancing every evening, often in masks, I shall find a mask for you as my partner.'

Her eyes were merry. 'And when it's time for unmasking I should be recognized and immediately sent back to France!'

'No! If you should be discovered not even the Grand Duchess would dare to dismiss the Empress's own embroiderer! But that won't happen!'

Still amused, she shook her head, believing he was flirting with empty promises. 'I have no wish to become a laughing stock in a ballroom or anywhere else. Sewing for the Grand Duchess is a pleasure and I'll not risk losing that privilege for anyone.' Tilting her head, she matched his flirtatiousness. 'Is that quite understood?'

His grinned. 'Of course, but not accepted. Meet me by the side entrance to the ballroom at nine o'clock. I'll bring a mask for you. Then tomorrow morning you shall have your first riding lesson.' He remounted and looked down at her again. 'Why are you shaking your head?'

She laughed. 'Because I'll not be there.'

He grinned still wider. 'I can't believe that you would disappoint me. So until later!' He saluted her with his whip and rode off, increasing his pace to a gallop, intending to catch up with the rest of the riding party.

Marguerite watched him go, a smile on her lips. She yearned to go dancing again. Often in cellar cafes she and Jan, holding hands, had whirled with other dancers as they had joined in Russian country dances. She knew from what she had heard that Catherine, being young and so lively, had such dances included in the programme of her Oranienbaum balls, which was not possible anywhere else when the Empress was present.

Although she would not have gone anywhere near that ballroom entrance the matter was settled for her anyway when a note from Konstantin was delivered to her. He had been summoned by the Empress to attend her immediately at the Summer Palace, but added that he hoped to return soon.

After not having seen either the Grand Duchess or Tom in the two weeks since her arrival Marguerite saw them both on the same evening. She had been given directions how to find the Grand Duchess, who had sent for her at last but from the most unlikely place. Catherine would be awaiting her in the upper park, which lay a considerable distance from the Palace.

It was a longish walk and the Palace was left far behind, completely hidden by trees, when Marguerite spotted some of Catherine's ladies-in-waiting far ahead. They looked like pastel-hued mushrooms as they chatted to pass the time, two of them practising some dancing steps. Then she saw Catherine and Tom standing together where the park rose upwards to a plateau. He was making sweeping gestures, throwing out his arm as he indicated different aspects of it. The vast, seemingly unending, plateau was obviously one of the areas that he had felt unable to change in any way. Even viewing it from afar Marguerite could see the wisdom of his decision, for it was a vista of untended natural beauty in complete contrast to any other part of the great park. She increased her pace, passing the ladies, who paid no attention to her.

Catherine was the first to see her approaching up the slope and beckoned with a graceful hand. 'Come, Mam'selle Laurent! There's something I want you to see.'

Tom had turned quickly at her name and his face tightened at the sight of her. As he watched her come up the long slope desire for her swept through him again. Slim and beautiful in her simple clothes, her full breasts enhanced by the narrowness of her waist, she was unaware how the slanting evening sun was burnishing her hair or how her every movement was full of sensuous grace.

Marguerite gave him a slight smile that offered no hint of her innermost feelings.

'Isn't this the most beautiful place, Mam'selle Laurent?' Catherine exclaimed at once. 'So quiet and peaceful! I feel as if I could stay here for ever! And, as Mr Warrington has shown me, the rarest of wild flowers nestle here in the moss and grass. I want you to collect and press at least one of each, and then you shall embroider them all on a cape that I can keep always!'

Marguerite was taken aback. 'Is this task to be completed before anything else, Madame? I've yet to see the gown I'm to copy.'

'Oh, that can be sent to one of your seamstresses or to the other atelier. You have this new task now.' Then Catherine added a cautionary warning with amusement: 'Incidentally, don't risk your life on the bridle paths again. Captain Dashiski informed me that he almost knocked down a French seamstress when out riding. Did he alarm you? The Empress has sent for him, but I shall chide him when I see him again if he caused you any harm.'

'No, Madame,' Marguerite replied. She was grateful that he had let Catherine know of her presence, which was what mattered. 'He has exaggerated the incident beyond recognition.'

Catherine laughed merrily. 'Yes, that is what he would do! He has a glib tongue in his handsome head! But now to the matter in hand.' She became serious again. 'Mr Warrington will tell you where to find the flowers that you don't discover for yourself, because some are so tiny in this northern clime, more to be expected on mountain slopes. You shall come daily until your task is done. Remember I want every one! Then you shall start work on the cape immediately.'

'Why not embroidered silken shoes to match?' Marguerite suggested, being as well practised in the art of accessories as she was in original designs for garments. As she had expected, Catherine welcomed the suggestion with enthusiasm.

'That would be delightful!' Giving a nod, she swept away with her quick, light step to rejoin her ladies, who had become restless and bored with waiting. As they all set off to the Palace Tom and Marguerite were left facing each other.

'Thank you for bringing the letter and package from Sarah,' he said. 'I found them waiting for me yesterday. I've been away from here for a few days.'

'I left her in good health,' she said at once, determined to bring the presence of his wife between them, 'but longing for your return. She misses you very much.'

'I hope to get home again soon to see her,' he said, his eyes never leaving her face. It was as if he could never get enough of looking at her. 'You didn't come to the house either time when I was there.'

'It was only right to let you and Sarah be together on your own as much as possible when you are away so much.'

'That was unnecessarily considerate of you. The house was full of her new acquaintances most of the time.'

She caught the edge to his voice as she moved away from him, looking downwards as she went to see what flowers were there. When she came to a wide cluster of little white star-shaped flowers encircling the base of a tree she stooped to pick one. She laid it on her palm as she straightened up again. 'What a miracle it is that something as delicate as this bloom can blossom so far north!'

He had followed her to stand by her side. 'It's a purely northern flower. I was here in time to see them appear like a white carpet everywhere under the trees. At home in England bluebells come with the same profusion. That is just one of the reasons I want this area to remain undisturbed, except where paths can be laid for the Grand Duchess to follow without getting grass stains on those shoes you are to embroider for her.'

'So you persuaded the Grand Duchess that a wild flower area should be kept?'

'She needed little persuasion. At first she was surprised that I was reluctant to lay out a formal garden here, but then she became enthralled by the idea of having a quiet and undisturbed place that could be her private domain.'

138

'But for a little while it will be mine too. I shall enjoy the task she's set me.'

'You'll need to cover a wide range to discover all the flowers. With this warmer weather new ones will surely be appearing every day.'

'Tomorrow I must come properly equipped to deal with this undertaking.' She had wandered on, wanting to put a little distance between them, and paused to pick another tiny bloom here and there. 'I don't want any of the flowers to droop before I get them back to the Palace.' Straightening up, she looked slowly around. 'Yes, I can see how the Grand Duchess fell in love with this very beautiful place. It's so peaceful and a world away from her palace life.'

'People can fall in love with places – and people – without ever expecting it.'

She held her breath, fearing he would say more, but he just stood watching her, making no move. Then, as she turned and went back again, he strolled along beside her.

'How have you been spending your time here since you arrived?' he asked.

'Walking and reading. It has been quite a holiday. Now my work will start again and the Grand Duchess has given me this most welcome task. I'm going back to my room now to write out the order for all I'll need from my palace workrooms. I shall write to Sarah as well and tell her about it. Then both letters can go with a courier in the morning.'

He thought of the letters that Sarah sent him, full of outpourings of love from the heart and yet physically she could never respond to his passion, her fanatically intense modesty ever a barrier between them. How often he had seen her lovely face contort, her eyes tight closed, as she suffered his tender exploration of her body. At least she was not terrified as she had been on their wedding night, huddling in a corner of the room and crying out that she loved him while refusing to share their bed. He believed that if he had allowed it she would have reverted to her childhood custom of bathing in a robe like a nun to hide what she thought of as shameful nakedness. He had wondered many times what poison her dragon-faced mother had instilled into her mind from an early age. In spite of all his loving efforts he had been unable to dispel it.

'I shall also write to Sarah this evening,' he said, 'and then my letter can go too.'

She was relieved that in speaking of Sarah he seemed to have acknowledged that there was an insurmountable barrier between them and it made her feel more at ease.

'Will it be another fine day tomorrow for me to begin my work?' she asked hopefully. 'You should be able to tell me. Gardeners are always supposed to be able to foretell the weather.'

He laughed quietly, glancing up at the sky, which was clear of cloud, and gave a nod of reassurance. 'I think I can promise you sunshine.' Then he turned to her again with his curve of a smile that awoke memories in her of another man in another time. As before, it had the unwanted effect of endearing him still further to her.

She nodded, wordless for the moment, before returning his smile. 'Thank you, Tom. I'll see you then.'

He watched her go. Although he had thought she would turn and wave that did not happen and eventually she disappeared from his sight with a flicker of her skirt through the trees.

At a palace window Catherine was deep in thought as she stood looking in the direction of the plateau, even though the trees masked it from her view. She was heedless of the chatter of her ladies in the room behind her. One day when she and Peter were ruling Russia she would build a palace of her own there in that lovely place, the beauty and delicacy of the architecture to match the perfect surroundings. It should be her retreat where she would receive her lover and closest friends. Yes, one day when the crown of an Emperor's wife was hers.

Twelve

F ortunately for Marguerite the month of May was proving to be exceptionally mild and it was bringing many more flowers into bloom. As always in the mornings before leaving the Palace she collected a basket of food covered by a white napkin, liking to stay all day at her task if the weather remained dry. She could have had a flask of beer too, but she preferred to cup her hands and drink the clear water from a stream on the plateau. A palace carpenter had made her a flower press, which enabled her to deal at once with the blooms she picked. She sketched one of each variety in meticulous detail and painted it afterwards from a box of watercolours that had been found for her.

She had become used to Catherine coming almost daily to watch her at work for a little while, always taking away a few flowers to tuck into her hair or between her breasts. Since her inspiration for a flowered cape had come suddenly, Marguerite concluded that the original reason for herself being here was in case a pregnancy during the summer months should need adjustment to imperial garments. Yet now it could only be through a desire to maintain an attractive appearance, for all would expect the Grand Duke to be the father, his supposedly successful operation being widely known.

When June arrived it was in a burst of exceptional heat that amazed everybody. Soon there was the shimmer of dragonflies over the upper and lower lakes and a delicate azure mist of harebells appeared. As the days went by tiny pansies spread themselves in carpets and the humble butter-cup arrived in profusion. Here and there the yellow and pink lady's slipper peeped out amid feathery grasses.

At the start Marguerite had sent her design for the cape and shoes to Jeanne in order that both should be ready for the embroidery when the first pressed flowers and coloured drawings arrived. Since then she had sent a continuous flow of her work by palace couriers, allowing progress to be made by her Frenchwomen.

Tom came every morning to see if she needed any assistance, but so far she had more than enough specimens to keep her busy. She always became a little tense in his presence, but as he was busy in another part of the park he never stayed long. He had already promised that no paths would be laid until she had finished her work, which was proving to be taking much longer than she had expected as new blooms constantly appeared.

She was packing up her paints one evening when Tom's shadow fell across her. Looking up, she saw him standing bareheaded and silhouetted against the golden sun.

'Oh, it's you, Tom. This isn't your usual hour.' She took the outstretched hand he offered and sprang lightly to her feet.

'It's such a perfect evening that I thought perhaps you'd take a walk with me before going back into the Palace.'

'Yes,' she said, taking off her hat and letting it drop on to the grass. 'I need some exercise after kneeling and sitting all day.'

It seemed natural that they should turn away from the Palace and begin wandering deeper through the groves of the area where she had happened to be. There was no need to talk. It was too peaceful here for inconsequential chatter and they strolled in harmony. Now and again she looked up at the canopy of foliage when they passed under the branches of a tree, seeing how every leaf seemed translucent in the amber sunlight of the northern evening.

After a while when it was about time to turn back she paused, leaning against a tree and closing her eyes, her expression reflecting her total contentment in this beautiful place.

'What are you thinking about?' Tom asked, setting the flat of his hand on the bark beside her head.

'Nothing really,' she answered softly. 'I'm just listening.'

He smiled. 'What can you hear? It seems very quiet to me.'

'That's what I can hear: the quietness. It makes me realize that no palace is ever silent. Always doors opening and shutting, voices and clattering feet and rustling skirts and the thump of the guards' boots.'

'But you've been painting here on the plateau every day. Haven't you been aware of the quietness before now?'

She opened her eyes and saw his smiling face close to hers. 'I've been too absorbed in my work.'

Then all words dried in her throat as he stepped closer to her. Immediately she would have moved from the tree, but swiftly he cupped her face between his hands.

'Don't draw away from me any more, Marguerite,' he implored lovingly. 'We tried avoiding each other, but that was useless. Now at Oranienbaum we have kept up a pretence that hasn't fooled either of us.'

'I won't listen to what you're saying!' she cried out, something close to panic in her eyes. 'I didn't hear what you said!'

His whole face was drawn by long-suppressed passion and it was as if she had not spoken. 'The first time I laid eyes on you it was as if all my life I had been waiting for that moment.'

'Don't say that, Tom!' Her expression was desperate and she would have jerked free, but his arms clasped her to him and he stopped her protests with his hungry mouth on hers. That mouth, so like Jacques's and just as ardent, hurtled her back in time, and suddenly the plateau could have been anywhere in Paris where she and Jacques had once loved and kissed. She was aware of him drawing her down with him on to the carpet of dry leaves. He kissed away the tears running from under her closed lids, not knowing how he was recapturing the past for her, and his caressing hand found her bare breast within her bodice.

'You and I were meant to be together, my darling,' he said lovingly.

'You're wrong!' Mentally she spun back into reality. 'There can never be anything between us!'

'How can you say that?' He gazed reassuringly down into her desperate face. 'We've been given this once-in-a-lifetime chance to be on our own here every day. Nobody to question us or to observe. We're as alone here as if we were on another planet.'

'But we can't let this happen, Tom!' Her voice broke.

He ran gentle fingertips down the side of her face, aware that she was being torn by conflicting emotions. 'Darling Marguerite, I want to make love to you,' he entreated. 'Don't you see what has happened? This secret place is our own. When we return to St Petersburg nobody else shall ever know it was here that we truly found each other.'

He would have kissed her again, but she turned her face aside and cried out despairingly, 'This can't be!'

'But Fate is being kind to us.'

She was unable to answer him, seeing no kindness in the circumstances that had created this terrible situation. All she knew was that she was on the brink of an abyss and somehow she had to force herself back from it. Even as she doubted her sanity in letting these moments happen she made no resistance as he kissed her again with even more passion than before. She was reminded of ecstatic moments in quiet places where she and Jacques had made love, her whole body alive to his, but they had had no responsibility for anyone except each other.

Summoning up all her strength of will, she broke away

145

from his arms and scrambled to her feet. He remained where he lay, his head bowed in wretched disappointment. She stood staring down at him, her chest rising and falling breathlessly.

'We have to promise each other that we shall never forget Sarah again! Never!'

For a few moments he neither moved nor looked up at her. Then he rose to his feet to stand facing her. Both knew there could be no going back to the guarded friendship of before. Barriers had been broken down. But as he reached for her again she drew back a step once more, shaking her head. He regarded her gravely.

'No matter what we say or what promises we make, you and I both know that this isn't the end between us. There's too much feeling between us. Nothing need stop when we have to leave Oranienbaum. There are always ways to meet that will not hurt anyone else.'

'You mean Sarah!' she said almost angrily. 'Why don't you say her name? No, Tom. This short time we've spent alone here is all that there could ever be for us. We must not meet on our own here or anywhere else again!'

'What difference would that make to what is between us?' He had dismissed her outburst and continued to love her with his gaze.

She uttered a sound in her throat like a sob and turned to run back the way they had come. Swiftly she gathered up her paintings and the rest of her belongings into her basket, snatched up her hat and set off down the long, grassy slope, her feet slithering in her haste. He had followed in time to watch her go. She ran all the way as if fleeing as much from herself as from him.

Next morning Tom went to the plateau as usual, but saw from a distance that there were several ladies of the Court waiting together. It could only mean that the Grand Duchess was with Marguerite and as he had urgent matters to see to elsewhere he decided to return later. He had to see Marguerite as soon as possible. She must be persuaded into seeing that his other life with Sarah need not be a barrier to keep them apart.

Catherine had been to see how Marguerite's work was progressing. She knew for certain now that she was pregnant again, but although there should have been no need to hide her condition this time she was in no hurry to let it become public knowledge. It was why she had wanted Marguerite to be at Oranienbaum with her in case she needed discreet adjustments to her garments. In the meantime the cape would set a fashion while at the same time it would be a useful garment in disguising the inevitable expansion of her figure. Later she would take pride in her condition, knowing it would please everybody, especially the Empress.

As Catherine left the plateau again, she thought of the moments in the forest on her first ride after arriving at Oranienbaum when she had broken the news to Sergei that she was pregnant.

'So soon?' he had shouted furiously in the echoing forest, making her clamp her fingers over his mouth even though no one was anywhere near. She understood his fury, for he knew as she did that once her condition became known she would be cosseted and made to rest, concern for the baby uppermost, and steps taken to keep them apart, their love-making totally curtailed.

'Hush, my darling,' she cooed to him. 'We have the rest of the summer here at Oranienbaum. Let us make the most of it.'

He was difficult to pacify. It was if he wanted to completely reject the part he had played in her present condition. The Empress's condoning of their liaison was akin in his mind to his having been put to stud, and he found it humiliating. Now, all too quickly to suit him, there was to be living proof of their union!

Seeing him so tight-lipped with fury, Catherine wondered again if he still loved her, but with her own passion for him far from assuaged she thrust her misgivings aside.

For the whole of the day Tom was occupied in directing workers in the installation of a great fountain. When it was time to call a halt until the morning he went to bathe and change out of his working clothes before he set off eagerly for the plateau. There he ran all the way up the slope.

It took him a little time to find Marguerite, for every day she searched new areas. When finally he sighted her he halted abruptly, seeing she was not alone. One of the maids from the Palace was assisting her. Neither had seen him and he drew away to wait until Marguerite dismissed the maid and he could take her into his arms again.

But Marguerite had seen him out of the corner of her eye. She had chosen the only possible way to guard against any more meetings on her own with him.

Turning her head as she and the maid left the plateau, she saw him waiting not far away. For a long moment or two her gaze held his and then, although it tore at her, she looked ahead again. That glimpse of the torment in his face had shown her that he realized that she was resolved that all was over between them almost before it had begun.

He stood as still as one of Oranienbaum's marble statues, watching her until she was gone from sight.

It took Marguerite much longer than she had expected to finish collecting the plateau's many flowers and their leaves, even with the maid's daily assistance. She had seen Tom twice from a distance, but that was all. Yet she believed he had come to the plateau several times to see if by chance he would find her alone again, but as there was such an abundance of trees and tall bushes it was impossible for her to be sure whether or not he was there. Then one evening a letter was delivered to her. Breaking the seal, she saw that it was signed by Tom. It was very short.

By the time you receive this note I shall be on my way back to St Petersburg to see Sarah for a short while, but do not suppose I shall ever forget that special time we spent together.

Sinking down on to a chair, Marguerite bowed her head as she crushed the letter in her hand. There must have been some magic in that lovely place that had taken all reason from them and left this aftermath of yearning. She had always despised women who enticed away the husbands of friends and she bitterly regretted having come perilously close to that treachery.

Straightening up again, she read the letter through once more and was able to see now with a clearer mind that he seemed to have accepted that there could never be anything more between them. Then another interpretation came to her. Did he mean that in spite of a setback he would not give up?

The thought disturbed her deeply. At night her sleep was restless. Sometimes she would get up and rest her arms on the sill of the open window, seeing the park in the ever-lasting daylight of the White Nights and listening to the birds singing as if it were morning instead of a little after midnight. Often to welcome the sun, which barely slept itself, a ballroom gathering would pour out of the Palace on to the lawns as if from a cornucopia in their jewelled and colourful clothes, Catherine and Sergei in their midst. Led by musicians, they would all pass out of her sight as they danced on their way in the golden glow. Sometimes Marguerite's own feet danced as if of their own volition until the music could no longer be heard.

Daily she longed for work to keep her mind occupied and away from thoughts of Tom. With her task at the plateau finally at an end and a network of paths already being laid there, she was impatient to take up her needle again. Having sent the last of the flowers and paintings to Jeanne, she was at a loss with nothing to do. She had not come to Russia to be idle. But Catherine was not yet ready to release her.

'No, Mam'selle Laurent, I'd like you now to choose one of those little flowers and let it inspire you in a new design for a gown for me. Is the cape finished yet?'

'It should come from St Petersburg any day now, Madame.'

The design for the new flower gown was finished when Jeanne brought the cape herself, together with the finished shoes. Marguerite was glad to see her.

'I took the chance to come,' Jeanne said conspiratorially when they were together in Marguerite's small salon. 'We've all been so curious about this orange palace.'

Marguerite laughed. 'As you've seen for yourself now, it's not even pale orange! Whatever made you think it would be?'

'One of the Russian seamstresses said it was named after the orange tree. I never thought it would be blue and white! So that was a real surprise to me!'

'I asked about its name when I came here. In this climate an orange tree would be so rare and valuable that only the imperial family ever has one. Thus this lovely palace has the same status, which is how it was given its unusual name. But of course it could be orange in colour at any time, because it seems from what I've heard that a different hue is often used whenever a palace has to be repainted.'

'My first thought when I saw this palace was that it looked as if it had come out of a fairy tale. There can't be another like it.'

'I can't answer that, although they say the Catherine Palace is the loveliest of all. There's even a room set with amber.'

Jeanne threw up her hands in astonishment. 'What wealth! The Empress has many more palaces than she has toes on her feet!' Her peasant blood was stirred and she frowned angrily. 'It's not right, is it? Just like at home. The rich are rich and the poor can starve.'

'Don't let us talk of palaces any more,' Marguerite said, impatient for news and not wanting Jeanne to start on hotheaded talk just now, for once started on her favourite topic it was difficult to stop her. 'I want to know what has been happening with all of you. You're not a good correspondent.'

'I hate writing. It wears my brain out trying to think what to say. Everybody sent greetings to you, of course. Now I'll start with Sophie.' Jeanne began to tick off her fingers. 'She has become betrothed to her nice Valentin Vaganov, but the marriage is not yet arranged. It suits Sophie, because she's preparing a trousseau for herself and it's not finished yet. He wants the wedding to be held when his sister and her husband and their family can come from Moscow and, if possible, when his brother is home from sea. I have come to know the rest of the Vaganov family very well through my friendship with Olga. She has sold some of my lace in her shop and is willing to sell more.'

'That's splendid!'

'As for Violette, she has been going through escorts like a hot knife through butter.' She gave a snort of disapproval. 'She has a lieutenant now, a shifty-looking fellow in my opinion, but she seems very taken with him as she is with all her men at first. Rose and Isabelle are with the Pomfret girls for most of their free time, although I've noticed that Isabelle sometimes stays away as if she has had enough for a while of their endless chatter of young men and hair styles and clothes and fripperies.' She sighed, wearied herself by her chatterbox daughter on occasions. 'But then Isabelle has always had a quieter nature than my Rose, who is still as giddy as a headless chicken. I would knock some sense into her if it could be done that way.'

'She's a very pretty girl.'

'Too pretty for her own good. Mr and Mrs Pomfret are so hospitable and Sophie and I have been to their house for tea.' She grimaced. 'I think they wanted to see Rose's mother and aunt for themselves. We must have won their approval or else we wouldn't have been invited a second time and yet again last week. There's always plenty of young company under their roof, where, I'm thankful to say, Mrs Pomfret ensures that the young women are strictly chaperoned.'

'Maybe Rose and Isabelle will end up with English husbands.'

'Perhaps they will. There are more young Englishmen working and training with businesses in St Petersburg than I had ever realized.'

'What of you, Jeanne?'

Jeanne chortled. 'No romance for me! That's all in the past as far as I'm concerned. But Jan van Deventer has been asking after you.'

'Oh?' In the wake of the emotional turmoil she had been through with Tom she felt barely able to tolerate his forceful presence. 'How is he?' she added automatically.

'As handsome as ever. He came by ship with a load of paintings, which he displayed at the Dutch Embassy, and sold every one. He must be making a mint of money! He's awaiting another shipment any day now, which is why he has to stay in the city until it arrives.'

'You told him I was here, did you?'

'Yes. When I happened to meet him on the bridge one day.' Jeanne was watching her closely, curious to see if Marguerite showed disappointment that he had not yet come to see her, but there was no sign of it. It was, she thought, as if Marguerite were numb to any feeling at the present time. It worried her. What had happened during this time at this oddly named palace?

'So you didn't see any of his paintings?' Marguerite's tone was flat.

'No.' Jeanne paused. 'Are you well? Is everything all right?'

Marguerite raised her eyebrows in surprise and forced a

little laugh. 'Yes, of course! And everything will be even better when I've seen the cape that you've brought.'

The box was opened. Jeanne folded back the layers of white muslin and Marguerite lifted out the cape. All the lovely flowers, which she had collected through the conflicting emotions of pleasure and distress, covered the cream silk in their wonderful colours. Waist-length and collarless, it was a work of art in itself. She slipped it around her shoulders and looked at her reflection in a mirror.

'It is superb,' she said quietly. 'You and Sophie and Violette have created a masterpiece. The Grand Duchess will love it.'

Jeanne beamed. 'We hoped you'd be pleased.' She turned to open the second box containing the shoes and held them up. The tiny flowers even covered the heels. 'The imperial shoemaker did his work well!'

Jeanne stayed overnight and as soon as she had left again next morning Marguerite took the cape to Catherine. As expected, she was delighted with it, putting it on at once and slipping her small feet into the shoes.

'Oh, how beautiful!' She turned and twirled before a tall pier glass, spinning the embroidery into rainbows of colour as she tried to catch a glimpse of it from every angle. 'I'd like a gown to incorporate these flowers over the skirt! Yes! That's what I want!'

'May I return to St Petersburg to organize that project?'

Catherine hesitated only briefly. 'Yes, mam'selle. You have done well and may leave tomorrow if you wish.'

Marguerite was relieved that she could get back to her companions. Although she trusted Jeanne's skills and management, she did not really care to be forever at Catherine's beck and call. Two nights ago when she had been unable to sleep, a new design for a gown for the Empress had come into her head, and she had gone from her bed to sketch it out. She believed that when made it should be just as spectacular as the peacock one.

153

That evening Catherine danced non-stop in her new shoes. Then in the morning a blow fell for her as well as for Peter in a command from the Empress for the grand ducal court to move to the country palace at Peterhof. She needed to have them nearer whenever important matters had to be discussed. The Grand Duke roared and stamped in temper like an ill-tempered child when informed, but he had to obey the woman he loathed. In private Catherine was in despair. She was being torn away from the freedom of Oranienbaum to be under Elisabeth's ruthless domination again.

Yet she could guess the reason. Although in the main Elisabeth lazily left the governing of the country to her ministers, there were always some matters that needed attention and that she chose to pass on to Peter. Couriers came almost every day with letters and documents for him, all of which he ignored, never breaking the seals. It was most surely her exasperation with him at failing to carry out his duties yet again that had resulted in this curtailment of liberty.

Marguerite had to wait several days until there was a courier carriage going back to St Petersburg. During this time she designed the new gown and gained Catherine's approval of it. Then at last there was a carriage transporting on its roof a large box of the Grand Duke's model soldiers that were going back to the Winter Palace in readiness for his return. She could travel with it.

She was in the courtyard, watching her baggage being fastened on to the roof beside the box, when she saw Konstantin Dashiski coming towards her.

'May I accompany you?' he asked, smiling widely at her.

She was laughing in surprise. 'But where are you going?'

'The same as you! Returning to the city!'

'In a courier's carriage, Captain Dashiski? I think there's another, grander equipage waiting for you somewhere else.'

'One set of wheels is as good as another. Do you object to my company?' He was teasing her.

'No, Captain.' She shook her head, her eyes merry, suddenly extremely glad of his light-hearted presence. He would distract her with his company from thinking about all that had happened since her arrival at Oranienbaum and already he had taken away any sad thoughts she might have had at this time of leaving about Tom and what might have been.

'Not a captain any longer,' he was saying. 'The Empress has chosen to promote me. I'm a major now, but to you I'm Konstantin.'

'Congratulations, Konstantin.'

He bowed his head in pleased acknowledgement. 'I thank you, Mam'selle Marguerite. I hope that sometime in the future you'll let me make amends for being unable to take you dancing that evening a while ago. I came from the Empress at Peterhof to bring her command to the grand ducal court, which is why I'm here at Oranienbaum again. But Her Imperial Highness told me you had already left here for St Petersburg some days ago, which is why I didn't start looking for you.'

'She did not know, but I've been waiting for a carriage. But why are you returning to the city when you have the chance to remain in the country? I've heard that mosquitoes are a plague there now. There have been some at Oranienbaum, but usually there was a sea breeze where I was working on the plateau there that kept them at bay.'

'Back to Peterhof, you mean? No, I'm going to have what's left of the summer at my own estate.' He had fully intended to go straight to his country house after leaving Oranienbaum, but he had sighted her and her luggage from a window and decided it would be a deal more enjoyable travelling in her company than being on his own. It was also no great diversion to go via St Petersburg instead, and if he had not known that his mistress was waiting for him in the country he would have stayed on in the city to see more of this intriguing Frenchwoman.

'I'll only be in St Petersburg overnight before escaping from the mosquitoes,' he said when they had settled in the carriage. 'Dine with me!'

She shook her head, smiling. 'Impossible! I've far too much to do when I arrive.'

He grimaced comically in disappointment, causing her to laugh again. 'Another time perhaps?' he said.

'Perhaps.'

A footman, having seen that Major Dashiski was not going to travel in the equipage waiting for him after all, came at a run to transfer a basket of refreshment, for the courier carriage was already moving. Turning the handle, he threw the basket in before slamming the door again. Breathless, he watched it speed away.

Konstantin pulled the basket into a more secure position. 'At least you can share a picnic lunch with me. Now you said something about working on the plateau at Oranienbaum. What were you doing there?'

She told him about the task she had been given and how she had enjoyed it, but all the time she was relating it her thoughts were uncomfortably haunted by Tom, and she changed the subject as soon as was possible.

As the journey continued Konstantin opened his basket of food to share with her. It had been intended solely for him, but there was plenty for both of them. He unfolded the single napkin on to her lap. Then he poured her wine into the glass while he drank his out of the only other container available, which was the top of his own silver vodka flask that he took from his coat pocket. It was an enjoyable carriage picnic.

At a fork in the road near St Petersburg when the journey was almost over Marguerite failed to notice another carriage passing in the opposite direction on its way to Peterhof. Its solitary passenger, who was reading with his long legs stretched out in front of him, also failed to glimpse her in the matter of seconds when their windows were level.

Yet he stirred and put aside his book. Snapping open
his fob watch, Jan took note of the time. Not much longer
now. On the opposite seat he had some rolled-up paintings in secure coverings. He would give first choice to
the Grand Duchess before showing the rest to the
Empress. These had all arrived by the second shipment,
which had been delayed, and caused him to wait impatiently for it.

He had expected to spend that time with Marguerite, but
had learnt from Jeanne that she was at Oranienbaum. Then
yesterday Jeanne had informed him that the Grand Duke
and Duchess had moved to Peterhof, which meant that
Marguerite, since she was in attendance on the Grand
Duchess at the present time, would be there too. This news
had coincided with the arrival of the second collection of
paintings. During the winter and between business commit-
ments in Amsterdam, he had completed a number of other
paintings himself, some of which he also had with him as
well as earlier work that previously he had not offered for
sale.

Although he had always had sketching materials with him
on his journeys, this time he had also shipped, in a
stout wooden box, plenty of powdered colours, oils and
brushes as well as his palette. Having started to paint again
during the winter he had found that he had taken to the
easel again. Just as Dutch painters before him had given
their works hidden meanings, he had done the same with
his painting for Marguerite, creating a little mystery within
it that she must solve for herself.

His thoughts went back to the night in Riga when he had
turned to see her for the first time, her beautiful face aglow
with pleasure at the good news she had to tell, her eyes
sparkling and the candlelight turning her hair red-gold. She
was entirely unaware how she had taken his breath away.
He had not known then that Hendrick was acquainted with
her until later in the evening, but she had lingered in his

mind throughout their business talk over the meal that had been served to them.

'That girl,' he had said at last, idly twisting the stem of his wine glass with his fingers, 'the one I was talking to when you sighted me. She was French. You've no idea who she is, have you?'

'I didn't notice her.'

'A beauty in her own way. She mistook me for someone else.'

'That could be the Frenchwoman Marguerite Laurent.' Hendrick told him why she and her companions had come to Russia and of the care she had taken of Sarah Warrington on the journey. 'She probably thought you were the Englishwoman's husband.' He began looking around for a waiting-maid. 'Now let's have another bottle of wine.'

Jan looked unseeingly out of the carriage window at the passing landscape, which was as flat as the eye could see. That night in Riga had fixed Marguerite in his memory. He had also learned where to find her again. Never before had a woman lingered on in his thoughts as she had done.

Thirteen

In the sewing room Marguerite was greeted warmly by her fellow Frenchwomen. Isabelle was particularly glad to see her and eager to show her latest work, which Marguerite studied and praised. Isabelle had all the signs of becoming her best seamstress and embroiderer and was almost certain to rival Jeanne before long.

'You're doing wonderfully well, Isabelle. I'm very glad to have you in my work team and I've a special task in mind for you.'

The girl glowed with pleasure. Jeanne always checked her work, but never with any encouraging word.

Marguerite sought out the trimmings she had brought from France. There she found the opaque, opal-hued sequins that she wanted. They were of no intrinsic value, having been bought cheaply on a Parisian market stall, but she intended they should be used to enhance the truly spectacular gown she had designed at Oranienbaum for the most powerful woman in the land.

'There's a letter from Paris waiting here for you,' Violette said, fetching it for her. 'We've recognized the writing.'

Marguerite also saw immediately that it was from Madame Fromont. Although she had written quite regularly to her, knowing how interested she would be to hear about them all, it was the first she had had in return. Sitting down, she read it aloud to them. Their former employer wrote that she had been so pleased to receive two letters, but she could tell from the contents that at least one other had failed to arrive. Although she was housebound she kept up with fashion news and told of new trends. She also gave news of the women still working in her old atelier, two of them being regular visitors, and with her hired companion looking after her she was content. She sent her good wishes to them all.

There was a little silence when Marguerite finished reading. She looked around at their faces. This voice from Paris had touched each one of them and they all sat motionless with a faraway look in their eyes.

It was Jeanne who broke the spell. 'Well, it's good to know the old lady seems happy enough. Now let's get back to work.'

Marguerite was about to leave the sewing rooms when the dressmaker figures of the Empress and the Grand Duchess caught her eye.

'What's happened to the Empress?' she exclaimed with a frown. 'Have her breasts sagged that much?'

Jeanne nodded. 'So it seems. We received her new measurements yesterday, hence the extra padding. The courier who brought them told us that not only has she put on weight, but she is not as well as she used to be. But then everybody knows she leads a strange sort of life with all her lovers and her drinking and whatever goes on at her private parties.'

Marguerite said nothing. Plenty of tales circulated about the Empress's excesses and debauchery, but how much of it was true she did not know.

Preparation for the work that she was to take with her took time in the selection of fabrics, the cutting and everything else, but as soon as all was ready she took time to see Sarah on the morning of her departure. She was thankful that her friend would never know of those few brief and dangerous seconds on the plateau when the past had almost overcome the present, for most surely it was Jacques whom she had sought in Tom's arms, not Tom himself. Yet why did she still have doubts?

But Sarah was not at home. The housekeeper informed Marguerite that Mr Warrington had taken his wife to Oranienbaum that morning, having promised her some while ago that she should see the results of his work in the park when everything was finished. Marguerite recalled how she had been included in that promise, none of them having known at the time that she would see it for herself.

'When Mistress Warrington returns, please tell her that I called,' Marguerite said as she left again.

Back in the sewing room she found Isabelle ready and waiting to accompany her to Peterhof. She had decided earlier that if she took an assistant to get the flower gown completed as quickly as possible she would be able to return earlier to her atelier. At first she had intended to take Rose, but she felt there was always something devious about the girl and decided against it. Isabelle, upon hearing that she had been chosen, had blushed with pleasure. Marguerite thought she was becoming quite pretty in an elfin way.

The journey to the Palace of Peterhof did not take long. As they passed through the couriers' gate Marguerite saw at once that Peter the Great's first country palace was truly beautiful to behold with its amber-hued walls enhanced by white and gold baroque ornamentation, a formal garden spread like a vast and beautiful carpet around it. Gilded statues caught the sun's blaze and fountains shot arrow-high into the sky, the spray full of rainbows, while terraced waterfalls cascaded in an endless crystal flow. Isabelle was wide-eyed with wonder.

'How splendid it is!' she exclaimed in awe.

As soon as they were settled in their rooms Marguerite was told she had been summoned by the Empress and she did not delay in going the short distance to see her at the Summer Palace. She took with her a collection of fashion dolls prepared by Jeanne from the new designs, including one dressed in what she had come to think of as the opal gown.

When Marguerite rose up from her deep curtsey after entering the Empress's salon she could see a change in her. Although nothing could dim Elisabeth's imposing presence and she was still a handsome woman, it was easy to see that self-indulgence and dissipation were showing the first signs of taking their toll. There was a loosening of her face's firm contours and slight bags under her eyes, but her well-designed stiffened bodice disguised any fault in her figure, her breasts showing plump and firm beneath it.

'All excellent.' Elisabeth's voice was slurred by alcohol as she waved aside the fashion dolls, each of which had been held up for her approval. 'I shall want all of these when I'm in Moscow again.' Her beringed finger suddenly pointed sharply at Marguerite and she added thickly, 'But when the time comes you'll bring the one with those opal sequins to me yourself, Frenchwoman! You've done enough running about on behalf of the Grand Duchess, making her fancy capes and other such nonsense. You shall attend me solely from now on. Why else did I bring you here all the way from France? Now get back to St Petersburg today and take up your sewing for me!'

Marguerite left in dismay. At Peterhof she went immediately to see if she could speak to the Grand Duchess, but without success. She was informed that Catherine was having her first sitting for a portrait by a Dutch artist at the Empress's instructions and was not to be disturbed.

Marguerite, about to turn away, stopped on a sudden thought. 'What is the artist's name?'

'Jan van Deventer.'

Marguerite raised her eyebrows. Jan had said he painted when he had the time. Obviously he was more talented than he had led her to believe. It could only mean that the Empress must have seen something of his own work and liked it.

Isabelle looked up from her stitching and paled when Marguerite broke the news to her. 'You're going back this evening? I'm to carry on here embroidering the flower gown all by myself?'

'I have to obey the Empress, but I don't want to disappoint the Grand Duchess. You did much of the embroidery on the Grand Duchess's cape and it was faultless. I have every confidence in you, but I shall send Sophie here in the morning.'

Abruptly Isabelle shook her head and straightened her back. She knew her skills had improved greatly during the past months, which she believed had much to do with feeling safe and unafraid. In addition, Marguerite's praise had boosted her self-confidence. Her frown cleared.

'No, I want to do the work myself. That should make me a true imperial seamstress when it is done.'

'Indeed it will!'

Once more Marguerite returned to St Petersburg. She thought the routine of her life had become as restless as that of the Imperial Court, always moving from one palace to another. At least the rest of the summer seemed destined to be peaceful.

Sarah had not returned from Oranienbaum, but had written that she was staying in Tom's accommodation. So with the Imperial Court away at Peterhof there was nobody to stop her from watching him at work or prevent her from wandering freely in the park where sometimes she would sit and read.

With the fading of summer Jan appeared again. Marguerite came downstairs to the domestic hall one evening and found him waiting for her. With his tricorne hat under his arm, which he had doffed at her approach, he seemed taller and broader than she remembered, not having seen him for some time. He gathered both her hands into his and drew her to him.

'You've been most elusive! When I arrived you weren't here at the Winter Palace, but at Oranienbaum. Later when I went to Peterhof where I was told you would be, it was only to find that you had vanished again. Have you been avoiding me?' It was a challenge thrown out with a lively look in his eyes.

'Of course I have!' she replied, laughing.

He shook his head, amused. 'I have been under pressure of work that has kept me at Peterhof until now. The Empress commissioned me to paint the Grand Duchess's portrait.'

'Yes, I congratulate you.'

He inclined his head in acknowledgement. 'That led to one of the Grand Duke and a stream of commissions. But now I'm here again. Let's begin by having supper together. Before long I'll be sailing back to Amsterdam. You and I have no time to waste.'

To her surprise he took her straight to the apartment he had rented in the Dutch quarter of the city. It was on an upper floor and a plump, middle-aged maidservant of his own nationality, named Saskia, bobbed when they entered and took Marguerite's wrap from her.

The salon was spacious and well furnished in what Marguerite assumed to be the Dutch style and the tall stove was tiled with blue and white scenes that he said were from Delft. She went to look at the paintings on the wall and Jan came to her side to give her the titles and the artists' names. There were views of the city of Amsterdam with its busy port, but she found most interesting two of the Van Deventer family home. The house stood with its stained-glass patterned windows overlooking a canal and the second one showed its rear courtyard and a lush garden beyond with flower beds full of tulips. Both had been painted by his brother Maarten.

Next to these was a painting by another Dutch artist that showed a woman in a dark bodice and rust-red skirt sweeping the black and white tiles of a floor, the whole scene full of light from leaded windows. Marguerite thought it beautiful and lingered before passing on to a portrait of a strong-faced man in his sixties, looking fully out of the frame, a ruby velvet cape over his shoulder. Except for the neatly pointed beard the likeness was unmistakable.

'That must be your father!' she exclaimed.

'No, it's a self-portrait by my late grandfather. He painted it just before we received the news that our father's ship had gone down in a great storm somewhere off the Dutch East Indies.'

She turned to him sympathetically. 'What a tragic time that must have been!'

'Sadly we lost our mother soon afterwards. A fever took her. Maarten was only twelve at the time. It was fortunate that Hendrick was already married to Cornelia and she mothered the lad throughout his grief.' Then he straightened his grandfather's portrait, which was very slightly askew. 'I like to have the old fellow with me.'

'You were very fond of him?' She studied the portrait again. There were the same clear, demanding eyes as his grandson's, the same experienced, sensual mouth.

'We all were. He was a travelling artist when he was young, but when he became successful he bought the house in Amsterdam that you've just seen and a studio with an adjoining gallery where he exhibited the work of other artists as well as his own. Hendrick has no talent for painting and he went to sea for a few years, but Cornelia gave him an ultimatum and he came home to stay. Unless, of course, he obliges me by bringing paintings to me as he did at Riga where you and I first met.'

'Do they live in the family home?'

'No, that was bequeathed to me and the studio and gallery too.'

'I hope your portraits of the Grand Duke and Duchess are hung where I'll be able to see them.'

'I've no idea where they'll be.' He had moved to hold a chair out ready for her at a damask-covered table at one end of the room, a three-branched candelabrum on it giving an extra sparkle to the glasses and a glow to the red wine in the decanter.

It was laid with a cold collation and included many small bowls holding a variety of traditional Netherland side dishes, such as tasty pickles, sliced cucumber in a piquant liquid, and cooked apple dusted with cinnamon. She found it all delicious. As they ate, sitting opposite each other, he told her how he had suddenly found himself commissioned by the Empress to paint the two imperial portraits.

'It was purely by chance. She happened to see a painting of mine that I had no intention of selling her, but I had picked it up with others by mistake.' He shook his head incredulously. 'Fortunately before she made any decision I managed to distract her from it by showing her one by Jan Fyt. I reminded her that she already had a still life by him in the Winter Palace, which her father had bought when in the Netherlands on his great tour.'

'Yes, you pointed it out to me. A still life with a dead hare, some fruit and a lively parrot. I remember thinking it a strange assemblage until you told me more about the symbolism in Dutch art of that period. So tell me what happened next.'

'It seems she took a liking to my work and, after asking me several questions, she gave me that double commission.' He gave a soft chuckle. 'She took it on trust that I could capture a likeness, because the painting she liked was not a portrait.'

'What was the subject?'

He looked steadily at her for a few moments before he replied, 'It's best that you see it for yourself.'

'I should like that very much.'

They had finished eating and she went to sit on a sofa while he crossed the room to a cupboard and took out the painting. It was small and he had had it framed in a finely carved and gilded frame. He handed it to her before sitting down beside her.

She gave a little gasp of pleasure, holding it between both hands. 'How beautiful!'

It was a view of St Petersburg held in the wonderful luminous light that at times seemed to hold the whole city in an ethereal glow. But surely that single small figure on the bank of the Neva was herself? She looked up at him quickly, her eyes inquiring.

'Yes, it's you, Marguerite,' he said, sitting down beside her, 'and I painted it for you. I thought you would like a memento of the city for your wall when you are back in France one day.'

'It's a wonderful gift and I'll treasure it all my life!' she declared fervently. 'Even if I never go home again.'

No sooner were the words out of her mouth than she was startled by what she had said. What subconscious conviction had risen to the surface in such an unexpected way?

He seemed equally surprised, but made no comment. 'That frame is heavy. Let me put it to one side for you.'

'I hardly like to let it go.' She let him take it, but he propped it up where she could continue to see it before taking his seat beside her again. 'Thank you a million times, Jan.'

He smiled. 'I'm glad it pleases you.'

Then without warning, although there was ample space between them, his nearness disturbed her and she was gripped by the old sense of withdrawal, aware of how painfully raw she still was from what had passed between Tom and her. Jan, sensitive to her mood, realized that she was still as far from him as she could be, even though he had hoped that the painting would form a bridge between them. The faintest shadow had crossed her expressive face and he had seen the sparkle go from it. As before, he sighed inwardly with exasperation that he seemed unable to break through to her. It was the reason he had not pursued her more closely, thinking to give her time to recover from whatever it was that was keeping that abyss between them.

167

She was glancing at the clock, which was chiming the hour. 'I must leave now. How quickly the time has flown!'

He did not go at once to fetch her cape, but went instead to pull out a drawer and take a key from it. 'Keep this,' he said, holding it out to her. 'You might like to come here in my absence. There are books on the shelves that I'm sure you would like to read and it would give you a sanctuary of your own whenever you want to escape the Palace. Saskia will be keeping the place clean and in good order. She would always see that the stove was lit for you when winter comes.'

'That's extremely kind of you.' She was on the point of refusing, but she hesitated, thinking how often she had longed to get away on her own for a little while.

He took her moment of hesitation as acceptance and put the key into her hand. 'Good! If you want to return hospitality to friends you will be able to do that too. As you've seen for yourself this evening Saskia knows how to present a simple meal.'

When they came out into the street he had the painting wrapped under his arm and would have hailed a carriage, but she wanted to walk. 'Let's enjoy the last of the White Nights. Already darkness is coming earlier each evening and there won't be many more.'

'Sometimes at the height of summer one could imagine it was the middle of the day,' he said as they set out together.

'That's true,' she agreed.

There were always people about everywhere, partying in boats on the river and canals, sitting on their balconies with glasses of wine in their hands, or just strolling, often with children frolicking along. It was as if sleep was temporarily abandoned by all except those who had a heavy day's work ahead of them. Always there was music coming from somewhere, either in song or in the sound of a violin or a balalaika and sometimes the melodious notes of a harpsichord drifting from open windows. Tonight was no exception.

It was now common knowledge that demolition for the building of the new Winter Palace would be started quite soon. When they came to the area, she asked him how long he thought it would be before it was finished.

'The general estimate is nine to ten years altogether.'

'So long!'

'Thousands of craftsmen, many from Europe, will descend on it once the actual building work is completed. Their specialized tasks will take a very long time. After all, it's to be the grandest palace in the world, so it is said.'

Somehow she knew in her very bones she would see it finished. Maybe she would never go home to live again. Did it mean that she was already putting down roots? But even though she had been in Russia for nearly a year surely it was too early yet to feel a true closeness to what was still a very alien land to her?

Yet so much of it was being absorbed into her blood. She loved the old Russian fairy tales that she had heard from various sources and she had found a tattered but readable French book in the market on its history. She knew now that this great country's name came from the Russ, as the Vikings had been called when they came up the great rivers to invade and to trade. She read of the Mongol hordes that had overrun the land, but eventually been defeated, and how the first tsar had moulded a nation together and made Christianity the faith for his people to follow. But none of the subsequent tsars could compete with Peter the Great, who had brought Russia out of the darkness of superstition and ignorance and into the world of art, literature and the sciences.

Suddenly she turned a shining face to him. 'Be sure to come back to St Petersburg when this palace is finished and fill it with beautiful paintings!'

He looked down into her face. She stood there in total abandonment to her dream for him like a loving woman

169

giving herself. With tenderness he put his hands against her cheeks and lowered his head to kiss her gently.

'If it lies in my power I shall do that,' he promised, low-voiced.

She had not responded to his kiss. It had been too swift and too light for any reaction, but oddly it had moved her in a way she could not comprehend.

Next morning Igor hung the painting for her. She sat on her bed and gazed at it again. Although it was quite perfect in every way there was something about it that puzzled her, almost as if it were missing some vital addition. Yet what could it possibly be? She had been vaguely aware of it at the time of first setting eyes on the painting and yet there was nothing she could pinpoint. The little mystery would continue to intrigue her and add to her pleasure. In all her life she had never received a gift she would treasure more.

Fourteen

J an sailed for home without Marguerite seeing him again. After a while, particularly when there had been a harassing day at work, she went to his apartment for a quiet hour or two.

The peace of it was particularly welcome after Jeanne and Violette had clashed in one of their noisy quarrels or there had been a hitch over a faulty fabric or some other worrying matter. She would have coffee served to her in the Dutch way by Saskia, for Jan had always preferred it to tea just as she did, although both had been luxuries beyond her purse when she had worked in Paris . . . If the Dutchwoman was not there, she would make her own, always buying a fresh portion of coffee beans to replace whatever was used. She began to think of the apartment as her own 'hermitage'.

Jan had not taken his grandfather's portrait with him. Sometimes, glancing up at it, she had the fanciful notion that he had left it for the clear gaze of those penetrating eyes to keep a watch on her.

Isabelle, flushed with success, had arrived back in the city shortly before the return of the court to the Winter Palace. The Grand Duchess had worn the finished flower gown to the end-of-summer ball and it had been greatly admired. Marguerite, knowing Elisabeth's savage ways, guessed that it had given her malicious satisfaction to inform Catherine that she had lost her favourite designer.

Elisabeth's eyes gleamed when she saw the exquisite

embroidery of the opal gown: the entwining leaves of a vine in a delicate pattern had the opaque sequins hanging in small, shimmering bunches like grapes all over the skirt, which parted in the front to reveal the palest green under-skirt. She would wear it in Moscow for the New Year cele-brations and the Frenchwoman must bring it personally. It would add proverbial salt to the wound she had already inflicted on Catherine.

Sarah had returned from Oranienbaum to the city on her own. 'Tom is staying on for a while. There is something else he has been asked to do. How lovely it is there, Marguerite! But I was ready to come back here as soon as summer lost its warmth. In your last letter you mentioned that you would be going to Moscow later on and I also wanted to see you before you left.'

'It won't be quite yet.'

They talked on, Marguerite flinching inwardly whenever Tom's name came into the conversation.

Sophie and Valentin were married on a windy day that was blowing the coppery leaves from the trees. Her compa-triots gave a party for her on the previous evening and she realized how much she was going to miss their daily company.

'You must all visit me often,' she cried, kissing and hugging each of them in turn.

When morning came they all helped her dress in her cream velvet gown. On her head she wore the pearl-studded and fan-shaped Russian headdress that Valentin's late mother had worn on her wedding day.

In the church the Frenchwomen were outnumbered many times over by the large gathering of Valentin's relatives. Jeanne would have liked to sit down, but that was not the custom for any service and there were no seats anywhere, everybody standing for the entire ceremony. Sophie was as conventionally radiant as brides were supposed to be and Valentin stood very straight and proud. There was an exchange of rings, vows were made and prayers said as the traditional gold crowns were held over the bridal couple's heads. When they emerged from the church the first snowflakes of winter had begun to fall.

The celebrations followed with feasting and many toasts. Afterwards there was music and dancing as well as the singing of Russian love songs by three of Valentin's male cousins, who had magnificent baritone voices. The highlight of the occasion for Violette was meeting another of the bridegroom's relatives, Grigori Batalov, a colonel of the Imperial Guard, who was there with his dull little wife, only her diamonds giving her any sparkle. He was a fine-looking man in his mid-fifties with a straight, military bearing, and Violette recognized instantly the predatory look that he gave her from under his hooded lids as they were presented to each other.

'Your servant, mademoiselle,' he said in a strong, deep voice. 'I hope you are not missing your own country too much while you are here.'

'At times, Colonel,' she admitted, 'but I have settled down quite well.'

After that she knew his gaze was following her wherever she was in the room and she made a point of being charming to his wife, sitting with her for a while. Although later Grigori Batalov partnered Violette only once in a dance it was long enough for a secret rendezvous to be arranged for the next evening. His wife, watching them out of the corner of her eye while chatting to someone, had recognized all the signs. She sighed inwardly, fluttering her fan, and wondered how long this new mistress would last.

Marguerite, having lost an important member of her work force, promoted Isabelle to take over the delicate embroidery that Sophie had done best. She had also decided to take the girl with her again when she went to Moscow, not knowing what amount of work might await her there.

That first snowfall had vanished the next day, it being

said that snow had to fall three times before it stayed, but soon winter's grip was on the land. Again the Court was stirring and before long the picturesque exodus took place once more. The Court was to stay for a while again at the Holy City of Kiev where Elisabeth could once again seek forgiveness for her sins in the cathedral there.

Marguerite intended to arrive in Moscow before Christmas. Isabelle, although excited at the prospect of seeing Moscow, was privately not so eager to accompany Marguerite as before. She had met a young Russian, named Mikail Legotin, who spoke French fluently and came from a well-appointed home. She knew, because unknown to anyone else, she had had tea there on her first visit. Since then she had been there many times.

It had happened when Rose and the Pomfret girls had run ahead of her, afraid they would miss the boating trip on the Neva that had been arranged. They had not seen her trip and fall headlong. Even if they had, she was not sure that they would have come back for her, being more likely to call over their shoulders to hurry up and come along as the boat would not wait. But she had landed on the doorstep of the Legotin family home, hitting her head severely on the handrail, just as Mikail opened the door to come out.

Square-shouldered and sturdily built with kindly blue eyes in a strong-chinned, freckled face, his curly reddish hair rebelling against the ribbon holding it back under his tricorne hat, he had bent down immediately to help her to her feet.

'Are you hurt?' he had exclaimed with concern. 'You've cut your forehead! There's a bump coming up like an egg already!' When she had swayed, feeling dazed by pain and shock, a trickle of blood running down her face, he had called to his sister indoors, 'Anna! Come quickly!'

Together they had helped her into the house. As she lay on the sofa his mother had bathed her wound from the bowl of water, which Anna had fetched, and bound it up until the bleeding stopped. By then she had begun feeling better and was able to sit upright and drink tea with them. That was how it had all begun. But he was her secret. All too often at the Pomfret house when one of the young Englishmen paid her attention, Rose was unable to resist flirting him away from her. She did not want that to happen with Mikail and was waiting the chance to ask Marguerite about it. There was also another more serious matter that she wanted to discuss, but there should be plenty of opportunities to talk on the long journey to Moscow.

Isabelle knew she would miss Mikail achingly, for she lived for the times when they could be together. When he discovered she could sing he would accompany her on his lute, either when they were on their own or for the benefit of his family or, more often, at gatherings of his friends, which were fast becoming hers too. Sometimes he would sing with her, having a good voice himself. She had come to realize that music was an integral part of Russian life.

He always held her hand when they walked together, but it was only recently after they had been to a fair on the ice one evening that he had kissed her for the first time, declaring that he loved her. It had been the happiest moment she had ever known. They were both aware that nothing could come of it for a time. He had his medical studies to finish with a local doctor and that would take another two or three years. Although his family approved of her, he knew there would be implacable opposition by his father to an official betrothal before he was qualified.

'But then I'll start a practice of my own and we shall marry, Isabelle. Nothing shall keep us apart!'

It was then that he had given her a ring to symbolize the bond between them: a ruby set in gold. She had shed tears of joy. For the first time in her life she felt truly loved. She wore the ring on a chain around her neck. Nobody else had seen it.

Yet at the same time it was as if a black cloud, which

she had managed with time to drive from her horizon, had risen again like an ominous threat. How would he feel about her if he knew her stepfather had taken her virginity from her in childhood and that she was a murderess? The thought kept her awake at night and troubled her by day. At least she would be able to unburden herself to Marguerite, who had been so compassionate when she had made her original confession.

Marguerite, all unaware, made ready for the journey ahead. Jeanne was to be left in charge and Agrippina had loaned two of her best seamstresses to cover the gaps that would be left by Isabelle and herself.

On the morning of departure Isabelle received a last-minute love letter from Mikail, wishing her a safe journey and expressing his longing already for her return. She had just enough time to write an equally loving reply. She left the letter on the shelf where Igor would collect and deliver it. He had long since become friendly with all the Frenchwomen and saw himself as their special messenger and informant.

Rose's sharp eyes had seen Isabelle put the letter there and guessed who the recipient would be. When Isabelle had taken to going off on her own more than usual Rose, becoming curious, had followed her one day and seen her meet a young man, each transparently overjoyed to see the other. From behind a post she had watched him assist Isabelle into one of the rowing boats for hire on the canals before taking the oars to row away, both of them talking and laughing together. Apart from being piqued that Isabelle had not told her about him, Rose experienced a shaft of unreasonable jealousy.

Nobody in the sewing room noticed when Rose, passing the shelf, took the letter and slipped it swiftly into her apron pocket. Later she slid the blade of a knife carefully under its wax seal and read it. Then she sealed it up again, a triumphant smile on her lips. She would deliver it to Mikail

Legotin. He had looked far more entertaining company than all the young Englishmen she had met, most of whom had begun to bore her.

Marguerite and Isabelle discovered they would not be travelling on their own. A courier, who was a quiet, pleasant man, was already in the carriage. It smoothed the journey for them, even after they had to transfer to sledges not long after leaving St Petersburg, for there was always a change of good horses at posting stations and he ensured that they had accommodation that was as comfortable as his own. Sharing a room with Marguerite meant that Isabelle could at last pour out her worries in private to her.

'I used to think I could never endure marriage with anyone,' Isabelle said after they had talked for a while. 'The horror of my stepfather always loomed up at me. But,' she added wonderingly, 'since meeting Mikail I know my love for him would sweep all my terrible memories away.'

'Yes, that is how it would be,' Marguerite said reassuringly, for even if all Isabelle had said of him was seen wholly through the eyes of love he still sounded kind-hearted and sensible.

'But how can I be sure that Mikail won't think ill of me?' Isabelle exclaimed desparingly, her fists clenched in her anguish.

Marguerite looked into the girl's unhappy eyes and although she regretted what she had to say it had to be said. 'As you know only too well, after the way you were abused from childhood onwards he would know on your wedding night that you were no longer a virgin. You will have to decide whether to tell him the truth beforehand or suffer his hurt and disappointment that another has already possessed you. The possibility has to be faced that he might fly into a jealous rage and not be prepared to believe anything you have to say. It could destroy all chance of a happy marriage for you both.'

'How cruel you are to say all this to me!' Isabelle's

voice broke on a terrible sob, bowing her head in her abject misery.

Marguerite put a comforting arm about the girl's shoulders and spoke gently and encouragingly to her. 'No, it's to help you face facts. Yet you seem to have forgotten the most important fact of all, which you must never forget. If he truly loves you then there is nothing – and nobody – that could ever separate you from each other.'

For a little while Isabelle did not speak. Then she raised her head slowly, her lashes wet from her tears, her decision painfully made. 'Then one day I must tell him,' she said in a broken voice, 'whatever the outcome. But not for a long time yet.'

When Marguerite and Isabelle arrived in Moscow they saw the Kremlin looming ahead with its high, rust-red walls and turrets topped with snow. Their sledge swept through the great gates and they were in a city within a city. Palaces and cathedrals, churches, barracks, armouries and fine houses were to be seen on all sides. The Empress was residing in the largest palace of them all.

The first news the Frenchwomen were given was that Catherine had had a terrible miscarriage and had hovered between life and death for thirteen days. She was now recuperating, but still very weak. Marguerite wished she could see her, but that was impossible. Nor could she manage to gain access to the Empress's presence and none of the court ladies knew what was expected of her other than that she should present the special gown on New Year's Eve.

Irritated by being idle, she visited the sewing rooms in the Palace where she could see plenty of rich gowns in progress, but the woman in charge was hostile, perhaps fearful of being usurped. Marguerite soon left. After that, although it was bitterly cold, she and Isabelle visited the cathedrals and churches both for private prayer and to view the magnificent interiors. They gained permission to enter a great library and afterwards they spent much of their time there.

Isabelle's prayers were always for Mikail's understanding when eventually she told him everything. She knew it was impossible to hope for a letter for a long time yet, even if he wrote an answer immediately to the one she had left for him. It had taken twenty-three days for her and Marguerite to journey to Moscow and that was because there had been no bad snowstorms to hinder them and good horses all the way. But she wrote to him, not caring how long her letters took to reach him, for it comforted her to write of her love and helped her to bridge the distance between them.

In St Petersburg Mikail was writing regularly to her, but unbeknown to him the letters never left the city. After his first meeting with Rose, who had brought Isabelle's letter to him, he had entrusted each one of his own to her. She had said that she knew the footman who collected letters to give to one of the couriers that rode horseback to Moscow, and she could ask for the letters to Isabelle to be included. That would ensure speedy delivery. It also meant that he saw Rose far more often than he had originally intended. She was lively and pretty, a born flirt, who knew how to entice and encourage. He had known girls like her before and enjoyed her easy kisses. The old adage went through his mind of having a good girl to marry and a bad one to bed.

Unexpectedly Marguerite received a letter far sooner than expected from Sarah. It had come with an English acquaintance, who had travelled to Moscow on business. She had written that Tom would soon be coming on his own to Moscow as she could not face the long journey in such cruel winter weather and was staying at home. The rest of the letter held inconsequential news about mutual acquaintances. Marguerite crushed the letter in her hand despairingly.

On New Year's Eve Marguerite and Isabelle carried the opal gown between them to the Empress's apartment. A

light cloth covered it, because Elisabeth wanted nobody to
see it before she appeared in it, not even her ladies. When
Marguerite and Isabelle entered her presence she stood in
her petticoats, tightly corseted with the padded panniers
protruding over her hips. Standing against the background
of her crimson silk-panelled room and velvet bed-hangings,
she looked proud and beautiful, ready to be adorned in a
gown that would truly do her justice.

When Marguerite had finished lacing the back of the
bodice Elisabeth chose the jewellery she would wear. Then
she regarded her reflection in a looking glass and gave a
smiling nod of complete satisfaction.

She gave no word of praise, but turned to Marguerite.
'You will attire yourself in whatever happens to be your
best gown and await instructions in the Malachite Room.
Now go!'

Marguerite, uneasy at this inexplicable command, hurried
away with Isabelle, both of them trying to guess what the
reason might be. She had an apricot-silk panniered gown
to wear, which she had made for Sophie's wedding. When
Isabelle had fastened the back of the bodice for her, she put
on a pearl necklace and earrings that her sister had given
her on a natal day.

'You look lovely!' Isabelle enthused, standing back
admiringly.

In the Malachite Room pillars of the rich green stone set
off the cream and gold of the decor and great vases of the
same mineral stood on rosewood cabinets. She could hear
the palace orchestra in the stateroom nearby. After studying the paintings, some of which were French, she sat down
to wait. Before long two ladies of the Court entered the
room.

'Who are you? What are you doing here?' one demanded
arrogantly.

'I'm here at Her Imperial Majesty's instructions.'

The woman shrugged and turned away to sit gossiping

with her companion, both ignoring her. When there came the distant sound of a fanfare announcing the arrival of the Empress in the stateroom they both sprang up to give a final touch to their hair and fuss with the frills of their low-cut necklines in front of a gilt-framed pier glass. But it was some time before the marquetry-ornamented double doors were opened by a footman and they went out into the corridor leading to the stateroom.

Marguerite had remained seated, but the footman nodded at her. 'You, too, mam'selle.'

'What's happening? I don't understand.'

'You're being given the chance to watch this evening's Portrait Ceremony, which doesn't happen very often. It's when Her Imperial Majesty gives a small diamond-framed miniature of herself to be worn only by her most favoured ladies. The two who were in here, Baroness Boristova and Countess Mikalova, are the lucky ones tonight. It's one of the highest honours the Empress can bestow.'

'That will be interesting to see!' As Marguerite left the room she thought how unexpectedly magnanimous it was of the Empress to allow her to be present. It showed how pleased she was with the gown.

Marguerite entered the enormous, glittering room and swiftly took up an unobtrusive place by the wall. Many hundreds of sumptuously dressed people were present, gathered on both sides without any crowding in such space to allow a wide aisle where the two ladies were advancing side by side towards the foot of the imperial dais. There, under a crimson canopy, the Empress sat grandly in her shimmering gown. The double-headed Russian eagle was emblazoned in gold on the velvet hanging behind her. Peter was on her right and on her left was Catherine, who looked thinner in the face, but any pallor that might be lingering in her cheeks was hidden by the skilful use of cosmetics.

Elisabeth stood as the two ladies before her dipped in their deep curtsies. Countess Mikalova stepped forward first and her citation was read out to the assemblage. When it was finished Elisabeth took one of the two miniatures from a cushion, held by a page on one knee, and pinned it on her, afterwards kissing her on both cheeks.

As she withdrew Baroness Boristova stepped forward. Elisabeth, bland-faced, regarded the woman's smug expression with inner hatred. This was the creature who had dared to laugh when once she had slipped and fallen in an undignified manner. As if that were not enough this detestable creature had spread gossip that she had to pay her lovers to perform! She, whom men had always adored and still came to with love and passion!

'Wait!' she ordered sharply when the citation was about to be read. 'There has been a great mistake! Baroness Boristova is not deserving of this honour with her contemptuous duplicity and infamous lies! Take her from my sight! I never want to look upon her countenance again!'

Revenge was so very sweet. The Baroness had turned ashen, taking a step back in shock before bursting out words of denial and appeal. Elisabeth waved her away in disdain and the stricken woman almost fell into the arms of her husband, who had rushed forward while the rest of the Court stood as if frozen. The courtier who had read the first citation received a signal to continue. His voice boomed out clearly again as the weeping Baroness was led away.

'The second portrait is awarded to Mademoiselle Marguerite Laurent, for her matchless skills and inspiration in creating masterpieces for Russia! These will be saved for posterity in order that in future centuries her work will still be seen and admired.'

Konstantin, who had seen Marguerite come into the room, had been edging his way behind the other spectators to reach her. He was in time to give her a thrust, for she seemed rooted to the floor.

'Go on! You can't keep Mother Russia waiting!'

The silence in the great room was almost palpable. Marguerite began the seemingly endless walk up the shining, parquet-patterned floor to the dais. Some of the spectators were not altogether surprised by this development, for the Empress had rewarded others of humble station in her time. Among the elderly were those who had witnessed Peter the Great doing the same. Yet what shocked everybody, even though they had seen the Empress wreak vicious tricks on numbers of distinguished people before, was the terrible humiliation of the Baroness and the supplanting of her by a seamstress. For that reason alone a wave of hostility from many of those present swept towards the young woman advancing towards the Empress, the glow of hundreds of candles highlighting her hair to flecks of copper and gold. They watched almost in disbelief as the Empress smiled and spoke to the Frenchwoman while pinning the miniature on to her bodice.

Then the ceremony was over and the orchestra struck up for dancing. There were congratulatory gatherings flowing around Countess Mikalova, but nobody came to Marguerite, except Konstantin. He was suddenly in front of her, smiling widely.

'My felicitations! Well done!' He took her hand ready to draw her into the dance as soon as the Empress took the floor. 'But,' he added in a low voice only for her ears, 'although you've gained court status with the honour, don't be disappointed if you're not allowed to keep the miniature.'

'Why should that be?'

Couples were lining up behind the Empress and her partner, their hands linked high. Konstantin drew Marguerite into the line and the dance began.

'We can't talk about it here! Nor should we leave before the Empress, but there are about three thousand people present tonight and we'll not be missed for a little while. We can come back in time to welcome the New Year.'

In the throng it was easy to slip through a door unnoticed and they went along the passage to the Malachite Room.

'Now tell me,' she said when they stood facing each other. The thought of surrendering the miniature did not trouble her in the least. She had no wish to be involved with the Court, who in any case had shown clearly enough they did not want her in their midst.

He turned from tugging at the bell-pull. 'Sit down, for God's sake, Marguerite. We want a drink before we talk.'

A footman came at once and a few minutes later brought cognac, wine and vodka on a silver tray. Konstantin dismissed him and poured the drinks himself. By then she was seated on a sofa and he gave her a glass of wine before returning to the tray, where he downed three vodkas before pulling up a chair to sit opposite her, a fourth in his hand.

'That's better,' he said with satisfaction.

'So what do you think will be the outcome of tonight?' she queried.

'The Empress made a tool of you this evening to settle in the cruellest way possible some real or imagined slight inflicted on her by the Baroness,' he said bluntly, keeping to himself how he alone had known of it beforehand. 'I've no doubt at all that whatever gowns you've made the Empress will be stored with the rest of her discarded garments, but whether they will ever see the light of day again is questionable. She is a devious woman. You've served your purpose this evening. Don't pin any high hopes on the outcome.'

Marguerite raised her eyebrows. 'That thought never entered my head.'

'I'm glad to hear it. But there is a credit side to all this.'

'Oh? And what may that be?'

'It's because the Empress acknowledged you before the whole Court that your new status cannot be eradicated. It means that socially you are equal now to anyone in that stateroom.' His voice took on a teasing note. 'You and I could marry tomorrow without a single objection being raised.'

She flung back her head and laughed. 'What a ridiculous situation! I'm certain the Empress expects me to return to my sewing rooms in St Petersburg as soon as possible now to carry on as if this evening had never happened.'

He frowned. 'Maybe, but at least for the time being make the most of the new privileges to which you are now entitled. We can avoid the boring court functions and attend the rest. So let us enjoy some time together.' A smile spread across his mouth again. 'You'll be able to unmask freely at the end of a ball without being afraid of being sent back to France as you were before. It will be fun!'

Fun. Yes, she believed it would be. Nothing else he might have said could have been more persuasive. His words had made her realize that work, laden with responsibilities, had dominated her time since the day she had arrived in St Petersburg. There had been traumatic happenings, as with Tom, and some happy occasions linked with Jan as well as with her fellow countrywomen, but unbounded fun coinciding with no work on her hands was something not to be missed. A burst of excited anticipation rang in her voice. 'Very well! And I shall make my own mask!'

His face shone with triumph. 'Tomorrow evening I shall dance you off your feet!'

They returned to the stateroom where couples were twirling in a gavotte and they were soon lost amid the other dancers, not knowing they had been observed. Elisabeth's sharp eyes missed nothing.

When Tom arrived three weeks later he tried in vain to see Marguerite, for she was always out having riding lessons or at a party or some other social function. Isabelle, who had not met him before, even though she had been in the same taproom when he had come for his wife in Riga, was glad when he called. She thought him a pleasant man and was thankful for the diversion of his company whenever he stayed for an hour or two while hoping for Marguerite's return. By now she had been looking daily for a letter from Mikail, but nothing had come and she was beginning to be anxious. Her self-confidence, which had been built up by both his love and her success at work, began to crumble and self-doubts assailed her more and more as Mikail's letters failed to come.

As for Tom, she had supposed at first that he was simply calling on Marguerite as a friend, but now she had her doubts. There had been a glint of anger in his eyes when she had mentioned that Captain Dashiski was giving Marguerite a wonderful time in a round of banquets and balls, gaming parties and masquerades. Nor did he seem appeased when she added that she herself had been with them sometimes to plays and concerts. His face always clouded with disappointment when he found that Marguerite was absent yet again and she began to feel quite sorry for him. She tried talking to Marguerite on his behalf.

'He always tells me when he's coming again. Why won't you make time to see him?'

Marguerite sighed. 'If I happened to be here I would see him, of course.'

'He's in love with you, isn't he?'

'Yes.' The answer had come without expression.

'But he's a married man!' Isabelle flushed and bit her lip. 'How foolish of me to say that! It's just that he has such a sweet wife.'

'Yes, he has. She is my friend and my loyalty is to her.'

'If he's not taking no for an answer tell him something! Say you're going to marry Konstantin Dashiski!'

Marguerite jerked towards her. 'What made you say that?'

Isabelle stared at her. 'He's asked you, hasn't he?' Then she was overwhelmed by her own outspokenness. 'Forgive me, please. I didn't mean to pry. Nor have I any right to tell you what to do.'

'It's all right, Isabelle. I will see Tom. You said he'd be coming tomorrow morning? I'll postpone my riding lesson with Konstantin.'

When Tom arrived Isabelle showed him into the room where Marguerite waited and then left. He had discarded his greatcoat and fur hat before entering and stood, well dressed in a crimson coat and knee breeches with high-booted feet set apart as he and Marguerite faced each other across the short distance between them.

'How are you, Tom?' she asked, thinking with anguish that nothing had dispersed the charm he still held for her, even though now she knew it for what it was, a nostalgic illusion that the man she loved was still to be found in this passionate Englishman.

He ignored her query. 'Why wouldn't you see me until now?'

'You know that I've been very busy. Mostly enjoying myself. As I'm sure Isabelle has told you, I continue to design and she makes each one up for the fashion dolls, but otherwise we have nothing to do. I'm negotiating her return in a courier's sledge to St Petersburg, even if I have to stay. She is eager to get back there. Do sit down, Tom.'

Although she took a seat herself he continued to stand. Again he ignored what she had said. 'I came to Moscow specially to see you.'

She shook her head wearily. 'I hoped you were not going to say that. Don't let us get into some pointless discussion about something that can never be.'

'Listen to me! It's you I want with me for the rest of my life! Nobody else!'

She regarded him incredulously, rising slowly to her feet again. 'You're out of your mind! Sarah loves you! She lives for you!'

'She thinks she does, but she's never been a wife to me as I would have wished. She lives in some airy-fairy dream of love and will go on cherishing some idealized image of me wherever she is. She shuts out of her mind anything that threatens to bring her down to earth and that includes the marriage bed!'

'Don't you care anything for her?' Marguerite demanded angrily.

'Of course I do. Who wouldn't respond to her gentle charm and her vulnerability, just as one would to a help-less child or a dependent kitten? I was captivated by her when we married, but it was not long before I realized that I had made a terrible mistake. That's why I sought work abroad, wanting to get her away from her dominating mother and hoping that we could build up a good relation-ship, but it was not to be.' He flung out his hands despair-ingly. 'Sarah suffocates me with her cloying, unrealistic devotion! Even if you had not come into my life I could not have gone on much longer in these circumstances.'

In her own mind Marguerite felt intense pity for him and for Sarah that they were such a mismatched couple, but there was nothing she could do to solve the matter for either of them.

'How you settle the crisis in your marriage is entirely between you and Sarah,' she said, managing to keep an even tone in her voice, 'but my life is my own and you can have no part in it. I was attracted to you, because you reminded me so much – and still do! – of someone I loved and lost before I left Paris. In you I was seeking the past, refusing to see that it had gone for ever.'

'But I can be your future instead!'

She shook her head firmly, tortured by the decision she had made. 'No, Tom.'

'No matter what you say I'll not be turned away! There is nothing in this world that can stop me making you my own. You and I belong together for the rest of our lives!' He was moving towards her, wholly confident that he had only to take her into his arms and all her resistance would melt away. 'My dearest love!'

'But I'm going to marry Konstantin Dashiski!'

The words were out almost before she realized it. He halted, rooted by shock, total disbelief in his eyes. She saw his face drain white before his colour flooded back, rising up from his crisp cravat to flood up his cheeks in crimson-hued rage. He swung up his hand as if to strike her, but almost at once he let it fall again to his side. Then, to her sorrow, she saw a terrible sadness sweep over his whole face and he sank into a nearby chair, his elbows on his knees, his hands hanging down limply, his head bowed in abject misery.

'I don't know how to bear this,' he said very quietly.

She had never seen a man so devastated. This breakdown into such terrible despair was dreadful to see. He looked utterly broken.

'Don't, Tom,' she pleaded, dropping to one knee beside him. 'I've never wanted to hurt you, but it has to be.'

After a few moments he raised his head abruptly and looked at her with a rallying fierceness she had not expected to see. 'I'll not give up! I'll have to see you wed before I'll ever accept losing you!' Then he seized her face between his hands and devoured her mouth passionately in a long kiss that she could not escape. She remained kneeling, shocked and distressed, as he stood up abruptly and went from the room.

When Isabelle came looking for her she had not moved.

Fifteen

The Empress was in a dressing robe having her finger-nails manicured and buffed when Marguerite was able to see her.

'Your Imperial Majesty,' Marguerite began, 'I'm at a loss to know what is expected of me. I'm still designing your gowns and sending my drawings to my seamstresses at the Winter Palace, but I wish to be there to supervise. When may I return?'

'Have you no desire to be a lady of my court, Frenchwoman?'

'It is a great honour, but I came to Russia in order to use my skills to create for you.'

'I see no obstacle there. You have excellent needlewomen carrying out your dictates and you continue to serve me as my designer. It would please me if that state of affairs could continue after you have married Major Dashiski.'

Marguerite gasped. 'I've not . . .'

'Not accepted him yet? I'm aware of that. As a member of my bodyguard he had to ask my permission to marry you and I granted it. There's another matter. You have not attended any of the formal court functions since the evening I granted you my portrait, although I've seen you at every ball. I hope you will soon amend that absence in Major Dashiski's company. Now you may go.'

Marguerite was furious as she left. She was not a Russian subject to have her personal affairs settled for her. She was French-born with the right to make up her own mind about anything and always would be! If she had not become drawn to Russia and enjoyed her work here so much she would have left with the next convoy for France!

Yet would she have wanted to leave Konstantin? He had made her happier than at any time since she had come to this country, except perhaps for some of the times she had spent with Jan and that special evening when he had given her the painting. She had brought it with her to Moscow and it was hanging in her present room. Although she had tried so many times to discover what hidden meaning was there it still evaded her.

On the evening of her investiture as a portrait lady, Konstantin had joked about her new status enabling them to marry without question, but he was quite different when he seriously asked her to marry him. They were at a private party given by friends of his when he drew her away from the dancing into an alcove draped in silk that partly concealed them from the sight of others.

'I have something to ask you,' he said quite solemnly as they sat down together. 'Will you marry me, Marguerite? I realize we haven't known each other for any length of time, but it's long enough for me to have fallen in love with you and to believe that we could enjoy being together for the rest of our lives.'

Although he had taken her by surprise she looked searchingly at him before she spoke. 'I think we could,' she answered reflectively, 'but we both need more time before any decision can be made.'

'Not in my case. If you wished to marry me tomorrow I'd be off to the church to wait for you now!'

She could see that he was desperate to marry her. For herself, he was all she liked in a man: intelligent, good company, serious when it mattered and yet able to enjoy life to the full. By the very nature of the career he had chosen, he was courageous too. She had become immensely fond of him in a very short time. Was that the most sensible form of love? Friendship and affection and laughter without any of the heart-tearing turmoil of highly charged love? She would have to wait and see.

Isabelle left for St Petersburg in the French Ambassador's entourage. Not that he knew that Marguerite had managed to secure a seat for her with three of the French maidservants. Isabelle would have enjoyed their friendly chatter more if she had not been weighed down by the dreadful conviction that Mikail had forgotten her, for in all the many weeks she had been away she had not received one letter from him.

When back again at the Winter Palace she sent word to him by Igor that she had returned, but feared the worst. Yet he came the same evening and as she appeared in the doorway, looking timorous and uncertain, he was overjoyed to see her and ran to snatch her up in his arms and twirl her around, making her petticoats flutter like flags.

'You're here again, my love!' he exclaimed exuberantly. 'I've missed you so much!' Then he realized she was weeping and set her feet on the ground again, one arm still around her as he tilted her face to his. 'What is it? What's wrong?'

Then it all came out. His lack of letters, her fear that he no longer loved her and had found someone else. It took many loving kisses and much reassurance on his part to finally convince her that nothing had changed between them. It never occurred to him that Rose had had anything to do with the disappearance of his letters, supposing that carelessness or wrong delivery, both of which were not uncommon, had been responsible. Yet when he mentioned having become acquainted with Rose and how helpful she had been there was no doubt in Isabelle's mind as to what had become of the letters.

Isabelle decided to say nothing to her erstwhile friend. It would only create an unpleasant atmosphere at work and, on a surge of regained self-confidence, she was buoyantly triumphant in knowing that all Rose's wiles had failed to take Mikail from her. She longed to believe that Mikail loved her enough now to understand with compassion whenever she should choose to tell him the dark secrets of her past, but at least for a while she could still put aside that terrible test of his devotion.

In Moscow Marguerite began attending formal court functions with Konstantin. She wore the Empress's miniature each time and, far from having it taken from her, she received an imperial nod of approval at its display. It became noticeable that even the Court was warming to her, partly because it was unwise to snub anyone whom the Empress favoured and it had not escaped notice that the Grand Duchess always acknowledged her.

She was soon in demand as a partner in the dancing, Konstantin being unable to monopolize her. He knew himself to be envied by many men, but as yet she would not accept a betrothal ring from him. He wanted to give her other jewellery, but she would not allow it. Her stubbornness exasperated him, but at the same time he admired her for it, having known too many avaricious women in his time.

When the announcement came that the Empress would soon be returning to St Petersburg Marguerite faced the fact that Tom would be there. Recalling how wild with love for her he had been, she thought there was no telling what risks he would take with his marriage while trying to make her reconsider all he wanted from her. She would not let poor Sarah endure the misery and despair of knowing that the husband she adored longed to be free of her. There was only one solution.

That evening Marguerite finally agreed to marry Konstantin after he had proposed yet again. It was in the troika taking them to a party being given by one of his fellow officers. He gave a great shout of joy that she had finally agreed, making her laugh, and he bundled her into his arms to kiss her heartily.

'Darling Marguerite! You've made me the happiest man alive!' Eagerly he took from his pocket the diamond-and-pearl betrothal ring, which he had optimistically carried with him on every recent occasion they had been together. Pulling off her glove, he slid it on to her finger. Triumphantly, he kissed her hand and then her mouth. Out of the fondness she felt for him she responded warmly, certain they would have a good life together. She had peace of mind. After all, she had known one great love in her life, which was more than many people experienced, and could not expect anything like it to come again. And yet? What was it that seemed to echo faintly in her mind from a far distance? She dismissed it as irrelevant.

'We'll be married before we leave Moscow,' Konstantin declared, passionately eager for her.

'Yes!' It was what she wanted. When she arrived as a married woman in St Petersburg it would mean that Sarah would retain her happiness and Tom would soon become resigned to her marriage. 'Let us have a quiet wedding.'

'No chance of that! The Empress will want to be there! She has honoured you and I've served her well as her body-guard.'

They had arrived at the house where the party was being held and he threw back the fur coverings to jump out and help her alight, not noticing in his jubilant mood how subdued she had become. Inevitably through the Empress's presence the marriage would be a grand occasion, and she had a sudden feeling of being swept out of her depth.

Konstantin burst out with the news of their betrothal as soon as they entered the crowded room that was golden with candlelight, pastel-hued gowns mingling with bright uniforms and the crystal gleam of raised glasses. Many toasts were proposed to the betrothed couple during the supper with the smashing of glasses in the traditional way.

Marguerite was not aware that some of the women giggled and whispered maliciously behind their fans until she caught a particular glance from one and then another of them. In both women it was a curiously mocking glance as if they were amused by something unknown to her. Momentarily she was puzzled, but promptly forgot the incident in her enjoyment of the party. All the officers wanted to dance with the bride-to-be, but as the proceedings became more riotous Konstantin, more than a little drunk himself, took her away.

'I'll make you happy, Marguerite,' he declared fervently, holding her close to him before they parted for the night. 'No matter what happens you'll always be the one I love. Promise me you will remember that.'

'I promise,' she answered, soothing away the anxious frown from his forehead with her fingertips.

He caught her hand and held it in his own as he looked into her eyes again. 'Within a week you'll be my wife. We'll never be parted again.'

It suited the Empress that there should be no delay with the wedding, for she was restless now to return to St Petersburg. She showed her approval by promoting Konstantin to the rank of colonel. The resident seamstresses began sewing the bridal gown of cream silk trimmed with gold lace and preparations for a marriage banquet at the Palace were made.

On the wedding morning Marguerite wished so much that Jeanne and Sophie could have been there to help her dress instead of two of the Empress's own ladies. She thought how much she would have welcomed the presence of Violette, Isabelle and even Rose too. Konstantin had no family, except an uncle in Moscow, who would attend the ceremony, and two cousins who lived too far away to be there.

Konstantin's marriage gift was a parure of emeralds and diamonds, consisting of a necklace, bracelets and earrings, all of which Marguerite had to wear. On her head she wore a traditional Russian fan-shaped headdress, a gift from the Empress, which was similar to Sophie's on her wedding day, except that this one sparkled with diamonds. With a sable cape around her shoulders against the cold, Marguerite left the Palace, accompanied by the two ladies.

A great number of people were present in the gilded magnificence of the cathedral and thousands of candles were burning. Konstantin was waiting in dress uniform and gave her a wide, reassuring grin as he took her hand to lead her to the splendidly robed priest, who stood among others equally richly clothed. It was long service with much ceremony and chanting. She and Konstantin made their vows, the symbolic crowns held above their heads, and wedding rings were exchanged. They were married. As they turned to leave Konstantin bowed low to the Empress and Marguerite gave a deep curtsey before they advanced on their way, her hand resting on his wrist.

It was then that one of the great doors of the cathedral burst open and Jan stood there with snowflakes flying about him.

'No, Marguerite!' he shouted hoarsely as if refusing to believe he had come too late, his voice seeming to echo endlessly in that vast interior.

Instantly guards rushed at him and he, struggling and fighting, was hauled away through the door and out of sight.

Both Konstantin and Marguerite had halted, he in surprise and she in shock.

'What will happen to him?' she asked, white-lipped.

Gently Konstantin propelled her forward with his hand over hers on his arm. 'Prison. Maybe a flogging first.'

She stopped again, looking at him in dismay. 'No! You must see that he is released.'

He was beginning to lose patience, aware of the stares and whispers all around them, a smothered laugh here and there. 'Yes, yes. Now let's get out of here.'

Outside there was no sign of Jan. She refused to get into the bridal sledge until Konstantin had instructed a captain of the guard to see that the Dutchman was released without charge. Only then was she reassured enough to take her seat.

'Who the devil is he?' Konstantin demanded as they were driven away from the cathedral. 'How do you know him?'

She explained, adding that Jan had been kind in letting her spend time in his apartment while he was away. Konstantin glowered.

'You're never to go there again!'

She caught her breath at his words, taken aback at being given such a sharp order, but then she supposed that he was racked by jealousy. It was the first time she had seen another side of his character beyond his normal good humour.

'You don't have to be concerned,' she said reassuringly. 'Perhaps he thought I hadn't known you long enough to be marrying you and was just anxious for me.'

Her calm words had their effect and he looked at her with recovered cheerfulness. 'From now on I'll be the one watching over your well-being.'

Although he kissed her as if sealing his purpose he was resolved to give orders at the Palace that the Dutchman was to be barred from visiting Marguerite at any time.

The Empress attended the wedding banquet, but left before ladies escorted the bride to the bedchamber. Konstantin's roistering fellow officers had plied him with plenty of vodka and he was very drunk when he staggered naked beneath his dressing robe from the adjoining bedroom to the marriage bed.

'You look beautiful, Marguerite,' he slurred, throwing off the robe to fall into the bed beside her. Then he pulled her under him and took her forcefully before rolling away to snore immediately.

In the morning he was full of remorse. He awoke to an aching head and the sight of Marguerite brushing her hair before a mirror. Sitting up, he met her reflected gaze with an apologetic downturn of his mouth.

'I drank too much last night in my joy at winning you for my wife,' he said.

She thought how skilfully he had made his apology. 'I think you did,' she remarked dryly, not considering him wholly to blame, for she believed that several times his glass had been spiked.

He forgot his headache when he saw with relief that she was not angry with him. His eagerness for her returned and he held out a hand persuasively. 'Come back to bed, my beautiful wife. Let me make amends.'

She hesitated only momentarily. Jan had given their marriage a precarious start and their wedding night had been disastrous. It was time to begin again. She moved towards him and held out her hand to meet his. He drew her down beside him and gathered her close to kiss and fondle her, re-awaking her long suppressed desires with his skilful touch. He was an experienced lover and found her responsive to him in every way. Yet during a pause in their love-making when he leaned on an elbow looking down into her quiet, sleeping face, her hair spread like a coppery aura about her head on the pillow, he felt that in some inexplicable way she had yet to be truly discovered.

He recalled their first meeting. Although she had been frightened of the Grand Duke she had still retained that elusive air that had made him hope he might see her again. It was what made her so tantalizingly attractive, whether she realized it or not. Had there been a sweetheart or lover in Paris? A relationship she had chosen to end by coming to Russia? He found it hard to believe that Frenchmen would not have noticed her sexual allure in their midst. The thought made him wonder if she had been a virgin when he had taken her, but his memory remained hazy and he knew from other times of drinking too much that he would never be able to recollect one way or the other. All that mattered was that she was his now and he had won the Empress's approval again by this marriage.

'Marguerite,' he said softly, disturbing her sleep. Even as she opened her eyes he began caressing her again. He did not know that already she had discovered that fondness was no substitute for love when it came to intimacy. It was as if her heart had detached itself and vanished.

Sixteen

Marguerite was glad to leave Moscow. She had not liked the city, probably because it had become associated in her mind with the upsetting scene she had endured with Tom as well as Jan's alarming interruption at her marriage. There had also been two terrible fires and on both occasions she had seen the red glow and smoke from her window, reminding her agonizingly of the past. But now she and Konstantin were on their way to his country home in the vicinity of St Petersburg where they would stay until the end of his marriage leave. Afterwards they would be back once more in the most beautiful of cities and spring would have arrived.

The approach to Dashiski Palace was pleasing. The drive, bordered on either side by marble statues on plinths, opened up to a wide forecourt where the Palace itself was of moderate size. It presented a charming frontage painted rose pink with the customary white ornamentation laced by a liberal gleam of gold. Konstantin had told her that the reason that it was called a palace was only that it had once been imperial property.

'Now that you are here I'll spend more time in this house than ever before,' Konstantin said. 'In the past I've held the occasional house party, but otherwise I've preferred city life to wandering about here on my own. That's why I've used my rooms in the military quarters of the Winter Palace whenever the Court is in residence there.'

She was surprised. 'I thought this abode to be your family home.'

'No, my parents were both dead long before this place came into my possession.'

It was on the tip of her tongue to ask him why he had purchased such a mansion when he seemed to have had such little use for it, but already they were drawing up at the entrance. Their carriage had been sighted and servants, both men and women, were pouring out in a flurry of white gloves and spotless aprons to line each side of the wide flight of marble steps.

Marguerite acknowledged with a smile the bows and bobs as she and Konstantin mounted the steps together. She looked about her as they entered a grand hallway with a double staircase shaped like an inverted wishbone, the wide parquet floor shining like a mirror and intricately patterned. Although she had hoped to have an immediate feeling of coming home, that did not happen and she thought herself foolish to have expected it.

Konstantin threw aside his hat and seized her hand. 'Come! I'll take you on a grand tour!'

Her spirits lifted as he took her at a run, just as if they were excited children, through one lovely room after another, each leading into the next. Her cloak slid from her shoulders to tumble to the floor behind them as on they raced through room after room until finally they came skidding back into the hall opposite where they had started.

'Now upstairs!' But there he only rushed her along to the bedchamber that was to be hers and they collapsed breathless and laughing on to the bed together.

'That was a lightning viewing!' she exclaimed merrily.

'You'll have plenty of time to settle down here and discover everything more fully while I'm in St Petersburg.'

She sat up to look down at him, her laughter fading away. 'What do you mean?'

'Exactly what I said. You're mistress of this house now. You'll want some time to take charge and order everything to your liking. It's only an hour's drive to the city and I'll be home as often as possible, although I'm sure to be extremely busy for the next few weeks.'

'But I'm still the Empress's designer! She made it plain to me that she would expect me to carry on even after our marriage.'

He propped himself on an elbow. 'Just think rationally for a moment, Marguerite. We've nowhere to live yet in St Petersburg. I have to be near the Empress when I'm on duty and you can't share my rooms in the Winter Palace's military quarters. Nor can you return to where you lived as a seamstress before becoming my wife. I would not allow it.'

She gasped, springing from the bed. 'Have you been planning all along to isolate me here?'

'No, that's not the case at all.' He hoped she was not going to be difficult and sat up, resting an arm across his up-drawn knee as he spoke on a gentle note, intending to placate her. 'There's nothing to stop you working from here with a trip every two or three weeks to show your designs to the Empress, and we'll find somewhere to stay together overnight. There will always be a carriage here at your disposal. Remember never to take it out with less than eight horses as befits your social position. You can go riding too. In fact, the time should pass pleasantly for you. You'll be able to visit and also receive those who have country homes around here. You can hold card parties and soirées. There are about thirty rooms under this roof, so why not have one fitted out for your design work? I know you would want to be here to supervise those alterations. If you wish, you can have friends to stay in my absence.' He smiled with satisfaction at having pointed out all the advantages to her.

Anger coloured her cheeks. 'You don't understand! I've been longing to get back to St Petersburg. Jeanne is capable enough to be in charge of any sewing room, but I know from the letter she sent me in Moscow that she has been looking forward to my return and an easing of her burden.'

He narrowed his eyes incredulously. 'Did you imagine

that after our marriage you could take up your stitching again with no more change than as if a peasant had made you his wife?'

'No, indeed not! But I thought we should be living in the city and I could visit the atelier at least twice a week for an hour or two just to deal with any crisis and keep an eye on the work in progress.'

He rose from the bed to come around to the foot of it and stand facing her. 'You can do that whenever you go to see the Empress, but otherwise you shall remain here until we have a city residence. Then you can take your place at court again with me.'

He was like most even-tempered people in disliking quarrels, but in this he had to make a resolute stand. It was not as if he wanted to be apart from Marguerite, but the Empress had stipulated that after the marriage his wife, although remaining her designer, should live out of St Petersburg, for he would have extra imperial duties now that he was a colonel. There had been a promise in her tone and he was certain that further promotion would be his if he carried out her wishes to her satisfaction.

'Then for the time being we must take an apartment for a short period,' Marguerite said firmly, determined not to be brushed aside. 'Since you will be so busy, I shall look for a suitable place for us.'

'No!' His patience finally snapped and he wanted no more. 'We could be jumping the gun, as the saying goes,' he stated sharply. 'The Empress mentioned something about arranging a suitable city residence for us. It could jeopardize my future if it should appear to her that I was not prepared to wait for her favour. You know how temperamental and difficult she can be.'

Yes, she knew, but she had never expected to find their marriage dominated by a third person, even though it was the Empress. 'But I'll need a pied-à-terre,' she insisted determinedly.

He was already bored with the argument. 'Very well. So find a small apartment to rent for yourself, but where I can stay with you whenever you're there.'

She realized that it was the best she could hope for at the present time, able to tell nothing would sway him from awaiting the Empress's indulgence.

He was relieved there had been no tearful scene, not knowing her well enough yet to realize that was not her way. It had been like walking on a tightrope, compelled for his own good to obey the Empress and yet not wanting to quarrel with Marguerite. His wide smile showed his relief and he reached out to hold her close.

'We'll soon be together all the time,' he murmured, beginning to unfasten her bodice. 'That is my promise to you.'

She let him lift her on to the bed, where he began to make love to her for the first time in the mansion that already seemed like a prison to her.

As the days went by Konstantin became increasingly restless before he decided he could wait no longer before returning to his St Petersburg. The Empress had allowed him four weeks' leeway in which to become accustomed to marriage under his own roof, but he missed city life with all its pleasures and was soon thoroughly bored in his country retreat. It had nothing to do with Marguerite, whose beautiful body was such a constant joy to him, for it had been the same previously whenever he had brought his mistresses here or somebody's wife for an amorous sojourn. He would have sold the house tomorrow if it had not been a gift from the Empress, but he did not dare to do that in case she ever decided to visit it.

Marguerite was equally glad to leave for the city with him, except that for her it would only be a short absence with the alterations at Dashiski Palace and some redecorating to oversee. They parted at the foot of the main outside staircase of the Winter Palace, he already back in uniform. He held her to him for several minutes, reluctant to let her go from his arms. Now that the time had come to leave her for a while he realized more than ever before the true depths of all he felt for her. He watched as she went off to the atelier and then he turned resignedly to go in the opposite direction to reach the Empress's apartment.

Yet as always when he saw Elisabeth again after an absence he instantly desired her, no matter that her beauty was fading and her figure being lost to extra weight, for her powerful sexual allure remained undiminished.

Elisabeth greeted him enthusiastically. 'Darling boy! You have returned early! Could you not stay away from me any longer?'

She enveloped him in her ample arms, her mouth upturned to his and he kissed her as she liked to be kissed. When he had gone to her bed for the first time he had been wildly excited by her, dazzled by her beauty, and over-whelmed by her generosity. Soon he had realized with pride that he was her favourite lover and he had been young then, only nineteen years old and newly commissioned. She had taught him many erotic ways to sexual pleasure and their relationship had always been totally satisfying.

When she had been so insistent that Marguerite should become his wife he had been puzzled as to the reason, for he had no illusions about her. Her own self-interest domi-nated everything she said or did, and he was certain some devious purpose lay behind her wish for such a marriage. It had only come to him by a chance remark that Marguerite had made quite innocently and his sudden enlightenment had almost made him burst out laughing. What better way to enforce her will on Marguerite than to marry her off to him! Fortunately he had no regrets.

Elisabeth almost purred with anticipation as she watched him shrug off his uniform jacket and sit to remove his high shining boots. She doubted that she would ever tire of him and would always keep him in tow, no matter that she took other men to her bed. By marrying him off to the Frenchwoman she had figuratively killed two birds with one stone. Most importantly she had permanently secured the best designer of gowns to be found anywhere, as it meant that Marguerite as his wife could never leave Russia and go back to France. Nor would there be any flitting off to Holland with the Dutchman, whom her spies had told her had been the Frenchwoman's escort for a time. Her purpose in raising Marguerite's status by making her a 'portrait lady' had been to make her acceptable as the wife of a nobleman and cause Konstantin no social embarrassment. What was more, by keeping the Frenchwoman at his country house most of the time, it gave him the freedom to come to her whenever she wished without any questions being asked. She did not want him harassed by a suspicious spouse. How pleasant she had made life for him!

In the atelier Marguerite found all her Russian seamstresses and apprentices at work, but no sign of her Frenchwomen.

'Where is Madame Jeanne?' she asked.

'In the French living quarters,' one woman replied.

Surprised, Marguerite hurried along to the salon where leisure time was spent. When she opened the door an unexpected scene met her. Rose, her cheeks flushed with anger and her mouth stubbornly set, was seated on a chair with her mother on one side and Violette on the other. Even Sophie was there, discarding her outdoor clothes, and had obviously been sent for. Only Isabelle stood apart, her face very white, staring at Rose with her eyes large with dread.

'What's happening?' Marguerite asked anxiously, closing the door after her.

Jeanne, who had been leaning threateningly towards her daughter, straightened up and burst out her reply. 'You may well ask! Rose is with child!' She turned on her daughter again. 'How long have you been doing it?'

Rose shrugged defiantly. 'It's none of your business! The

206

first time it just happened and then every time we met it seemed the natural thing to do. I wouldn't have told you now if you hadn't been clouting me for being late for work! I need cosseting in my condition.'

Jeanne was almost speechless with fury, making her choke on her words. 'You wicked girl!'

Violette was regarding Rose with exasperation. 'You've been a stupid little fool! Why didn't you come to me for some advice before you started playing with fire?'

Rose bared her teeth. 'Because I'm not a whore like you!'

Violette screeched furiously and would have hit her, but Marguerite intervened in time, gripping her wrist and lowering it. 'No! This is no time for violence! We have to talk over this situation calmly. Workers who become unlawfully pregnant in the imperial service are dismissed instantly. None of us wants that to happen to Rose.'

Sophie spoke up. 'She will have to marry the father.'

Jeanne gave a sharp nod of agreement and turned back to her daughter. 'I demand that you tell us his name!'

'I've told you that he's Russian and I expect he would marry me out of a sense of duty. He's that kind of man. But I don't want to be his wife and I'm not going to be!'

'When did you meet him?' Marguerite asked quietly. She was sharing the same misgiving that had already made Isabelle chalk-white.

Rose answered evasively. 'A while ago.'

'Was it after Isabelle and I went to Moscow?'

'It might have been.'

Jeanne took over again, giving her daughter's shoulder a sharp shake. 'Come on! Who is he and what is he? Does he work in the Palace?'

'No! You can stop questioning me, because I've no intention of tying myself up for the rest of my life with someone dedicated to a career that would turn my stomach!'

Marguerite looked across at Isabelle and their eyes met.

The girl gave her an almost imperceptible nod of permission before turning her face away in distress.

Jeanne had caught the exchanged glance. 'What is it you know, Marguerite?'

Marguerite looked directly at Rose. 'Is the father-to-be a young man named Mikail Legotin?'

There was instant confirmation in Rose's explosion of hysterical tears and she drummed her fists on the chair arms and stamped her feet in temper. 'I'll never marry him! You can't make me!'

'Indeed I can!' Jeanne shouted furiously, slapping her hard across the face. 'You'll get your cloak now and we'll rout him out! Where does he live?'

Only Marguerite noticed Isabelle rush from the room. She became deeply anxious for the girl, but could not go to her yet. Rose was kicking and bellowing, holding on to the chair as Jeanne tried to wrest her from it.

'Wait, Jeanne!' Marguerite caught the woman's arm to restrain her. 'Although I happen to know where he lives I'll not tell you until you've calmed down. By all means go to see Mikail. He must be informed. From what I've been told of him, I'm sure it would be as Rose has said, even though I believe him to be in love with someone else.'

'I know he is!' Rose spat out her words. 'That was the fun of it for me! And that's all it was for me. Not a life-long commitment.'

The anger seemed to drain from Jeanne and she regarded her daughter with a stricken look in her eyes. 'I always knew you thought only of yourself, but I didn't know you were heartless too. Was this young Russian the first for you?'

Rose's gaze shifted. 'Of course he was.'

Nobody present believed her and Jeanne did not pursue it. She turned her back on her daughter and spoke in a tired voice.

'Rose and I will visit the young man this evening. In the

meantime we must all get back to work, but first of all I want to talk to Marguerite on my own for a few minutes.' As soon as the others had gone Jeanne sat down in the chair that Rose had vacated and gestured for Marguerite to sit down too. 'I shall press for a marriage and hope that the young man in question is fond enough of Rose to persuade her into it.'

'Is that wise? I can only foresee unhappiness for them both.'

'That's the price they must pay,' Jeanne replied harshly. 'The sooner Rose is tied down from her irresponsible ways the better.' Then her face seemed to crumble. 'Yet I know I have to consider the alternative to a marriage. It would be so difficult to hide her condition from others as it advances and we can't use the artifices and furbelows that disguised the Grand Duchess's pregnancy. If Rose should get turned out of imperial employment she'll never get anything well paid in good working conditions again.' Her mouth became tremulous. 'Then there's the confinement to consider and the baby. Whatever can be done?'

'Let's take each stage as it comes,' Marguerite suggested, concealing her impatience to get to Isabelle. 'If the young couple are not to wed we can start by letting the apprentices make fuller working aprons for everyone. That should keep the Russian seamstresses from noticing anything amiss for quite a while to come. Leave the rest for the time being. You know we will all help in any way we can.'

When Jeanne returned to the sewing rooms Marguerite accompanied her to see if Isabelle had gone back to work, but she was not there. Thinking the girl must have sought the refuge of her own room Marguerite hurried to it. When there was no reply to her knock, she tried the door. It was not locked and she went in, but the room was empty.

Wondering where Isabelle could have gone, she searched several other places in vain before it occurred to her that perhaps the girl had felt faint from shock and gone outside in a desperate need for air. Hurrying downstairs, Marguerite came to a woman washing a tiled floor.

'Have you seen a seamstress in an apron come this way?'

The woman sat back on her heels to look up at her. 'About ten minutes ago and at such speed that she slipped and almost fell on the wet floor.'

Suddenly afraid, Marguerite rushed on until she met a groom entering the domestic hallway from outside. She put the same question to him.

'Did you see one of my seamstresses anywhere outside?'

'A girl ran out of the palace gates when I was on my way to the stables. Would that have been her?'

She did not stop to answer. Outside the gates she dodged the traffic and saw that a small crowd was gathering on the bank of the Neva. Full of fear, she ran along and was in time to see people reaching down to haul the seemingly lifeless body of Isabelle from the arms of a rescuer in the river. With water streaming from her hair and her arms hanging limply she looked like a puppet released from its strings. Then the crowd blocked out the sight of her and she was lowered to the ground.

Swiftly Marguerite elbowed a way through the spectators. The rescuer had clambered out himself and was kneeling on one knee as he pulled Isabelle face downward across his other knee and began pumping the water out of her. It was Jan.

Marguerite dropped down beside him. 'Will she live?' she asked fearfully.

'With luck she will,' he grunted, not looking at her as he continued unceasingly in his task, using such force that she hoped Isabelle's ribs would not crack. Then after some seemingly interminable moments the water escaped with a great gush from the girl's throat and she began to cough violently. Some of the crowd began to disperse, but the rest lingered on to watch the end of the spectacle as Jan took off his coat and wrapped her in it. Then he gathered the girl up in his arms, but turned away from the direction of the Palace.

'Where are you going with her?' Marguerite demanded, hurrying to keep up with him. 'She needs rest and warmth and care!'

'That's what she'll get in my apartment. Saskia will look after her.'

'You don't even know her!'

'Yes, I do. I'm acquainted with the Legotin family. They have bought paintings from me since my return, and I've met Isabelle several times at their house.'

'I didn't know!'

He gave her a mocking glance. 'You weren't available to tell, being in the country. In any case, she's not going back to the Palace unless she wishes it. Something quite terrible must have happened there to make her want to end her life in the river.'

They had reached his apartment. She followed him up the stairs into the room where she had spent many quiet hours in the past. During the next hour she helped Saskia massage some warmth back into Isabelle's limbs and body before wrapping her in soft blankets to rest and recover. Leaving her to sleep, Marguerite returned to the salon while Saskia went to make coffee. Jan had changed out of his wet clothes and sat writing at a desk, but he put down his pen and turned on his chair to inquire after Isabelle.

'She's almost asleep.' Marguerite, suddenly enervated by the shock of all that had happened, sank down wearily on the sofa. 'You saved her life.'

'I happened to be crossing the river on one of the ferry-boats and saw her throw herself in. So, as I swim and happened to know what to do, I dived in myself.' A grin widened his mouth. 'In the Netherlands falling into canals is not uncommon, although mostly those people are drunk.'

'But this was a flowing river. Far more dangerous.'

He shrugged her comment away. 'Now I want to know what it was that made that poor girl feel she no longer wanted to live.'

Since he had done so much for Isabelle she felt compelled to tell him. He listened without comment and then shook his head sympathetically. 'So Isabelle has had her heart broken and Mikail is going to find his life shattered when he returns home from his studies today.'

'It's a tragedy,' she said sadly.

The fragrant aroma of coffee preceded Saskia as she brought it in. She was prepared to stay overnight to care for Isabelle, but Marguerite shook her head over her cup.

'I'd like to sit at her bedside if you have no objection, Jan?' she requested.

'None at all.'

'Saskia will watch over Isabelle now while I return to the atelier and tell my companions what has happened. Later I'll come back with my overnight valise and bring some fresh clothes for Isabelle.'

At the Palace she found that Sophie had waited with Jeanne and Violette for her return and Marguerite told the three of them what Isabelle had attempted and of her subsequent rescue. Jeanne shook her head wordlessly, her eyes full of sorrow, and she walked with the pace of an old woman back into the atelier. Later when Marguerite returned to Jan's apartment in early evening she walked part of the way with Jeanne, who was now wooden-faced, and a mulish-looking Rose. They were on their way to the Legotin residence.

Isabelle was lying awake and at Saskia's persuasion had managed to eat a little food. She was very weepy and leaned over to cling like a child to Marguerite, who had taken the vacated chair at the bedside.

'Why did Mynheer van Deventer have to save me?' she cried pitifully. 'I don't want to go on living without Mikail. I thought he truly loved me, but I realize now that when

Rose could take him away so easily he would never have cared enough for me to overlook my past.'

'Hush,' Marguerite said soothingly as the tears flowed copiously again. 'You've had a great shock, both mentally and physically. We'll talk things over when you've had a full night's sleep.'

She held Isabelle until she slept and had just eased her on to the pillow when Jan came into the room.

'It will be a long night for you,' he said, low-voiced in order not to disturb the sleeping girl. 'Saskia has gone home to her family, but I'll take a turn with you. I'll call you if she wakes.'

Just then there came the sound of feet pounding up the stairs and such a hammering on the apartment door that even Isabelle stirred. Jan crossed the hall and as he opened the door Mikail, wild-eyed, flung himself in.

'Where's Isabelle?' he demanded in a shout. 'I must see her!'

'Not tonight,' Jan said firmly, barring the way.

'You can't keep me from her! I know she's here! I have to talk to her!'

In the bedchamber Isabelle gave a little cry, propping herself up on an elbow. 'Don't let him come in!'

Marguerite moved swiftly to close the bedchamber door, but Mikail had heard Isabelle's voice. Giving Jan a great thrust he dived past him and into the room, where he flung himself down on his knees at the bedside, snatching Isabelle's hands into his.

'It's you I love and always will, Isabelle! Rose meant nothing to me. Forgive me! Nothing like that will ever happen again!'

Distraught, she tried to wrench her hands free. 'No, it's Rose you must marry! She's carrying your baby! I could never have been your wife in any case. You wouldn't have wanted me when the truth came out!' Her voice was getting pitched higher and higher. 'My stepfather raped me and used me from my early childhood and in the end I killed him! Did you hear that?' She gave a hysterical laugh. 'I'm a murderess!'

What he had heard made him gasp, but he did not lessen his grip on her and spoke fiercely. 'It's as well you rid the world of such a man! If you had not I would have sought him out and killed him myself!' Then his voice broke. 'Oh, my darling Isabelle, what you have suffered. I'll never let any harm come to you ever again.'

Jan, seeing how Isabelle was in too hysterical a state to take in what he was saying, wrenched him to his feet and dragged him from the room, leaving Marguerite to soothe the girl.

'Now,' Jan said grimly, throwing him down into a chair and standing over him, 'what right have you to come here tonight? I assume you'll be marrying the young woman you've made pregnant.'

'No.' Mikail sat forward and shook his head dejectedly, his tone bitter. 'Rose created a most terrible scene before my parents and her own mother, saying I was too dull and bookish for her ever to marry me. Then when I said that for the sake of the baby we should go through with it, she screamed out that she didn't even know if the baby was mine.'

'So what happens now?'

'As some doubt will always remain, my father will pay for the upbringing of the child all the time I'm studying, which I shall repay as well as taking on the financial responsibility afterwards. Otherwise I'm free.' His tone was bitter. 'Somehow the pregnancy is to be kept a secret in order that Rose is not dismissed, but how that will be managed I do not know.' Mikail dropped his head into his hands. 'What a fool I was! To think that I almost cost my beloved Isabelle her life!'

Marguerite appeared in the doorway. 'Isabelle will see you now, Mikail.' As he jumped to his feet and would have rushed past her, she made him pause. 'Take your time in talking to her. She's still in deep despair.'

He nodded and went quietly into the bedchamber. Marguerite and Jan were left alone. He told her all that had been said as they stood together, both alert in case Isabelle should cry out again. But all seemed to be well. Suddenly, taking Marguerite by surprise, Jan took hold of her chin between his finger and thumb to tilt her chin as he looked searchingly into her eyes.

'Why did you marry Dashiski?' he asked. 'I had just arrived in Moscow when I heard of the marriage at the cathedral. I tried to get there in time to stop you.'

'You should not have done that. You could have been imprisoned for months.'

'It was worth the risk. You don't love him.'

Somehow it seemed pointless to make any pretence. She answered with perfect truth. 'I'm very fond of Konstantin and we enjoy being together.'

'But to my knowledge you had not met him when I once told you that I knew somebody else stood between us.'

She turned away, clasping her hands together. 'I hope that dear ghost has been laid.'

'Who was he?'

It seemed a time to speak frankly about everything. 'When I was working in Paris there was somebody whom I loved with all my heart, and we would have married if he had not died in tragic circumstances. Then that night in Riga a stranger, whom I mistook you for, reminded me so strongly of my lost love that he brought back the past and I foolishly tried to recapture that time through him.' She shook her head at her own folly. 'Konstantin is different in every way. That is why I'm content to be his wife.'

'That doesn't sound a very stimulating relationship to me. I could have made you feel alive! Not as you are now!' Momentarily his tone became derisive. 'Just content!'

'That is how I wish to be.'

'Don't tell me that! I must have been mad that night in Riga to let you go. I even spoke of wanting you for my wife at another time.'

'But you were joking.'

'Yet I said it with more truth than I realized at the time, not knowing it was the beginning of the love I have for you!'

Although the room was warm she went to stand by the stove as if cold, not looking at him. 'It would not have made any difference.'

'My brother told me afterwards whom you were meeting. So it's Warrington, the English gardener, who's been your link with the past! He has a wife!'

'She is my friend and that was the insurmountable barrier. By marrying Konstantin I've put the past away and everything has been solved for me.' Turning her head, she met his eyes steadily. 'Now my marriage makes a barrier between the two of us.'

'Oh, Marguerite,' he said sadly. 'What have you done to your life and mine?'

'I've told you all that needs to be said between us. You know more about me now than anyone else. Continue to be a friend to me, but without any more talk of love.'

'There's more ways of showing love than talking about it.'

Mikail's voice interrupted them, making them both turn sharply towards him. 'I've been talking about love too.' He looked very serious, but relieved. 'Isabelle has forgiven me. We've put the past behind us, both hers and mine. It means that we are making a fresh start together. So I'm leaving now to let her rest.'

Marguerite ran forward and kissed his cheek out of joy for them both before going in to Isabelle. Jan nodded approval and gave him a cognac before he left.

Although Marguerite kept her vigil at Isabelle's bedside, only letting Jan take her place for a short while, the girl

216

slept all night. In the morning Isabelle thanked him emotionally for all he had done for her.

The three of them breakfasted together and then Marguerite and Isabelle returned to the Palace. At the moment of parting Marguerite remembered she had not given Jan back the key to the apartment.

'I don't have it with me,' she apologized. 'It's at the Dashiski Palace, but I shall return it next time I come to St Petersburg.'

'Keep it,' he said firmly. 'Someday you may need a refuge.'

His words lingered with her. It was then that she remembered that Konstantin had forbidden her ever to go back to the apartment. But she had just spent a night there and would keep the key, even if she never returned.

Isabelle took her place in the sewing room as usual. Rose, who avoided meeting her eyes, had moved her chair to another table. The apprentices were already at work on the new aprons for everybody. But these proved unnecessary, for three weeks later Rose, pale and unsteady, but bright-eyed with relief, came to work after spending the previous evening with Violette. Jeanne guessed immediately what had taken place and gave her daughter a hearty clout.

'You behave yourself in future, my girl! Nobody would help you a second time and I'd turn you out myself!'

Rose took heed of the warning, but soon began to resent the constant curb that her mother put on her freedom. There were no more comings and goings without her being cross-questioned and her absences timed. Worst of all, her mother sometimes accompanied her when she went to the Pomfret house.

Before leaving the city for the country Marguerite found a small, pleasingly furnished apartment for herself in one of the city's magnificent mansions. She knew Konstantin would not have wished to be seen entering a building less grand in any way. Sarah was her first visitor and would be her only one, for there were no facilities for entertaining there.

Her life with Konstantin took on a pattern of their being together for brief intervals, she always sending word to him whenever she arrived. During these times their social round was much as it had been before their marriage until she left the city again for the quietude of the countryside.

She and Sarah always met at some time before she returned to the Dashiski Palace. After a while it was noticeable how listless Sarah had become with Tom constantly absent and her health not all it should be. Marguerite was concerned and invited Sarah to stay with her indefinitely, hoping the country air would bring some colour back into her friend's pale cheeks. Her invitation was gladly accepted.

Seventeen

Sarah was thankful to stay and after a few days felt much better. Here at Dashiski Palace she had Marguerite's company each day and liked being busy untangling embroidery silks for her, pressing a piece of work when it was finished and performing other small tasks. Marguerite, knowing that she would never betray a confidence, told her one afternoon of how Jan had saved Isabelle's life and also how the whole incident had come about.

'I wish that girl had had the baby and allowed Tom and me to adopt the poor unwanted little thing,' Sarah sighed wistfully.

'But would Tom have allowed it?'

'I believe he would allow anything that made me less tearful all the time, but I've become so terribly homesick, more than ever before. There are days when I no longer want to get up in the morning, dreading the day ahead. At least when we were living in France an aunt and several English friends visited me from time to time. I was able to go home to see my mother during her last days, but here my father's funeral was long over before I heard that I had lost him. Now I feel so completely isolated from my roots.'

'Why haven't you told me this before? I could see that something was wrong.'

'Because I know I'm being weak and foolish to feel abandoned all the time.'

'But you have made so many friends in the English community.'

'Acquaintances – not friends. Over the past weeks I have refused so many of their invitations that sometimes they forget to ask me now, which is a relief to me. Tom and I have never been apart as much as we have been since coming to Russia. He is so impatient with me at times and he never used to be. Even when he's working not far away, he doesn't come home for two or three days at a time as often as he used to do.'

Marguerite was deeply concerned, able to see that her friend was suffering from melancholia. 'Have you talked to Tom about feeling lonely?'

'Yes, but he says he has so much to do now and that it will be different in the winter when we can be together all the time.' She raised her linked fingers up and down in her distress. 'But I don't want another horrible winter in Russia. I want to go home to England! I had a letter last week from my brother's wife Anne. She has just had her seventh child. If only I could have been there with her! She and I have been friends from childhood. It would be such a joy to me if Tom and I could live nearby and, since my brother David is away at sea again, I could help her with them.' She dropped her face into her hands with a sob that shook her through. 'I hate this vast country with its cruel snows and its millions of poor, suffering people owned like chattels. I think of England with its gentle countryside and soft weather and how the primroses come in the spring and so much more.'

Marguerite moved to put a comforting arm about Sarah's shoulders. 'Does Tom have any idea how homesick you are?'

'No. I'm so afraid of making him angry with me. He is so short-tempered at times. He never used to be. Everything I say or do seems to annoy him.'

Her words revealed a deterioration in their marriage that struck at Marguerite's heart. She knew the change in Tom came from his present distress over her rejection, but with time that breach could be healed between the two for whom she cared so much.

'I think you should write him a long letter and tell him all that you have told me. I'm sure he will be more understanding than you suppose. He will have felt homesick too at times. I've heard it said that no man longs more for his own country than the Englishman abroad. Perhaps when his summer work is finished he could take you home for a winter vacation.'

Sarah looked up hopefully. 'Do you think he would consider that?'

'Tom is a kind man. Ask him and see what he says.'

Sarah wrote to Tom that same day, a long plea for him to grant her this dearest wish to go home for a visit. When a reply came he wrote that he was considering her request. It left her hopes high.

From the start of Sarah's visit Konstantin had not been pleased to find a permanent guest under his roof, although he was courteous to her at all times. As a result he came home less and less to the Dashiski Palace. Nor did he and Marguerite meet often at her little apartment as now she rarely stayed overnight, not wanting to leave Sarah too long on her own. There had been no more talk from him of receiving a city residence through the Empress's munificence, and Marguerite did not pursue the matter, knowing he would be angry if she refused to move into a property with him all the time Sarah was her guest.

It was early September when Tom arrived. Joyfully, Sarah ran to meet him. They were coming across the hall together, he smiling down at her with his arm about her waist, when Marguerite came to the open door of the salon. Seeing her, his face tightened.

'This is the first time I've seen you since your marriage,' he said, but made no attempt to offer good wishes, 'and now there is an important decision to be made. Sarah has her mind set on a visit home. I thought it over carefully and we shall leave as soon as our possessions are crated and ready.'

Sarah gave a delighted cry. 'Darling Tom! How good you are to me!'

Marguerite was intensely relieved. 'You have made a wise decision. In all honesty I should be afraid for Sarah's health and state of mind were she to stay here much longer without seeing her homeland again.'

He nodded in understanding before turning to Sarah with a softer look, for she was now too overcome with happiness for speech. 'It shall be more than a visit. Our house in St Petersburg will not be needed any more. I'll never take you away from England again.'

'Oh, Tom!' Sarah exclaimed breathlessly, hugging him close, her cheek pressed against his shoulder. 'How wonderful! We're going home at last!' She closed her eyes ecstatically. 'Home!'

While Tom supervised the packing and crating of their furniture and effects, Sarah stayed on with Marguerite for the last few days. It was already autumn.

When Jan came riding up to the Dashiski Palace Marguerite saw him from the window of her designing studio and went to greet him. He was handing over his tricorne hat and riding gloves to a servant in the entrance hall, his tall frame silhouetted against the sunshine outside.

'Welcome, Jan,' she said genuinely, glad that he harboured no ill will towards her.

He turned buoyantly, throwing out his arms as if he would have embraced her. 'How well you look, Marguerite! The country air suits you, I can see.'

Yes, she thought to herself, but not this house. 'Come! Sit down and let us talk.' She led the way through gilded double doors. 'Sarah Warrington is staying with me. Do say you will stay to dine with us.'

He accepted gladly and drew up a chair nearer hers. 'Is she in good health?'

'Oh, yes.' She told him all that had happened and of the arrangements made.

He nodded approval. 'That seems an ideal solution. Did you know that Isabelle and Mikail are building up their relationship again? I said goodbye to them only yesterday.'

'You're returning to the Netherlands?'

'I'll be going from here straight to the wharf as the ship sails at four o'clock tomorrow morning. I heard a couple of months ago that there are some fine Dutch works going up for auction just before St Nicholas's Day, a couple of Rembrandts among them, and I intend to be there.' Then abruptly he put a question to her. 'Now that Sarah is going home, have you ever thought of going back to France?'

She gave a little laugh of surprise. 'Why should I do that? Konstantin would never want to live there and my home is in Russia now.'

'Then life is being good to you?'

'Yes, indeed. It will be better when we have a permanent residence in St Petersburg. I have to admit that I do not feel at home under this roof. Even allowing for it being a country house there is a transitory air about the place as if it's never allowed anyone to stay and really care for it.'

'Maybe,' he answered seriously, not taking his eyes from her. 'But perhaps it's more than that. I think the restlessness is in you, just because you haven't truly settled down.'

She did not want to pursue the matter and told him about her studio. 'I have your painting on the wall there.'

'Focus your roots in that,' he advised, still serious. 'It will give you a home wherever you are.'

She thought he was right. One familiar object could be an anchor in any alien surroundings. 'Tell me all that is happening in the art world, and have you done any painting yourself recently?'

She felt completely at ease with him as their conversation flowed. Gone was the old tension of the past. It was if the marriage band on her finger was a talisman working against the turmoil of his intensely male attraction for her. Instead she was serenely conscious of him with every fibre of her being, telling herself that having him as a friend had made him important to her in a way that had not been there before.

Sarah was pleased to see Jan and at dinner he shared his attention equally between her and his hostess, making the duration of the meal the most enjoyable for them both for some time. Afterwards the three of them played cards, he teaching them an amusing game that neither of them had played before and afterwards Sarah played the harpsichord at his request.

When Jan was ready to go it was quite late and since the White Nights had already ebbed away the sky was dark and starry. Jan's horse was brought for him. He and Marguerite stood alone, facing each other.

'I wish you bon voyage,' she said gently, sorry to see him leave. 'I'll look forward to the first thawing of the Neva's ice in the spring. Then I'll know you'll be back again.'

For a few moments he did not speak, only looking at her deeply. She knew he was about to kiss her and lost all will to move. Suddenly his arms went about her and his kiss was both hard and tender and, above all else, loving. Then he broke away and swung himself into the saddle.

'Take care,' he said, looking down at her. 'If ever you feel yourself to be in danger, seek the help of the Comte and Comtesse d'Oinville. They alone could have influence on your behalf.'

'Nothing will happen to me,' she answered reassuringly. 'You are the one embarking on a dangerous voyage once again. God be with you, Jan.'

'And with you, Marguerite.'

He rode away. She had no qualms about having let him kiss her and the pressure of his mouth seemed to linger on hers. She hummed a little tune under her breath as she went upstairs to bed, Sarah having already retired.

Eventually the day came for another farewell when Tom came to take Sarah away to England with him. He was at her side as she and Marguerite stood together at the head of the flight of steps down to the waiting carriage.

'Always write to me,' Sarah implored huskily, for both knew that the likelihood of their ever meeting again was remote.

'I will,' Marguerite promised and they hugged each other for the last time. As Sarah hurried down the steps Marguerite turned to Tom and gave him her hand. 'Farewell, Tom. I wish you well.'

He kept his grip on her fingers as he had once in the past, and she was suddenly uneasy. 'But I'm coming back to Russia,' he said quietly. 'Of course I shall stay for a while in England to make sure Sarah is happily settled near her sister-in-law.'

'But you must never leave her!' she protested vehemently in dismay. 'You're the entire world to her!'

He smiled. 'Not when she has those nephews and nieces whom she can engulf with love. I'm not deserting Sarah. I shall visit her from time to time. Did you think you had seen the last of me, my love? I could never stay away from you. I know you are going to need me in time of trouble as never before. You'll not stay loyal for ever to a husband who is more often in the Empress's bed than he is in yours.'

He turned from her and went down the steps to take a seat beside his wife. Shocked beyond measure by his words, she acknowledged almost automatically Sarah's wave as the equipage departed. She remained standing there for several minutes, scarcely able to believe that she had heard Tom's words correctly. There had been no malice in his tone. It was as if he had assumed she knew about Konstantin's supposed infidelity and was enduring it in silence. But it could not be true!

Slowly she went back indoors. Then, unbidden, there came into her mind any number of small signs that could be slotted together. There was Konstantin's rapid promotion in the Imperial Guard from captain to colonel in a comparatively short time and his certainty that the Empress would grant him a grand residence before long. She recalled the maliciously amused glances from both men and women on her wedding day and the whispering behind fans that frequently followed her. Now the reason was clear. They had been mocking a woman in their midst too naive to realize that her husband was the Empress's lover and that the marriage would not change that situation in any way. No wonder Jan had tried to stop the wedding and just this evening had given her that strange warning. He had heard the ugly facts as had Tom. It was an old adage that the wife was always the last to know and in her case it seemed to be true.

Sinking down on to a chair as if in a daze, she recalled how Konstantin had mentioned that the Dashiski Palace had once been imperial property. Now she understood why. It had been a gift to him from the Empress! No wonder he wanted a wife out of the way in the country, allowing him to be unhindered by domestic ties whenever he went to the imperial bed!

A gust of fury consumed her, making her head snap back, high colour glazing her cheekbones, and she clenched her fists. She would not stay under this roof another night! She would go to Jan's apartment. He had once offered it to her as a place of refuge and she needed it now.

Going swiftly from the room, she gave orders in all directions and, catching up her skirts, she hurried away up the stairs. Two maids followed in her wake to start the packing.

She left Dashiski Palace an hour later and without a backward glance, taking with her Jan's painting, a valise and a travelling box, the rest of her belongings to be sent on to reach her in time to accompany her home to France. After she had confronted Konstantin she would set off at once.

She cared nothing for the hazards of the journey she would make, although winter was already showing itself in the bare-branched trees standing amid carpets of yellow, russet and ochre leaves under an afternoon sky of pale icy blue.

She thought of her Frenchwomen, whom she would be leaving behind. None of them would wish to accompany her. Sophie and Isabelle had their futures settled and Violette was living now in a fine apartment, only coming to the atelier to embroider and avoid loneliness whenever her besotted general was on duty or with his wife. As for Jeanne, she had too much loathing of her husband ever to risk meeting him again in Paris, while Rose, much subdued and subjected to her mother's strict rules, would be compelled to stay with Jeanne, whether she wished it or not.

Reaching the city and being driven through the streets, Marguerite was amazed to see how much the building of the new Winter Palace had advanced over past weeks, already looking as if it had always belonged there. Its long frontage, still windowless and bare of ornamentation, gave the illusion of stretching for ever where it overlooked the Neva.

The coachman and the groom carried her travelling box up the stairs to Jan's apartment. Immediately she felt safe and more at home than she had ever done at the Dashiski Palace. That night, emotionally exhausted, she slept in the bed that Isabelle had occupied and did not wake until morning when Saskia, entering the room, exclaimed aloud with surprise at finding her there.

Sitting up, Marguerite scooped her hair back with one hand. 'I'm here to stay for a few days,' she explained.

'I'm sure Mynheer van Deventer would be pleased. I will heat water for your bath and then prepare your breakfast.'

'But I brought no food with me.'

'The bakery is almost next door and I was given instructions always to be prepared for your coming.'

As the woman left the room, Marguerite folded her arms

across her up-drawn knees, her expression thoughtful. Jan had realized that when eventually she discovered the truth about Konstantin she would not wish to remain under his roof. She closed her eyes in gratitude for his thoughtfulness.

Knowing that Konstantin was normally at one of the city barracks in the morning, she walked there as it was not far from the apartment. An orderly showed her into his office. He was writing at his desk, but he sprang up from his chair, pleased and surprised to see her.

'You are looking very fine,' he said, his gaze sweeping her up and down. 'I was intending to come out to the country to see you now that we can have the place to ourselves again.' He reached out to take her into his arms, but she drew back. 'What's the matter?'

'I want our marriage to be dissolved.'

He stared at her in disbelief. 'What are you talking about?'

'I will not play second fiddle to the Empress any more! All the world seems to have known about it, except me.'

He raised an eyebrow and a resigned expression settled on his handsome face as he lodged his weight on the edge of his desk to look steadily at her. 'So old gossip has finally reached you. It was what I have always feared. I admit I was one of her lovers when I was younger. It is only duty that keeps me in her tow these days. Nothing else.'

'Don't lie any more,' she countered in exasperation. 'As I want nothing from you except my freedom it should be a simple affair for lawyers to end our marriage.'

He narrowed his eyes incredulously. 'Do you suppose it would be as easy as that for us to part? You're a Russian subject of the Imperial Throne through your marriage to me and the Empress would never permit it! Apart from anything else, she brought you here all the way from France to design for her, honoured you with one of the highest awards she can give and approved you as my wife.

To reject all that would be tantamount to treason in her eyes.'

'You're exaggerating!' she exclaimed impatiently.

'Indeed not! Mention this matter to her and you'll find yourself shut away in a convent somewhere.'

'She would not dare!'

He sighed. 'You would be at the mercy of a ruthless woman. You must have heard how she seized the throne by incarcerating a child, the rightful Tsar Ivan IV, in a fortress where he exists to this day. It has happened to others who have crossed her in minor ways. Do you imagine that she would deal more leniently with you for displeasing her?'

Marguerite had turned pale, horror possessing her. 'This is a monstrous regime!'

He saw how she shuddered. It was a pity she had found out the truth, but it should not be too difficult to mend matters.

'I happen to love you, Marguerite,' he said genuinely, 'whether you believe me or not. Don't suppose I'd ever let you go even if the idea is running through your mind of leaving Russia secretly. I'd follow you to Paris if need be.'

'But it is all over between us. You have had a long relationship with the Empress!'

'I don't deny it. But not any more, you must believe me!' He took hold of her by the arms. Although she went rigid, he did not release her and brought his face close to hers. 'I'm telling you in total confidence that in a matter of months Russia will be at war with Prussia, which is increasing its military power under Frederick II to become a dangerous threat to Europe as well as to us. Great Britain is allying herself with Prussia for reasons best known to herself, probably because George II is of German descent, whereas France and Austria will be our loyal allies. There's even a chance that Spain will eventually become involved. There's a great deal of coming and going happening everywhere. I'm telling you that although I disliked Sarah being constantly under my roof, my lengthy absences from you have been through my regimental duties and nothing else!'

'But the Empress . . .?'

'Her final benefaction was my promotion to colonel, granted upon our marriage. Why else do you suppose a city residence has not been granted to me as it has to others?'

'I never wanted us to be dependent on her munificence!' Her tone was bitter.

He saw she was angry and resolute, but he gave a forceful reply, becoming the accuser. 'In recent months you would have stayed by your own choice in the country with Sarah in your care,' he pointed out sharply, 'even if I had asked you to share a new home with me. I've been waiting for you to decide who comes first in your life. Is it I or do you have another lame duck like Rose to whom you will be giving preference?'

She was puzzled and indignant. 'I have never thought that I was putting anyone or anything before you. I don't understand.'

'For the past month we have had our own house here in St Petersburg, independent of all imperial benefaction. It was up for auction and I bought it. If you wish to live in it I'll take you there this evening.'

'I have a place to stay.'

'Not your little pied-à-terre, because I've cancelled that, and I forbade you ever to return to Van Deventer's place.'

'I'll not be browbeaten!'

He sighed, seeing that his modified confession, persuasion and bullying had been to no avail. Now finally he spoke from the heart. 'Give me another chance, Marguerite. As I said before, I love you and I hope you will eventually come to love me as much.' There was a rueful twist to his mouth. 'Did you think I haven't known that you've never felt as much for me as I do for you? Maybe it's been good to get the past into the open, because there's no reason why everything should not go well from now on. There shall never be any more secrets between us.'

She regarded him sharply. 'Do you mean that?'

'Yes, with all my heart. Let me show you the house. You may take your time before making a decision as to if and when you will move in with me. In the meantime live wherever you like, but don't turn away from me.'

He watched her reaction to his plea that flitted across her expressive face like a passing shadow.

'I'll see the house,' she conceded almost inaudibly, 'but as yet I can make no promises.'

The mansion had gilded balconies overlooking the Neva and was painted the colour of dawn. All the rooms were spacious with high ceilings, the parquet floors laid out in intricate designs. The grand hall and some of the salons were furnished finely with effects that had belonged to Konstantin's late parents and had been taken out of store. He had taken up residence quite recently and servants moved about discreetly.

When they had returned to the first salon she had viewed Konstantin waited while she went to the window and stood looking out, her back to him.

'I need time,' she said quietly.

'You shall have it, but grant me a favour. Furnish the rest of this house for me, but in your taste. Redecorate anywhere and everywhere if that is what you wish. If you do come to live here one day I want you to be happy with everything in it.' Then he added dryly, 'Even me.'

The winter passed slowly. Marguerite did as he had wished, changing colours, having damage repaired, windows well fitted and faded silk panels replaced. She added elegant furniture and draperies, which had been imported from France. There were some paintings, but not one of them pleased her. She wished she could have asked Jan's advice when he returned, but she could not risk being with him any more if ever her marriage was to be mended.

It made her gall rise to continue designing for the Empress, but it had to be done and she kept a detached attitude to her work. She continued to live in Jan's apartment, although after a while she began going to court functions again with Konstantin, seeing that in every way he was trying to make amends. With the coming of spring she knew Jan would soon be returning and the time had come for a decision to be made. She left the apartment and moved into a bedchamber of her own at the dawn-coloured mansion.

That night Konstantin made love to her for the first time in many months.

Their marriage settled to its mending. He did everything in his power to please her, refusing her nothing. He gave her lavish gifts of jewellery and would have bought her anything she admired had she wished it. It was as if he were courting her all over again. She had no illusions, knowing that beautiful women were his weakness and that he was surely most vulnerable where the Empress was concerned, but he had given his word that the relationship was over. She had no choice but to believe him. It was all in her part of shutting a door on the past.

Eighteen

In spite of some sporadic sunshine it was a chill day when Marguerite set off to the Summer Palace with some designs for the Empress. On the way she passed the vast site being cleared by thousands of serfs for the new Winter Palace.

She knew she would find all the Court gathered when she arrived, for Catherine had become pregnant again and should give birth at any time now. She was thankful that the Grand Duchess would not have to endure giving birth in a roomful of courtiers as was the custom in France.

She sensed the heightened atmosphere as soon as she entered the Summer Palace by the grand entrance. Gone were the days before her marriage when she took humbler ways into the palaces. On the stairs she met Countess Shuvalov, a pretty woman, who was one of the few at court genuinely friendly towards her.

'The Grand Duchess has been in dreadful labour since yesterday!' the Countess exclaimed in distress. 'I went past the birthing room earlier today and her cries were quite terrible to hear.'

Marguerite was dismayed. 'Let us hope her torment soon ends and that all is well.'

Suddenly there was a rush of footsteps and two of the lady courtiers appeared at the head of the flight. 'We're telling everyone!' they pealed excitedly. 'Russia has an heir! The Grand Duchess has just given birth to a son!'

'How soon may we offer congratulations to her?'

Marguerite asked, glad to have received such good news.

Their painted eyebrows raised in surprise. 'She has fulfilled her duty and has been left to herself,' one said. 'It is Her Imperial Majesty who is to be congratulated on gaining an heir! She took charge of the future Tsar Paul immediately. He is to have a room next to hers.'

They departed again in a flurry of frills, their perfume lingering on. Marguerite looked questioningly at the Countess.

'The Empress will rear the child,' she explained.

'But Catherine?' Marguerite queried with concern.

'You heard what was said,' the Countess said regretfully. 'She has done what was expected of her and hereafter will have no say in her son's care or upbringing.'

'The poor woman! To deprive her of her newborn baby! How cruel!'

'That is what happens when an imperial child is born.'

Marguerite was full of compassion for Catherine. She had enjoyed designing for her until the Empress had put a stop to it. Then that powerful woman had almost wrecked her marriage to Konstantin, but she was resolved that there should be no more imperial meddling in her life. She would make a first stand against it by visiting Catherine as soon as possible.

'I'd been hoping to see the Empress today,' she said, 'but I'll have to return for that task another time.'

The Countess put a hand on her arm. 'Don't leave yet. Drink a glass of wine with me to celebrate the birth of Russia's heir to the throne.'

They spent a pleasant hour together before the Countess went to offer her congratulations to the Empress, but Marguerite did not accompany her. Instead, she took the opportunity to spend some time in the Summer Palace's splendid library.

She had been reading for more than two hours when the door burst open and Countess Shuvalov reappeared.

'Do come with me now, Madame Dashiski! I've been at

the celebrations in the Empress's apartments and that dreadful woman Madame Vladislatova has just told me that she went to see the Grand Duchess, who asked her for a drink of water and to help her change her nightshift. She refused both requests as being beneath her dignity!'

'How could anyone be so heartless!' Marguerite exclaimed, already on her feet.

Together they hurried to the birthing room, passing the entrance to the Empress's apartments on the way where in the great salon noisy celebrations were in full swing with laughter and the clink of glasses.

As Countess Shuvalov opened the door to the birthing room neither she nor Marguerite was ever to forget the pitiable scene that met them. The windows, ill fitting as were so many in the palaces, were letting in a cold draught that had chilled the whole room. Catherine, hollow-eyed and exhausted, was lying in the rumpled bed, her nightshift and the sheets still stained with birth-blood. She raised her head wearily.

'Oh, my dear ladies,' she cried huskily, 'could you in all mercy fetch me a drink of water?'

There was a jug on a side table. Marguerite filled a glass and the Countess held it for Catherine as she drank thirstily before sinking back on to the pillows.

'The Empress has taken my son from me,' she said wretchedly. 'As soon as he had been bathed and wrapped in his swaddling clothes the priest christened him, and then the Empress told the midwife to carry him into her apartments.'

'Had nobody attended to you?' the Countess demanded, outraged.

'They forgot all about me in their excitement that Russia has an heir. The midwife never returned. I wanted to go from here to my own bed, but I hadn't the strength to move.'

Marguerite leaned forward. 'Tell me where I can find a

fresh nightshift for you. We'll not let you lie in this condition for another minute!'

While the Countess went in search of the midwife Marguerite found what was needed and put it ready.

The Countess returned soon afterwards with the sulky looking midwife, who had been plied generously with vodka at the Empress's celebrations and whose apron pocket jingled with the gold coins received from those present.

The midwife did everything for Catherine that was needed, but with ill grace, angry that her moment of glory had been cut short. Lastly Marguerite brushed and combed the bereft mother's hair from its tangles to hang softly to her shoulders. Then, with a robe over her fresh nightshift, Catherine was carried by a footman back to her own bed. There Marguerite and the Countess settled her comfortably against propped pillows, the midwife having been left to strip the soiled linen from the birth-bed.

'I thank you both so much,' Catherine said in gratitude. Then the Countess left to return to the celebrations, saying she would look in periodically to ensure that all was well.

'Stay with me for a little while, Marguerite,' Catherine requested.

All formality between them had vanished. They talked as friends. As Catherine had had nothing to eat since early the previous day the Countess had ordered a light and nourishing meal for her, which a maidservant brought in on a tray. Marguerite sat with her until it was finished. Seeing that Catherine was ready to sleep, she removed the tray and then pulled the curtains closed over the windows against the noise of the city's celebratory fireworks.

As she was about to leave the room, Catherine propped herself up on one elbow, and spoke with a fierce rise of defiance in her voice. 'I'll not be crushed by what they have done to me!'

'Well said!' Marguerite endorsed approvingly.

'Make me a gown in secret for my first appearance in

public that will outshine everyone! Even the Empress!'
'It shall be done!'

The décolleté gown was the rich blue of lapis lazuli, heavily embroidered in gold to depict the wings of the imperial eagle spreading from the bodice up across the shoulders. Elisabeth's nostrils flared with jealousy, knowing that she was being outshone. Such a gown should have been made for her! Catherine was wearing it proudly and with a new authority, her chin tilted high, commanding the respect of all the Court as mother of the heir. Although she still radiated her delightful charm, having smiles for everyone, she was also warning that she could be formidable.

None could have guessed that inwardly Catherine was heartbroken, not through being separated from her baby, to which she was becoming resigned, but because the Empress had sent Sergei to Sweden on a diplomatic mission. There he would remain until sent to another foreign destination. It meant he had fulfilled a purpose in fathering her child and Catherine knew she would never see him again. What hurt her most of all, illustrating that he had truly grown tired of her, was that callously he had made no attempt to see her before his departure.

Out of pique over the gown Elisabeth delayed in letting Catherine see her son for the first time since he was born. When eventually she was allowed a few minutes to view him in his cradle he was wrapped in black fur, querulous through being too hot, red-faced, and damp with sweat. She was powerless to intervene and was sad as she left him.

It was a long time before she saw him again and by then he did not know her, the maternal bond lost to them both beyond recall.

Jan's days were busy from morning until night from the time of his arrival. A large number of commissions for portraits were awaiting him, but first of all he had to hang all the paintings he had brought with him in the gallery of the auction house.

Konstantin accompanied Marguerite to a private viewing. Since it had become clear to him that his wife seemed to regard the Dutchman simply as an obliging friend, he had decided to accept the invitation that they had received.

There were already a large number of people in the gallery when they arrived, but Jan came across to them immediately. He had not met Konstantin before and Marguerite presented them to each other. Then he turned to her, his eyes searching hers.

'I hope I find you well, Marguerite.'

'Yes, Jan. Congratulations on having this fine gallery for your exhibitions!' She could almost read his thoughts, knowing all he would have wished to ask her had they been on their own, but she kept her smile fixed and her air distant. It was not only because of Konstantin's presence, but also for the reason she had to get on with her life as it had been laid out for her. It was for the sake of all three of them.

'If you should find any painting that you would like, one of my assistants will be pleased to oblige you.' With a bow, he left them.

Konstantin soon chose an oil painting of Russian battle troops in triumphant action during the Swedish war while Marguerite enlisted the service of an assistant to mark out several of the works of art for herself. She could see that Jan was being lionized by the society gathered there. It was doubtful whether she or Konstantin could have drawn near enough to speak to him again had they wished it, and they left without his noticing their departure.

It was the following evening when Konstantin referred to their visit. He was sitting in a winged chair, relaxed and at ease, his long legs stretched out and crossed at the ankles, a glass of wine in his hand.

'After this forthcoming war is over I'll commission the

Dutchman to paint our portraits. I had a word with one of
the assistants before we left and was told he was fully
booked at present. In any case there wouldn't be time before
I leave with the regiment.'

She looked across anxiously from where she sat. 'Is it to
be very soon?'

He shrugged. 'I heard today that we could expect to march
in about ten days' time. Two weeks at the most.' Then,
putting aside the glass, he rose to come across to her. Sitting
down on the stool by her feet, he took her hands into his
and looked up into her face, his own gravely serious. 'I
shall send letters whenever possible, but never lose faith
that I'll return. Reports often get confused in wartime. If
news should come that I'm dead and toasts are drunk in
memory of me, don't raise your glass. You will know in
your heart that I'll be coming back to you somehow and
sometime.'

It was a most extraordinary declaration of his love for
her. She knew from gossip, deliberately spoken in her hearing, that he had not been true to her when she had been at
the Dashiski Palace, but now she saw that at last it was she
alone who would always be first with him before all others
in his life. He, who until recently had been so consistently
unfaithful, was now desperately afraid that he might lose
her to someone else in a lengthy absence.

'I'll remember,' she promised quietly in reassurance.

He drew her down from the chair on to his knees and
held her close to kiss her deeply and hungrily as if it was
already the moment of their parting. Then he carried her
upstairs.

The paintings were duly delivered. Marguerite was
delighted with all she had chosen. There were two charming and slightly risqué French paintings, which the assistant had told her were by a new young artist named
Fraganard. Both pictures had made her smile while at the
same time her seamstress's eye had been held by the almost

rustling sheen of the silken skirts worn by each of the young women depicted with ardent young men in their boundoirs. Konstantin regarded the subject matter with very male appreciation and insisted on hanging them side by side.

She had also chosen five paintings of Dutch domestic scenes, all vibrant with life, even in the calm setting of a black-and-white-floored interior or a simple courtyard at the rear of a house. It added to her pleasure in them that through Jan's instruction she was able to understand much of the symbolism in them. There would be other viewings when the next shipment came in from Amsterdam and she looked forward to buying more paintings in the future.

Catherine was away from the city at Tsarkoe Selo, staying at the Catherine Palace, when Marguerite received an invitation to visit. It had been built long before the Grand Duchess was born and had been named after the wife of Peter the Great, who had reigned as Empress Catherine after his death. On two previous occasions Marguerite had taken designs to the Empress there and to her mind it was the most beautiful of all the palaces and a fit setting for the Grand Duchess. Presently painted in the Empress's favourite shade of rich blue, it had a frontage of enormous length, said to be the longest anywhere in the world, with beautiful windows and a spectacular entrance, the roof crowned with gilded statues and pinnacles. Elsewhere still more gilded figures at the magnificent fountainheads gleamed vividly in their soaring veils of sparkling water.

She was directed to the Amber Room, a dazzlingly beautiful room with inlaid amber panels and further enriched with Florentine mosaics and sculpture. There Catherine sat at a rosewood desk, rereading letters she had received that day. She kept up a flow of correspondence with foreign intelligentsia, many of whose writings she admired tremendously. Apart from her intellectual pursuits, she had a new man in her life and was in a happy frame of mind. She looked up with a smile as Marguerite entered and put the letters aside.

'I'm so pleased that you were able to come today,' she said welcomingly, moving to a sofa where Marguerite could sit beside her. 'I went riding early just in case. The Grand Duke is in St Petersburg, not wanting to miss any of the preparations for war, although he is in a constant rage that his beloved hero, Frederick II of Prussia, is now our feared enemy. It must have been a sad day for you when you heard that France had become involved in this war of several nations, even though she is allied to Russia.'

Marguerite nodded in exasperation. 'Why must men always believe that fighting is the only way to settle disputes?'

Catherine made no comment. She understood Frederick II's motives. Sometimes conquests on the battlefield were necessary to extend and consolidate a nation's power, but she could not expect the Frenchwoman to view the situation in that light with a husband soon to be risking his life in the fighting. 'Tell me what has been happening in the city. I believe there is plenty of military activity.'

'Troops are everywhere. The Empress has been reviewing the regiments, wearing an appropriate version of their uniforms, and they cheer her tremendously. Konstantin and his fellow officers are forever bending over maps and discussing regimental matters when they are not rejoicing that they are going to war. They seem to think Russia has been at peace for far too long. It will only be a short time now before they march, which is why I must return home again soon. I just hope that this conflict will not be of long duration.'

'Just as long as Russia is victorious,' Catherine stipulated. Then she changed the subject, talking about a book she had just finished and fetching another that she wanted

241

Marguerite to read. They did not speak of the war again.

After two very pleasant days together during which they had gone riding, played cards with others staying there and watched a play performed, Marguerite arrived home to discover that Konstantin had received his orders sooner than expected. He was waiting to depart, looking very handsome in his red and green uniform with its gold buttons and epaulettes. He greeted her with intense relief that she had returned in time for them to say farewell.

'Thank God you're back in time! I was afraid I should have to leave without saying farewell to you.' He crushed her to him, kissing her passionately in the knowledge that it might be a long time before he held her in his arms again. Then it was time for him to go.

'Be careful!' she urged, suddenly afraid for him.

He nodded wordlessly. Putting on his leather helmet, which was crowned with a black fur crest, he adjusted the gold chinstrap before mounting his waiting horse and riding away.

Soon afterwards she left the house herself to find a place among many others where she could see his regiment go by on its way out of the city. She did not have long to wait. There were cheers in the distance and then the soldiers could be sighted. The commanding officer on a black horse came first, looking neither to the right nor left with a proud, chiselled profile, Konstantin and fellow officers riding in his wake. Although Marguerite waved Konstantin did not see her. The fifes and rat-tatting drums went past and the colours of the regiments fluttered high. Now came line after line of soldiers as if for ever, black tricorne hats set straight, polished buttons shining and long-barrelled muskets across their shoulders. Many more regiments would join up with them on the way to meet the enemy.

On and on they came to the continued approbation of the watching crowds and then hundreds of horse-drawn cannons rumbled by followed by the endless streams of wagons carrying stores, firearms, ammunition, food and everything else an army needed on campaign. Marguerite stayed on as many did to see the hundreds of spare horses that followed in the rear. Yet that was not quite the end of all there was to see. Last of all came a great swarm of camp followers. Among these were the sweethearts and wives who did not want to be left behind on their own for months and perhaps years. Outnumbering them were the countless whores, who waved cheerfully as they went by. Apart from pleasuring the men, they would also help the other women cook for them, dress their wounds and hold their hands when they were dying. Most carried bundles of possessions, but there were many carts of every kind loaded with belongings, children riding on some of them.

Marguerite admired the women's courage. They would all face untold hardships in the time ahead and silently she wished them well.

That night she paused on the stairs on her way up to bed when a footman hurried across the hall to answer a hammering on the door. As he opened it Jeanne rushed in, her face white and panic-stricken. She sighted Marguerite at once and rushed to the foot of the flight.

'Rose has gone!' she cried out frantically. 'She says she's never coming back!'

Marguerite hurried back down to her. 'Gone where?' she queried, putting an arm about Jeanne's waist to guide her towards a salon.

'She went with the soldiers!' Jeanne wailed in despair, holding out the note she was clutching before collapsing into one of the salon chairs. 'Wouldn't you have thought she would have learnt her lesson? Oh, the silly, wicked girl!'

Marguerite read the note. Rose had stated briefly that she had felt like a prisoner under Jeanne's eye all the time, and now she intended to be free of all dominance for the rest of her life. She could earn her own living anywhere with her sewing and with time she would get back to France.

'How can you be sure that Rose left with the troops today?' she asked. 'Perhaps she has taken ship somewhere?'

Jeanne, her tears flowing, shook her head. 'She had no money, except what I allowed her from her wages. I've also kept a private check on her purse to make sure she didn't earn anything extra by following in Violette's footsteps. Ever since that affair with the young Russian I haven't been able to trust her out of my sight.'

Marguerite thought to herself that therein lay the root of the trouble. Jeanne had curbed the girl's freedom too much in every way. 'Perhaps if you promised to be more lenient with her in the future she could be persuaded to return.'

'But she's gone!'

'She's not beyond reach yet. If I asked Jan to go after her—'

Jeanne sprang to her feet. 'Do you think he would?' she cried desperately. 'I'd be forever grateful! Tell him to tell Rose—'

'He'll know what to say if I have your word that you'll give Rose the independence that she craves.'

'Yes! I will!'

While Jeanne returned to the Palace Marguerite went to put her request to Jan. There had been nobody else to whom she felt able to turn. It was a great deal to ask and she knew that since the trouble Rose had created for Isabelle he had no time for her.

He was no longer living at the small apartment, but had moved to a more luxurious one close to the gallery. When she arrived a Dutch manservant admitted her and left her waiting in the hall. Moments later she heard a woman's soft laugh before a door was closed and Jan appeared, a smile still lingering in the corner of his mouth, although it vanished the moment he saw Marguerite's taut face.

'What is it?' he asked without preamble.

She told him with equal bluntness, adding Jeanne's promise that was to be relayed. When he sighed and shook his head over what she had said her hope sank.

'It was too much to ask of you,' she said quickly, turning away. 'In any case, you have company. I'll go myself.'

He caught her arm and jerked her about. 'You'll do no such thing! I haven't refused you. It just amazes me that after all this time you still think like a mother hen about your Frenchwomen. Go home now. If I can find the wretched girl I'll bring her to you.' He held up a hand when she would have thanked him. 'Save your thanks. I haven't found her yet.'

He never did find Rose. Although he arrived among the camp followers in the early morning when most of them were astir he searched in vain. His inquiries brought no result, but it was to be expected that Rose would try to blend in unobtrusively. He waited until troops and camp followers were on the move again, scanning the women as they passed by. Finally he remounted his horse and returned along the route by which he had come.

Rose laughed to herself. Luck had been with her. Returning to the camp after relieving herself behind some bushes, she had seen him speaking to one of the sentries and had dived out of sight behind a cart. After that she had dodged him all the time. It had been easy enough in such a large gathering. Finally she had left undetected by carrying one of the babies and keeping her face averted.

As soon as it was safe she dumped the baby back with his mother and eased the bundle holding her best gown and other necessities on her arm. She would leave the camp followers and make her own way whenever she came to a place that suited her. Ahead of her lay freedom. She walked with a light heart. One day it would be through the gates of Paris.

Nineteen

Isabelle's marriage to Mikail took place the following year. The wedding was a happy occasion and all the Frenchwomen were present, including Sophie, who was with Valentin and their little son Alexei. Jan was there as well and he and Marguerite sat side by side at the wedding feast.

They saw each other quite frequently, although always at social functions when he was usually with one pretty woman or another. A new theatre had been built in the city and she attended plays and concerts there with him. Nothing had changed between them. It seemed to her that the air still seemed to vibrate around his powerful presence and at unguarded moments his eyes frequently dwelt on her with a look she chose to ignore.

'How is Dashiski?' he asked. 'Have you had any recent news of him?'

'Not for a while,' she replied. 'In his most recent letter he was jubilant over the Russian victory at Memel, but sadly there were heavy casualties.'

'Some wounded from another skirmish were shipped in yesterday from the port of Riga.'

'I know. I went to the hospital and stayed to help in whatever way I could. They were all officers and I knew several of them. Most of them were taken home to be nursed by their families. Only those too ill to be removed remained there for the time being as well as the few there of other ranks.'

He raised his eyebrows. 'What did you do? Take names? Guide relatives to bedsides?'

'Yes. And a little more than that.'

'You still continue to surprise me, Marguerite.'

She was amused, thinking how often their relationship rose and fell through anger, hostility, laughter and the warmth of friendship, but never without an element of danger. 'You should know me by now.'

'I haven't even begun.'

She knew from his tone how he would be looking at her, but she turned to speak to the man sitting on her other side.

A few weeks later Jan returned to the Netherlands for the winter. The highlight of the snowy season was the birth of the Princess Anne to Catherine. As before with her son, the Empress whisked the baby away from her, but this time she did receive aftercare.

Then the old year of 1757 gave way to 1758 and yet another year of the war went by. The fact that England was fighting on the enemy side, mostly against the French in North America, did not affect the English settlement in St Petersburg. They were not harassed in any way and, with the war being fought so far away, life in the city continued as normal, except for the absence of many young men. Yet there were always more than enough for the Empress to take to her bed, for she still exuded a sexual magnetism that men less than half her age found irresistible.

Although her health was failing her bouts of debauchery seemed to invigorate her and counteract her excessive drinking, leaving her good looks intact, except for a high colour in her cheeks, which paint and powder skilfully disguised. Her lust for beautiful clothes remained equally unabated and Marguerite's designs continued to delight her.

The Empress was kept informed of the war's progress by frequent despatches and, although not all the news was good, all Russian victories were joyfully celebrated with lavish banquets and balls. There was a short period of court mourning when little Princess Anne died at the age of fifteen months. Catherine grieved that a young life had been cut, but since she had only been permitted to see the little girl once since the christening her sorrow was not what it would otherwise have been.

On that one occasion she had taken Marguerite with her when she had gone to see her children at Oranienbaum, where they lived away from the Court. Neither toddler Anne nor her brother, who had stood side by side for the meeting with their mother, had known Catherine and were shy of her. Marguerite had been struck by the plainness of young Paul. He was quite ugly-featured and it was almost possible to believe he was the Grand Duke's son after all. Yet Catherine had viewed her children with a mother's eye and thought him handsome.

The year slipped by into another, following much the same pattern as before, except that Marguerite included Jan on her guest list whenever she gave supper and card parties, as well as more formally when she had people to dine. The war continued with its ups and downs, although Frederick II was beginning to weaken, drawing back in many areas under Russian and Austrian pressure. All the time the new Winter Palace grew in size and grandeur like a glorious bud bursting into flower.

It was in the late summer that a great battle with many casualties was fought between the Russians and the Prussians. Shortly afterwards the Empress sent word to Marguerite that Konstantin had been wounded and was being brought back to St Petersburg. It was what Marguerite had feared all the time and she hoped desperately that he would survive the voyage home, for there were often as many dead as there were living when the ships came in.

When the estimated time drew near for his arrival she went to stand with others whenever a ship arrived, scanning those brought ashore on stretchers and looking into the faces of the walking wounded in their tattered uniforms, many of whom had to be helped ashore. Jeanne always accompanied her, hoping that Rose would have thought better of running away and taken the chance of a voyage home, for quite often camp followers helped with the nursing on board.

It was a September day full of pale sunshine when Marguerite and Jeanne stood together and watched the pathetic flow of stretchers and hobbling men come ashore. Then suddenly there was Konstantin being carried on a stretcher down the gangway.

'There he is!' Marguerite exclaimed.

Jeanne watched her run to him, but he made no sign that he knew his wife. His head was bandaged and whatever other wounds he had suffered were hidden under a covering blanket. She saw Marguerite's grave expression as two grooms from the Dashiski carriage took over from the stretcher-bearers to carry him carefully. It was obvious that he was in too poor a state to be jerked about in a carriage over the cobbled streets and must be borne by hand.

Jeanne turned her attention back to the ship with little hope that Rose would appear, but she could not leave before she was sure. Suddenly she stiffened and her heart began to pound as she stared almost in disbelief at a one-legged soldier on crutches, his uniform torn and dark with old bloodstains, coming ashore. She took a tentative step forward and then another before suddenly breaking into a run.

'Louis!' she screamed out.

He jerked up his head incredulously and exclaimed as if he were a boy again: 'Maman!'

Reaching him, she wrapped her son in her arms and they wept together in their joy at their reunion. Her one thought was that although the war had taken away her daughter, it had given her back her son.

At the Dashiski house Marguerite had sent for Isabelle's husband, now Dr Legotin, and he came at once, bringing a young nurse with him. With her help, he cut away Konstantin's uniform and saw that his patient's body bore the scars of two healed minor wounds, but the one in his shoulder was festering badly. He cleaned it as best he could, Konstantin groaning with pain and scarcely conscious, before binding it up. Then Marguerite and the nurse bathed the patient, put fresh linen on the bed and put him into a nightshirt. Mikail stayed the whole time, giving a hand in the lifting, and deeply concerned as to whether Konstantin would recover.

'Give him plenty to drink,' he advised both Marguerite and the nurse, who would be staying to help with the care, 'because he lost a lot of blood when he suffered that wound, and try to feed him plenty of light and nourishing food. I'll look in again later.'

He left the room, but on the way downstairs he saw that in answer to some heavy knocking at the entrance it was being opened wide. Immediately he recognized one of the Empress's most important ministers, Count Batalov. He had come striding in, accompanied by four palace guards.

'Where is Colonel Dashiski?' the Count demanded of the footman who had opened the door.

Mikail spoke out strongly, causing all in the hall to look up at him. 'I'm Dr Legotin. My patient is very ill and cannot receive visitors.'

'Her Imperial Majesty has been informed that he was on the ship that arrived today and I have instructions to remove him immediately to the Palace where he can be attended by her own doctors.'

Mikail spoke sternly. 'You must go back to the Empress and explain that to move him again now could be fatal! He is in a very weak state.'

The Count regarded him contemptuously. 'One does not question an order from the Empress! So get out of the way!' He moved to the foot of the flight.

'No!' Marguerite had come to the head of the stairs. 'Dr

Legotin is right! I'll not allow it!'

The Count knew her and shook his head wearily. 'Be reasonable, Madame Dashiski. I have no choice in this matter. Your husband is to be taken to the Palace immediately.' He began to mount the stairs. 'I don't want to cause you or Count Dashiski any distress.'

'Do you want to deliver him dead?'

He stopped and looked at her uncertainly. The doctor had already warned him. He could imagine the Empress's terrible wrath if Dashiski did die after he had ignored those warnings. 'Very well.' He gave in reluctantly. 'I shall inform Her Imperial Majesty.'

After he and those with him had gone she and Mikail exchanged smiles of relief.

'Well done!' he said. 'That fellow would never have taken notice of me. And take heart. We've a fight on our hands to pull Konstantin through, but we have a chance to break the fever now that it's certain he can stay where he is.'

Marguerite returned to Konstantin's bedside and sat down to continue to put cool damp cloths on his forehead. Once he opened his eyes and knew her. He raised a hand towards her and she took it.

'I thought you were a dream, Marguerite,' he said almost inaudibly before closing his eyes again.

The nurse had returned with an egg-nog and managed to spoon a little into his mouth. He was sleeping again when once more there came a thunderous knocking on the door. Marguerite sprang up in alarm. Had the Count returned to repeat his demand? Once again she rushed to the head of the stairs and was in time to see the door opened to two palace guards, who promptly stepped in to stand rigidly to attention on each side of the entrance and it was the Empress herself who swept in. She looked up at Marguerite, her expression frantic.

'Where is my darling boy? Is he really dying?'

'My husband is sleeping,' Marguerite replied coolly.

The Empress was already on her way up the wide staircase, holding her skirts so that her twinkling feet were unhindered and at the same showing inadvertently her heavily swollen ankles. At the top of the flight she stood for a few moments to recover her breath, her hand pressed to her chest, before she was able to speak. 'Take me to him!'

Marguerite led the way and signalled for the nurse to leave as the Empress burst into the room and flung herself down by the bedside in a billowing of skirts. She snatched up Konstantin's hand and pressed it to her lips.

'Speak to me, my darling! Say that you know your beloved Elisabeth is here!'

Marguerite stood as if frozen, pressing her back against the wall in the shock of what she was hearing. Tom's words came back to her. Still the endearments flowed.

'You must not die, dearest heart! How would I live without your loving arms?'

Konstantin stirred and his eyes opened. As when he had looked at Marguerite, there was momentary recognition. He mumbled something, although neither woman comprehended what he said. Yet Elisabeth took his response eagerly.

'Yes, you know me and you will get well and strong again. I shall take you with me now and care for you myself.' She began rising to her feet.

'I cannot allow it!' Marguerite stepped forward. 'The doctor insisted he is not to be moved.'

Elisabeth swung round, her eyes blazing and struck Marguerite full across the face. 'How dare you forbid me, seamstress!' she thundered. 'Konstantin does not belong to you! Nothing belongs to you! Not this house or anything in it! All of it is mine! He spent his last night before going to war with me!' She prodded a finger into her own chest. 'You've only had him as a husband because I allowed him a wife! Now I'm taking him back where he belongs to get well again!'

She made for the door, giving Marguerite a great thrust out of her way as she went from the room. Descending the stairs, she gave orders to the guards below. They in turn signalled to two more, who had been waiting outside with a stretcher. They came running up the flight to take the sick man from his bed. Marguerite had to watch helplessly as Konstantin was wrapped in a blanket and then carried from the room. She went to the window and saw him placed along the seat of the waiting coach, the Empress cradling his head in her lap.

The nurse had returned to the room and as Marguerite looked dully towards her she hurried across. 'Your lip is cut, madame! There is blood! Let me see to it.'

Marguerite sat numbly while the nurse tended to her. She supposed one of Elisabeth's rings had slashed her and she could feel that her lip was swollen. But that was nothing compared with all that had been revealed during that terrible scene.

She had truly believed that there was no longer anything between Konstantin and the Empress, no matter what had happened in the past, but now she realized that he had lied to her consistently, even to telling her that he had purchased their house himself. Instead, it had been given to him by his lecherous benefactress, together with everything else. How could he have been so weak, so greedy? Yet she knew the answer. The truth was that he had never been able to free himself from the spell that Elisabeth could cast over men.

When Mikail called in later he was dismayed to hear that Konstantin had been taken away after all. He also saw that Marguerite was still in a state of shock and tried to cheer her.

'I trained under one of the imperial doctors. Dr Samsonov is a good man. I'm sure he will do his best for your husband.'

She nodded. 'I know he'll not lack care.'

'Would you like to invite me to have a glass of cognac with you?'

She was jerked out of her lethargy as he had hoped. 'Forgive me! I should have offered you some refreshment from the start.' Then she smiled, realizing that he thought it was she who was in need of it. 'I'll pour it myself for both of us.'

He sat with her for quite a while and she was glad of his company.

'Shall you visit Colonel Dashiski tomorrow?' Mikail asked.

She shook her head. 'After what happened here with the Empress today I think the Palace will be barred to me.'

'Was it so bad?'

'Worse than anything you could imagine.' She touched her cut lip significantly.

He whistled under his breath. 'I see what you mean! But I'll find out your husband's condition from Dr Samsonov and report to you.'

'Will there be anything to report, do you suppose?' she asked anxiously.

He hesitated. 'He should not have been moved, of course. But he survived the voyage, even though the state of his wound had deteriorated on the way. Provided his fever subsides and his strength is built up again we can allow ourselves to be hopeful.'

After Mikail had left again she wandered aimlessly about the house, remembering how she had gradually come to find pleasure in its graceful rooms and fine proportions. Now it seemed like a prison. Yet, in spite of her bitter disillusionment, she would have to stay until Konstantin was on the path to recovery. His life was at stake and if he should express a wish to see her in extreme circumstances she would go to him. The Empress would not deny his request.

Before she went to bed a note from Jeanne was delivered, giving the good news of finding her son, who had been fighting as a mercenary in various conflicts over the intervening years. Marguerite was so glad for them both and read the note twice over.

When finally she went to make ready for bed she sat for a long time looking at Jan's painting. Once again it was like an anchor to her. Something to contemplate and ponder over, always intriguing her even while it gave her peace. She knew that even if Jan had been in St Petersburg, she would not have turned to him this time in her troubles. This was a matter she had to sort out for herself and her whole future depended on it.

Several weeks went by before word came from the Palace that Marguerite was permitted to visit the invalid. She went full of trepidation that Konstantin had taken a turn for the worse, for he had hovered between life and death for quite a while before Mikhail's reports had begun to be hopeful. She found Konstantin in bed still looking very ill with an almost translucent pallor beneath the remains of his tan. He was propped up against pillows in a room in the Empress's apartment. He gave the bedcovers a pat for her to sit down there and she did as he wished.

'Why haven't you been to see me?' he demanded irritably in greeting, not noticing that she had failed to kiss him. 'I've asked for you to come many times.'

She had no intention of worrying him with the true facts of the case in his present condition. 'I believe you were too ill at first to have any visitors. We can talk about all the other reasons when you are home again.'

'Nothing wrong, is there?' he inquired querulously with a frown.

'Everything is in order.'

'Good.' Then his expression softened, showing his pleasure in seeing her. 'I've missed you, Marguerite. I want to come home, but I haven't put a foot out of bed yet. The Empress fusses over me all the time. It's almost as if she relishes having me shut up here all to herself.' He raised himself up, catching at her hand. 'See if you can get those damn doctors to say I can come home.' Then he fell back again on the pillows, momentarily exhausted by the small exertion he had made.

'I'll do my best.' It seemed to her that the Empress had taken jealous possession of him as she had done with both of Catherine's children. 'But I must go now. I was only allowed two or three minutes.'

He swore fiercely in exasperation. 'I can't take much more of this molly-coddling!' Then, as she reached the door, he sat up again. 'I love you, Marguerite. You do know that, don't you?'

'Yes, I do,' she replied.

Closing the door after her, she paused for a few moments, a hand over her eyes in despair. All fondness for him had long since drained away, leaving only tolerance. Yet he did love her. She knew it, but in spite of his present attitude towards the Empress he would ever be held in thrall by her, no matter how much he might long to escape now or at any other time.

She told Mikail of Konstantin's request, but after he had spoken to Dr Samsonov he reported that it was in vain.

'The Empress will not hear of him leaving yet. At least you know he is receiving good care, and his recovery does seem assured.'

A few days later Marguerite received a summons from the Empress to attend her. Expecting to hear some report on Konstantin's progress or even more lenient visiting to be conceded, she arrived at the appointed time. Elisabeth greeted her smilingly as if nothing untoward had happened between them. 'Well, Madame Dashiski? Where are the new designs?'

Marguerite looked at her in astonishment. Did the woman imagine that everything could go on as before?

'There are none, Your Imperial Majesty. My designing days are at an end.' She saw Elisabeth's eyes narrow for a matter of seconds as they looked at each other in full under-standing.

'What nonsense!' Elisabeth exclaimed dangerously, the smile gone from her face. 'Your work must continue. Such talent cannot be discarded so easily.' A deep threat came into her voice. 'I'm sure you wish to be at home when Count Dashiski returns after his convalescence.'

Marguerite thought of the warning Konstantin had given her some time ago when she had wanted to defy this cruel, despotic woman, but she would not be beaten down this time. 'Naturally I do. Where else should I be?'

Elisabeth thought how swiftly she would have had this proud-faced creature shut away for defiance if she had not wanted the continuation of gowns made up from those ima-ginative designs.

'I shall be sending your husband to the Catherine Palace to recuperate. He has a persistent cough left over from his fever, but that will soon go. You shall accompany him and supervise his nursing. In such a setting your own work should flourish extremely well. Is that agreeable to you?'

Marguerite realized a bargain was being struck, but still she was not ready to acquiesce. 'It would be better for Konstantin to remain at home now that the winter is here.'

'No. Now that I am about to depart for Moscow he can no longer remain under my care. Since the doctors have agreed with me that he should be in harmonious surround-ings to stimulate him out of his listlessness, the Catherine Palace is ideal. It's only a short journey from here and he has always liked being there.'

Marguerite saw that further opposition would be useless. Elisabeth had made up her mind and there was no chang-ing it. 'How soon should I be ready to leave with him?'

'According to the doctors, he will be fit to travel next week.'

When the day came they travelled in a closed sledge through the snow-covered countryside. Konstantin, who had not yet regained his full weight, still had the look of an invalid in his features, but he was in high spirits at being away from the Palace at last. Yet he had not lacked company during the latter weeks of his recovery, for fellow courtiers and friends had come to see him, bringing bottles of vodka and plenty of talk and laughter. But now the Court had departed for Moscow for Christmas and it would be quiet again at the Winter Palace.

'Now we can make up for lost time, Marguerite,' he said cheerfully as they were driven along.

He had been too ill to know anything of the terrible scene with the Empress that had taken place at his bedside and Marguerite had said nothing about it to him. But as soon as he was fully recovered their parting must come about, for she knew that he would still go running to the Empress whenever she crooked her finger.

The Catherine Palace looked extraordinarily beautiful in the snow. The lack of leaves on the trees enabled a full vista of it to be seen from the approach through the gilded gates. The white marble statues bordering the drive all wore caps of snow and the curious winter light enhanced the Palace's golden splendour.

Servants ran to help Konstantin into the Palace, but he refused their assistance, making his own way up the snow-cleared steps with the aid of a cane. Indoors the welcome warmth from the tall, handsomely tiled stoves enveloped the two arrivals. Konstantin hurled his hat and gloves aside and flung off his sable coat, letting it drop to the floor.

'I feel better already!' he declared.

In many ways it was a lovers' palace – not only because of the beauty of both its exterior and interior, but because it was possible to dine alone without the intrusion of servants at a table that could be raised up through the floor, fully set with dishes for the meal. Sometimes Marguerite and Konstantin took advantage of it, but not as lovers.

'I have the desire, but not the strength yet,' he said

regretfully when they parted one night at her bedroom door. She made no reply.

At first the time passed comfortably for both of them. There was a splendid library in the Palace where they both liked to read. Soon they had plenty of visitors, people they both knew, who were living at country estates in the neighbouring district, but when Konstantin was totally exhausted afterwards Marguerite had tactfully to limit the visits.

Unless it was snowing hard or dangerously cold she took a daily walk. Paths were cleared daily between snowfalls until there were high white walls each side, making it impossible to see anything except the tops of the bare trees. Konstantin, using his cane for support, took his exercise indoors along the enormous length of the exquisite golden enfilade that went on and on through many rooms.

'It's like walking through the gates of Heaven,' he joked wryly one day.

At first she went with him, but he felt increasing humiliated by his slowness in regaining his strength and by his constant attacks of coughing, which frequently made him halt for minutes at a time.

'Don't follow me about!' he snapped irritably at her one day. 'I don't need you to watch me all the time!'

After that she did not accompany him, but instructed his valet to be in range unobtrusively, for the parquet floor was well polished. Once he deliberately left his cane behind, but fell so heavily before he could be saved that it was sheer good luck that he did not break any bones.

As Konstantin slept a great deal in the daytime, Marguerite worked during these hours, taking the colours of the many beautiful rooms as her inspiration. The glorious Amber Room with its inlaid amber panels, which she thought must be a wonder of the world in itself, gave her the idea for a gown of ruched cream silk with amber beadwork. An azure drawing room with silk-upholstered, blue-flowered walls inspired another, and even the Pompeian greens in her own bedroom resulted in a unique design.

She and Konstantin spent Christmas on their own, but when they were invited to a party at New Year he insisted that they go.

'After all those weeks in bed and then coming here I need to see some life again,' he declared. 'I'm going mad from boredom in this place.'

He was also becoming increasingly concerned over his lack of libido. One night he came to Marguerite's bed, but it was useless and he sat on the edge of the bed in despair. She began to wonder if his persistent cough indicated that he was more ill than the doctors had realized.

It was a bitterly cold evening when they left the Palace and although they stayed overnight after the party it was even colder when they returned. Inevitably his cough became worse within the next few days, forcing him to stay in bed. Marguerite sent for the nearest doctor, but a two-day blizzard delayed his coming. When he did arrive Marguerite had sat up both nights at Konstantin's bedside and been constantly in attendance by day. Coughing had racked him and with dismay she had seen blood on the handkerchief that he held to his mouth.

After examining Konstantin the doctor shook his head gravely when he and Marguerite had left the bedroom. 'I regret to tell you that your husband is very ill, madame. He has inflammation of the lungs and his strength is waning. I do not think he is long for this world.'

'But surely there is something that can be done!' she cried.

He shook his head. 'I will give you a stronger potion to ease the coughing and a sleeping draught to help him through the nights, but he must have been suffering from this illness for some time. My supposition from what he has told me is that it dates from the fever of the lungs he contracted when he lay wounded on the battlefield overnight in the rain before he was found.' His eyes were sympa-thetic. 'Care for him, madame. He is one of Russia's heroes. Make his time, be it long if he rallies or shorter than we would wish, as content as it can be.'

The doctor departed, saying he would call again from time to time. Marguerite, heavy-hearted, returned to the sickroom.

After a while Konstantin did rally and was able with help from his valet to dress. The effect of being up again invig-orated him and he began to talk of returning to St Petersburg.

'As soon as the thaw sets in,' he added, knowing that Marguerite would not let him venture out in the cold air again.

His cough, eased by the doctor's potion, was much less troublesome and he had become convinced that he was going to recover in spite of the enervating tiredness that overcame him at times. By the spring he would be well again. As February passed and then March even Marguerite had begun to raise her hopes again and chose a date in mid-April for their return to St Petersburg.

He always went to bed early, sometimes to read, and she would go in to see him before she retired to make sure that all was well for the night. Then one evening, shortly before their planned departure, he sat against his pillows almost asleep when she entered, his book fallen from his hand. As she went to remove his book she saw there was a change in him, a waxen paleness to his face that filled her with alarm. He looked up at her.

'Do something for me, Marguerite.' His voice was almost inaudible.

'Yes, what is it?'

'Undress for me here. Let me see you in all your beauty once more.'

Tears sprang to her eyes. She began to remove her clothes and when she was naked something like a smile touched his lips.

'I never saw another woman as lovely as you or one I loved more.'

Swiftly she sat on the bed and put her arms around him. 'Don't go, Konstantin!' she cried out imploringly, able to see he was slipping away.

But his eyes had widened sightlessly and suddenly blood gushed like a fountain from his mouth in a haemorrhage nothing could stop.

Alone in a carriage Marguerite followed the hearse with the coffin to St Petersburg. It was the day they had planned to return and the snow had gone, leaving only patches in hollows and in places under the trees.

Although she was the widow, she had been allowed no voice in the funeral arrangements, for the Court had returned from Moscow and the Empress controlled the whole procedure. A great number of people were present at the service where Konstantin was laid to rest in a vault of Elisabeth's own choosing in the Peter and Paul Cathedral.

Twenty

Catherine was in love again, but this time more deeply and more ecstatically than ever before. She felt as if she had been reborn and never before had there ever been such a love between a man and woman. Gregory Orlov was a tall, splendidly built and handsome young lieutenant, who had fought so courageously and successfully at the Battle of Zorndorf that he had become a hero, admired and respected by fellow officers and his men alike. Women found him irresistible, enhanced as he was by an aura of daredevil bravery, and he had taken full advantage of all the opportunities that had come his way when not at the gaming tables or at drinking parties.

When Catherine had seen him for the first time it was at a distance, but she knew she would know no peace until meeting him. She arranged it and soon after that he became her lover. He was one of five equally courageous and physically well-built brothers in the same Guards regiment. Here was a man who was not her intellectual match in any way as her previous lovers had been, nor could he discuss the books she read nor engage her in the deep and stimulating discussions that she so enjoyed. But sexually they were ideally suited and he gave her nights of great passion beyond anything she had experienced previously. Above all else he was as totally in love with her as she was with him.

They could not see each other often enough. Sometimes at night she slipped out of the Palace to go to him, disguising herself by dressing as a man, a tricorne hat tilted well down over her eyes, a tie-back wig covering her hair. Unbeknown to her, none of the guards were deceived and exchanged amused glances. As with the majority of those who came into contact with her, however lowly their status, they liked and respected her too much to betray her, even though it was through them that plenty of salacious gossip about her and her lover resulted in the domestic quarters.

Catherine always returned before the Palace stirred and once found that the door she always left unlocked had been bolted unwittingly against her in her absence. Fortunately a servant on duty came to her rescue and let her in. She dared not think what would happen if the Empress should ever get word of her nightly absences.

Yet everyone could see that Catherine was in love. There was a glow in her face and a sparkle in her eyes while her delicious charm, which drew people of all ages to her, seemed to create an aura about her. She had never been happier, except that she had begun to be deeply afraid of her husband.

She spoke to Gregory of her fear one night as she lay in his arms. 'Peter has always disliked having me as his wife, but as time has gone by he has come to hate me and never more so since he became devoted to his present mistress. That horrible Elisabeth Vorontsova! He has told me that he will marry her when he gets rid of me after the Empress dies!'

'Beloved Catherine, I'll never let him harm you in any way,' Gregory vowed, holding her close. 'I'd defend you with my life if need be!'

He took very seriously the threat she had received, for the Grand Duke would be capable of anything once he had all the power of a tsar. Personally, he despised Peter as did his brothers and other officers, all of whom considered the heir to the throne to be a traitor to Russia with his adulation of Frederick II. Most believed Peter to be weak-minded with his eccentric behaviour, wild laughter and weird capers, often at the most solemn of occasions.

Catherine, with her compassion for others, went to call on Marguerite in her widowhood, even though she had been at the funeral and expressed her condolences that day. She knew that Konstantin had long been one of Elisabeth's favourite lovers, as did everyone else at court, but she, ever alert and observant, had seen how often Konstantin had looked in Marguerite's direction with something deeper than affection in his gaze.

When Catherine was shown through to where Marguerite received her, she was surprised to see on the way that dust-sheets covered much of the furniture in the hall and some paintings had been removed from the walls. Through an open door she saw that the library furnishings were similarly covered and some of the shelves had been emptied of books. She was shown into the Yellow Salon, where Marguerite, dressed in black, came forward to greet her. This room was still in order and immediately Catherine asked the reason for the dustsheets elsewhere.

'I'm leaving here,' Marguerite replied. 'I'm only taking pictures and books as well as a few other items that I purchased for myself. This house belongs to the Empress.'

'Has she told you to move out?'

'No, but she purchased this house for Konstantin and told me at his sickbed that it was not mine in any way. So now he has gone I have no place in it. I have rented the apartment that the Dutch painter Jan van Deventer once occupied. If I could have severed all links with the Empress I would have done it, but I'm still forced to the task of designing for her.'

Her words confirmed for her listener that she had known of her late husband's infidelity.

'If only you could have still designed for me!' Catherine exclaimed fervently.

'If only,' Marguerite repeated with a rueful smile.

'But one day you shall design for me again!'

Marguerite appreciated the kindly vow, but as the omnipotent Elisabeth was still only in her late forties it could be a long time to wait. She hoped to be back in France long before Peter gained the throne.

Two days later Marguerite moved into the Dutch apartment and, because of the many times she had been there before, it felt like a homecoming. Although everything that had belonged to Jan had gone, the tall blue-and-white-tiled stove was still a fixture to warm her when winter came again. The furniture she had bought was already in place, made ready by a young Dutchwoman named Marinka. The girl had been recommended by Saskia, who was now housekeeper at Jan's present apartment and his caretaker again in his absence.

As she had expected, Jan came to see her as soon as he landed back in St Petersburg, seeming to fill the small apartment again with his presence. He looked strong and in good health, his well-brushed dark hair tied back with a ribbon bow. There was a prosperous air to him too in a well-tailored grey-cloth coat and knee breeches, his cravat white and crisp with a narrow edging of Dutch lace, his shirt cuffs similarly trimmed. He had heard from Saskia that she had been widowed, and he strode restlessly about the salon, looking at everything and noting without comment the painting he had given her on the wall.

'What are you doing here?' he demanded. 'Why aren't you still living in your fine mansion? Or at Dashiski Palace?'

She thought he seemed almost angry with her and could not understand why. She gave him a brief explanation and received a sharp look from him.

'So you're coming to your senses after all. That debauched court was no place for you,' he stated. 'Why don't you go home to France?'

'I can't at present. All the time I'm of use to the Empress

with my designs I'm trapped here. It would go against my whole nature to deliver inferior work and in any case she would see through my ploy and find some devious way to punish me. Remember that I'm a Russian citizen through my marriage and subject to her whims and her ruthlessness. But that doesn't mean I don't intend to break those chains when the time is right.'

'How?'

'I don't know yet. I have to be careful and carry on as usual until she feels confident that I've no thought in my head of leaving Russia. Once, after I was married to Konstantin and spoke of returning to France, he warned me that the Empress's spies would make sure I didn't get a passage on any ship to my homeland and that I would be followed and brought back if I went by road. Perhaps, now that I've moved here, I'm already being watched. In any case, if I wished to get a passage home, whatever the conditions on board, no French vessel has come in yet this year.' She shrugged. 'Maybe the British Navy is blocking French ports. At least this conflict can't last for ever.'

'It shows no sign of it abating yet, although for Russia everything seems to be going well and great gains have been made. But Frederick II isn't beaten yet.'

She became exasperated with his pacing about. 'Do sit down and have a glass of wine with me. You're like a prowling tiger.'

He flung himself down in a chair and watched her as she poured the wine. As she handed him his glass he caught her wrist, looking up into her face. 'Marry me, Marguerite! That will make a Dutchwoman of you and, as the Netherlands aren't at war with anyone, you'd be free to return to your homeland.'

For a long moment they looked into each other's eyes. 'Take your wine,' she said calmly, 'and don't make wild suggestions. I'll do it my own way.'

He took the wine, gulped a mouthful, and as she sat down

opposite him he regarded her cynically. 'Are you still moon-ing over that Englishman?'

She flushed angrily. 'Although we've known each other a long time you have no right to cross-question me in this way!'

'Answer my question anyway.'

'If you were referring to Sarah's husband, I'm not languishing after him or anybody else.'

'Come now. There is still someone making a barrier between us and I know you never loved your husband.'

A gasp escaped her at his outspokenness. 'I was fond of him when we married!'

'But he wore out your affection with his promiscuous ways. Am I right?'

She sighed heavily. 'Everybody seemed to know of his long-standing relationship with the Empress except me.'

'That's why I tried to stop your marriage.'

'I realized that later. Yet in spite of everything I know that Konstantin loved me and it was no fault of his that he could not break free of her.'

'You're very forgiving.'

She shrugged. 'I just know that his last words to me did much to mend matters between us. I'm thankful that I can remember him for all that was good between us.'

'I'm glad to hear it. Bitterness destroys.' He paused. 'Let me paint your portrait, Marguerite. I've long wanted to ask you, and this seems to be the right time for it.'

She raised her eyebrows. 'From what I have heard you have plenty of court commissions waiting for you to fulfil.'

He ignored the evasiveness in her answer. 'I've sketched you many times, holding an image of you in my mind, but now I want to capture you in oils. Come to my studio tomor-row. You've never been there. And,' he added as an addi-tional incentive, 'you'll be the first to see the paintings I've shipped back with me this time.'

She had long wanted to see his studio. Although she could

269

no longer afford to buy works of art, Konstantin having left tremendous debts that she had managed to settle, it would give her enormous pleasure to view Jan's latest acquisitions before they went on sale or for auction in the gallery.

'I will sit for you,' she said, 'but you need time to settle back in to your apartment again.'

'Then come tomorrow afternoon and we'll discuss the portrait,' he said, putting aside his emptied glass and rising to his feet. 'There's no point in delaying a start.'

She rose too. 'You're forgetting something. In this case, time has to be paid for in one way or another.'

He glowered. 'You must be out of your mind if you think I'd charge you! In any case I intend to keep the portrait for myself.'

'So I guessed,' she replied, amused by his fierce indignation. 'But in exchange I want a self-portrait of you.'

He realized she had been making gentle fun of him and his expression cleared. 'You shall have one,' he promised willingly, knowing immediately that he would paint the two portraits in the Dutch way of portraying a betrothal or marriage, with each individual looking towards the other.

When Marguerite arrived at his apartment he took her into the salon. As they entered he suddenly remembered that she had only been to the apartment once before. That was when she had wanted him to find Rose and he had not been alone. That affair had not lasted, nor had others since then, which was to be expected when she alone was the woman he wanted with every fibre of his being.

She was also remembering the glimpse she had had of his visitor and was careful not to sit in the same place.

'Have you any special pose you want to hold?' he asked. 'Is there any particular object you would like to stand on a table beside you, such as an arrangement of flowers? Some sitters like a book to indicate their intellectual interests. If you want to hold a rose or some other blossom as many women do, that can be easily done.'

'There are no roses blooming in April!'

He looked amused. 'That's no problem. I could paint you in a bower of roses if that was what you wished.'

She laughed. 'Now you're making fun of me. Maybe I should have a needle and a skein of silk thread?'

He frowned seriously. 'Not for this portrait. No, not for this one.'

'What do you visualize for me then?'

'Just you. A new beginning. No adornments.' His gaze fastened on her hand. 'No wedding ring.'

She answered quietly. 'In spite of all Konstantin's infidelities I owe him the respect he deserves for losing his life as a result of service to his country on the battlefield. I'm still in mourning for him.'

'Then you might as well sit for your portrait in black!' he gave back sharply.

Even as she caught her breath at his unexpected flare of anger Saskia appeared with a samovar. Marguerite welcomed the interruption, thinking how often she and Jan had clashed in their long relationship. She and Saskia chatted as the porcelain cups were set out with a plate of little cakes made with fruit and nuts that Marguerite remembered were made from a Dutch recipe.

When the woman was gone again Marguerite looked over her cup at Jan. 'We either discuss my portrait sensibly or cancel it altogether.'

He compressed his lips ruefully. 'I apologize for my outburst. But, as I said yesterday, I want to portray you setting out on a new path, the past behind you.'

'Then let us postpone the portrait for three months. I need that time at least to adjust to the changes in my life. By then perhaps I shall have formed a plan as to how to leave Russia.'

'I hope that doesn't mean I'll not see you until then.'

She shook her head. 'No, of course not.'

'Then we'll dine together this evening.'

271

Her refusal was firm. 'Not tonight You're in too uncertain a temper for me to feel relaxed in your company for a while.'

'Then let it be in two days' time. By then all the paintings in the gallery will be properly hung and I'll be in an exuberant mood.'

She laughed. 'Very well. Why do you still buy and sell the work of other artists when you could paint all the time here in St Petersburg?' she asked him. 'Your portraits are always in demand and any landscapes or other scenes would be too.'

'I admit my work here is profitable. The extra income is useful as it enables me to risk backing young artists whose work I believe will make its mark on the art world one day. Without my support they might starve and then their paintings would be lost for ever. There's a young Dutchwoman among them, whose flower paintings are exquisite.'

'Do you have any of her work here?'

'Yes, there's one. My assistants unpacked it today. I believe the Grand Duchess would like it and I intend to offer it to her first, which is why it will not be on public show at the opening, although you shall see it. There are also some French paintings that I bought when I was in Paris last November that you may like to see.'

'You were in Paris!' she exclaimed. 'How did it look? Do you think much has changed since I was there?'

He told her at length about his visit, for she asked him many more questions and it pleased him to answer them, although there was something he had been waiting the whole time to tell her.

'I wish I had known you would be in Paris,' she said at last. 'Before you left last autumn I could have given you a letter for my former employer, Madame Fromont, whom I've spoken about sometimes. It's such a very long time since I've heard from her and I only hope that the cause is the disruption in the post by war and not that she is ill or otherwise incapable of writing.'

'I remembered all you had told me about her and I went to her address.'

'You did?' she exclaimed joyfully. 'How very kind! Was she well?'

He frowned. 'That's another reason why I wanted you to come today. I have bad news, I'm sorry to say. She had died the previous week.' He saw immediately how much she was saddened by what he had told her, and he paused considerately before continuing what he had to say. 'But the very pleasant woman who has been caring for her knew my name from your letters and went with me to vouch for my reliability to a lawyer. He gave me a letter for you.' He took it from his pocket and gave it to her.

She opened it in silence and read it through before looking up in astonishment. 'Madame Fromont has bequeathed me her house and its contents in the hope that one day I'll return to France and design for Versailles.'

His face was expressionless. 'How opportune. You'll have a home waiting for you when you effect your escape.'

She smiled sadly, her thoughts still with the letter. 'Madame Fromont was always annoyed that the Comtesse d'Oinville would never reveal to other women the source of the clothes she wore to Versailles. Now through her kindness in providing me with a home in Paris it's as if Fate is encouraging me to leave Russia at the first opportunity.'

'It seems like it,' he remarked dryly.

She looked up brightly. 'You could stay whenever you come buying in Paris! I should be so glad to see you.'

'That's most generous of you.'

They met quite frequently as the weeks went by, but almost always in the company of other people, for she never knew when or if she was being watched night and day. She often saw, but chose to ignore, the question that lingered luminously in his eyes under his lowered lids. Yet to let him make love to her might set off events beyond her power to control and she wanted to avoid anything that could further complicate her life at the present time.

Towards the end of July Marguerite arrived at his apartment for the first sitting for her portrait. To oblige his whim she wore a yellow silk gown that she had never worn before. Before coming she had removed her wedding ring and put it away. It was right that she should make a fresh start. A new beginning, Jan had called it.

He took her straight into the finely panelled room that he had made his studio and where the windows gave good light, particularly at this time of year. She looked about observantly. Canvases were stacked against the walls and a handsome chair was set on a draped dais. A prepared canvas had been propped ready on its easel and on tiered shelves were flagons of oil and rows of jars containing coloured pigments. There were white and black, vermilion, a variety of browns, yellow, red ochre and several greens as well as azurite and smalt, both of which gave a deep-blue colour. A pestle and mortar stood on a table beside shallow bowls of colours already ground and mixed. His palette was lying in readiness. Containers holding brushes were right beside it and some paint-rags were at hand.

She stepped on to the dais and settled herself in the chair. He came across to take one of her hands and rest it in her lap. Then he propped her elbow on the wooden arm of the chair before turning her chin slightly to the right. He stepped back to regard her pose professionally. 'Are you comfortable?'

'Yes, I am.'

After that he took up his palette and selected a brush.

'Here we go.' He gave her a smiling glance before he disappeared behind his easel.

He had told her once that he rarely spoke when he painted, although his sitters could talk as much as they liked. So he was as silent as she had expected he would be and it was wonderfully quiet in the studio.

It was a time to be reflective. A spell in her busy life in which to think of many things. She thought first of Sarah. It was almost a year since she had heard from her, but there would be letters on the way somewhere. Tom had been absent at the time of Sarah's writing. She had related proudly that titled clients had engaged him for projects months ahead, for a change was taking place in the world of great gardening. Sweeping landscapes with lakes, man-made or otherwise, had become fashionable for the parks of great houses in England, whole villages being relocated if they spoiled the desired view, so that Tom with his skills was greatly in demand. As for Sarah herself, she was happily helping to care for her brother's children and even added that she scarcely had time to miss Tom.

So it was as he had predicted, Marguerite thought, and with so many projects to fulfil, as well as the war making travel difficult, it was highly unlikely that he would ever return to Russia. She supposed that sometimes he would wonder how much of his plans, if any, was being used for the glassed-in roof garden on the new Winter Palace.

Marguerite pondered over the intensity of relief that had swept over her when she had read that letter from England. Was it that she was still not totally sure of her feelings towards Tom and to see him again after a long time might ignite again that attraction between them as instantly as it had been aroused in that hostelry in Riga? At least she would never have to risk that test now.

There would have been no call for him to create sweeping parkland at the new Winter Palace, as it was in the heart of the city and fast approaching completion. She knew the Empress had viewed each stage in its progress and it was said to be more magnificent than anything previously built in Russia, maybe in the whole world. Marguerite remembered how she had always had the conviction that she would see it finished. Now, unless she soon found an opportunity to escape the Empress before that day, it was likely to be her destiny.

She had turned over in her mind many ideas for getting away, but each one had a flaw. Whatever way of escape she took it would have to coincide with the Empress being at a distance from the city, because she could not risk being sent for unexpectedly and her absence discovered too soon.

Her thoughts turned to her Frenchwomen. With the exception of Rose, from whom no word had ever been received, all were totally comfortable with their lives in St Petersburg. Sophie was looking forward to the birth of her second child and was blooming in her pregnancy.

As for Jeanne, life was being good to her and not only in her being reunited with her son Louis. When Agrippina had retired, the two sewing ateliers had been amalgamated and Jeanne was totally in charge. She had bought a pleasant apartment, where Louis was living with her. As he had been fighting with the enemy as a mercenary he would not normally have been taken on to the ship that had brought him to St Petersburg. It was as the battle had ended and he lay with his leg smashed by a bullet that he had had the wit to steal the coat of a dead Russian officer lying beside him, but with the comradeship of soldiery he had shoved the man's identification papers into the corpse's blood-stained shirt. Then, half-fainting with pain and loss of blood himself, he had drained his last strength as he struggled to put on the coat before losing consciousness. When he had recovered his senses he found he was minus his leg from the knee down. It had been hacked off by an army surgeon in a battlefield tent.

Since he had called out in his own language during his delirium and with French being natural to an educated Russian officer, his true identity had never been suspected in the general turmoil. He had been given a crutch as soon as he began to make a recovery. Soon he had been shipped off to St Petersburg, never supposing there would be truth in the plausible reason he had given of having family there, for his one thought had been to reach some place where he could lose himself from the eye of authority.

But that was all in the past and Louis had become quick and nimble on the wooden leg a palace carpenter had made for him. At Sophie's suggestion Valentin had decided to employ him as an assistant in his pharmacy. Although at first it was only for selling potions and pills in the shop, Louis had become interested in the mixing and blending of herbal remedies as well as in the other ingredients used, an interest that Valentin was encouraging.

Marguerite's thoughts turned to Violette, whose curves had become more than ample from her rich and lazy living, for she no longer embroidered or made her own gowns. She now had more jewellery than she could wear, went driving in her own carriage with a coachman in livery and six black horses, had an even larger apartment than before and was still adored by her generous elderly lover, who was now a general. He had provided well for her in the event of his demise, which he thought was his own idea, not realizing that Violette had instilled it. If she took younger lovers from time to time he did not know of it.

Only Rose's fate was unknown, but Marguerite believed that, whatever troubles and dangers the girl encountered, she would come through it all to suit her own ends as she had always done previously.

Jan took the rest of the summer to finish the portrait, for her sittings were spasmodic and long-standing orders for his work had to be filled. When she questioned him as to the progress of his self-portrait for her he made a quick excuse.

'Pressure of work is delaying me. Be patient, because it would suit me much better to paint it at my Amsterdam studio during next winter.'

She knew it was a reasonable request and did not question him about it again, knowing he would keep his word.

In any case he would have to bring it to her in Paris if all went well for her in the meantime.

He had not let her see her portrait before he had given it a final touch. It was September and the day before his annual departure.

'Now,' he said, taking her hand as she stepped down from the dais for the last time, 'come and see yourself.'

She was startled by the way her likeness seemed to breathe with life. Had a pulse throbbed in the throat it would have seemed perfectly natural. He had portrayed her looking slightly to the right as if someone had just spoken to her and there was a smiling look to her eyes. Maybe it was when he had broken his silence occasionally that he had managed to capture that look on the canvas.

'Does it please you?' he asked with a frown of concern when she remained silent.

'Very much,' she replied. 'I'm just overcome by what you have done.'

'It was not a hard task to paint the woman I love.'

She shook her head slightly. 'Jan . . .' she began uncertainly.

He made a dismissive gesture, his tone impatient. 'Forget what I said. You have made up your mind always to keep us apart just because of someone you can never have.'

She almost voiced a fierce denial, but she bit it back. For the moment, in all honesty, she was uncertain as to whether there was any foundation for his accusation. Abruptly he turned away and picked up her cape from a chair to hold it for her. She knew he had seen how he had caught her off guard, and his face was set. Yet she did not want them to part on a discordant note.

'I'm also forgetting your last remark too,' she said determinedly. 'Tomorrow you sail home again. Let us part as friends. Say you will still come to supper with me this evening as we arranged?'

He nodded stiffly, but did not smile. 'I'll be there.'

That evening when Jan arrived Marguerite was relieved to see that he was his usual agreeable self, nothing of the anger in his eyes that she had glimpsed earlier. She had chosen a good wine and Marinka had prepared an excellent meal. Over it they talked non-stop as they always did. It was after the dishes had been cleared and Marinka had gone home that he stood looking at his own painting on the wall.

'You haven't realized yet what is missing in *Morning in St Petersburg*, have you?' he asked.

She had just seated herself, but she sprang up again and went to his side. 'So there is something! I've always felt it. You've never mentioned it before. Tell me what it is!'

He laughed and shook his head. 'No, you have to discover that for yourself.'

'At least give me a clue!' she implored eagerly.

He turned to her. 'Is it so important that you should know?'

'Yes! I've been continually tantalized by this beautiful painting and it has made me exasperated with myself many times for not being able to define its secret meaning.'

His frown was serious as he looked down into her upturned, hopeful face. 'Then you shall have your clue. It is in this one night when you shall not send me away!'

His arms swept about her, almost lifting her from her feet as he crushed her to him, his mouth coming down on hers with such a force of pent-up passion that a thrill of voluptuousness swept over her, sending a violent tremor through her whole body. Without realizing it, she had became pliant in his arms, responding almost without her own volition by cupping his head in her hands as if to hold his kiss to her for ever. It was a sudden total abandonment on her part, for in spite of all her efforts against surrender he had brought her to the point of no return and she no longer wished to escape his sudden, ardent domination. A fierce yearning for him, long denied, possessed her utterly.

She made no move as he began to strip her lovingly where she stood until, defeated momentarily by the tapes at the back of her bodice, he snatched up her scissors lying beside her sewing box and cut them through. Only when she was released from her garments, standing as naked as Venus rising out of the sea, did he take his time as slowly and sensuously he caressed her, his lips and hands travelling over her lovely curves and inlets while she stood like a poised dancer, hands softly by her sides, her head tilted back as she exulted in his tender exploration. When he lifted her up she looped her arms about his neck and rested her head against his shoulder. He carried her through into the bedroom, which had also been his in the past, and laid her on the bed.

She watched him toss his own clothes aside and there was a wild turmoil inside her, a physical yearning of a force beyond anything she had ever experienced before. In total happiness she welcomed this strong and beautiful man, his muscles taut as ropes, into her warm embrace. For a few lingering moments he leaned on his forearms as he looked down into her eyes.

'I have wanted to be with you like this since the first moment I saw you, my beloved.'

Then his mouth covered hers again before moving to her breasts and he began making love to her with his lips and his hands, alternating between infinite tenderness and a demanding adoration. The aura of candle-glow gave a golden bloom to their bodies as hers became as familiar to him as his own. When at last he entered her with a loving violence she clutched at him and they were swept away together into such a tide of ecstasy that she reared against him, her back arched, and cried out in her joy.

He made love to her in many ways throughout their night together, the imminence of his departure in the morning giving intensity to this brief time they had together. Once when she was resting her head on his flat stomach after pleasuring him he stroked her hair with great gentleness.

'Is it so impossible for you to speak of love to me?' he asked quietly, his voice heavy with regret. 'Not once in this whole night, not even at the height of passion when you abandoned your whole self to me. Yet I know the reason why. It has kept us apart in the past and it will ever be the same in the future. I fear, my beautiful Marguerite, that you'll never come to the truth of the painting I did for you.'

But she slept and did not hear him.

Cherishingly, he drew her up into the circle of his arms and kissed her closed eyelids. After a little while she stirred to smile sleepily at him and he made love to her again, for it was almost time to leave her.

He was dressed and about to wake her when she next opened her eyes. She sat up immediately, sweeping her hair back from her face. 'Is it time for you to go?'

'Yes. As you know, it's an early sailing and I've left my departure to the last minute. But there's something I have to tell you before I go.'

His serious expression alarmed her. She swung her feet to the floor and reached for a robe to slip on. 'What is it?'

'Your Englishman will soon be back in St Petersburg. He is presently in Moscow. I heard of his forthcoming return yesterday evening just before I came here. According to my source, the Empress has summoned him for his advice concerning the roof garden at the new Winter Palace.'

'You knew and yet you didn't say!'

It was an exclamation of surprise and not a reproach, which in his sensitivity on the matter he supposed it to be.

'No doubt he will be calling on you. So there'll be plenty of opportunities ahead for both of you to make up for lost time.'

'Jan!' She was deeply hurt that after such a night as they had shared he should speak so cuttingly, not knowing that it came from his utter despair.

'Farewell, Marguerite.' He left the room and went across the hall.

'Wait!' she cried, intending to stop him, but she slipped on the hem of her untied robe and fell to one knee as the outer door closed after him.

On her feet again, she ran to the window and struggled to open it, but the catch was stiff and would not move. Helplessly she stood with her palms pressed against the glass and watched with overwhelming sadness as he strode away down the street without a backward glance. He had spoken as if he never expected to see her again.

By the time she had dressed and run almost all the way to the wharf the ship flying the flag of the Netherlands was already on its way down the river. She suddenly realized that as she stood alone in the sparkling morning mist that was drifting off the water the scene was exactly as Jan had captured in his painting. Yet he had never intended it to be the scene of farewell that it had just become. She knew its true meaning now and it was all too late.

Twenty-One

A ny plans for escape that Marguerite might have settled
upon would have had no chance of being carried out
as the Empress became difficult to please as never before.
She found herself summoned to the imperial presence
several times a day over some change of mind as to detail
of trimming or colour.

Then, just as the Neva was beginning to draw in a veil
of ice over its surface, Tom arrived from Moscow. By sheer
chance Marguerite, who had just left Elisabeth yet again,
saw him before he sighted her. He was advancing towards
the Palace even as she was leaving it. She stood and waited,
knowing this meeting was inevitable and preparing herself
for it. Then she was gripped by anxiety, seeing that he was
wearing a black cravat, which was a sign of mourning.
Perhaps he had lost a parent, she wondered desperately, or
maybe someone else close to him. But with a dreadful inner
conviction she knew it must be Sarah.

When he looked up and saw her waiting for him a serious smile touched his lips. 'My dear Marguerite,' he said
in greeting.

'Not Sarah, Tom!' she implored in a last faint hope.

He nodded. 'I'm sorry to have to tell you I lost her at
the end of last February.'

'How did it happen? An accident?'

His voice was quiet, heavy with sadness. 'No. She caught
a severe chill on an exceptionally cold day while playing
snowballs with our nephews and nieces. There was no

saving her.' Then he saw how the tears were filling Marguerite's eyes. 'I know what a shock this must be to you as it was for all who knew her. I have a letter for you from her at my accommodation, which she wrote shortly before she died. Although at the time neither she nor I knew that I should be returning to Russia she was convinced that one day I would be able to deliver it to you.'

'Sarah was the kindest and gentlest person I've ever met,' she answered in deep distress, her voice choked. 'There was so much goodness in her.'

'Indeed there was,' he acknowledged and paused before he spoke again. 'You have suffered bereavement too. When I asked after you I was told that Count Dashiski had died. My condolences.'

There was a flat note in his expression of sympathy, which did not surprise her, for she knew he had hated Konstantin from the moment she had told him that they were to marry. Automatically, she inclined her head in acknowledgement.

'I'm to see the Empress this morning,' he continued, glancing at his fob watch. 'It's to discuss the planting of the glassed-in roof garden on the new Winter Palace. May I see you afterwards? I could bring Sarah's letter to you. Where do you live now?'

With her thoughts full of Sarah, she told him. In the past she would have been wary of his company, but his drawn face showed that he was devastated by his bereavement. Moreover, she longed to read that last letter from Sarah, and he would have called on her with it sooner or later.

'You may be all day at the Empress's beck and call,' she warned, 'but after some shopping I shall be at home for the rest of the day.'

'I'll come as soon as I can.'

It was early evening when he arrived, looking extremely harassed.

'I couldn't get away before now,' he declared exasperatedly. 'I was to and fro between the old Winter Palace and the new. When I gave the Empress a full report on what I had in mind after seeing the finished layout of the roof garden she was not satisfied. She kept sending me back to see if her own idea for a patch here and there would be suitable for certain of her favourite flowers, which I had already incorporated. I could have told her without those futile trips. It was all a waste of time!'

Marguerite was pouring him a glass of cognac. 'Sit down and calm down,' she advised sagely. 'Tell me, has your original design for the flower beds and bushes been followed?'

'There have been some changes, probably on some whim of the Empress. She doesn't seem to know her own mind at the moment.' He took the cognac gratefully. 'I needed this.'

'Did you see much of the new Winter Palace's interior?'

'Only from the flights of some very fine staircases to the roof garden, but that was viewpoint enough for me to see from the paintings on the ceilings to all the gilded plaster-work that it is a palace to outshine any other.'

'It is almost finished, I believe. Then all those hundreds of rooms will have to be furnished, many more there than in the old palace, which I've heard is to be demolished. I suppose there will be plenty of celebrations when the Empress finally takes up residence.'

'If she lives to do that.'

Marguerite looked at him sharply. 'What do you mean?'

'The change in her since I saw her last is almost beyond belief. All those pointless orders that I followed today did not come from a logical mind. I pity this country in her hands.'

'I know she is leaving all government matters to her ministers, but there is nothing new in that. I've been told many times that they have always carried the burden for her. She slurs her speech, but that is because she is still drinking excessively. Sometimes when I visit her with

285

designs she has a glass in her hand and is too incoherent for me to understand what she is saying.'

'A terrible woman!' he exploded, remembering what else he had heard of her that day.

Marguerite smiled slightly. 'It's fortunate for you that I'm the only one present to hear you say that. Even as a foreigner you could still get imprisonment.'

He looked across at her ruefully. 'I didn't mean to come here and pour out my grievances.'

'I'd like to hear more about Sarah if you don't find it too harrowing to speak of her. I have missed her letters so much.'

'I know she did write to you. Maybe not as often as she would have wished, but she had a full-time task. She was like another mother to the children, teaching them and playing with them, and then comforting them in their bereavement when their mother died in childbirth. She was so assiduous in carrying out her responsibilities that it was not generally realized that her strength was running out like sand in an hourglass.' He passed a hand across his eyes and his voice caught in his throat. 'Had I been home more I'm sure that I would have seen what was happening.'

Marguerite was silent. She could picture how Sarah, excited by his homecoming, would hide all her troubles and difficulties from him just as she had done when they had lived here in St Petersburg.

'If she had taken care when she first felt ill, maybe all would have been well,' he continued quietly, 'but there was the new baby to care for and she gave no thought to herself.'

'Yes, she always would consider others first.'

They both sat in silence for a few moments before he spoke again. 'When a diplomatic communication came from the Empress requiring my services again, it took a little time for me to finish the work in hand, but I don't intend to stay in Russia for more than six or seven months this time.' He did not add that originally he had intended to remain permanently, but circumstances had changed through her widowhood and he foresaw a far better outcome.

'I suppose you'll have orders waiting for your return?' she was saying.

'Yes, plenty. But I had already decided, even before I received that imperial demand, that the time had come to keep my promise to you that I would return. I had already secured a passage on the first neutral ship that I could take to get here.'

Too late she realized that she had given him the opening to voice what she did not want to hear. 'Don't speak of that now, Tom, or ever again.'

'Forgive me.' He was truly apologetic in his blunder. He had not intended to say what he had done, but seeing her sympathetic face and being in her sensuous presence again he had been momentarily overwhelmed. Yet his loss of Sarah had been like losing half of himself, making him realize how deeply he had loved her. For the present time her demise overshadowed him as it did this lovely woman, who had been her loyal friend and whom he desired so much. He was determined this time not to rush anything between them, but to build up her trust in him until she would be ready to leave for England with him as his wife.

'Who is helping now to look after the children that Sarah loved so much?' she was asking.

He had recovered himself. 'My mother. She is well organized with nursemaids and governesses. The children are fond of her, but it is Sarah whom they loved.'

'As did we all,' Marguerite said sadly, closing her eyes briefly on the pain of loss.

He stood up to leave and took Sarah's letter from his pocket. 'I'll go now,' he said as he handed it to her. 'I'm sure you'll wish to read this on your own.'

Thankful when the door had closed behind him, Marguerite sat down to break the seal of the letter and read the shaky handwriting. Sarah had written from her bed and, although she had known she was dying, her concern was not for herself, but for those whom she would be leaving. It was a very short letter and, judging by the shaky handwriting, it had been difficult for her to find the strength to hold a pen. It opened with an affectionate greeting and was followed by a single poignant paragraph.

> I had always hoped that one day we should meet again, dear friend, but it is not to be. Tom will miss me more than he would ever suppose at the present time, because you have filled his thoughts and longings ever since we left Russia. I knew almost from the start how he has desired you and if you can find it in your heart to comfort him in his sorrow I should be so grateful. Yet your love has long been elsewhere. Maybe by the time you receive this letter you will have found where it lies.

Her signature was indecipherable amid a splatter of ink as if the pen had dropped from her hand in her exhaustion.

Marguerite, deeply distressed, sat for a long time pressing the letter flat against her breasts with both hands.

By now it had become clear to everyone that the Empress was failing fast. There would be no move to Moscow this Christmas. Although Elisabeth barely had the strength to move about, she had not lost her taste for vodka or handsome men, or her love of beautiful clothes. Her ladies had to dress her in a new gown sometimes four or five times a day.

Peter rubbed his hands in joyful anticipation. His chance to reign in the country he hated was coming at last and he took a savage delight in constantly taunting Catherine as to how his mistress would supplant her.

'She'll make a better empress for me than you! It was a great mistake that the old harridan made when she had you brought all the way from Pomerania to marry me! If she had seen my Elisabeth first you would never have been considered. So it's high time I gave thought to putting the matter to rights in the future.'

Over past months with control growing lax under Elisabeth's weakening grip, Catherine had been visiting her son at Oranienbaum. Paul was now eight years old and he had soon lost his shyness of his mother as she came often, bringing little gifts and staying to play with him.

On 23 December Elisabeth suffered a severe stroke and two days later she died. The glorious new Winter Palace from which she had intended to continue her reign stood ready at last, but now that was not to be. Peter was exultant at her death and would have moved into the Palace that same day.

'It would not be seemly, Your Imperial Majesty,' his ministers protested. 'We beg you to wait until after the funeral.'

'Very well,' he conceded. 'We'll see the old bird in her tomb first.'

They left, shocked by his disrespect. But later that same day they were further appalled and also infuriated to learn that he had sent a peace agreement to Frederick II, whose armies had been about to surrender unconditionally. Not only had he ended the war at entirely the wrong moment, but he had restored to his hero all the captured lands, including the entire German empire, for which thousands of Russians had given their lives. He then installed a Holsteinian regiment to replace the Imperial Guard, who were ordered with every other Russian regiment to wear the hated German uniform, causing rage among them to simmer and burn. Meanwhile Catherine had sent for Paul and had her son with her at last.

Although Elisabeth's embalmed body, wearing a gold crown and magnificently gowned, lay in the Palace for six weeks, Peter held celebratory parties where he crowned his mistress as empress and everyone invited had to wear their brightest clothes to dance and drink the night away.

In contrast Catherine, now in real fear of what her future might hold, realized she must guard her every move from now on and not raise the slightest public criticism. She wore deepest mourning and behaved in an exemplary manner, spending a great deal of time in prayer by the coffin. Afterwards, when the body had been moved to Kazan Cathedral, she appeared every day to kneel for hours beside the catafalque as the public filed past it in respect. Through her constancy she gained the high approval of the bishops, her devout presence emphasizing the fact that Peter had not been near.

The funeral route was packed with people when the day came, but Peter shocked everybody by laughing raucously and shouting as well as dancing about and pulling faces like a naughty child, both in the funeral procession and at the solemn service itself.

Peter had not yet given much thought to his coronation, apart from having decided to wear the filigreed gold, bejewelled and fur-rimmed crown of Tsar Ivan the Terrible, which he considered would be quite a joke. Drunk with power, he turned his attention to the wealthy Church, interfering in its affairs and infuriating its bishops, not caring that he was creating new enemies. Inevitably as the weeks went by the tide of opinion began to turn against him. In contrast Catherine was gaining friends and Gregory and his brothers were prepared to give their lives for her.

The month of May found Catherine living in constant dread. She and Peter had taken up residence in the new Winter Palace. Every part of it delighted her with its beautiful decor that had taken thousands of artists and craftsmen countless hours to complete, but since many of the hundreds of rooms were still empty the choice of furnishings was left to her. Daily she received French cabinetmakers and agents with books and drawings of what they could supply. She saw them all in her own apartment, which was at the opposite end to that of Peter's in the vast Palace. One of his first acts had been to banish her there. 'It will save me from having to see your face more often than is necessary,' he had sneered vindictively. 'I am totally sick of the sight of you. The sooner I'm rid of you the better!'

As soon as Catherine had moved into her allotted apartment it was announced from there that she had sprained her ankle and had to rest for several weeks. Through Marguerite's skills she had concealed her pregnancy so far, for Peter would know he was not the father, and now those who came to visit always found her lying on a couch with a silk coverlet over her. Her isolation enabled her eventually to give birth secretly to Gregory's baby, aided by her loyal maid. The newborn infant was immediately whisked away to foster-parents, who would never know their charge's true parentage. Nobody in the Palace even suspected that anything untoward had happened.

Yet Catherine's fear of Peter never left her. Mercifully she had still been resting with her supposedly sprained ankle when he had given Elisabeth Vorontsova the title of Mistress of the Court and ordered that homage be paid to her. This was deeply resented by the courtiers, particularly the ladies, who already loathed everything about Vorontsova from her ugly facial looks to the way she spat as she talked, showering saliva or, which was worse, bits of food when she laughed while eating. Her new title completely turned her head that evening and, flinging out her arms to all present, she made a foolish declaration.

'In my honour at becoming Mistress of the Court on this auspicious occasion, all gentlemen shall curtsey and all the ladies bow to me!' She and Peter thought it a hilarious joke, particularly when two elderly courtiers fell, one having to be helped away after breaking his arm. It was reminiscent of the late Empress's cruel games and filled the courtiers with trepidation.

At one important social and political banquet when Catherine was present Peter humiliated her most cruelly. He was seated with Elisabeth Vorontsova at his right hand at the long and glittering banqueting table, and she rose with everyone else to drink the loyal toast to the imperial family. As his empress, Catherine also remained in her seat, but as the guests sat down again he sprang up, his face contorted with hatred, and shouted at her, 'You should have stood for the toast too, you idiot!'

The shock that prevailed was almost palpable as guests gasped or stared at him. His insult had amounted to a declaration that he no longer saw her as his rightful wife.

On yet another public occasion he humiliated Catherine even further by demanding in a loud voice that she surrender the insignia of the Order of Saint Catherine. All present knew it was one of the greatest honours in Russia since only tsarinas and the wives of heirs to the Russian Throne could wear it. Catherine had an inherent right to it until the end of her life.

Catherine, already pale, felt the last vestige of colour drain from her face. She had always been intensely proud of having been awarded the Order by the late Empress on her betrothal day. To her it had been particularly symbolic, making her feel truly as one with the vast country that she had come to make her own. In silence and with great dignity she removed the decoration and handed it to a footman, whose expression was as shocked as that of everybody else. Only Peter and his mistress were unaware how once again he was being despised for yet another of his outrageous actions.

Nor was Peter's next move popular with people in general when he decided without consultation and for no imminent reason to go to war with Denmark. Although the army was still made up of vast numbers of men, there were many hundreds of families, highborn and low, who were mourning sons, husbands, lovers and fathers lost in the recent conflict from which nothing had been gained. Peter was excited by the prospect of this war since it was not against Frederick II, whose health he would toast on every possible occasion and whose likeness he wore in a large ring on his finger. Now and again he ordered the defences of the city to fire volley after volley of cannon fire just to heighten the atmosphere. It was an extension of the many war games that he had played so often.

Catherine watched from a window when he reviewed every one of the regiments before they went marching off to the port of Kronstadt, where they would await the order to sail when the time was right. She had not been idle in gathering support through the Orlov brothers to counter whatever Peter had planned for her, but for that she needed money. When King Louis of France refused her request she turned instead to the British Ambassador. Through him the financial aid that she wanted came through speedily from England, cementing a future good relationship, which was France's loss.

By now it was June and Catherine had no doubt that soon Peter would want to marry his mistress. She hardly dared guess what her own fate might be if everything went wrong. Even now, at any moment of the day or night, she could expect to be bundled away and shut up behind bars at some far distant location. She might even be smothered by a pillow over her face while she slept or murdered in a so-called accident.

Her alarm increased when Peter ordered her to Peterhof Palace, not far from where he would be staying with Vorontsova at Oranienbaum. Catherine knew that there she would be an even more vulnerable target away from the city. Once again she was separated from her son.

Although others from the Court went with her to Peterhof she did not know if Peter had sent assassins among them. Upon arrival she let them take up their accommodation in the Palace with its labyrinth of rooms in which an attack on her could come from any direction. Instead, as Gregory had advised her, she stayed in a pretty little pavilion in the park with just her maid, Chargorodskaya, and a manservant she could also trust implicitly. Every time she heard carriage wheels and the clip-clop of hooves she summoned up her courage, determined not to show her fear should the worst be about to happen. She trembled with relief when they went safely by.

Marguerite came to see her at the pavilion and upon entering her presence curtseyed deeply. She had not spoken to Catherine since before the old Empress had died, although she had seen her kneeling black-veiled by the catafalque in the cathedral. Out of respect for court mourning, she had waited a suitable time before coming to see what Catherine would wish to have designed for her.

'How good to see you, Marguerite!' Catherine swept forward with a rustle of her black mourning gown to raise her up by the hands and greet her fondly, relieved that this time the carriage wheels had brought a friend and not someone intent on her arrest. She was more anxious than ever today, having received a letter from Peter to say that he would be coming from Oranienbaum to see her the following day. She was convinced that he would arrive with soldiers and it was then she would be taken away. The Frenchwoman's arrival was a welcome diversion. 'It's been a long time since we last met. You must stay to dine. Now tell me your news. I need to be cheered at the present time.'

Marguerite thought to herself that she had little to tell. She could not talk about Jan, who had failed to return in the spring. Saskia had received no news of him, but promised to let her know if he should appear. Her heart ached every time she passed the gallery, which remained closed, and she tried in vain to keep him from her thoughts. Tom, who since that first evening had made no reference to having come back to see her, seemed to find consolation in talk-

ing about Sarah. As a result, in their mutual sorrow, they
were building up a new relationship. It was as if they were
beginning again and they saw each other frequently, which
eased her loneliness.

'I've been sketching a lot for myself recently,' Marguerite
said, having related whatever news she had been able to
give about mutual acquaintances, and was glad to have a
topic that would lead to the purpose of her visit. 'Having
time on my hands since no longer designing for the late
Empress, it has given me the chance to draw a few buildings and landscapes.' She shook her head in smiling regret.
'The results are very amateurish.'

'I have no talent in either sketching or painting, although
my French governess did her best to encourage me when
I was a child. I could see no point in sitting at an easel out
of doors when I could have been riding over the land I was
expected to paint.' Catherine gave a little laugh at the
memory. 'You have a gift for creating beauty in the sphere
of embroidery and design. Did you bring any mannequin
dolls with you today?'

'No, because I thought you would wish to discuss your
coronation gown.'

A flicker of anguish crossed Catherine's face. It would
not be she who would be wearing a coronation gown, no
matter that ever since coming to Russia she had worked
constantly towards the day of sharing power with justice
and wisdom as Peter's empress. 'It's a little too early to
think of that. As yet I'm still in mourning for the late
Empress. But if that coronation day ever comes for me it
will be your design that I shall be wearing.'

Marguerite hid her surprise that Catherine should have
spoken so strangely and indecisively. She had expected to
find her full of enthusiasm and eager to talk of fabrics and
motifs and colours, but she seemed very tense, her hands
full of nervous little movements. Their conversation turned
as it invariably did to the arts, Catherine commenting on

many people's disappointment that the Dutch painter had not returned this year. Then, as usual, she wanted to know about the concerts Marguerite had attended and the plays she had seen at the new theatre. Each time Marguerite had been with Tom and she mentioned that he had finished his project on the roof garden.

'Ah! The English gardener. I remember him at Oranienbaum.' Catherine gave a little sigh. 'I had planned to have a beautiful little palace on that lovely plateau one day.'

'It's an old saying that dreams can come true,' Marguerite said, puzzled by Catherine's mood, for this new tsarina should always be able to have anything she desired. Was it that she believed that her husband would always consider his mistress's wishes before hers? Everyone with any connection with the Court, however indirectly, knew of the vulgar Vorontsova and how he doted on her.

'Which palace park is the English gardener working on now?' Catherine asked.

'He had no further imperial commissions, but he is busy all the time on other private parks.'

They talked on. Then, as it was such a beautiful day, a damask-covered table, glinting with crystal and silver, was set out under the trees, and they ate alone. Afterwards some courtiers, both men and women, who were staying at the Peterhof Palace came across the lawns to the pavilion. They had brought a violinist with them and there was an impromptu recital. Somehow the day trickled away into an evening of cards, still out of doors, until at last everyone departed. Catherine had already insisted that Marguerite should stay the night, and the maid supplied her with everything she needed.

Before getting into bed Marguerite stood for a while at the window looking out at the park still fully visible in the daylight of the White Night. She could see the shimmer of the Gulf of Finland just beyond some trees. Although she had intended to spend no more than three or four hours at Peterhof, which was the average length of her visits combining business and pleasure, there had seemed to be a kind of desperate need in Catherine to keep her close at this time. It was as if, in spite of having two loyal servants at her beck and call, she was strangely ill at ease and needed a friendly presence with her.

It was very early morning and Marguerite, who still found it difficult to sleep sometimes during the light summer nights, had been lying awake for a little while when she heard the click of a boot heel. Immediately alert, remembering Catherine's unusual nervousness, she feared at once for the woman's safety She sprang from the bed and looked out of the room. The door leading to Catherine's rooms had been opened. Deeply alarmed, she ran through to see Alexis Orlov, whom she recognized instantly, hovering on the threshold of Catherine's bedroom as Chargorodskaya shook her from sleep.

'Madame! Alexis Orlov is here! He has an urgent message for you!'

Alexis had used extreme caution when entering the pavilion, using a key that Catherine had given Gregory, for he had not known if she was already under guard. Fortunately that did not seem to be the case. At the maid's signal he entered the bedroom at once and dropped to one knee as Catherine sat up in bed, instantly awake.

'Madame! There is no time to lose! You must dress and come with me now! It's feared that forces moving against you may overtake you at any time now! The army has rallied to you! You are to be declared Empress of all the Russias in your own right in St Petersburg today!'

Marguerite flew to dress too. She matched Catherine's time and ran after her out of the pavilion to the waiting coach, Chargorodskaya hobbling in their wake, for she had lost a shoe on the way and had not dared to stop and put it on again. The manservant, who had been awakened too, was fully dressed, and with his powdered wig slightly askew he ran out in their wake. None of them noticed that Catherine was still wearing her beribboned nightcap, and the three women clambered into the waiting carriage, skirts bundled high, and it bowled away even as they flung themselves on to the seats. The manservant had just managed to leap up at the back of the carriage in time, losing his wig in the process, and his shaved head gleamed in the sun. The carriage departed by the unguarded way it had come. Catherine and her fellow passengers hung on as the wheels splashed through wavelets on the shore before lurching back on to the land to take the road to St Petersburg at a rollicking speed.

They had gone some way when Catherine became aware of something tickling her face. She brushed her cheek, thinking it was a fly or even a little spider, and then realized it was the ribbons of her nightcap. She burst out laughing.

'See what I'm still wearing! My nightcap!'

She pulled it from her head and spun it merrily on a forefinger. Marguerite laughed too and Chargorodskaya giggled, promptly taking care of it. There was still more merriment when the maid revealed her shoeless foot. Their laughter eased the tension. Catherine knew that she had exchanged one perilous situation for another, but she was high-spirited and exhilarated, her mood infectious.

Alexis, up on the box beside the coachman, pistols ready in his hands in case of any ambush or pursuit, recognized an approaching carriage as belonging to Monsieur Michel, Catherine's French hairdresser. Knowing from experience that all women wanted to look their best for any occasion, he signalled to the coachman to stop. As the Frenchman put his head out of the carriage window, Alexis shouted to him.

'The new Empress has need of your immediate attention!'

Moments later Monsieur Michel was changing carriages. With Marguerite and the maid holding hairpins and brushes, he dressed Catherine's hair simply but superbly, in spite of being jogged about and losing his balance more than once as the wheels thumped over ruts and dipped into dusty hollows.

When they reached the city limits Gregory Orlov was waiting on horseback beside a grander open carriage, other mounted officers and a mass of foot soldiers with him. He saluted her with his sword. Catherine, about to alight, paused with a theatrical sense of occasion on the step of the dust-streaked equipage that had brought her to this fateful moment, and bowed her head forward and to the right and left in traditional greeting.

Instantly a great burst of cheering rose up from the foot soldiers and they shouted that she was the little Mother of all the Russias, their beloved tsarina and their rightful ruler. She gave them all a little wave before she was handed into the waiting open carriage.

Marguerite and Chargorodskaya had remained seated where they were and their coachman urged his horses forward, making sure that he was in the direct wake of the officers on horseback before the foot soldiers could close in to shut him off from the imperial carriage. He did not want to miss seeing what happened next. As a result his two passengers had a superb view throughout Catherine's triumphal ride as she was escorted joyfully from one barracks to another throughout the city, being met every time with loyal support that increased her following procession. There were no ordered ranks, only a mingling of regimental uniforms, and here and there mounted officers rode together or singly as if sailing on a moving ocean of men.

Only once was there a tense and dangerous moment when they met a double line of muskets ready to fire from a regiment uncertain where its loyalty should lie, but the sight of Catherine, rising to her feet in the carriage to face them, swayed the day. Weapons were lowered and exuberant acclamation reigned. By now great numbers of other people had joined the throng, word of the coup d'état spreading everywhere. The many genuine smiles that Catherine had bestowed on soldiery and civilians in the past, in addition to her reputation for always being gracious and considerate, even to the humblest of individuals, had finally brought her the total acclaim for which she had always aimed.

Rumours about Peter's instability, later fuelled by his inexcusable behaviour in the funeral procession, which had been witnessed by the huge crowds that had lined the route, had aroused misgivings in many thoughtful citizens as to how he would rule. Now here, without doubt, was a ruler they could trust.

At Kazan Cathedral Catherine alighted and entered to find the Archbishop, standing at the altar with a grouped semi-circle of other bishops, waiting to bless her as the new Empress. She sank to her knees before him and bowed her head thankfully and reverently.

When she emerged there were cheering crowds as far as she could see, and the whole host followed her to the Palace, filling every available space in front of it and overflowing all around. Marguerite, who had now left the carriage, was in the midst of the crowd when Catherine appeared on the balcony with young Paul. People were still cheering when Marguerite left to return home and put down on paper the design for Catherine's coronation gown, which she had had in mind for some time.

Later Catherine made an even more memorable appearance, wearing the gold-braided dark-green uniform and tricorne hat of one of her regiments, and riding astride a red-bridled white horse, a sword in her hand. She was ready to lead her army against any hostile forces that Peter might muster, although she dreaded the thought of Russian against Russian and hoped desperately it would not come to that. No word yet of the coup d'état would have reached the regiments waiting at Kronstadt to embark for Denmark and, dangerously, they far outnumbered those in St Petersburg.

In addition to gaining their loyalty she had yet to win over
the navy waiting to transport them. She had already sent
an envoy to the naval commander in charge of the port's
fortress as well as to the army commander. All she could
hope for was that Peter would not reach either of them first.

She cast a happy look at her own loyal soldiers, now
formed into orderly ranks, seeing that they had discarded
the hated Holsteinian uniform they had been forced to wear
and had found old regimental coats to don instead. They
were almost delirious in their pride in her and burst forth
once again into a spontaneous cheer.

The fifes and drums began to sound and Catherine rode
forward followed by the Orlov brothers riding just behind
her, the tramp of the soldiers' boots drowned in the cheers
of the crowd waving them on their way to Kronstadt. The
momentous day, which had had such an early start for
Catherine, was still only in mid-afternoon.

At Peterhof a very different scene was taking place. Peter,
having been told that he would find Catherine at the pavilion, mounted the steps of the entrance, his mistress at his
side. He frowned with displeasure when the door was not
immediately opened for them from within. Elisabeth
Vorontsova, eager to witness Catherine's final downfall,
reached out a hand to open it herself, but he stopped her.
One of the men from the party of courtiers who had accompanied him from Oranienbaum ran quickly up the steps to
perform that duty and stood aside as Peter led the way into
the charming blue entrance hall.

'Catherine!' he bellowed loudly, his voice echoing.
'Present yourself at once!' Then, when she failed to appear,
he stamped his foot impatiently. 'It's no good skulking in
a corner! I want you here! Now!'

Somebody spoke behind him. 'I fear she has gone, Sire.'

Peter whirled round to face the courtier. 'What do you
mean? She would never disobey my command!'

'One of the guards has just this minute reported that the

Lady Catherine left here at a very early hour this morning.'

'No!' Peter roared in disbelief, ignoring Vorontsova's whine of disappointment. 'She would not dare!'

He turned to throw open the nearest double doors and began charging through one room and then another, convinced that he would find her, all the time shouting her name hysterically in his temper. When he did not discover her in any of the ground-floor rooms he rushed upstairs. Those of his party gathering in the hall could hear his high-pitched shrieking as he continued to search in vain. Now and again something crashed as he hurled a vase or a porcelain figurine against a wall in his frustration. Once he toppled a Roman bust. When he returned to the head of the stairs, scarlet-faced with rage, a chancellor of his court came forward, an unfolded message in his hand, and stood looking gravely up at him.

'Your Imperial Majesty, I have just received word that the Lady Catherine is in St Petersburg, where the army has rallied to her! She is being declared empress in your stead!'

Peter turned ashen and uttered a kind of frenzied scream of fury, arching his back as if he had been shot in the chest, and shaking his clenched fists into the air. His one thought was that Catherine had thwarted his plan to have her incarcerated and had put his life in danger instead of hers. Then he gave way totally to panic.

Nobody could keep pace with the orders that he shouted out as he ran about like a dog chasing its tail. Someone brought him a decanter of burgundy and a glass, and he gulped down glass after glass as if he thought it would give him strength at this time of crisis. Vorontsova sobbed noisily as she watched his wild antics. He was drunk when he finally sat down and the chancellor was able at last to give him sound advice.

Peter did not even raise his head as he mumbled his replies. No, he did not want to go to Kronstadt where the troops would still be loyal to him. No, he would not ride at their head and march them to the city to put down the insurrection.

In the end the chancellor lost patience with such cowardice and did the unthinkable by wrenching the Emperor to his feet. With the waters of the Gulf of Finland lapping the shore of Peterhof it was not long before Peter was bundled aboard a vessel and found himself bound for Kronstadt with Vorontsova at his side while attempts were made to sober him up. But Peter's failure to rise to the moment had lost him the day. Catherine's envoy had reached the fortress first. A shout from Peter's vessel that the Emperor was on board only met with a refused entry by the commander, a cannon blast across its bows a hostile threat to sink it in the event of defiance.

The chancellor still did not give up hope for Peter, who sat weeping. He tried to persuade this pathetic emperor that he could still win the day if he went ashore and addressed his troops courageously, but Peter sprang up in terror at the suggestion and bolted from him. When they found him it was if he had sought the safety of the womb again, for he had tucked himself away in one of the darkest corners of the hold, seated with his knees drawn up to his chin and his arms covering his face.

Soon afterwards he was landed back at Oranienbaum and went straight to bed, emotionally exhausted. Later, when a declaration of abdication was brought to him, he took up his quill without a murmur of dissent and signed it.

It was only when he heard the fate decreed for him, which was exactly what he had planned for Catherine, that he once again gave way to tears, high-pitched shrieks and protests.

'No, no, no!' he cried, falling to his knees and totally without dignity.

He was to be incarcerated in a fortress a great distance from St Petersburg, from which he would never be freed. Although he would be allowed some privileges, he would not be permitted to take Vorontsova with him. It was impossible to tell which of them shed the most tears or made the worst scene.

The Orlov brothers were made responsible for seeing him installed at the fortress. Marguerite happened to be with Catherine when she received an urgent message from Alexis. Marguerite saw how she turned ashen and read the contents twice as if to convince herself that what was written could be true. Then, her face wrenched by distress, she turned distractedly to Marguerite.

'Peter is dead!'

'Oh, no!' Marguerite was equally shocked.

'Alexis has written that it was an accident. Some kind of struggle. But everyone here and abroad will always think I had him murdered!'

Marguerite did not doubt that would be the case. All the time Peter was alive he would have been a potential threat to Catherine's security on the throne, for there would always have been those prepared to launch a counter-coup d'état, seeing him as the true tsar. It was obvious to her that the Orlov brothers in their fierce loyalty to Catherine had decided to dispose of him for her. There was also the possibility, considering that all five were proud men with great love for Russia, that at the same time they had taken private revenge for the terrible humiliation they had suffered in being forced to wear the hated Holsteinian uniforms.

Peter was not given the pomp and ceremony to be expected at a former tsar's funeral and was buried in civilian clothes.

With her new power Catherine was resolved to be as good to her people as she would be ruthless towards her enemies. She began writing what she called her 'Great Instruction'. It was her blueprint for ruling wisely and justly, ensuring that there were fair trials in the courts with the accused innocent until proven guilty and abolishing all forms of torture, which was used so widely in Europe. Free schooling for both boys and girls was to be introduced with no corporal punishment allowed, and many other great improvements and benefits that would show the world that Russia was an advanced and enlightened country, both stable and strong and an example to all.

Pausing at her writing, she gave a thought for herself. She would extend this palace by another, which should be her own Hermitage in the heart of St Petersburg. A smile curled her lips. Maybe she would need to go on extending if the works of art and other treasures she intended to buy never stopped flowing in.

Twenty-Two

It was announced that the Coronation would take place at Moscow's great cathedral in September. While Catherine spent the intervening time making changes for the good of her people as well as renewing alliances with England and other countries that Peter had severed, Marguerite and Jeanne supervised the sewing of the gown that Catherine was to wear on the great day. Already it was almost finished, many embroiderers having worked long hours.

'You really did excel yourself with this design,' Jeanne said admiringly when she and Marguerite left the atelier to go into her room to talk.

Marguerite smiled as they sat down together. 'It is my Russian swansong.'

Jeanne looked at her in dismay. 'What do you mean?'

'I feel the time has come for me to leave Russia. If I'm to set my life on a new course I must do it now.'

'But you've already done a host of new designs for the Empress that have yet to be made up. She will always want you on hand.'

'I've already spoken to her about the matter. She is very understanding.'

'But you've never expressed any wish to leave Russia!'

'I know. Part of my heart will always remain here. How could anyone ever forget that wonderful golden light that often suffuses the whole city as if it has escaped from the glories within the palaces? I've grown to love this country in all its seasons, perhaps most of all in its snows, even though that may sound strange. Yet who could not respond to those glittering days when hoar frost gives its own beauty to everything?'

'Yes, it's pretty enough,' Jeanne admitted in an understatement, seeming to think about it for the first time. 'Where shall you go? Back to France? You're not intending to marry Tom Warrington, are you?'

'He has not asked me.'

'But he will if he thinks he is about lose you.'

'Inwardly he is still grieving for Sarah. There is nothing binding in our relationship.'

Jeanne snorted. 'That is more or less what you said about Jan van Deventer when all the time you were in love with him, whether you realized it or not.'

'I know I was now,' Marguerite admitted frankly. 'That's why I need to leave and make a fresh start for the second time in my life. I could not endure to stay here watching and waiting for him for ever in vain. When he did not come back in the spring it was exactly what I had feared when we parted. He will never come back now.'

'So what are your plans?'

'I'm going home to France. One of the Empress's diplomats is leaving for Paris the day after the Coronation and the Empress has generously allowed me to accompany him and his retinue in a carriage to myself. As you will remember, Madame Fromont bequeathed me her house and so I'll have a home waiting for me. There is also the money that I have saved, and that will enable me to establish my own dressmaking salon with a full atelier of seamstresses. All that I have done here should give me an open door to design and make for the ladies of Versailles.'

'You don't sound very enthusiastic, but I've no doubt that you'll be a success. My old man is surely dead from drink by now. So I'd come with you and be your head seamstress if it were not for having my son here and looking forward to grandchildren one day. I had hoped you would design his bride's wedding gown.'

'I can still do that. I'll arrange a meeting with her.'

'That's good of you.' Then Jeanne narrowed her eyes on a sudden thought. 'Tom worked in France before he came here, didn't he? I suppose he could get work there again.'

'No doubt he could.'

'You're not telling me anything more for the present, are you?'

'I've told you everything. But I will add that, as you know, I have been through one disastrous marriage and, much as I long to have a family, I don't intend ever to make the same mistake again.'

Marguerite got up to leave, but before she reached the door Jeanne spoke again, making her halt.

'Where shall I send the Dutchman when he comes looking for you one day? Paris? Or England?'

Marguerite turned, her face full of anguish. 'He would have returned in the spring if he had still wanted me. Now, if by some rare chance he does ever return, it will be for his work here and nothing else. That's why I have to leave.'

Jeanne sighed and made a little gesture of sympathy as Marguerite went from the room.

As expected, Tom reacted to Marguerite's decision to leave Russia in much the same way as Jeanne had done.

'Leaving?' he echoed incredulously. 'Surely not now when you and I have become so close?'

'So we have, Tom, and I'm glad of it.'

'But I thought that at last you truly cared for me!'

'I do, Tom. But not as you would wish. That could never be. This has been a time of reparation for Sarah's sake without anything that would have caused her hurt in her lifetime.'

'But she wanted more for us! When she knew she was dying her dearest wish was that you should take her place as my wife.'

'I don't doubt that was what she wished, but she was too understanding to impose that request upon me, wanting only that I should find love in my life.'

'Haven't you found it with me during this time we have been together?' he entreated.

She shook her head. 'No, Tom.'

'I've been so careful this time not to rush you into anything! Do you think I've not wanted to kiss and hold and possess you every minute that we've been together?'

'Of course I've known, dear Tom,' she said compassionately, thinking how often lust could be confused with love and that that was basically what he had always felt for her, even though she had not realized it when Sarah was still alive. 'I understood at once why you put a limit on your stay in Russia this time. It was because you thought that now you were a widower and I had lost my husband six or seven months would be all the time you needed to win me for yourself. But that was never a possibility. In any case, I could never replace Sarah. You'll love her until the end of your days, no matter who else you take into your life.'

His face was stark as if accepting reality for the first time. As she left him she thought how she would always remember the happier times when Sarah had been with them.

On Coronation Day Marguerite was waiting at the cathedral to be able to arrange the Empress's gown to perfection before she made her stately way up to the altar and the pomp and ceremony of crowning that awaited her there. The cheers and shouts of 'Little Mother!' could be heard long before Catherine's coach drew up outside, escorted by cavalry, having been timed to travel slowly in order that the enormous crowds could glimpse her dazzling appearance when she passed by. Then Marguerite was so busy for a hectic few minutes, bending and kneeling to eliminate the slightest unruly fold in the Empress's skirt and smoothing out the hem that she scarcely looked up.

It was not until the ceremony was over and the crowned

Empress came back with immense dignity through the bowing and curtseying of all present in the cathedral that Marguerite was able to take in her truly magnificent appearance for the first time.

Catherine held the gold and bejewelled spectre in her right hand and the jewel-studded orb in her left, her rustling silver gown glowing with the gold-embroidered, double-headed Russian eagles that patterned her skirt profusely, a single one enhancing her bodice. This imperial pattern was repeated on her purple-velvet mantle edged with ermine, which flowed from her shoulders. The rise of her breasts showed above a deep frill of silver lace with diamond ornamentation, the pure sparkle of which was echoed in her glorious new crown. It rose bulbously, dazzling the eye with its diamonds like so many captured stars and topped by a priceless ruby that flashed its fire. Marguerite caught her breath with pleasure as many others had already done. Catherine gave her a special smile as she went by to emerge from the cathedral into the autumnal sunshine and meet the thunderous cheering of her people.

A short time later when the Court was back in St Petersburg again, Catherine gave a great ball at the Winter Palace and Marguerite was invited. When the evening came she joined many hundreds of guests flowing up both sides of the enormous double staircase of white marble in a vista of tall pink pillars and gold ornamentation. At the head she went through the open gilded doors and on past the rotunda within to enter the vast golden stateroom hung with enormous chandeliers of crystal where three thousand people or more were gathering and moving freely about. She thought that indeed this beautiful palace was truly out of a magical Russian fairy tale.

She stayed long enough to talk to a few people whom she knew and have some refreshment from the silk-draped and flower-trimmed buffet tables in an adjoining salon of almost equal size. Then she faced Catherine with a deep curtsey for the last time. The Empress rose to her feet and kissed her farewell on both cheeks.

'May good fortune go with you, Marguerite,' she said fondly. 'My coronation gown, which is truly your masterpiece, shall always be kept here in Moscow.'

Next morning Jeanne, Isabelle, Sophie and Violette gathered to see Marguerite depart. They had previously given a farewell party for her, together with husbands and, in Jeanne's case, a son and his betrothed. All of the French women were wiping their eyes as they hugged and kissed her in turn. Then she stepped into the carriage, the signal for starting the journey having been given. The convoy moved forward, escorted by armed guards. From the carriage window she waved to the little cluster of her friends until they were lost from sight. She was not aware that from a distance Tom had also watched her depart.

Some time afterwards at the now empty Dutch apartment Marinka returned, as Marguerite had instructed, to dust and give a last wash to the floors in order that everything should be left spotless for the next tenant. She had just finished her task, the soapy water in her bucket almost as clean as when she had started, when there came a knock on the door. Wiping her hands on her apron, she went to open it. Jan van Deventer stood there.

'Is Madame Marguerite at home?' he asked with a frown.

'No, mynheer. She has gone.'

He saw now that the hall was empty of furniture. 'You mean she has taken other accommodation?'

Marinka shook her head. 'She has left Russia.'

His face set grimly. 'For England, I suppose.'

'No. For France. To Paris. She intends to open her own dressmaking salon there.'

He seemed to look even fiercer. 'How long since she left?' he demanded. 'A month? Six months?'

'No, mynheer. About two weeks and a day.'

'Then she is still on Russian soil. Thank you, Marinka.

You've been extremely helpful.' He turned and went away down the stairs.

He had only arrived in St Petersburg that morning, having made the long journey over past weeks from Archangel, where he had followed up the trail of a young local artist, whose work had proved to be as good as he had been told. He intended to offer one of the three paintings he had purchased to the new Empress.

At the Winter Palace he was surprised when Catherine gave him an audience as soon as his name was presented to her. He was smiling broadly when he left again and it had nothing to do with her taking all three paintings. She had commissioned him, as well as another agent known to him and with whom he would cooperate, to buy up on her behalf any great private collections of works of art that came on to the European market and he knew of two already, one of which was in England and the other in France. He could tell that she intended to fill her beautiful palace with the greatest treasures to be found anywhere in the world. A highly intelligent and intellectual woman, who loved beauty in all its forms, was about to change and benefit Russia for evermore.

In her carriage Marguerite looked out at the endless grassy plains. Horizons in this country, stretching as it did halfway across the world, always melted away into the sky as if it had no end and no beginning. How small everywhere else would seem to her in the future! Even her homeland, in spite of its size, would surely seem strange and almost miniature to her after all this time. Soon she would be in Riga, where so much of importance had begun and where her last link with Russia would be severed. Yet she would always have the pearl-and-diamond brooch, pale and sparkling as the Russian snows, which Catherine had given her as a keepsake.

Suddenly there seemed to a commotion ahead and her carriage stopped abruptly. Before she could make any move to look out of the window the door was jerked open and Jan, his clothes dust-streaked from days of hard riding, threw himself into the carriage and on to the opposite seat.

'Now,' he said, frowning at her as she sat speechless with astonishment, 'I gave you a year to discover for yourself whether or not it was I whom you wanted or . . . somebody else. I believe you have made your decision.'

She drew a deep breath. 'Yes, although I thought I was never going to see you again and that the painting you gave me would remain unfinished.'

A guard had come to the window, looking anxious. 'Are you all right, madame? This gentleman insisted on coming to your carriage.'

'Yes, indeed,' she replied with a smile.

As the guard disappeared and the carriage rolled on again, Jan moved across to sit beside her. 'So what is missing?' he asked urgently. 'Tell me, Marguerite.'

'I had been searching for some hidden symbolism such as there has been in so many Dutch paintings, but finally I solved the mystery on the morning that I thought I had lost you for ever. You had painted me standing alone, but there should have been a second figure at my side.' She rested her palm against his face as she looked deeply into his eyes. 'You, whom I love, my dear Jan.'

He answered her softly, drawing her to him. 'I have waited a long time to hear you say those words and,' he added with a smile, 'to finish that painting. Now I have a great deal to tell and much to hear from you.'

That night in the Riga hostelry she was awake for a little while after their passionate reunion, Jan's arm around her as he lay sleeping. Careful not to disturb him, she raised herself on one elbow to gaze down at him.

Already she was looking forward to living in the house with the stained-glass windows that overlooked an Amsterdam canal. She could picture how reflected sunlight on the water would make rainbow patterns dance across the ceilings. It would be a place to put down roots and raise a family. As for the house in Paris, that would always be a pied-à-terre for them both. Maybe in time to come when the heir to the French throne was old enough to marry, she would design for his young bride. In the meantime the ladies of the Netherlands would want fine clothes created for them too.